NEW
UNDER
THE SUN

KEVIN MAJOR

NEW
UNDER
THE SUN

A NOVEL

Cormorant Books

**Canada Council
for the Arts**   **Conseil des Arts
du Canada**   ONTARIO ARTS COUNCIL
CONSEIL DES ARTS DE L'ONTARIO

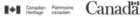 Canadian Patrimoine
Heritage canadien   Canadä

The publisher gratefully acknowledges the support of the Canada Council for the Arts and the
Ontario Arts Council for its publishing program. We acknowledge the financial support of the
Government of Canada through the Canada Book Fund (CBF) for our publishing activities,
and the Government of Ontario through the Ontario Media Development Corporation, an agency
of the Ontario Ministry of Culture, and the Ontario Book Publishing Tax Credit Program.

LIBRARY AND ARCHIVES CANADA CATALOGUING IN PUBLICATION

Major, Kevin, 1949–
New under the sun : a novel / Kevin Major.

ISBN 978-1-77086-057-5

I. Title.

PS8576.A523N48 2011   C813'.54   C2011-904035-2

Cover art and design: Angel Guerra/Archetype
Interior text design: Tannice Goddard, Soul Oasis Networking
Printer: Friesens

Printed and bound in Canada.

This book is printed on 100% post-consumer waste recycled paper.

CORMORANT BOOKS INC.
215 SPADINA AVENUE, STUDIO 230, TORONTO, ONTARIO, CANADA M5T 2C7
www.cormorantbooks.com

ACKNOWLEDGEMENTS

The writing of this book persisted because of the support and knowledge of many people and institutions, and to them I extend deep gratitude:

Anne, Luke and Duncan
Linda McKnight and Marc Côté
Selma Barkham, Joan Clark, Ingeborg Marshall, Alan Macpherson, Anna Porter
Archaeologists, in particular Robert McGhee, Priscilla Renouf and James Tuck
The Centre for Newfoundland Studies, Memorial University
The Newfoundland and Labrador Arts Council

New Under the Sun is a work of fiction. It imagines the lives of historical figures beyond what history has recorded.

KM

In memory of the peoples who first ventured to this land.

SHANNON

HOME IS NEVER HOME anymore. Shannon anticipates nothing but the landscape.

The rest of the country at her back. This, the final thrust of the journey begun on the edge of the Pacific a week ago — the frigid swat of the North Atlantic on deck, across the Cabot Strait, dead in the face, Shannon bundled in a ski jacket, some space-age fabric gloves and a boiled-wool toque.

It is May. She loves it.

In British Columbia everything grows. In Newfoundland nature is a blessed snarl, humans an imposition. You have to want to come here; you have to want to fight to stay. You are not seed on fertile ground. You are a fish washed up on rock. She feels welcomed just for making the decision to return. And when the ferry's horn announces the docking, it is a blaring decree to take hold or be left sputtering for air.

She has never seen the ferry terminus at Port aux Basques except with fog licking its barren rock, its clusters of houses some rarefied spectrum. Who would paint a house turquoise but someone fraught with hope? Or that fog-burning yellow?

She drives off the boat with a resolve that hasn't penetrated her skin in years. The place names up the Northern Peninsula of Newfoundland are fuel to the homecoming — Steady Brook, Bonne Bay, Port au Choix, Bide Arm.

Begin again at the beginning. Demarcate the past.

SHE GREW UP IN a place called Conche, on the northeastern edge of the peninsula. Then it had six hundred people. Now there's half that number. The closest of the three Parks Canada sites included in her new job — the Norse site at L'Anse aux Meadows — is more than a hundred kilometres farther north. The others — the Basque site at Red Bay and the Maritime Archaic Indian site in L'Anse Amour — are both in southern Labrador, farther away still. A safe enough distance between her past and her present.

Yet she decides she must first set herself down in Conche and dutifully impose herself on her relatives. Otherwise, once they get wind of her return, it will only confirm her status as a thoughtless prodigal.

In her twenty years away she's lost the Newfoundland trait of arriving at the home of relatives unannounced, expecting food and lodging. Instead, she's emailed ahead to a nearby B&B, and it's there she turns up, at the end of a long day's drive from Port aux Basques.

Her name is a dead giveaway, of course, and she has to own up to being related to the Carews who live in Conche. And once Isabel, the owner of the B&B, has figured where to put her on the Carew family tree, she feels it necessary to offer an excuse for choosing her establishment over the home of a relative. 'My sister moved away, and Aunt Bertha is not getting any younger.'

'She's not well, certainly, not since the cancer.' Shannon's inadequacies as a blood relative are suddenly glaringly apparent.

'Of course,' is what she manages.

'Her girls are after her to go to the Home in St. Anthony, but she says no, not as long as she can cope by herself. She's been going downhill since Billy died.'

That would be Shannon's Uncle Bill, Bertha's husband. She knows that much, that he died, three years ago. She still sends and receives Christmas cards, if sporadically.

'They were very close.'

'They was so, too.'

Isabel seems to have bonded with her despite any qualms she might have. Shannon feels redeemed.

Her tiredness proves a tenable excuse to take to her room for the night. What she wants is a shower and a bed. She escapes the offer to join Isabel later for tea. There's a need to quit her company while she is ahead.

After the shower and completion of her nightly rituals, she props herself up in bed with a pen and notebook. Her goal is to make a list of relatives. Some will have died, and no doubt there's a batch of youngsters to be added to the list, but she will at least have the congenital core straight as possible in her mind.

There are deplorable gaps in her memory, but this Shannon conveniently attributes to fatigue. She slithers down between the sheets, her dread of the day ahead only partially dulled. Her dreams are of frightful meetings with nameless, but vaguely familiar, relations.

SHE WAKES TOO EARLY. Not managing to get all the much-needed sleep. The incomplete list of relatives rests on the bedside table, tangible proof of her ragged connection to her past.

What Shannon has is a roster of relatives whom, as ashamed as she is to admit it, she cannot call by name. Some of the younger ones will have moved away, to Alberta mostly, it can be assumed, but there remain a number, generally advanced in age, and in various states of health. Of them, only with Aunt Bertha, her mother's much older and only sister, has she maintained contact.

When her mother was alive, Shannon could count on her to keep her up to date, but a dozen years is a long time to be getting only a few lines scratched below *Season's Greetings*.

Breakfast for her usually doesn't extend much beyond coffee, but she yields to Isabel's expectations and agrees to toast, a poached egg and bacon. Something to last her into the day, given she doesn't know what the day will bring. 'Light on the butter,' she says.

'Bertha will be surprised to see you,' Isabel calls out from behind the kitchen counter. It's as subtle as she is capable of making it. It does at least channel Shannon into a possible starting point for when she actually arrives in Conche.

'I'm thinking it's a bit early to be barging in on anybody.'

Isabel turns to her with a smile that suggests she sees her as the 'mainlander' she has been the past twenty years.

By the time she finishes eating it is still not clear to Isabel, who is now sitting across from her with a cup of tea, how her day will unfold. Isabel's rural sensors have detected a need for action.

'Would you like me to call her, dear, to let her know you're coming?'

Shannon is quite capable of doing that herself, of course, and to have Isabel do it would only acknowledge her self-doubt. Yet, the proposal spreads over Shannon like a mild sedative. She's sure that once she is past the hump of that initial encounter, the day will be much simpler.

'That would be good of you, Isabel. If you don't mind. If she's not well, then perhaps a more familiar voice would be better.'

Isabel has risen to her feet and is on her way to the phone before Shannon finishes. Shannon takes to the washroom to brush her teeth and fix her hair, thinking it best if she keeps up the momentum she has now inherited. When she shows up again in the kitchen she's in a rain- and wind-proof jacket, a daypack hanging on her shoulder. She's ready to head off.

'She remembers you, dear, well enough. I told her not to go to any trouble. But you know Bertha, she likes to be good to people. She's gone off now to make a few tea buns.'

Perhaps the extended breakfast was not such a good idea. Nevertheless, Shannon is set now, and soon out the door, with one final piece of advice from Isabel. 'Bertha's hard of hearing. But don't let on you know that.'

CONCHE, SHANNON ADMITS, IS a strikingly beautiful place. She gave no credit to its scenery when she was growing up there. What teenager pays attention to where she lives, except to wish it were someplace different? Only after she moved away did she realize what she'd left behind.

For three centuries Conche was part of the French Shore, a portion of the Newfoundland coast where the French held fishing rights. Every summer ships loaded with cod fishermen from Brittany and Normandy sailed into the harbour. In the middle of the 1800s the Irish turned up, too, settled in and scraped a living from the ocean under the noses of the French, their faith in God and St. Patrick their dubious protection.

Whenever Shannon summons up her childhood, it is invariably with a sense of the staggering presence of religion in the place. As she drives into Conche the first building to seize her attention is the Catholic church. She often thinks it was the Church as much as anything she was escaping when she left.

Her relatives could never understand or forgive her suspicions about the Church. Especially her maternal grandmother, who immersed herself in Catholicism. Her life was her family and the Church, in importance the two often in the reverse order. The same couldn't be said of her grandfather, whose faith, she suspects, was never as strong as his weekly piety made it appear. She never knew him to miss Mass on a Sunday, except if he was away to the Labrador fishery, or for the months he spent in the hospital in St. Anthony when he was dying.

She grew up in spite of the Church, perhaps, then grew beyond it. Except for funerals and weddings, she hasn't darkened the doorway of a church since she left. Yet the primacy of religion in her youth comes rushing back the minute she enters Aunt Bertha's house. A framed picture of the Virgin Mary hangs in the back porch, and below it a mirrored crucifix.

A door leads from the back porch into the kitchen. It's an older house, built by Uncle Bill in the late forties, she would guess, after he and Aunt Bertha were married, once he came back home from his time in the navy. The house is two-storey, a variation on a saltbox, square and simple. She remembers it as being immaculate, rightfully enough.

Aunt Bertha is still house-proud, even if she is no longer as able a housekeeper. Shannon knocks at the door and opens it at the same time. Aunt Bertha rises from the kitchen table to meet her. She must be over 80, a mite of a woman in height, though she has not gone thin as women of such an age are inclined to do. She's not lost the squareness of her build, her breasts and stomach of near equal extension. She was always a solid woman. Shannon's mother, in an uncharacteristically candid moment, once said that she had to be built like a concrete block to hold her own against Billy's temper.

Shannon remembers her trying to compensate for her height by wearing shoes with a bit of a heel. Those days are past. She shuffles toward her in home-knit slippers. The smile that spreads across her face is only slightly reticent, despite the fact that she hasn't seen Shannon in so long.

'God bless ya, my love,' she says. 'God bless ya.'

Bertha's embrace is brief and somewhat spiritless, but that is due more to her health than the length of time that has passed since Shannon's last visit. The touch of Bertha's cheek against her own causes Shannon to stiffen slightly. The skin is loose and chilled, and there's a faint sour smell, an indication that Bertha's age is catching up with her ability to take care of herself.

'You haven't changed a bit,' Shannon says.

She has changed, of course. In any case, Bertha is indifferent to such comments, except that this one leads, conveniently enough, to the state of her health. It's the natural starting point of their conversation, and it settles Shannon comfortably into place at the other side of the kitchen table.

'Since Billy passed on I haven't been meself. That's what they tells me anyway. I'm not too far gone, I s'pose, thank the Lord. It's not yer mind you got to worry about, is it, maid? If you goes in the head, then you don't know the difference anyway. It's the rest of you you got to live wit'. Me stomach's been awful queer the past few months, and I half thinks the darn ol' cancer is back. They said they got it all the first time, but you never knows wit' that stuff, do ya? I haven't told me doctor. I haven't got the strength to go through another operation. If the good Lord wants me, He can take me.'

Which is an admirable attitude, although Shannon thinks better than to acknowledge the fact. 'That's hardly like you, Aunt Bertha.'

All that's needed is a few words to lead her on. Shannon gets the full account of her condition, or as much as Bertha is able to keep straight in her mind. As she runs out of narrative, the timer on the stove buzzes, signalling a natural intermission. Shannon takes on the task of retrieving the buns from the oven, as well as steeping the tea, and the pouring of it into the pair of china mugs that Bertha has previously placed on the table.

'I can manage, you know,' Bertha says, 'but I'll take a hand when it's offered.'

Shannon's busyness is taking the dread out of her entry back into the fold. She had anticipated something much more awkward, more directed toward her and what she has been doing the last dozen years. There's no escaping some of it.

'You're not married?'

'Not yet.'

'Good for you. Do what you wants. Marriage is not for everyone, is it?'

Coming from Aunt Bertha, it's a surprise, a relief.

'Tiffany had her man — if you can call 'en that — and then had to get rid of 'en.'

Where Tiffany is positioned on the family tree Shannon is not quite sure. She presumes Tiffany is a granddaughter.

'Not before she born three of the sweetest little boys you ever laid eyes on. Lucky thing they is in Grand Prairie, I say. She'd never make any life for them around here. Her mother does what she can for her, and that's not easy either, wit' her arthritis.'

That would be Gail. Or Beverly.

'I misses her. She was such a good help to me, but there's nothing I can do about it. Fred had no work once the plant cut back. They all goes where the grandchildren is. I s'pose you can't blame 'em. Gail thinks the world of them boys.'

'And where's Beverly now?'

'Still in St. John's. She haven't moved. She retired from the job she had wit' the government. I never sees her much. She comes home once a summer, that's about all. It's a long way to drive, maid. I could go live wit' her and Reg, but they got the dogs, you know, and I got no friends in St. John's. Or St. Anthony, either, except Cy's oldest is there. As long as I can do the few things I needs to do for meself.'

'You're happy enough.' It's lame, but it's what Shannon can manage and still sound as if she has followed the trail of relatives laid in front of her.

'As happy as the Lord needs me to be, I s'pose.' At that she blesses herself and nods her head in affirmation of her lot in life.

Tea buns at mid-morning needs a major readjustment of the dietary ethos that took hold during all those years in BC. There's no disappointing Aunt Bertha, however, and with dabs of butter melting over the opened buns, and a touch of bakeapple jam, it doesn't take much for Shannon to give in. Aunt Bertha has always been known for her way with a tea bun. Shannon thinks of it as a perfect homecoming ritual.

She has a second one with a second cup of tea and her Aunt Bertha is charmed.

Shannon works at trying to settle herself even more, for there is more family business at hand. It is useless to try to avoid it, for she knows it will only surface behind her back once people know she was in the place.

She decides she would rather pre-empt the gnarly speculation that is bound to fill the telephone lines.

'And what is Jerome up to these days?'

Her directness confuses Aunt Bertha, even though she tried covering the question with an indifferent tone of voice.

Bertha starts to raise her teacup, but puts it back onto the saucer. 'I hardly ever sees 'en, to tell the truth.'

'Did you wonder about Mom? Did you wonder what was going through her mind when she married him?'

It's out of the blue. It's not that Shannon wants to be unkind, but something tells her it would be no better if she tried working her way around the questions. They came blundering back as soon as she was in sight of Conche.

'Your mother ...' Bertha sits, searching for words.

Shannon knows she should feel like a shit. But doesn't. She figures it takes someone who feels less sorry for herself to feel like a shit.

'Your mother didn't have it easy,' Bertha says.

Shannon has heard it before, anticipates what's next.

'She was left with the two of you after your father died. No insurance to speak of. Not enough education. You knows that yourself. She had her hours in the plant, like they all did.'

'So Jerome comes along ...'

'He didn't just come along, maid. He was here all the time.'

Shannon won't say anything else. She knows it's ungodly selfish of her to be dragging Bertha into it. She also knows Bertha is the only one she is willing to talk to about it.

Jerome, as long imbedded in Shannon's mind, is the prick of a man who set his sights on her mother and dragged her into a marriage that turned out to be hell for her, and hell for her two daughters. Contrary to what it now must seem to Bertha, Shannon has dealt with it. Otherwise, she knows she would have never come back to Newfoundland, and certainly not to Conche. Dealt with it as far as she has ever been able to deal with it, given that she hasn't set foot in the place since her mother's funeral. Of course, there are questions. There are always questions.

Shannon just wants to breathe the air of Conche. To think herself as deserving as the next person of filling her lungs with it. Like the teenager she was when she left. Sucking in the first draw of a cigarette on a Friday night, after all day determined to never smoke again.

SHE SPENDS A COUPLE of hours in the afternoon walking about, chatting with people in a convenience store, rediscovering a few relatives. Bertha insisted that she come back for supper, which she agreed to do, partly to make up for her behaviour, partly because she is wondering if there's not something more Bertha might be telling her.

The house where Shannon grew up is there. She feels little attachment. It now has insipid pastel vinyl siding, and a new side porch. The house is set back from the main road. The path leading to it is the path that defined her teenage years. It was a path she took at the end of high school and never truly set foot to again.

She assumes Jerome and his wife are inside. Jerome's 'new woman,' as they used to say. The woman who set up shop less than a year after Shannon's mother passed away. Shannon knows nothing about her, other than she was from somewhere in Labrador. Nor does she wish to know anything. When her mother died the house was there as her mother left it, and anything that should have been passed on to Shannon or her sister Patti was there as well.

Her mother's will, in all its simplicity, said everything was to go to Jerome. Whether the will was made under pressure from him, or whether her mother didn't have the strength of mind to realize what interest Patti and Shannon had in anything belonging to her, Shannon could never be certain. And at the time didn't much care. She had no wish to contest the will. What little the house was worth would have been soaked up in lawyer's fees. Shannon had memories of her mother that didn't include

Jerome, and a few pictures, and that was what she wanted. A few months before her mother died — and, Shannon likes to think, unknown to Jerome — her mother had given her the wedding ring from her marriage to Shannon's father. To Patti she gave the engagement ring. They had been bought in 1967 in Corner Brook as an interlocking pair.

There were times in recent years when Shannon wished she had a few things she valued — a Royal Albert plate that had belonged to her mother's own mother, a jewellery box, a certain few Christmas ornaments. When she again saw her sister, some years after the funeral, Shannon discovered she felt the same, that there were some things more rightfully theirs, things they didn't know the whereabouts of anymore. Eventually, Shannon wrote Jerome and asked for them. The letter was never answered.

Which led her to think he doesn't have them anymore, or that neither he nor his wife have any wish to give them up. Or give in to a request of Shannon's, given he knows how much she detests him. She takes it for an assertion of control over her that he never had when she was growing up.

Her walk about Conche is not without its positives. She revisits some of the places she would go to as a teenager to work her way through what was happening at home. They are oddly very much the same, not that nature's formations shouldn't be after twenty years. In the face of how much she has changed, she expected a difference. There is a narrow channel between some shoreline rock that hid her, where she studied for final exams, where Jeffery Walsh had most of what he wanted, but not all. It was the retreat, if only ever for a few months of the year, for mostly the shoreline was lashed with freezing cold wind and drifted in with snow.

When she thinks of Conche, it is not the natural beauty she remembers, but the endless housebound months. What happy memories there are come from summer bonfires, the few temperate days of autumn. When she went to the Caribbean for the first time, for the inevitable beach holiday in her mid-twenties, what she noticed immediately was how teenagers growing up there live most of their lives outside the house. It struck her as entirely liberating.

Her own teenage years led her, after the ride of university, to seek a job with Parks Canada. It dropped her into the great, endless outdoors. Over time, she became somewhat more domesticated, and created within the confines of the various apartments she rented quite attractive and liveable space. But there remains the untempered urge to get out from under anything that entangles her for long.

WHEN SHE DWELLS ON her teenage years now, she realizes it is something of a miracle that she came through them without getting pregnant. It is one of the great ironies of her life. Now, when she feels the urge to have a child, the man of the hour is not to be found.

When she was sixteen, not only were they to be found, but she could hardly get rid of them fast enough. They had picked up the scent of sex, amplified by the towering guilt emanating from the Catholic Church. She had a steady stream of boyfriends over the last two years of high school, though none for very long. Not that she was anything but poised and level-headed through it all.

She was an honours student, bound for university, and, unlike most girls in her class, had set a direction for herself — to get out of Conche the minute she graduated. Still, she realizes now the pattern of relationships must have generated a reputation of sorts. She hardly thought about it at the time, nor truly cared. There was not the remotest chance of a long-term commitment, and they all knew it. They all knew she would have them forgotten as soon as she was free of Conche. And indeed they have been obliterated from her memory, except for the first, of course, and the intermittent awkwardness of a succeeding few.

Including Jeffrey Walsh, whose penis she remembers as never being able to make up its mind what it wanted to be doing. Between the wedge of rock, on succeeding summer nights, she discovered that bravado and actual performance don't necessarily bear a close relationship, that the male can be as intimidated as hell by a female with greater expectations than his own. Jeffrey eventually rose up from the intimacies, so to speak, with his self-respect intact, but it was only with considerable patience on her part. She suspected his version of them was somewhat different from her own. She even suspected him of being eager to break off the relationship so he could enhance a version of it for his friends and not feel guilty. It was her first, and lasting, demonstration of male self-absorption.

A lesson learned and carried on to university, though she had less cause to make use of it. By that time she had tamed considerably. Her first roommate in residence, also a girl from the outports, but with considerably more common sense, led her to being more selective in her dating practices, and led her to the student clinic and the pill. Oddly enough, taking the pill coincided with diminished sexual activity, forcing her to the realization that her outport high school view of the world was rather all too perverse.

The university years in St. John's worked a miracle. After some initial floundering, she fell into courses which began to unleash her thinking. She gravitated eventually toward Cultural Geography and Ecology.

It was something more than job training, but as it happened Parks Canada and her honours undergrad degree proved a practical and useful fit. During her first posting in the North she was met head-on by a crisis involving the local Aboriginal community over hunting rights. She was at the bottom in the management and decision-making hierarchy, but her input turned out to be constructive, and, in the long run, avoided a nasty confrontation. Word of it must have found its way to the bureaucracy in Ottawa, for within a year she was offered a second posting, this time on Baffin Island, with significantly more responsibilities.

On Baffin she came to terms with what she was all about. It was an interval of what she liked to think of as substantive personal release. Her life in Newfoundland was a distant, but vivid, memory. Her friends were all from somewhere else; none of them had ever set foot in any part of the country east of Montreal. She dragged her closest friend, Marta, into the dregs of her youth, until she concluded Marta must have been thoroughly sick of hearing about it. Marta pressed her for the stories, and drove Shannon to tears half the time. It must have been Marta's Scandinavian penchant for the dark recesses of the soul. Whatever it was, it was therapeutic.

And then they would laugh and laugh, and get steadily drunker on tequila. It was Marta who went with her to Jamaica. It was with Marta she shared that first beach holiday, and with whom she shared their beach-roaming Rodney for a night.

When all was said and done, and she and Marta went in different directions — Marta back to Norway one year and Shannon on to British Columbia the next — she was left thinking she'd forged a whole new take on herself and what the years ahead might bring. She and Marta still keep in touch, and she was, in fact, the first person Shannon told about the new job. Marta has promised to come to Newfoundland, especially since the job encompasses the Norse settlement at L'Anse aux Meadows. Marta has promised to come and bring her husband and their three-year-old.

Shannon is pleased Marta managed to get what she wanted. The job and the husband and the kid. She's entirely happy for her and has told her so. And Marta, she knows, is entirely hoping the new job works out for her.

IT WAS MARTA WHO shored her up when, on long cold Arctic evenings together, certain realities struck their deepest. It was she who kept telling Shannon that she was very good at what she did, that she had a decisive level of comfort with Aboriginal cultures, a durability in the face of tough situations.

In other regards she couldn't boast equal success. When she left the Arctic behind, post-Marta, Shannon fell into a number of relationships, all, ultimately, to no end.

The successful relationships were with unmarried women of her own inexplicit age. As always, she had proven to be a listener, an empathetic friend. She would sincerely miss a number of them. She called them her sea-kayaking sisters, for that indeed is how they spent a good deal of their time together.

She purposely sold her kayak in preparation for leaving British Columbia; a fresh start her intent, unencumbered by defining paraphernalia. Perhaps take on an indigenous activity. Snowshoeing. Something to thrust her into the landscape. She wants to feel that she has parted ways with the rest of the country, that she is truly coming home. The parables have always been the most memorable aspect of her Catholic upbringing.

BRITISH COLUMBIA SHE NEVER found to correlate particularly well with her take on the world, such as it is. She never thought BC entirely true to anything, except how it blends its multitudes of retirees with its furtive pot growers. It seems to her a place of huge secrets sunk among huge trees. All the while she was there she longed for a lengthy vista, but rarely got one, except over salt water.

She wanted the place to come clean. She was speaking personally of course, perverted by her liaison of the two years just past. His name was Kim. Like his name, never quite real. The name Kim, like Jamie or Crispin, always struck her as rather lame, never quite right for a man. It sounds good on a curly headed tyke, but on a six-foot-two male it never measured up. And couldn't even be shortened to something with some heft.

Of course, in BC such insight is meaningless, given its population mix, even though the Kim in question is thoroughly Caucasian. He was raised in Prince Rupert, the son of a logger. A no more white, wholly British Columbian male is likely to be found. He smelled of Douglas fir.

He is a strapping brute of a Kim, and in the shower, water falling from his pecs and suds streaming to the forest between his legs, his name seemed irrelevant. She could lose herself in that charmer, and often did.

In the broad sweep of the bed, it was the same. The morning following, invariably a different matter. Even on weekends Kim liked to be up and away. Doing something. While she would have been content to lie there reading, her head propped against his chest, Kim was wanting out of the bed and in motion. She found that to be a disadvantage of BC's subtropical climate. It rarely gave cause to hunker down, surrendering to a snow-storm. It lacked weather extremes of most sorts, and although it had more than its fair share of rain, it was generally warm rain, and Kim, she sensed, relished the way wet clothes outlined his physique.

Was there conceit at play? Undoubtedly. A reasonable amount of conceit she has no problem with, especially when it is enveloped in such pronounced physical attributes. Unfortunately, Kim's conceit weighed heavier than most.

He was 35, somewhat younger than his housemate. Her house, his mate. It was at her invitation that he took up residence, and therefore she had no cause to resent it when she left for work in the morning and he was sitting on the front steps finishing his coffee, in anticipation of where his day would bring him. He had a job — a tour guide for a private outfit in Port Alberni — but it was seasonal, which meant he had months of lingering within daily reach of her place. Doing what was never entirely clear, so she gave up pretending to be interested. Without exception though he was back in the nest by dark, as food was about to go on the table.

Theirs was a traditional arrangement. He provided the sex, she provided the food. She was confident he wasn't two-timing her, for he hardly spent a night away in the off-season. Life was reasonably good, and they talked of making it permanent.

The idea of a husband and two kids — she thought two was a reasonable number to fit in during her remaining fertile years — sounded appealing. Not desperately appealing, for she is never desperate about anything. In any case, it never found its way beyond the talk stage. And the talk stage came to an abrupt end the night, more than a year and a half into the relationship, when he revealed he was already a father. To a four-year-old in Port Alberni.

Her reaction: a year and a goddamn half into the relationship.

'What the hell are you? An ingrate who thinks I would be indifferent to the fact that the man I was expecting to be the father of my children has spawned one already? As if it were a blip in your past that has nothing to do with me? Is that the goddamn world you live in?'

'Just hold on a minute —'

'As if being a father is something you did to pass the goddamn time of day?'

'I didn't tell you because I didn't want to mess up our relationship.'

'Right.'

'It's the truth. I wanted to give it a chance to ... mature.'

'And today it finally matured. How fuckin' reassuring.'

'Don't swear at me. It doesn't become you.'

'It doesn't fucking become me. Really?'

'Shannon —'

'KIM!'

She calmed down after that. Screaming his suck of a name seemed to vent all she needed to vent.

It turned out he'd been paying weekly visits to Port Alberni, spending the day with the kid, returning in time to fill his unconscionable gut with whatever she had been toiling over in the kitchen. Occasionally he did stop along the way and purchase a bottle of wine to do his bit for the meal. How bloody good of him.

Nothing was the same after that. She gave him credit (as she said after to her female friends — a fraction of the credit he dared to think he deserved) for trying to make it up to her. He set more than a passing foot in the kitchen. It didn't become a logger's son from Prince Rupert.

Two months later he was gone permanently. Word had it he eventually moved in with the mother of his child. Perhaps, in the end, it all led to something worthwhile, Shannon reasoned. Perhaps the kid was better off with a live-at-home dad. Cheer up, Shannon, was the word from the sea-kayaking sisters. It wasn't meant to be.

Strange what truths arise as one paddles the open ocean. Strange what devastatingly accurate analyses of interpersonal relationships emerge in the face of salt-sea air. She'd had her fill of Kim, as she bluntly added, and it was time to move on. Eight thousand kilometres on, as it turned out.

She looked on the bright side. If Kim hadn't screwed up, she would never have given more than the usual passing attention to job vacancies.

By that time she had been Kim-less for only a few months, but she swore, as the flakiest of the sisters liked to say, she had 'centred' herself again, had re-established 'an equilibrium at the core.' She was just goddamn ready to move on.

NONOSA

THE LAND LURED HIM, secured him.

It was the slope of the hills in the distance, how it fell together, the belly and thighs of a pregnant woman. It was memory of Démas.

There was time without the lure of land — his people told of such a time — but Nonosa had no mind for it. Such headfuls did not feed his people. Broodings did not answer his question — what spread itself beyond those hills?

Frost still stiffened the moss underfoot, tufts of snow lay everywhere but on the open rock. Bare ice-worn rock, no noiseless trek as in summer, his skin boots brushing and scraping a crust. Ready game he was.

Though Démas was near birthing and the sun had hardly loosened the earth, Nonosa's curiosity had run too deep for him to stop any longer at the camp. Nothing could keep him from setting off at the first break of spring. Gone in the direction of the ascending sun, back with the story of what new the land held for his clan. Even if winter had been good, always there was the summons of something more.

Once, what he found so gladdened his heart that the three days of his journey back he pressed to two.

'Caribou in numbers to numb your eyes!' Conceit it was to some. Old men rubbed their hands in tight circles about their chests. Women laughed at his gestures to the night sky. It bred a fire-story as mesmerizing as any ever told to them.

'Only you,' Démas murmured and wrapped herself in him at every word. His heart swelled even more.

He curved his outstretched hands, held them apart. They twitched as if in the air between them he were about to grasp a dripping hunk of meat.

Now, what sights to fill his eyes? Nonosa quit his canoe. His muscles spurred a lissome, heedless stride. Only a bare notion of what lay underfoot, enough to skim past bog ice and not break through.

He was a relentless shank of a man, sinew taut beneath the covers of bear and caribou. Mantle hood bunched about the back of his neck, thin-worn skin cap loose about his mane of hair, its chin strap hanging.

In his head rumbled the words, their doubts bare. 'Follow the scrapings. Mark where they veer and scatter.'

The anticipation was too much for such rigour. Over rocks he ran, past scrub thickets, with joy as plain as daylight, unclogging his head of winter.

'Eager, Nonosa! So big in yourself!'

It cut his stride. He stumbled and pitched.

Still, Nonosa was the one to laugh, in the face of the foolish trickster.

'And shameless, too, Nonosa.'

Now the trickster laughed. Nonosa heard it through the scrawny fir and shook his head. He pressed on, reclaimed his stride, as wilful as before.

Over the scruff tearing at his skin boots, twigs stabbing at the soles of his feet. Had he more mind, less heart, he would have skirted the worst of it. No stopping now to amend his ways.

A fresh spring wind blew about him, too fine for laughter. Cooled the sweat on his face. Nonosa hauled away his skin cap, let the wind whisk the hair matted to his forehead.

Mantle and leggings fur clung to him, sweaty, vexing. Yet he bounded up the bare knob of the hill. So much will left in him yet.

It was as if Démas were giving birth at that very moment.

What lay before his eyes! He stood upright, leaned against the shaft of his spear, out of breath. Sensed the moment the mass of land had heaved and split, disappeared and reappeared for his forerunners. Thunderclouds encasing it, weighing it down, breaking it to pieces, casting it adrift. Water roaring against the land, the land rearing, only to fall against itself.

He had hardly believed.

His doubt, the fault of time? He needed this breadth of rock before him, snatching itself through time to water. Water with only the palest edge of shore, far, far beyond it.

That in one direction, and in the other — nothing. Endless water, as endless as ever was!

Even on such a clear day, even when he squinted his eyes again and again. Could water stretch so far? What would hold the fish? In the stories of his people there was such talk, of countless seasons past when such a place was known.

Laughed at the sight of it he did, in hope the trickster would hear him.

No voice, no wind. No one to believe in it but him.

He loomed above the crest of the hill. He slowly trod down it toward the water. All the while his head raced with the tale he would tell, though his footsteps were fitful, in dread of reaching the point where he could step no farther.

He stood on rocks, water swirling to kiss his skin boots. Before him the wild span of water. He bent down, touched it with caution, put the wet finger to his lips. His mouth twisted ruefully.

Nonosa took the full measure of his breath and struck both hands against his chest. The meeting place, water's ceaseless breath on rock, drawing in and heaving out, calling in rhythms for which there was no measure.

At the close of daylight he came to the land's end. Never again could he set out on a spring journey toward the sun.

ON NONOSA'S RETURN A great fire was built. Impatient young bucks of men — among them his brother, Tuanon — hauled hides from a storehouse and spread them around the fire. If they were not dry, if they had no heat, the aged would be forever grunting, breaking the spell of the stories with their coughs and farts, with mutterings about what the chill was doing to their bones. With the steam gone from the fur, they shuffled to their places, smiling faintly. The oldest, Coshee, nodded. The evening could begin.

The rest of the clan gathered, mindful not to keep a distance from the old ones. The children flung sticks into the fire as they would spears. Then curled among their mothers and stared at the fire, eyeing their sticks, watching to see whose would be the one to last the longest.

Only Démas sat apart from the others. Worried what they would think of her husband.

Nonosa rose to his feet before them, not without thought that the longer his silence the more they would hold to his words.

This night his thankfulness rang but briefly into the sky. 'You are the Spirits and we are the people. You are the Spirits and we are forever thankful.'

His haste brought the disapproving eyes of the old ones.

Nonosa found more words. 'The Spirits fill the land, fill rock, fill trees. The Spirits are the animals that feed us, the Spirits are the fish that fill ... seas.'

A good word for what he had seen. He had been the first to set eyes on it. To him fell the choice of what to name it.

'Seas? What are you saying, Nonosa?'

'Water so far it has no end.'

Laughter broke among the old ones. Licence to all the others, loudest the heedless children.

Except for the embarrassed turn of Démas's lips, it was of no consequence to him.

'Seas.' The word was raw, unyielding. He said it again. 'Seas.' It quelled some of the laughter.

'There was another name.' Coshee looked around him. Mothers buried the blather of their children in their chests. 'I have forgotten it. Somewhere past was such a place.'

'Seas?'

'We will take your name. It is as good as any.'

The story was his. From the sack he took his treasure, wrapped in moss and tender young fir boughs. Wound precisely, reverently with strips of hide. He loosened the strips gently with his teeth.

Held it high for them all to see. 'Sea-fish.'

Their eyes narrowed. No slender salmon or trout. Thick in its fore half, scraggly thin behind. Big eyes and a big fish mouth with a hanging stringy bit beneath the jaw. Blotchy brown except white along the gut.

A graceless fish, bereft of any charm.

But cooked it revealed its charms. A bowl of it was passed around. They peered and poked at it and pronounced it the tastiest fish to pass their lips. Flesh so soft, white as snow?

Nonosa enticed, encircled his people, wrapped them in his stories. Charmed away their doubts with words — cod-fish, sea-bird, sea-beast! Stirred words about in the wake of winter. The outright vow of a fresh kill warmed away the last lingering days of frost. Drew them from their dwelling place. They gave up their comforts for better days ahead. For seasons yet to show their barren ways.

'What good is resting here, if there is a journey to be made? What we do not know, do we not long to know?'

'You make your way with words, Nonosa.'

His people did the same. They followed Nonosa and his words all the way to the sea.

THAT NIGHT NONOSA CURLED into the back of Démas, his hand stroking the taut bulge of her belly. They chuckled at the sudden pokes beneath the belly skin. A hand or elbow, perhaps a knee. Nonosa smothered his laughter in her hair. Perhaps a little cock.

Démas clenched Nonosa's own cock. Surprised him, sharpened his glee. Stroked the swollen head to a mad and frenzied eagerness. Nonosa moaned at the throbbing bliss of it, and thrust and thrust wildly in the grip of her. He erupted, and sagged with unrelenting joy.

WITHIN THE BAREST SIGHT of the sea, Démas felt the baby drop.

Nonosa helped her from the canoe. Along the riverbank, they kept a pace as slow as that of Teraset, the midwife. His people never let childbirth stop what needed to be done. Clansmen had told him rough travel was good for a pregnant woman, helped clear the passage for the infant.

Démas grimaced, gripped his shoulders with both hands, her whole weight falling into him. Nonosa sank under her, straining to keep her upright.

The women came running. Scowled at Nonosa, as if he had been the reason for it. Teraset barked for shelter for his desperate wife.

Nonosa summoned Tuanon to their floating raft of framing poles. Found a patch of thick moss and circled it with poles, bound their tops together. Hastily covered it with hides.

Nonosa claimed the softest of the hides and cast it inside, then quickly built a fire.

'Démas.' He clenched her hands and raised her to her feet. Walked her to the shelter, his eyes pressed into hers, strained and narrowed.

'A child blessed by the Spirits. Your pain will pass.'

It was untrue. For with each surge Démas grew weaker. Outside the shelter Nonosa cringed at her deep-throated cries.

Three women surrounded Démas. They tied and tucked her hide robe above her rigid belly, strapped thicker leggings to just above her knees. They tied her unruly hair from her face, draped her arms about the necks of two of them to keep her upright. Her hands tightened into theirs, fell slack at the end of each spasm.

Teraset knelt before her, massaging her cold, naked thighs to keep away the cramps, all the time chanting, luring the child out. From time to time she would probe between Démas's legs, then shake her head. Then quickly nudge the legs apart.

Sweat streaked Démas's face. Rivulets of sweat reddened by ochre marked her neck. One of the women snatched a handful of moss and wiped her brow, then wiped blood seeping down her legs. The moss cast a shiver through the pregnant woman. For the moment it passed, but returned, a near-violent trembling.

Her helpers could hold her weight no longer, and let her slouch to the patch of hide. She squatted, both women kneeling behind her. They leaned her backwards while Teraset ran her hands to all parts of her belly. The midwife kept returning to a single spot, pressed her palm flat against it.

The contractions grew stronger, barely a pause between them. Démas — sodden, chilled, drained of strength — moaned and moaned louder.

Nonosa slipped inside the shelter, squatted nearby, both hands clutching a stick for balance, his heart stricken by what he glimpsed.

His wife fell back on the hide in exhaustion. One woman sat under and behind her, Démas's head and shoulders in her lap. The other knelt to the side, gripped a hand. Joined loudly in Teraset's chant, her voice ringing above it all.

IT WAS THE NEXT day before the child showed itself.

A tiny hand oozed out of the birth passage.

The fingers separated. So slowly, so fragile and extraordinarily pure. The women stared, incredulous. Their silence thickened the shroud of fear covering Démas.

As tenuously as it appeared, the tiny hand withdrew.

Not long after, the crown of the child's head emerged. In time, the sodden amalgam of its infant face. Teraset stroked the face with her thin, arthritic hand. She freed the air passages of their clogging slime.

The child filled its lungs with crisp and frosted air. The surprise of it, the elation of it, thrust the infant out.

Into the world came a girl, crimson with blood. Teraset tied her cord with sinew. The child fought for her life and lived, by the quick sense of the women who enveloped her and by the furs Nonosa had kept warm by the fire.

Her cry proclaimed a stalwart creature, soundly formed, blessed with an ardent will.

The women who surrounded Démas chanted now the mother's song. But the blood that flowed with the afterbirth did not stop. The women soaked it with moss, forced together her legs. The birth had made of Démas a wretched mortal. The force of her life drained away.

'Démas.' Nonosa called to her as the three women made way for her husband. 'A flawless girl. What shall we name her?'

'Shanaw,' she said, for they had decided long ago.

Démas hadn't the strength to open her eyes. Nonosa tried to warm her hands in his. They grew steadily colder.

Nonosa stared intently at her barren face and heard the thumping of his heart.

THEY TOOK DÉMAS'S BODY to where a rock face met near-level ground. They cleared the ground as best they could, then wedged the body, coated with red ochre, against the rock, the head turned inward. Then encased the body with a thick shroud of moss. They gathered rocks to cover the moss, though only a few were of the boulder size they wished. They implored the Spirits to take her before vile creatures came near.

The clan lingered in silent petition. Then only Nonosa remained. Many times he returned to pile more rocks upon the grave, and to sit, then lie, entirely sore of heart.

What drew him away were the hunger cries of the little one. No mother among them with milk in her breasts. What was he to do?

'Wait for the infant to die. Make a place with the mother for her child.'

'Not so, Teraset! Tell me another way.'

Such boldness vexed the old ones, turned them sullen at the sight of him.

Nonosa hacked the hair from his head and burnt it, in homage to the Spirits.

It did no good.

Again and again, day and night, the little one cried herself to exhaustion. Her crying turned to frightful whimpers, and less and less was the courage that it bore. Nonosa melted snow, encouraged her to suck water from his finger. It prolonged the agony.

He would go in search of another clan. It was all the hope he had. Among the clan perhaps a nursing mother with milk for the child. He would walk the course of the river back to the camp. Follow a branch of the river north to where the Nookwashish should be.

'The girl will die before you find them. Stay.' Coshee was not one for patience, yet he could hardly deny Nonosa his grief. 'Death we must abide.'

Nonosa refused to take his words for truth.

'You know little of this world, Nonosa, and nothing of the next.'

'It hurts no one for the child to live.'

'All around us — Spirits angry at your taunting!'

'I do not fear such Spirits!'

'Banish you, we will! For the sake of every one of us.'

Nonosa ran off, holding the child to his chest. Clutching a spear and a pouch of firestones, taking no time to gather provisions. He would hunt and fish, stave off the cold, question the sky, find shelter before foul weather struck. He escaped the eyes of Tuanon, ran past other hunters, the scampering children, the huddling old ones. Not thinking of himself, thinking of his infant daughter.

Only once did he stop while still in sight of the smoke from their fires. He tucked the infant inside his mantle, against the fur and his own flesh. He strapped her blanket fur to his waist and ran on. He ran to nightfall.

He knew the place for him and the child to rest the night. When he reached it, weary, wet with perspiration, he found the moss beds and fire pits where his clan had stopped on their way to the sea. He made a fire, in hope the sway of his body with hers was what had calmed her hunger cries.

The fire took hold. Nonosa uncovered his infant. Laid her naked on the blanket of caribou fur, a sorrowful wrinkle of a child. A piteous mound amid the long, mottled hairs of brown and yellowed white. She was alive. Barely so. Too weak to cry, a silenced slip of an infant.

'Shanaw.'

He called to her over the crackle of the fire. She glistened with his sweat, and stirred, if only with the slightest motion, the fire steaming the sweat away. He touched water to her lips and saw them part for more. A faint, piteous cry, barely human.

Nonosa wrapped her in the fur and held her to within a breath of his face, the child unable to open her eyes. He chanted charmed words, faraway words, words chanted to him by a mother and father long dead.

'*Little one, cherished one, blood of mine, Spirits' sign.*'

This little one, this cherished one, this withered one — a sign? Why would Spirits loose such pain? Was he not mindful of the Spirits since his first kill as a boy? Ever knowing it was them who gave of their store, not he who took it.

Why would they take his child?

He seldom tramped back from the hunt without a kill. Was it not the pitch of his spear, the keenness of his eye, his cunning tricks to outsmart his prey? Was it only at the pleasure of the Spirits that he made such kills?

Such thoughts dared enter his head and bring him grief! When all around him others had no doubts. 'You question too much, Nonosa.' Always said of him. Without fail, yet they had come to praise his skill with the spear. Depend on his clever ways.

He was the doubter, the questioner. Now the widower, the near-childless outcast.

He lay as near to the fire as was safe. Shanaw he held tight to him, bundled in the curve of his arm. He droned into the darkness and wished her sleep, all the while dreading she might not last the night.

The whispers of the wind, the trickster, were nowhere heard. The stillness fell around Nonosa with a fearsome gravity.

THE BREAK OF MORNING revealed the land, shepherded the contours of the hills. Shanaw was still alive.

The hills brought the memory of the infant's mother. The sun rose over them. In the rays of early morning, he found berries beneath the tufts of snow. Frosted red-berries left over winter. He burst their skins in his mouth, burst an icy tartness.

He dared not think the juice would feed the child. It might be poison to her tender stomach, might end what moments remained. He crammed the fruit into his mouth.

He revived the fire and laid Shanaw near it. Promised her that before the day was gone, she would have her belly filled.

He returned the child to her pouch against his chest and carried on. No prayer to the Spirits passed his lips. Alone, he would make good his promise, or see her die in the womb he had cast for her.

A warming sun filled the sky, glistened off the snow patches. A treasured day of spring.

Suddenly, he heard the trickster laugh. Nonosa embraced his swirling voice. 'Bold one,' he heard. 'Bold in your love.'

He hesitated. His broken step witness to unspoken words.

Nonosa strode with a plan. He sought the familiar signs, the markings, the rubbings, the ways of the caribou. He knew them well enough, could spot the shrubs where caribou had stopped to feed and then passed on. He caught the scent of animals moving fast.

Animals intent on getting to their calving grounds to have their young in peace, far from the herd of males. Away from other birthing cows he came upon a mother and her newborn calf. A calf so new it could not stand on its legs, but fell to the ground each time, its mother licking it still, the calf seeking her teat.

Nonosa lurked in the scrub. His instinct was to grip his spear and fling it at the easy game. He dropped the spear. He slipped the child from inside his mantle, wrapped her in her blanket fur. Her newborn scent lay open to the air. Near lifeless now, a limp, unknowing stray venturing near a nursing mother.

The mother, stretched on her side, raised her head to catch the scent. She dared not run away, her calf not strong enough to follow. Her ears twitched, her nose caught a foreign scent. A hunter playing his hunting games.

Nonosa approached the caribou with low, light-footed strides. The mother suddenly dropped her head. She lay rigid, confused. A lifeless beast, not knowing how to guard her calf, in dread of what might happen next.

Nonosa lay a hand on her flank. Her bony leg flinched, the hoof reared in defence. Nonosa's hand glided down the quarter — firm, faithful — and smoothed it to the ground. He held it there, knowing well it was her choice that it stay. He slowly withdrew his hand. When the leg did not heave, his fingers moved to the deep fur of her back.

His hand lay against the broad muscle, until the caribou knew the gentle weight of it, the steady measure of his intent. He stroked the spot and loudly hummed, his voice a firm and peaceful drone. It eased when he sensed a calm, rose again when she abruptly raised her head. She eyed her sleeping calf, then settled back.

When Nonosa felt her quiet, he moved the calf to a teat. In its half-sleep the calf carelessly mouthed the nipple. It slipped past the calf's lips and out again, drips of milk left hanging there.

Nonosa withdrew one of his arms from his mantle. He loosened the infant from her nest and gently led her along the sleeve until her head emerged. Her ghastly features had sunk deeper into themselves. Just as it looked as if there might arise a meek and sorry cry, Nonosa brought her to the teat. Drips of milk fell across her lips.

Seeped into her mouth. Shanaw stirred enough to like the taste. Her father led her lips to the teat and saw her face twitch faintly at the touch. Her lips settled around the teat. The infant began a weak, sluggish suck, enough to coat her mouth with milk.

Enough to fill her belly.

'NONOSA! COUSIN!'

At the edge of the calving grounds stood a hunter. Tall as Nonosa, thickset, hair hanging past the beaver fur that cloaked his shoulders. A half-circle of polished incisors traced the neckband of his mantle.

A Nookwashish. Remesh by name.

'What are you about, Nonosa?'

The caribou sprang up, tossed Nonosa, and Shanaw with him, backwards onto the moss.

Remesh's spear pierced her chest before the beast's four legs had found the ground. Long before she could nudge her calf in hope it might hold itself upright.

The spear felled the animal. Remesh rushed and cut its slender throat. With the struggling, bewildered calf he did the same. Remesh's lips broadened to a smile, hardly less glaring than the teeth he bore about his neck.

'Your clan moved again. I saw the deserted camp, the trail of you in the distance,' he said, gutting the animals as he talked.

Nonosa told Remesh his story. From the pouch he revealed the head of the child, her milk-soaked face.

Remesh, arch-hunter of the Nookwashish, head man at every test of strength, saw no wisdom in it. 'She will not live. She is too weak.' Though he had no mind to view more than her face. 'Milk of the caribou....' He twisted his mouth.

'Who among your women has milk for her?'

'Biesta, the only one.'

Nonosa could hardly think it — Biesta, Démas's sister.

'We have a newborn son!'

More news to astonish him. 'Biesta has taken to your marriage bed?'

'Lerenn gave me no boy children who lived.'

Nonosa did not dwell on it. 'We must hurry. Before the child dies.'

'A girl nursed at the teat of a caribou? If she grows into a woman she will be a rangy, hairy one,' Remesh declared, his amusement clear, as he took to gutting his game. 'Now, Nonosa, you expect the breasts of Biesta?'

'Are they not full? Is your son not growing strong like his father? One day he will want to wear a cord of polished teeth.'

Remesh, his hands red with blood, walked past Nonosa. He tramped off and cut two slender lengths of spruce. Crossed the legs of the carcasses, lashed them to the poles.

The two men set off.

Against his chest Nonosa felt Shanaw stir, felt the spit of milk mix with his sweat. In time another trickle. Nonosa lowered his head to sniff the air inside his mantle. Piss. A smile edged across his face.

Remesh stopped to strip away his upper fur. He fixed the fur beneath the poles set atop his shoulders.

'Sun on the bare chest. After winter, it does me good.'

At each shift of the poles, thick muscle swelled his shoulders. Sweat glistened across his back.

Remesh set a cruel pace. Tramped on without another stop until finally the poles were set to ground near his canoe. Nonosa groaned against his will, his shoulders chafed raw, the fur around them matted wet with blood.

THE PAIR EMERGED ALONG the path from the river, children scampering ahead of them. Sabbah, his aging aunt, the mother of Remesh, stood before Nonosa, dismayed at his squalidness, especially his senseless crop of hair.

Still, charmed she was to set her eyes on him. 'You have come alone, Nonosa?'

With stiffened arms he drew Shanaw from her pouch. The infant lay in his hands, scrunched and naked. She quickly soured and expelled a piteous cry. Though a cry it was, for all of the Nookwashish to hear.

They stared in disbelief. His aunt sent a young girl scurrying to a lodge and back again with fresh, warm fur. She covered the child with it, scolding Nonosa all the while.

Nonosa looked about. His eyes fell on Biesta, a child in her arms. His head stilled in surprise, she the pure portrait of her sister. She stood in a winter dress of doeskin, patterned with antler beads, fringed with bright breast feathers. She did not draw near, though ears she had for his every word.

The camp fell silent at his story. And at its end their eyes turned to Biesta. Women gathered around her, one taking her child. She leaned against another, silently weeping for her sister.

The question of Shanaw remained. To Remesh they looked for their answer. The infant gave another cry, hardly to be heard.

There could be but one response. 'What we have we share. The Kindred are one people.'

Sabbah gathered the infant from Nonosa and walked across the open ground. Biesta took the child in her arms. Kissed her amid her own tears. Quietly disappeared inside a lodge.

Remesh said, 'There will come a day when a Kanwashish mother will do the same for one of us.'

But no one gave Remesh the attention he expected from his words. He strode off, calling loudly to a bevy of young hunters to help him hang and skin the caribou. The rest of the clan encircled Nonosa, to share in the loss of his cherished wife.

And in time, to ask of the Kanwashish. Of Coshee and his health. Of the other old ones.

'None of them lost this winter, Nonosa. That is good. And your people shifting place again?'

'Yes.'

'A restless lot. No need to move on. Not yet.'

They pressed him for stories of the winter hunts.

'The Spirits are as pleased with the Kanwashish as they are with us.'

'But there is good reason to move. Seas I have found!' He charmed them with stories of the vast and wondrous seas, of endless sea-fish.

He went on and on. Many shook their heads and laughed.

'Keep this notion, Nonosa, and you will become Nonosa, the crazy man. The man wild with words.'

The Nookwashish recalled the Nonosa they knew as a boy, the boy who told impossible tales, the son who would not heed the wishes of his father, the cause of constant torment for his mother.

His father had died one spring by drowning, his mother the next winter with fever. Nonosa showed up in the Nookwashish camp the spring that followed, a young man with the gift of a yearling carcass strapped to his back. Seeking to take Démas home as his wife.

The Nookwashish took pity on him, against the doubts of the girl.

But Nonosa proved himself to her, turned into a sharper hunter than any among his clan. Démas bestowed on him her deep, enduring love.

NONOSA STRETCHED THE LENGTH of the sleeping pit his aunt had set aside for him in a corner of her lodge. His arm curled around his infant daughter, his sleep disturbed by thoughts of Remesh.

Boys together they had been, constant rivals whenever the clans had come together, Sabbah and his own mother forever scolding the pair of them. Nonosa's forehead still bore a scar where Remesh had flung a stick that cut it to the bone.

Their boyish games had given way to fiercer tests of strength. Remesh grew in bulk, just as tall, and broader than his cousin. With a boast-fulness to match his size.

'More boulders needed for the fire pit. Which do you choose?' Nonosa recalled the ring of his voice.

Rocks Nonosa could not dislodge. Remesh staggered under the weight of them, all the while Nonosa prodding him with names. Foolish names Nonosa had concocted, vexing his cousin at every step.

Then prowess of a different sort filled Remesh's head. 'Your cock no more long-lasting than the muscles of your arms! Don't you long to know the secrets of fortune between the furs?' He bent his arm stiffly in the air and laughed aloud.

Now, when their paths crossed, never was it without respect. Hunters more than cousins, the best in each clan. Few were the times their people went without meat. Nonosa had seen the spite in Remesh's eye when he told of the vastness of the sea. In the hunter's mind, he was certain, stirred a notion of some new prowess to be had.

Nonosa drifted finally to sleep.

Past daybreak he woke. Shanaw had gone from the curl of his arm. He jolted upright. Had he rolled atop her, smothered her?

'No worry, nephew. The little one cried again for milk. So fast asleep you were you did not hear. I took her to Biesta.'

Nonosa rose to go to Biesta's lodge. Sabbah motioned him to sit again, handed him a bowl of soup made from ptarmigan.

He ate with eagerness, for he knew Sabbah's way with cooking. In the soup floated young nettle sprouts, freshly picked.

'With Biesta I shared my secrets at the cooking pot. I do not say the same for Lerenn.'

'No fondness for Lerenn?'

'Fondness for her, yes.' She chuckled. 'For her cooking, no.' She poured more soup.

'Remesh has fondness for her. She was the prize of the Dohwashish. There were countless stories of her charms.'

'Remesh returned with Lerenn, proud as if he had felled a herd of stags.'

Nonosa had caught a glimpse of Lerenn when he first arrived. A potent lure, there was no doubt.

'*Beauty of face not a good wife makes.*' Sabbah's scrap of wisdom.

Nonosa finished the last of his soup. Sabbah took the bowl from his hands.

'Lerenn bore him two sons,' she said, more quietly now. 'The first lived but a morning, the other not at all. Remesh was not to be without a son. Biesta bore him a fine boy. Sojon will be as strong a man as his father. As good a hunter.'

'A clan must have its sons.'

'There will come many days when the Nookwashish will feast on his caribou.'

No more to be said. Sabbah's love rested first with her family. Her nephew — as much as she cared for him — would not be with the Nookwashish for long.

'This sleeping pit is here for as many days as you wish. The child will have her milk and grow. And Remesh will never go against the wishes of his mother.'

NONOSA FOUND SHANAW ASLEEP at the feet of Biesta. At her breast a second child, one old enough that his hand wandered about her neck, played with a string of antler beads.

'Already I feed him caribou broth. His father wants to give him bones to gnaw. Too hard on his belly.' She smiled. 'Besides, he has no teeth.'

Remesh suddenly filled the doorway. Biesta's smile fell away.

'Ah, Nonosa, your little one has found much to enjoy at my woman's breast.'

Nonosa stood shoulder-to-shoulder with him, close enough that he smelled his sweat.

'The child is alive. I have your mother to thank, and your wife.'

'Do you forget who led you here?' He let the question settle, then cast it off at his will. 'You owe nothing to the Nookwashish. Stay and make yourself one of us.'

Nonosa said nothing.

He could not rest with the Nookwashish. Nonosa's skill at the hunt made Coshee's threat to banish him a vacant one. The clan knew well what would become of them if their storehouses were not filled. As much as they honoured the Spirits, they had no wish to join them before their rightful time.

Nonosa would go, then return for Shanaw before winter reappeared. Later he came upon his aunt in her lodge, near the fire, hunched over Shanaw lying naked.

Sabbah looked up. 'Your daughter made you proud! Her first shit. A strong one. Her little body works well.'

She charged Nonosa with finding dry moss. He returned with so much his aunt sagged with laughter.

'Take enough for an infant bottom. Warm it by the fire. Rid it of twigs.'

Sabbah laid out a tiny covering of softened hide. 'Sojon's, when he was born.' She lined it with moss, wrapped it between the child's legs and around her waist. Secured it tight with thongs of hide.

'Now, little one. Your father will hold you in his arms, fearlessly.' Chuckling, she lifted the child and presented her to Nonosa.

Nonosa gazed into her face. Content she was, free of pain. Her preciousness filled his heart.

NONOSA WOKE AT DAYBREAK. He kissed the forehead of his daughter and placed her gently in Sabbah's arms. He smiled at Sabbah, gripped her hand for a moment, took his spear from where it rested against the wall, and left the lodge.

He found Biesta alone outside her lodge, airing sleeping furs.

It was another day of melting snow.

Biesta stood up slowly. The morning sun caught her ease, revealed the full detail of her face.

At once it was Démas — the wideness of her eyes, the turn of her mouth, markings of a generous heart.

Nonosa saw no shyness, no worry at who might be watching them. He kept a distance, for Remesh would hear of their meeting. Nonosa stood boldly tall, his spear resting against his shoulder.

He gathered relief in the way her eyes agreed with his. His daughter would not be without affection.

He took up his spear and walked away.

He strode a safe distance from the camp, only then looked back.

Biesta was bent again over the furs, her head in his direction now, her eyes catching a glimpse of his passage through the scrub.

SHANNON

SHANNON PUTS THE NOVEL down. Her taste in books generally runs to non-fiction, but she does have a liking for historical novels. She's not so sure about this fictionalized take on one of the extinct Aboriginal groups of Labrador, but it's not a book she can ignore. She needs to read anything and everything that has been written about the Maritime Archaic.

Her job was listed as a term position 'to analyze and make recommendations for expanded interpretation of the Aboriginal components of three sites — L'Anse aux Meadows in Newfoundland, Red Bay and L'Anse Amour in Labrador.' The Norse, the Basques, the Maritime Archaic and the Beothuks all in one job. The potential staggered her. The opportunity to go back to Newfoundland and Labrador was suddenly and unexpectedly staring her in the face.

Her application would never have seen daylight but for the fact she had the credentials and the job experience to back them up. In some quarters Parks Canada bureaucracy had a reputation for being anal, but Shannon sensed that if she made her case, the interviewers would have no choice but give her a fair hearing.

She flew to Ottawa for the interview and wasn't in the headquarters building in Gatineau twenty minutes before she knew they could hardly say no. She looked good in the interview, but looked even better on paper. She'd written an addendum to the application, demonstrating why she was particularly suited to the job and what she saw as its possible direction.

For two weeks she'd researched material relevant to one of the three sites — the Norse contact with Natives at L'Anse aux Meadows about the year 1000. There was little primary material, only what had been mentioned in the Icelandic Sagas — friendly trading in "Vinland" that over time gave way to violent encounters.

She knew there had to be a deeper story. Shannon found herself drawn to Gudrid, one of the Norse women who came ashore at L'Anse aux Meadows. Gudrid was indomitable, likely the most widely travelled woman of her time. Years later she would voyage to Norway, then on foot to Rome. At L'Anse aux Meadows she gave birth to a boy, the first European child born in the New World.

It was said by Thorfinn Karlsefni that she be Sæhildr, defender of the seas, but Gudrid, wife of Thorfinn, wished to call her by her Skræling name. Thorfinn was not pleased but did not argue long with Gudrid for she had just given birth to their first child, a son. Thorfinn chose to name him Snorri, to honour Snorri Thordarson of Hofdi.

The girl was alone on the rocks, looking out to sea. The people were troubled at the sight of her, for the days just past had been ones of poor trading with the Skrælings and there was fear of revenge from them. Some took it for a trick. Some thought her a lure to draw men to where they would be attacked by Skrælings hiding behind boulders.

She rose up and walked toward them. She stopped at the palisade which Thorfinn had built around his farm to keep out the Skrælings. The people all set their eyes on her and were satisfied she bore no weapons, though some were still uncertain of her powers to bring harm to them.

Gudrid had been the first to see her. Gudrid was sitting outside spinning wool. She motioned to her and the girl approached the opening in the palisade. Gudrid ignored the warnings of the others and ordered the guard to allow the girl past the gate.

The girl was striking of face. Her skin was covered in red ochre in the fashion of Skrælings. She bore large black eyes, clear and quick to move. Her mouth was small but well-formed, with lips only slightly parted until she spoke. Her hair was blacker than any ever seen before, combed tight to her head and shiny with grease. She was dressed in skin clothes that bore fringes of bone pieces and red ribbon cut from cloth traded with the Skrælings by other voyagers to Vinland.

She approached Gudrid and her child, for she seemed to know that Gudrid would be gentle toward her.

Gudrid pointed to herself and spoke her name and then pointed to the child and spoke his name.

The girl announced her own.

The people laughed at her forthright ways for in age she was barely a woman. The Skræling stared at them and spoke in her own language. Gudrid invited her inside the longhouse so she would be alone with her, although there were not many words spoken between them, for Sæhildr's tongue was strange.

Gudrid gave her milk from the cows. The girl liked it very much. She ate skyr and then salted cheese, which wrinkled her face.

The Skræling opened a skin pouch tied to her waist and from it took dried bits of food which looked to be meat. She put one piece in her own mouth, then offered some to Gudrid. Gudrid ate of it and showed a liking for its taste. This was very pleasing to the Skræling.

Snorri woke at that moment and began to cry. Gudrid took him in her arms and rocked him and began to sing to him a song.

The girl Sæhildr took much pleasure in this and began to hum with the singing. When Gudrid sang the words a second time Sæhildr sang with her.

The people who heard her in the other room of the longhouse laughed, for the Skræling stumbled at the words and had no knowledge of their meaning.

Gudrid called out to them, 'Do not laugh. She bears a love for children. She wishes one day to be a mother. In that she is no different than any woman.'

Then Gudrid held her son out to the Skræling and placed the child in her arms. The others were astonished, but again Gudrid called out to them. 'Do not be tormented at the sight of a young woman with a child in her arms. For no woman can show but love for a newborn child. She who would bring harm to a child is not human.'

Sæhildr was filled with delight at holding the boy. She rocked him in her arms and sang to him in her own language.

When Thorfinn Karlsefni entered the longhouse he was not pleased at the sight of his son in the arms of a Skræling and ordered him given back to his wife. Gudrid took him, but not without words to her husband. 'Am I not a Christian?' For Gudrid had become Christian before leaving Greenland.

Thorfinn then spoke, 'I have no wish to harm the Skræling. She must go back to her people, for this is not the place for her.'

Thorfinn stared roughly at the girl until she rose to her feet. The Skræling stood no taller than his chest. In her eyes was the look of a beast of the forest.

Thorfinn then spoke, 'Am I not right to distrust such a look in a woman?' He showed her his sword, not to harm her, but to frighten her.

'Husband, put away your weapon,' Gudrid answered. 'She bears no malice.'

At Gudrid's words Thorfinn returned his sword to its sheath. He reached for the arm of the Skræling to lead her out of the longhouse, but the girl growled like a beast and broke away from him. She held to the side of Gudrid.

Thorfinn's face grew harder. The Skræling looked at him and spoke in her own language. She was loud in her words, but neither Thorfinn nor any among them understood her.

She departed from the longhouse. She raised her open hands and called loudly toward the sea.

A Skræling man appeared from behind the boulders near the shore. He was tall and strong, with a face and arms thick with ochre. He bore a bow in one hand and arrows in the other.

Thorfinn held his sword in the air and shouted at him.

The girl Sæhildr left them and walked toward the opening in the palisade. Gudrid told the others to let her pass. She joined the man and he shielded her. Together they disappeared in the direction of the forest.

Thorfinn then spoke, 'Now this is as it should be — our people among their own and the Skrælings among their own.'

WHAT SHE HAD COMPOSED offered a more human perspective, she explained, sitting as it did at a comfortable distance from the centre of the gruesome encounters. A prime consideration, given that a considerable number of visitors to the Norse site at L'Anse aux Meadows are families, and interpretation of any Historic Site must always take into account diversity in visitor base.

Shannon was taking a calculated risk, based on a belief that in the right hands the imagined saga could take on a refreshing, maternal quality. Fortunately, it had landed in a pair of the right hands, and when one of the interviewers leaned forward and complimented Shannon on the 'deftness of the scenario' she had created, Shannon was guessing it boosted her to the top of the applicant pile. Shannon thanked her, knowing full well Parks Canada interview language rarely gets as spontaneous as what she had just witnessed.

The job was hers. Shannon was given a week to make a decision.

She needed a change. Her personal rut was only growing deeper by the month. On day three following the offer she sent the email confirming her acceptance.

DURING THE INTERVIEW IT was clear that Parks Canada considers L'Anse aux Meadows one of the jewels in its chain of National Historic Sites. The site has garnered a UNESCO World Heritage designation and every summer thousands of visitors stream to its cluster of reconstructed eleventh-century Norse dwellings. Still, it's common knowledge that the powers-that-be in the federal government have been clamouring for more Aboriginal content in the site's interpretation.

Up to this point the focus has been the Norse. The tourist trade would prefer the more lively and fearsome "Viking," but Norse is what they really were. Inside the turf-walled buildings, with fires blazing and animal skins spread across the seating platforms, with a great bearded Norseman and suitably robust Norsewoman telling stories — it all makes for a lively and informative, but rather one-sided, interpretation.

The known Sagas give some clue as to what happened, but every bureaucrat at Parks Canada realizes that the truth about events at any Historic Site can never be fully known. Shannon thinks that's where her invented, but entirely plausible, saga fits in. Not to go beyond the confines of Parks Canada of course. Rather, an internal tool to stir bureaucratic thinking on directions for a new interpretative plan, one that draws in an Aboriginal component, gives it due significance, but doesn't unhinge the carload of kids in the midst of their relaxing family vacation.

Shannon realizes she's on slippery ground, that it is not as simple as it sounded to her when she first came up with the approach. She is aware that archaeologists have a critical claim to the site, as narrow as their thinking might be at times.

Subsequent Aboriginal history definitely compounds the situation, as

Shannon knows well enough from past experience. It stands as the great unspoken consideration.

In any case, as Shannon proposed to the interviewers: Is there ever complete certainty about the past? Shouldn't they be looking for open ground among all the shards of argument? Open ground, it went without saying, acceptable to all stakeholders.

SHANNON PARKS THE CAR near the bottom of the path. The walk on this summer's day is not without its doubts. She is calm and admiring of the smartly planned, well-tended ribbon of plants along the fenced side of the path. A woman's affable touch, she thinks, a pleasant enough addition.

There is a screened door, and behind it a second door partway open. She presses the bell. It has a ring she doesn't remember.

The woman who appears has no reason to recognize her, nor does Shannon have any reason to recognize the woman. She assumes it's Jerome's wife. Shannon is momentarily startled by her appearance. The woman has Inuit heritage. Some generations past, but still evident.

'Hello.' The woman smiles quietly, as if she is not standing before a stranger. 'I think you must be Shannon.'

Shannon knows she shouldn't be surprised at the woman's response. In Conche, news and corresponding descriptions travel with unrelenting speed.

'We have the high school yearbook,' the woman says, her smile more pronounced. 'And you haven't changed all that much, from the pictures I've seen.'

Shannon finds a voice that is not in the least ambivalent. 'Is Jerome at home?'

'Yes, he is. Would you like to come inside?' She adds, 'My name is Marie.'

Shannon sees no point in a repetition of her own.

'Thank you very much.'

She avoids using the woman's name, unwilling to confirm that it's perfectly reasonable Marie should be there.

Jerome doesn't appear in the narrow confines of the porch. He stands in the middle of the kitchen. From a living room can be heard the clamorous chatter of TV.

'I'll turn that off,' Marie says. She exits and eventually eliminates the grinding Sunday sports program.

The brief period she is out of the kitchen is the time for Shannon and Jerome to acknowledge each other.

'You've heard I'm back in Newfoundland. I thought it useful if I came by.'

Useful is the wrong word choice, but that is of no consequence. The fact that she is standing before him is the situation at hand.

'Have a seat.' Shannon suspects it is no different than what he would say to anyone. In Newfoundland the kitchen is the room for visitors. She sits in one of the chairs.

'Like a cup of tea?'

It's rather too early in the game to be offering tea. Shannon sees the man is wading, needing somewhere to take a conversation.

'A glass of water would be fine.'

'We're not used to the heat. Too warm outside for me, this is.'

Talk of the weather holds no more weight. Yet she has no intention of being aggressive. She positions herself solely as the returning daughter of the first wife. To the house in which the foreigner spent eighteen years of her existence. Proactive curative strategy. Her intentions are merely social. She sees he could do with proof. 'How have you been keeping, Jerome? Well?'

'I can't complain.'

As tempting as it is to ask about his back, his eyes, his headaches, and his gout, she refrains. The echoes of ailments past are best left in the past.

'Prostate,' Marie says.

The word hangs still for a moment. The overweight Jerome is sitting at the kitchen table fiddling with a salt shaker.

'But he's good now,' Marie adds quickly. 'Thank the Lord.'

Indeed. Jerome has a personal saviour. Things have worked out well. Catholic, Shannon presumes, of course. But she is wrong.

'Pastor Levi calls it a miracle.'

Pentecostal. Marie's contribution to their married life.

'I can't complain,' Jerome brings forth again.

The dialogue needs redirection. Marie's own miracle might be next.

'I see you have made a few changes to the house.'

This jerks the arrow of discomfort skyward. Jerome brings the pepper shaker into play. Shannon knows she should attempt to alleviate the fears. To confirm her own strength, if nothing else.

Marie hands her a glass of water, and places a mug in front of Jerome. It has no tea in it yet, but that doesn't prevent Jerome from spooning in sugar and adding a prolonged stream of canned milk.

Marie moves to defuse the awkwardness.

'Jerome and his brother built the porch. What was there was a bit small and pokey. I don't know if you remember it.'

She thinks: I did go in and out of it for a complete childhood and adolescence.

The silence leads to the topic of the overhaul of the kitchen. New cupboards, new wallpaper. Thickly applied country kitsch.

'It's a big change,' Shannon says, pleasant enough. She realizes she has to bring a halt to the inanity, before Marie has her touring the house and the spaces upstairs, which Shannon knows she must avoid if she is to retain any semblance of civility, not to mention bloody personal equilibrium.

She refuses to linger on thoughts about the house. The conversation shifts to the inevitable — the exodus from the outports to Alberta, to which she has no opinion to add that hasn't been expressed a thousand times before.

Neither Jerome nor Marie mentions Patti, which only confirms for Shannon that nothing much has changed.

After no more than fifteen minutes Shannon stands up and sets herself on leaving, having told Jerome she's glad she came by, that it was something she's had in her mind to do since she came back, that she hopes the weather cools.

'Before you go ...,' Marie says and disappears upstairs.

Eventually she returns with a floral gift bag, a match for the wallpaper.

'These are yours. You should have them.'

SHANNON KNOWS WHAT'S IN the bag. She opens it only when she gets back to her apartment. Even at that the bag sits on the floor by the door for hours, until she decides opening it is less of a curse than watching it turn into a damn eyesore.

There's the jewellery box, the plate, three Christmas ornaments, though not ones she remembers. There is a collection of photographs, held together with a rubber band.

A picture of Shannon and her mother. Recently framed. She doesn't open the jewellery box, or look at the other pictures, but crams everything into the bottom drawer of her bedroom dresser.

The bottom of the gift bag still has its fluorescent price sticker. Likely from a dollar store.

She takes the next day off work and drives right back to Conche with a plant for her mother's grave. She hasn't been at the gravesite since her mother's death. She has a picture sent to her by the company she and Patti hired to engrave and install the headstone. It is modest and unobtrusive, as her daughters believed she would have wanted. Beside it someone has placed a gaudily coloured ceramic statue of the Virgin Mary. Shannon braces herself, but that does nothing to suppress the tears.

THE PLACE SHE HAS been renting since her return is in St. Anthony, the only community of any size in the area. During her years in BC she grew use to anonymity. St. Anthony doesn't offer much.

She has set up an office in the apartment, but a good deal of her time is spent on the road, back and forth to the Norse site at L'Anse aux Meadows. Her evenings are often spent alone, watching television, emailing friends in BC, reading. Immersing herself in Aboriginal history, real and imagined.

When the emails from BC, all so effortlessly animated, turn too short in comparison to her own, she experiences an emotion she hasn't known for several years — the hollowness that comes from quick, and likely permanent, separation from good friends. It's inevitable, she realizes, that the emails would start to peter out. That the time it takes for responses would no longer jive with the excuses offered in their opening lines. In her acceptance of that, loneliness bears down on her.

She fights it, of course. First by initiating an end to most of the correspondence. By the latter part of June she is keeping regular contact with only two of her BC friends. Two of the sea-kayaking sisters she has known for years. Who, since she left, have become a permanent couple. And who, now, suddenly, are using Shannon as a detached sounding board during the unfolding dramas of their relationship.

In the last email they talked of getting married, perhaps in the fall. It hadn't been a surprise to Shannon that their attraction to each other had heated up suddenly, something having sparked a change from the on-again, off-again partnership they'd had for years.

Shannon is halfway through replying to their last email when it suddenly strikes her that her own departure from the scene in some way propelled them in that direction. She can't believe it hadn't crossed her mind before.

She stops composing the email and moves away from the computer. She sits on the sofa with her coffee and reconsiders what took place over the months prior to her leaving BC.

She had made it known from the beginning that she was heterosexual, given that it was obvious a number in the group were not. Perhaps the breakup with Kim had released new doubts among the others, put a new set of possibilities on the table. Thinking about it now, months later and at the other end of the country, she can't understand why she had been so blind. So unreservedly naive.

In which case she's only too glad to have left and made room for whatever emotions were ready to race out of the starting gates. And from a distance attempt to analyze the dimensions of Jillian's relationship with her. The willingness to help check on her apartment when she and Kim were away, the snappy note left in her mailbox during the week following Kim's permanent exit.

When Shannon let it out that she had accepted a job in Newfoundland, Jillian had been the one to drop by unannounced with the hope that Shannon might somehow go back on her decision. Jillian had come alone, without Ursula.

What was there beyond wine-assisted reminiscence of their better kayak trips, and the expected hugs and promises to stay friends? So why is it obvious to her now that Jillian was making openings for something more? A matter of distance sharpening the perspective? She doesn't know, she just feels it.

Three months later, at Ursula's instigation undoubtedly, they are running their wedding plans by her. What Jillian might or might not feel toward Shannon now can't be of much concern. Jillian, it would appear, had the smarts to put that vacant segment of her life behind her. Does Shannon in the background, only an email away, complicate the picture?

Shannon concludes it does, decides it better to back off entirely. She returns to the computer and deletes what she has written so far in reply to their last message. She will answer, just not yet. In a few days.

SHE HAS EFFECTIVELY SEVERED herself from a life she no longer wants, but one she does miss. For someone used to a social life peppered with single-female escapades over the years, the new reality takes getting used to. She wants to think of it as a period of personal shift, and has made a conscious decision not to seek out much beyond work, her apartment, and her trips to Conche. How long that will last she has no idea, but for now she is determined to stick to the plan.

She does go to a restaurant now and then, to a club for a drink on occasion with some of the Parks Canada people she has met since her arrival, but she generally leaves early and always alone. There are times she desperately misses a physically well-armed man thrashing about the sheets at night, but another relationship is not something she is willing to endure at the moment.

SHE HAS HER PRIORITIES, and first among them is to take firm control of the work assignment, make of it something that will add significantly to her profile within Parks Canada. She has nine months to do the research, formulate her proposals with input from the Aboriginal community, write and present her report with recommendations. In her mind she has set out a timeline, and anticipates being able to stick to it. She has never been so regimented, acted with such purpose.

She knows she is not particularly well-liked among the present Parks Canada staff at L'Anse aux Meadows. Anyone sent in from outside to initiate change rarely is. The fact that she is a Newfoundlander helps, but only marginally. For some, in fact, it likely confirms a mistrust. Why would anyone come back after being away twenty years if not to demonstrate that she knows better than those who stayed? In the back of some minds there is the fear of losing their jobs, especially those involved in the re-enactments.

Shannon is tempted to say that if someone can play the role of a Norseman, he can likely get away with being a Native as well. Tempted, but not foolish enough to do so. She goes out of her way to assure them that they have no cause to worry, that, if anything, there would likely be more people hired, not less. One of the goals of the reinterpretation is, after all, to increase the profile of the site and up the visitor potential.

She is well aware just how dependent the local people are on the site for work, and for the boost it gives the summer economy. That and icebergs. What, since the closing down of the cod fishery in 1992, have become near–ghost towns the rest of the year come valiantly alive for four months, June to September.

Gros Morne National Park, at the southern end of the Peninsula, is the initial draw. That brings the tourist trade within four hours by vehicle to L'Anse aux Meadows. The local business strategy is maintaining the profile of the site so that people will want to make the trek up the length of the Peninsula. In fact, on a warm summer's day the drive is a jewel in itself.

Not that the fate of the L'Anse aux Meadows site is in her hands. It's absolutely not. She knows there's too much at risk to allow her to run untethered with any proposals. Whatever she recommends, powers greater than her own will veto it if it threatens to undermine local interests. Political powers of one stripe or another.

The political masters at the moment are a conservative and visionless lot. By consensus, boors in three-piece suits. Demonstrate something that smells of movement beyond the status quo, and sensors activate. The federal government is paranoid about change that might in any way engender controversy.

Ironically, change is what they have to initiate, in order to soothe the Aboriginal stakeholders across the country who feel under-represented in the interpretation of Historic Sites. To avoid at all costs the sight of them with placards blocking roads. Especially with an election a distinct possibility.

It's a careful balancing act, but one Shannon knows she can handle. She understands the need to go slow.

For several days in a row she doesn't show up at L'Anse aux Meadows. And when working in the apartment starts to feel claustrophobic, she decides it's time to shift gears, and pay preliminary visits to the other two sites.

She starts with the Burial Mound at L'Anse Amour. She decides not to inform the person responsible for the site, the head of Parks Canada at nearby Red Bay. She wants to be alone when she first encounters it.

The site itself is a modest, unobtrusive affair, located on a sandy terrace, the ocean not far beyond. In 1973 a construction crew, working on a new road into the community of L'Anse Amour, came upon the circle of boulders that shapes the mound. Clearly old and clearly manmade. The following summer a crew of archaeologists from Memorial University in St. John's arrived and began excavation. What they discovered was an ancient burial site — 7,500 years old, three thousand years before the Pyramids — one that for its age and complexity has few to match it anywhere in the world.

Once the excavation work was complete, the sand was returned and the boulders put back in place. Bare sand dunes surround them on three sides, and beyond the far side is a dwarfed, wind-warped ridge of coniferous trees, a buffer between the mound and the expanse of Labrador landscape.

This is what Shannon comes upon. Little different from what it must have looked like for millennia, except for the viewing platform and its interpretative plaques some distance away, next to the road.

The road leads to a community with only a handful of permanent residents. It sees very little traffic, and, as Shannon expects, the site itself is deserted. She parks her vehicle and walks to the viewing platform. She pays no attention to the plaques, choosing to lean against the railing and look beyond it to the mound.

Her reaction in the first moments is purely aesthetic. She is struck by how unassuming it is, a simple undulation in the landscape, a circular rock configuration that alone would escape any passing driver's attention.

Her impulse is to get closer. She steps away from the platform, descends the slight embankment, and slowly approaches the boulders. She has read every report written about the mound, and anticipates it now being a purely pedagogical exercise, giving direct form to the pictures she has seen.

Unexpectedly, her pace slows. She stops, the decision to draw closer aborted. She stands, her arms folded firmly in front of her.

It is partly the wind off the ocean. She feels the chill and pulls her arms tighter to her chest. She thinks herself the outsider — the jeans, the hiking boots, the bulky cable-knit sweater, a down-filled red vest. Her short trim hair, highlighted blond, brushed about by the wind.

The boulders recede. The sand gives way. She stands at the pit's edge, peers a metre and a half below the surface at the skeleton of a twelve-year old child. Buried with a cache of tools and weapons. A flute made from the hollow leg bone of a bird. A child buried face down, a large flat stone across its back.

She believes it to be a boy, although archaeologists have not determined the gender. She starts to sink forward, but catches herself, stiffens upright. When her eyes rest, she is looking into the distance, to the beach where the child would have played. Her upper body trembles, her eyes return to the circle of blackened, lichen-encrusted boulders.

NONOSA

I N THE BOW OF Tuanon's canoe she sat, without a paddle. Stiffly, her arms clutching something to her chest. Nonosa knew the person to be a woman, even from a distance. He stared at her, and at his brother Tuanon manoeuvring the canoe through the rough water, steadily closer.

For a paralyzing moment it was Démas. As if his wife were returning, as if she had crossed paths with his brother. He bringing her home.

Nonosa heard the baby cry. Saw the woman untie the front of her robe, bring the child to her breast. The cry rose sharply and was gone.

The riverbank was strewn with Kanwashish, startled, too, by the sight of the woman. For most knew her from the times the clans had come together.

Biesta — appearing out of nowhere? They turned to Nonosa.

An answer came from Biesta herself, though not one to satisfy them. She stepped from the boat. She stood before Nonosa, placed Shanaw in his arms. 'A healthy young girl.'

Hardly had the words left her lips when Biesta's head began to sway. Her body slumped to the sand.

Nonosa set the child in another's arms, dropped to his knees. He stretched out her legs. He extended one hand into the river water until the hand was ice cold, then laid it across her forehead. She stirred enough that she could be helped to a lodge. Hot broth revived her even more. She slept.

She awoke to find herself alone with Nonosa and his child.

'At night I made a fire,' she said. 'We huddled together under the fur I had strapped to my back. There were berries to eat. When we reached the river I followed it, as you said you would do when you left us in the spring. I walked for days, and then I saw the Kanwashish canoes.'

'The child could have waited until I returned to the Nookwashish,' Nonosa said.

Biesta took Shanaw in her arms and began to nurse her.

'Sojon has finished with my milk. No longer is he my child. Remesh insists Lerenn is now his rightful mother.'

Nonosa saw how eager Shanaw was for her breast, how much stronger a child she was than the one first brought to Biesta. Shanaw made a contented moan. Her hand wandered about Biesta's neck, playing with its cord of antler beads.

Nonosa was left alone with the child as Biesta slept. He laid her on a sleeping fur by the fire. She kicked her bare legs and filled his ears with bright and blissful sounds.

'Father,' he said, leaning over her. He formed the word more slowly, 'Father.'

She made more music, smiled and waved her arms and kicked her legs about.

Her smile filled him with pride. He was desperate to see it again, so he smiled broadly himself, puckered his lips, made odd little mouth noises. Shanaw's face stiffened. Her lower lip began to quiver. There came a pitiful whimper, only growing louder.

'You will wake Biesta. She needs her sleep. Don't cry, little one, don't cry.'

Nonosa mimicked chirpy birds. Hummed and grinned and wriggled his fingers. Hoisted her to his shoulder and rocked her back and forth. Nothing stopped her tears.

Biesta rose sleepily from the back of the lodge, took Shanaw in her arms. The child's cry turned back to a whimper, then faded slowly away.

'What will you do, Nonosa, when she no longer needs my milk? Will you wish I were still here to take care of her?'

The women of the Kanwashish would take care of her — that was the way. Yet he had no wish for her to be raised by women in another lodge, her father a stranger to her.

Was it time he took another wife? Was that the question from Biesta?

The thought of Biesta as his wife had already stirred in him. When he looked at her singing to the little one, he could only think she should be the second mother to his child.

Yet he dared not wish for her as a woman for his marriage bed. There was no stealing another man's wife.

Biesta looked at him. 'Remesh brought me to his bed for one reason. My duty is done, now the child is theirs. No longer am I of any use to Remesh. He has Lerenn and a son. That satisfies him.'

Nonosa said nothing.

'Only Sabbah knew of my going. Remesh was away to the hunt.'

'She also knows her son,' said Nonosa. 'She knows his temper.'

'Remesh does not own me! No parent gave me to him. I chose to deliver him a child, that is all. He gave me food, had clothing made for me while I bore his son. Now I am free to do as I choose.'

Nonosa knew of wives who went to live with other men, but only with the consent of the first husband, only when there were not enough wives for all the men who needed them.

'Remesh will command that you return.'

Biesta scoffed. 'He will find another wife soon enough. Let him travel to the Dohwashish and try his luck again.'

Raw words, thought Nonosa, for a young woman.

THAT NIGHT, AFTER SHANAW had fallen asleep, Biesta tucked her between furs in one corner of the lodge, in the sleeping pit Nonosa prepared for both of them.

'The child has not known her father since birth,' Nonosa had overheard Biesta say to the other women. 'It is right that she be there.' Still, it made for whispered talk, though Nonosa cared not that it did.

He sat close to the fire, inspecting his spears, readying them to strap together, for the next day the camp would be disbanded. Biesta sat near him. She poured water in a wooden bowl, added heating stones to it.

The firelight caught their faces, enough for an exchange of glances, enough for Biesta to see that Nonosa was not as intent on his work as it first appeared. One of the hide straps broke and he grumbled in mock anger. He glanced her way, caught the end of her smile.

He worked on, glancing again from time to time. She removed leaves from a small pouch, added them to the water. He caught their odour — fresh, pungent wintergreen. It kindled memories of lying flat to the ground in the mists of early morning, in wait for great long trails of caribou.

With a square of softened hide, Biesta soaked clean her face and neck. Sitting back on her legs, she untied her robe, eased it from her shoulders and let it fall in a mound around her waist. Her sudden display of nakedness — so shameless, so untroubled — swept over him.

Démas gone just one season past, and his passions ripening so quickly?

Biesta's hand curved down and around her breasts, the firelight flickering over them. In their rounded fullness such perfect, alluring flesh. Nipples of ripened berries. Their taste the taste of dew on wintergreen.

She bent over the bowl for more water, drew her breasts against herself with an outspread hand. She rose to her knees, her robe falling away. The dusky light caught the curve of her body, the passage of her hand along it. From beneath her breasts, slowly down one thigh. Biesta turned slightly, her back toward him now.

She bent a hand to wash her back. It failed to reach between her shoulders. Nonosa edged nearer to her, drew the cloth from her hand. Did not startle her, nor did he show surprise at her soft pleasure moans. He washed the upper reaches of her back, drew the cloth lightly, gently along her spine. Lingered before placing the cloth back in her hand.

He moved back to where he had been sitting, all the while staring at her, at her private moments of washing now traced by the motion of her arm. She finished, placing the bowl and cloth out of sight.

She eased herself between his sleeping furs, stretched and curled down one side of them.

The firelight revealed but the mound of her body. From time to time the mound stirred. He imagined an arm brushing over her breasts, one leg sliding against the other. If there was a reason not to follow her into the sleeping pit, if the memory of Démas was any impediment, it faded to a distant murmur.

He set aside the bundle of his spears. Added more wood to the fire. Sparks flew up, the flames intensified. He removed each of his skin boots, laid them down as he always did, their open ends in the direction of the fire. He untied the belt and its knife from his waist, set it aside. In the heat of the fire he peeled his thin mantle over his head. Hung it from the poles that framed the lodge.

The flames caught a lean and sturdy torso, darkened almost to russet by the sun, by the polish of red ochre. It bore a glistening sheen of sweat. A scar angled down his rib cage, remnant of a caribou hunt. His fingers ran along it out of habit, reminding him that his skills now at the hunt were equal to any man's.

His hide pants ended tight to his calves, just long enough for the skin boots to cover. He loosened the waist of his pants, peeled them to the ground. Lifted one leg and then the other, stepped out of them. He hung them overhead beside the mantle.

Nonosa stood naked before the fire, his legs apart. Heat rose up and collected between his thighs, inciting him more. He locked one hand around the other's wrist, stretched his arms their height above his head. He arched his spine and for the moment held the length of his body taut.

Cold grazed his back and rump. Nonosa slid between the furs, found the heat that had accumulated there.

His body curved into Biesta's, one arm wrapping around her. No modesty, no hesitant exploration. Hard as ever he had been, and she so eager she hardly turned to face him before her hand held his cock, rubbing it against her, probing the moist folds between her legs. He rolled above her, his mouth falling to her breasts, his tongue suddenly ravenous at her nipples. He reached one arm behind him and yanked away the furs, to have the heat and cold play about their nakedness.

She delighted in the heft of him, lingering in the pleasures of the entry. She twisted, wrapped her legs in him, seeking satisfaction equal to his own. He now the fervid, anxious one, eager to drive his shaft, drive the wave of delirium to its limits.

She gave herself to his wishes. Her legs tightened, he his full rigid length, the thrusting now a mad, visceral affair. She swept her hands down his back and into the curve beneath his buttocks, holding to his every stroke. When the peak came, he slowly, gently sank into her, exhausted flesh curving onto exhausted flesh.

He fell asleep in the odour of wintergreen, dreamed of vast herds of caribou.

THE KANWASHISH HAD PROSPERED into people of the sea. Multitudes of cod made mariners of their landsmen. Their success crowned them with courage.

Now, with the first signs of winter, it was the time to be turning inland again, to the camping grounds they had left that spring. Already one trip of the canoes had been made.

The morning broke, brisk, cloudless, promising a day of steady travel. Nonosa stood at the river, watched dawn shape it, reveal its breath of vapour. The camp had begun to stir.

To Nonosa rivers were the life creases of the land. They severed the infinite rock, yielded a home where a people might never suppose one could be. Rivers were the links between clans, the force drawing Kindred together, the concord letting them find space apart. Nonosa loved how each morning they were the first to draw breath again.

He was not long at the river when before him stood a groggy Tuanon, bare-chested, his skin pants askew. His brother scratched his head through a thick mess of hair, shivered with the cold. Tuanon and the other paddlers had done little but eat and sleep since their return from carrying Coshee and the older ones inland.

'No worse for your journey, brother?'

'Coshee bore the first joy of steering Teraset. But only out of sight of the sea. Then I, the privileged one! Each day I grew stronger at her moaning, and ashore I had only a dim echo in my ears!'

Nonosa and Tuanon fell against each other in laughter.

It quickened the dawn, brought the curious from their beds. Women emptied the lodges of their bundles, piling them on the riverbank.

The men, Nonosa leading them, stripped the hides from the lodge frames, the eager young climbing for the highest ones, unbinding the poles. The hides they rolled and tied, set in the bottom of the canoes. What poles were needed they lashed into a raft, for towing in the water behind.

The Kanwashish gathered about a shoreline fire for a last meal of fresh cod-fish. Biesta lingered outside the circle, Shanaw in her arms, staring out to sea.

She pointed north and east. 'There,' she said. 'No end to it, Nonosa?'

'We would not paddle far before our boats would be swallowed by the sea. But everything must have an end.'

Nonosa took Shanaw in his arms. He passed her to one of the women seated around the fire. The woman passed Shanaw to another, and her to another, all charmed by the health and vigour of the child.

'Biesta will live among us,' Nonosa announced. 'She has brought my daughter and I have taken Biesta for my wife.' He announced it with such boldness there would be no questioning him. Biesta gathered Shanaw to her, with great pleasure held the child tight to her chest.

IT WAS A JOURNEY of three days.

All the while Tuanon turned Nonosa's mind to caribou, the great fall hunt to follow. Tuanon could barely quell his elation at its prospect. Only the sighting of their camp stilled the excited chatter between canoes.

There was no waving of arms from the riverbank, no answers to their yelling. A silent few had gathered, in wait for the canoes to strike land.

Nonosa's eyes fell on a canoe overturned onshore. His eyes shifted — to a lone figure standing away from the riverbank. A terse cry sprang from Biesta.

The figure sharpened in its unmoving grimness. An unrelenting rock, outlined in stiff hide, only the trim of beaver fur moving in the wind. His eyes were fixed on Nonosa.

Child tight to her chest, Biesta rushed from the canoe, stumbled, ran up the riverbank to someplace beyond the lodges.

Nonosa called, 'Remesh! Cousin!' He climbed the riverbank, started toward him.

The cousins, the rivals, the husbands of Biesta, stood face to face.

'It was Biesta's choice to leave.' Nonosa pushed at Remesh with his words. And not without satisfaction, he pushed at him again. 'I have taken her for my wife.'

Remesh's thick hands latched onto his throat.

'Almighty tongue!'

Nonosa locked his own hands around Remesh's wrists, senseless against such hateful strength.

Remesh jerked him free. Nonosa rubbed his throat, regained his breath.

Remesh had no intention of bringing him to his end, for such a deed could never be right in the eyes of the Kindred. Neither was there a chance he would succeed. The rest of the Kanwashish had come running, feverish to attack.

When Tuanon drew back a stick to strike, Nonosa thrust himself between them. Another Nookwashish, one who had come with Remesh in the canoe, raced to his defence.

Coshee stood among them, out of breath. 'This is not the way of our people! Not the way of settling wife quarrels!'

That night, around a fire, the Kanwashish came together. It settled nothing. Nonosa charged that if wives were not plentiful, one man was not to have two while another did without.

'Nonosa did nothing to find another wife!' Remesh declared. 'His first barely cold when he took her sister to his bed.'

Biesta had not shown herself lest Remesh's temper be unleashed on her.

'Never for the woman to decide,' proclaimed Remesh.

'In wife quarrels,' Coshee shouted above him, 'we seek the guidance of the Spirits.'

There was silence.

'At sunrise you will both depart the camp. In canoe, each with a bowman. Remesh — turn upstream. Nonosa — down. By sunset on the third day will be known whose ways have been most pleasing to the Spirits. We will see who has returned with the greatest kill. That man shall have Biesta for his wife.'

Nonosa looked at Coshee. In the direction set for Remesh were the caribou crossings. Did Coshee despise him so much he would give unfair advantage to another clan?

Coshee beckoned Biesta to reveal herself. She came into the light clutching Shanaw to her. The child cried, Biesta soothed her with great diligence, leaving no doubt as to her choice of husband.

'Biesta — stay apart from these rivals until the troubles are past,' Coshee announced. 'Remesh, son of our dear Sabbah, shall take a sleeping pit in my lodge.'

Remesh declared it a place of honour.

Coshee had reclaimed the inland camp as his domain. The Kanwashish followed him, relieved to have escaped great grief between the clans.

All but his wife. 'Such foolishness, Coshee,' she muttered, as the Kanwashish dispersed.

'Teraset ...'

'Nonosa needs a wife. The child must have a mother.' Teraset was not to be silenced. She was old and crippled and hardly in her right mind. She had no reason to keep her thoughts to herself. 'Why does Remesh think he has a right to two wives? One is enough for any man, is it not? Is it not, Coshee?'

BY NIGHTFALL ON THE first day Nonosa and Tuanon reached the sea. They built a fire, settled on a well-worn spot. For shelter they used poles and hides left behind only days before.

Nonosa took to his spear. From caribou antler he had carved a slender tip, hollowed to fit over the end of the wooden shaft. Down one side of the antler tip he worked a hole. To it he tied a long cord of braided hide.

That night Nonosa slept but fitfully. The rhythms of the sea striking the shore were not enough to ease him into morning.

The morning brought great astonishment!

Neither Nonosa nor Tuanon could have predicted such a creature. So different was it from any creature they had ever seen, so different from any ever told about in all the stories of their people.

They crouched in awe of it. A grey, leathery mound of a beast. A giant seal? But flaunting a pair of bone shafts from its thickly bristled mouth. Nonosa clenched the new spear in his hand, drawing no closer than the rock that hid them from its view. Though it seemed not to move on land any faster than a seal, might it not surprise them and attack? What if his spear should wound it, could the creature not rear up and thrust itself at him?

'If we are hunters, this is our prey,' murmured Tuanon earnestly. 'If we are not, let us paddle back, heads hung to our chests.'

Tuanon was near pleading, the moment so intense it pushed Nonosa into the open. Nonosa rose his full height, rushed madly toward the beast, spear stretched above his head. Tuanon ran behind.

At the sight of the pair the beast discharged a great bellowing snort, its mat of whiskers flaring from its upper lip. It reared its blunt knob of a head. Tusks, the length of a forearm, lashed the air.

It flung ahead its foreflippers. A sudden lurch thrust the rest of it toward the sea. A second thrust would surely cast it in the water, where it was certain to escape, its flippers driving it beneath the waves.

Nonosa stopped, drew back his spear, flung it with a vigorous whip of his arm. It tore into the thick and wrinkled skin collected at the neck. Broke its stride. Yet the wounded beast pushed on, twisting its head wildly to rid itself of the spear.

The shaft fell away, the tip still embedded in the beast. From it trailed the cord, its end coiled around Nonosa's hand. He hauled the cord hand-over-hand until it jerked taut. Jerked the creature's head askew.

'Charge it, Tuanon! Charge your spear into its skull!'

Nonosa dug his feet into the sand, set his strength against the cord. The beast proved far the mightier, yet its thrust toward the sea was slowed, enough that Tuanon caught up with it.

The creature reared, then lunged. Its tusks flailed the air. Tuanon fell backwards, barely escaping their slice. Scrambled to his feet, and backed away. The beast within a last lunge of the water, he thrust the spear. Struck above one eye, left the beast to make but a final, flopping, useless stride. Its head sagged, bleeding onto the wet sand. The lap of salt water turned to red.

Nonosa held taut the cord. Tuanon raced for a rock. He lifted the rock to his chest, sent it smashing down onto the skull.

The brothers neared the carcass, wary still of what it might do. When they knew for sure it was dead, Tuanon jumped on top of it, arms triumphant in the air.

In time they drew hands over its hairless, wrinkled hide, awed by its toughness. Brushed their fingers against the rigid slivers hanging from its lip. Ran a hand down each tusk. Such an odd, misbegotten creature that for the moment they thought there might not be another like it in the world. Then came a wailing chorus from an island not far offshore and a surge of thick mounds rushing into water.

When the tumult ended they chose the creature's name.

LOADING THE ANIMAL ABOARD the canoe proved a dire task. Its stomach split, its guts aside, the creature was still a hulking aberration. The brothers heaved and strained, and in the end abandoned all hope of lifting it aboard.

Rolling it into the canoe proved no less a plight. The canoe sank into the sand, impossible to move. They hauled the carcass free, dragged it through the tide to low water. In a final scrap of energy they rolled the carcass aboard the canoe again. Then rested, the rising water setting the canoe afloat.

Just barely, and it would not bear their own weight in addition to the load. Now the task was walking the canoe upriver, perpetually knee-deep in frigid water.

But their conquering was complete. Only the voyage home remained.

They travelled all day, through a moonlit night. At dark on the third day, they glimpsed a fire, one lit in secret by Biesta. They fell onto the shore.

A crowd gathered. They dragged themselves to their feet. 'We lost hope, Nonosa,' said one. 'Remesh is long returned, his caribou hanging in our storehouse for all to marvel at.'

'And him to sit around Coshee's fire, gorging on victory.'

Suddenly, the Kanwashish no longer surrounded Nonosa and Tuanon, but encircled their canoe. In moonlight they beheld the beast. It lay on its back, its flippers wedged upright like broad and broken paddles.

'Walrus,' Tuanon told them. 'We have brought home a walrus.'

The only sounds were of incredulity. Tuanon shouted, 'Build up the fire, so you can see it in all its glory.'

Firelight spread over the marvel. A torch of dead sticks was brought forth to hold above it. At the sight of the creature's tusks falling from its bristled mouth there rose up a deep and awe-filled cry.

It brought Coshee, his right hand clutching a stick to aid him down the riverbank. The others drew back to give him a clear and open view, to wait in silence for his judgment.

He gazed at the carcass, did not betray his thoughts. He called on a clump of men to empty the canoe onto the shore. The carcass spilled out, a mass of fat encased in hide, an exotic feast of meat and bones at its core. There could be no doubt where victory dwelt.

'This world is full of strange sights,' Coshee declared, drawing all eyes to his. 'More sights in one life than I will ever know.' He turned to Nonosa and filled the night with the words Nonosa most wanted to hear. 'You have earned a wife.'

On the riverbank, in the light of the fire stood Remesh, not unlike the way he had boldly stood when Nonosa set eyes on him days before.

The Kanwashish looked up, waited for Remesh to speak, but he said nothing. Before sunrise he and his paddler had gone.

THAT NIGHT, WHEN BIESTA undressed and Nonosa held the full measure of her, without the shade of guilt that had tinged their previous night alone, he still could not separate the memory of Démas.

He lay with Biesta's head resting on his chest. He thought it pure and natural that he should remember his first wife's body against his own. He was certain that in time such thoughts would pass, but at that moment it was as if he were passing between two women, not yet separated from one, not yet giving himself wholly to the other.

SHANNON

SHANNON SHUTS THE BOOK in one fluid motion.

Her knowledge of the Maritime Archaic has its basis in archaeology reports, but she knows she'll go back to the novel. She's caught up in the story, against her will. It's the sex, what else?

In her opinion — and she has lots on which to base an opinion — the Maritime Archaic would have been preoccupied with basic survival. Their primitive existence would have had to be just that — primitive, without the sexual melodrama. She justifies reading the book by filtering through to what the author did get right. She takes it as research. It does something to fill a gap.

She thinks often of sex. In the months since she parted ways with Kim, she has deliberately avoided the possibility of entering another relationship. In any case, the move from BC had so occupied her that a man in her life could only have been a needless complication. Now that she is somewhat settled in St. Anthony, she allows herself to consider it. Not that there is any opportunity, given who she has met so far. In her experience, except for the occasional university student hired for the summer, Parks Canada terrain is not exactly a hotbed of alluring men.

She finds other ways to get a break from work. Even though Conche is far enough away that she feels no obligation to go there, every few nights she finds herself on the telephone to Bertha, and often on a Saturday she'll head off to visit her.

Invariably, it's a warm welcome. Bertha sees her as a family connection that has been salvaged, and since Bertha has no children or grandchildren living around her, Shannon takes on a new role, that of confidant, a willing listener and sounding board for her aunt's problems. Bertha has retained a sense of humour about her ills, the food is good, and in the end often they find themselves at the table, sharing stories, sometimes memories, and inevitably something to laugh about.

Even though Shannon tries to dissuade her each time she calls to tell her she's coming, Bertha uses the visit as a reason to cook a substantial meal, something far beyond what she would normally do for herself. It's traditional Newfoundland fare, and in an odd sense Shannon finds it something to look forward to. It draws her back. These are meals she remembers, but which she never did learn to cook properly herself, and as a result never attempted in all the years since she left home.

Food in Newfoundland is a social force akin to conversation. It sets people down on common ground. For most everyone loves a meal of salt cod and potatoes, or a boiled vegetable dinner with salt beef, and a partridge-berry tart. Massive comfort foods, universal in the outports. For the older generation at least, it hasn't yet been replaced by the box of chicken and fries from the local takeout.

Shannon's visits gradually evolve into cooking lessons. She wants Bertha to teach her the standard recipes, the ones that would have been passed down to her mother, and should have been passed on to her, but weren't.

Initially it is a way of diverting attention away from Bertha's health problems, but after the first session Shannon can see it becoming more than that. It's a way of reconnecting to the place that two decades ago she couldn't escape from fast enough.

When she was growing up her mother did most of the cooking. She recalls her father turning his attention to moose and caribou, and he had a knack for trout when he caught them, but otherwise the kitchen counter was woman's territory. And when Jerome came along it was invariably her mother who did the cooking. Shannon swore sometimes that was the most he wanted from marriage — someone to put a hot meal on the table three times a day.

Shannon admits she wasn't much help. She washed dishes. But as far as cooking went, her part was generally no more than reheating something her mother had made before she went off to her shift at the fish plant. Jerome could manage the microwave, though he rarely did. When Jerome worked, which was repeatedly the minimum number of weeks a year to qualify for unemployment insurance, his job sometimes took him overnight to Corner Brook and Stephenville. During which times he would stay with his sister and, as Shannon and Patti agreed, bring the delights of his personality to her family. And why does she recall those sporadic reprieves? It was more than not having the leaden male presence across the table. It was the food, the time in the kitchen, the three of them together at the table talking through the meal.

Shannon wants the essence of her mother's meals, the way of making them that she fails to remember. They are there for her to learn and, although Bertha finds it peculiar to have her standing at the kitchen counter with a notebook and pen, she is, Shannon suspects, secretly thrilled at the interest.

'The trick is good fish. If you haven't got good fish then it's just as well not to go at it.'

Duly noted. As well as Bertha's description of what constitutes good salt fish — not sunburnt, and not wet ... thick, but not too thick. 'Cook it a few times,' she says, 'and you'll soon find out what's good and what's not.'

She has on the counter a small piece that didn't make it to the bowl where the rest has been soaking in water overnight. Shannon holds it in her hands and rubs her fingers over it to get a feel for the texture, the salt and sun-cured flesh of the cod. Bertha instructs her in cutting a piece of salt pork fat into small cubes for the frying pan, to be rendered to hot fat and 'scruncheons' for spooning over the fish and potatoes once they're on the plate.

Here she is, she thinks — the wayward Newfoundlander reborn; home, where 'fish' means 'cod.' Where for centuries salt cod was its lifeblood, and held back starvation. Where millions of quintals of it were loaded into the ships of Newfoundland and Labrador bound for the corners of the world.

Shannon knows all this, yet it's been years since she's eaten salt cod. She hasn't been the Newfoundlander getting packages from home to reinvigorate her roots. When she and Bertha sit down at the kitchen table and settle into the meal, it's the climax of the day, and she's almost afraid to take the first forkful, afraid she'll be disappointed in the taste.

But it's delicious. It's basic, practical food. Good fish, good potatoes, hot fat and scruncheons. Sin and salt. Diet fare it's not, reaffirmed when Bertha unveils the partridgeberry tart.

It brings Shannon back, of course. The smell of it alone retrieves the memories.

When she glances across the table she sees a person for whom she now has great affection, more than for anyone else she knows. It is not the way Shannon normally looks into her life, but since there appears to be a major re-evaluation going on, why not ascribe a value to it?

Bertha is the only person it seems she loves unreservedly. Who else is there? Marta, but now they are too far apart. Patti? And there had been Kim. Bertha comes with the idiosyncrasies of someone who has lived eight decades in the same small corner of the world. She is wise in the world she knows, with no reason to change, and lots of reason not to. To Shannon it's as endearing as the way she keeps a tissue tucked inside her bra or up a sleeve.

Shannon sits across the kitchen table, eating fish and potatoes on a day in June. As close to 'home' as she is likely to get. And with all the nerve in the world.

SHE RETURNS TO WORK renewed.

Shannon realized from the start that the reference point for any Native issues in Newfoundland has to be the Beothuks — the Aboriginals who occupied the island when the Norse landed there, a millennium ago, then those who followed in the wake of Giovanni Caboto five hundred years later. The Beothuks had been driven to extinction by 1829, with the death of the last of them, the young woman, Shanawdithit.

It is the Native group Shannon knows best. In fact knows substantially better than most people, the Beothuks being a central topic in several undergrad courses and the subject of a master's thesis. A thesis started several years before, and remaining, as yet, incomplete.

Or, as she said in the resumé that accompanied her job application, 'ongoing.' Her friend Marta had convinced her she was capable of a master's, and had insisted she take it on if she were ever within reach of a university. Insisted it would put her another step ahead of the pack, as far as job opportunities were concerned. Once Shannon moved to British Columbia, with the possibility of university courses staring her in the face, her interest piqued. It came at a point in her life she was feeling particularly good about herself. The start was a seminar course once a week at UBC, which allowed her to overcome her misgivings about a return to academics after such a lengthy lapse. Followed by several courses online, and finally a six-month educational leave from her job and a term on campus, all of which allowed her to complete the required course work. What remains is the thesis. She doubts now if she will ever finish it, given the deadline is less than two years away. She hates to think of it as an aborted master's, but that may well be what it turns out to be. Something else she can, in some measure at least, blame on Kim.

She has the perfect topic for her thesis. At the time she started it she was on the ground floor of investigation into the subject, although she doubts now if that makes any difference. While she has lingered, a half dozen others have probably swooped in and usurped the raw material and put it to other use.

At the point she was searching for a thesis topic her supervising professor drew her attention to a recent acquisition by BC Archives — a newly salvaged collection of nineteenth-century journals and crude, but readable, duplicates of letters, discovered in an old house in New Westminster, material belonging to one William Cormack, a minor public official in the pioneer days of the city. The name meant little to most people, even those with a reasonable knowledge of the city's history. What made the find extraordinary were the portions of the papers which related to Cormack's life several decades prior to his settling in New Westminster.

William Cormack had lived in Newfoundland in the early 1800s and was a diligent observer and recorder of the history and customs of the Beothuks of Newfoundland, then still alive. In fact Cormack spent the last few months of his time in Newfoundland hosting in his own house in St. John's the last of the Aboriginals, Shanawdithit. Part of his journals and letters turned out to be a record of his contact with Shanawdithit. The archivists surmised that he made duplicates of the letters he sent to his friends in Britain, rather than repeat the same observations in his journal. The archivists were as excited by the duplication of the letters as they were by their contents, it being a rare early usage of what was then called 'carbonated paper.'

Once word reached Newfoundland of the find, there was an instant flood of academics from Memorial University showing up to scrutinize them, several of whom Shannon encountered in the course of her thesis work. The BC Archives rushed to have the material of most interest scanned to microfilm and DVD, a copy of the latter coming into Shannon's possession once her thesis topic was approved and her thesis supervisor had gone through the official channels. The originals remain in the vault of the Archives, although it's Shannon's understanding that there are negotiations underway to have the Newfoundland component of the material transferred to the Provincial Archives in St. John's.

In the years that followed the final waning of her effort to finish the thesis, every time she came across the DVD, carefully labelled and protected in its clear plastic case, she was ridden with guilt. Had she pressed on and forced herself to complete the writing, it would have all been behind her, degree in hand.

The degree has become more elusive than ever. The only thing keeping the possibility of it alive is the biannual fee she pays to the university to keep her name on the program. She hates the thought of all that money curling down the drain, and is now anticipating the time the deadline for submission of the thesis is past and she won't have to pretend she will ever get back to completing it.

In the past weeks the guilt has worked itself to the surface again, more intense than ever, given Shannon is now in the epicentre, so to speak, of the thesis. Its title — *William Cormack in Newfoundland, a study of the nineteenth-century colonial attitude toward Aborigines* — sits in her mind like the great unfinished task of her life. Fortunately, she doesn't have to work hard to convince herself that she has indeed learned a great deal that is of use to her in her present position, that by no means should it be seen as a wasted exercise.

The story of the Beothuks has to inform any process of reinterpretation. Her solemn regret is that her conclusions won't have the weight of a master's degree behind them.

CORMACK

Exploits Island, Newfoundland
27th October, 1827

Dear John,

Please forgive my hurriedness in getting to the point of my letter, but I have just come away from the most extraordinary of experiences. I have passed an hour in the company of the Boeothuck I told you about in my last correspondence. What has been my good fortune but to meet her face to face. Let me relate the detail, as much as my excitement will allow, if, in truth, my excitement will ever slow the eagerness of my quill.

The young woman has not the wildness of face to be expected of someone nurtured beyond the boundaries of civilization. Nor does she have the curtness of manner one might suppose of a human who has lived most of her life among the savage races. When I stamped the early winter

snow from my boots and stepped into the Peyton house on
Exploits Island I was not certain she was the one, my eyes
coming to rest on two young women undoubtedly close in age.
One stepped forward and introduced herself. Only then did I
know for certain the other, behind her, was the Red Indian.

I extended my hand. 'William Epps Cormack. Of St John's.
Of the Boeothuck Institute.'

'Mr Cormack. We received word of your coming,' Mrs Peyton
said, somewhat shyly, unused to visitors.

I confess I had to force my eyes away from the young
woman in order to properly introduce myself and try to put
my hostess at her ease.

'Mr Peyton is away, tending to the fishery,' she added
quickly.

'That is unfortunate,' I said to her.

I was not entirely disappointed, for it would mean one less
person to take my time, time I wished to devote to the aborigine.

Mrs Peyton turned then to the young woman, and held out
a hand to her. She did not take it, nor did she step forward as
was the wish of Mrs Peyton; instead, she held to the children
clinging to her skirts and nodded in my direction.

'This is Nancy April,' my hostess announced.

It is her English name, taken as she was in the month of
April, her sister and her mother having died of starvation. It is
a name I wish not to use. And never 'Nance,' which I find to
be even more common among some in the village. I gather it
is also the name Mr Peyton most often uses, since the time she
gave herself up and came to live with them.

'Shanawdithit,' I said and bowed my head. Though only
slightly so as not to embarrass her.

She joined us in the sitting room for tea, and once her
assistance to Mrs Peyton was complete, she appeared content

*in her chair, and not overly sorrowful, as I presumed she
would be. I was anxious to engage her in conversation, but
thought it wisest to first set Mrs Peyton at her ease, and have
Shanawdithit join us of her own accord.*

*Shanawdithit remained silent, and preferred not to return
my smile when occasionally I looked her way. I persisted in
the course of my conversation, until eventually I turned and
put quietly forth a direct question.*

'Do you think often of your people, Shanawdithit?'

*She seemed surprised by the question, perhaps more by the
suddenness of it, although I had tried to be comforting in my
tone. In time she answered, 'Yes.'*

*Subsequently, there have been several more words and
phrases. That she is an aborigine is only entirely clear when
she speaks. Her words are English, but of a ruleless
composition. I suppose it similar speech to that of the
aborigines of Australia and the Hottentots of southern Africa.
Its deficiencies come from lack of proper instruction, not from
any dearth of intelligence, as far as I can surmise. Indeed,
Shanawdithit is very capable in other ways. She moves about
the house with ease and confidence, and certainly has no
hesitation in undertaking what is expected of her, especially in
her dealings with the children.*

*'She sometimes likes to go in the woods by herself to feel
close to her people,' Mrs Peyton informed me. 'She says she
speaks to her mother and to her sister.'*

*Mrs Peyton's look left me with the notion that she indulged
Shanawdithit her fantasies, and with kindness. I did not pursue
the question, for I sensed Shanawdithit's reluctance to talk of
such personal concerns with someone she had only just met.*

*I trod lightly for I knew much depended on the relationship
we were about to initiate. My first time in her presence was*

one mostly of observance interspersed with a few well-chosen compliments, an attempt to set her at ease. She would have realized my great interest in her race — the Peytons no doubt told her of my journey five years previous across the interior of the Island in search of them — yet I had no intention of overwhelming her with questions. She is a woman with an austere and primal experience of life after all, and I — a white man. I know it natural she be wary of such men, especially in light of the tragedies some had inflicted on her people.

When her eyes were turned to Mrs Peyton, or she was for a moment occupied with pouring tea, I studied her features, thinking perhaps I would detect something unique to her race. Professor Jameson has often noted the angle of the jaw in certain tribes, or the prominence of cheekbones. In his laboratory he sometimes encouraged us to close our eyes and run fingers over certain specimens of skulls, the better to note the differences among them. But that I could touch the head and face of Shanawdithit. I had to content myself with holding fast to memory all I could, and, later, in the seclusion of my room, fill page after page with my notes, just prior to beginning this letter to you.

She is somewhat fairer in skin than the Micmac women, and in stature, a good deal taller. She seems to have eaten well, for she is sturdy of body and moves at times with a clever robustness that, had one not studied her face and her straight, coal-black hair, might lead one to think her another of the Newfoundland servants from Cork or Portsmouth. In complexion and curve of face she seems closer to the natives of the warmer countries, though her features were broader and less distinct than those of the Gypsy race.

Upon seeing her I recalled the portrait of another captive — Mary March, a miniature of her that I had seen at

Government House some years before. Indeed, I could see clearly a resemblance. I can only conclude the Red Indian women of Newfoundland to be a strong breed, the most intense feature being their black and penetrating eyes. It is what resides beyond those eyes that most interests me, and though it is difficult to bridle my impatience, I do so and should think at the moment I appear to Shanawdithit as no more than a polite and agreeable visitor.

It was in her presence that I decided to restrain my use of the designation 'Red Indian,' for it was obvious that the use of red ochre is confined to the wilds, and gives a false view of these people when they live among settlers. Indeed, red ochre is no more than a colouration applied to the skin, and once removed, leaves no indication that the skin was ever subject to it. These are not 'Red Indians,' but were more properly Boeothuck, the name they apply to themselves.

During this time on Exploits Island I have been graciously welcomed into the Peyton home, for there are no rooms to be had on the Island beyond those of the fishermen. Mrs Peyton has provided me with a bed and an array of meals, and though she may well protest, I will insist on payment, and one equal to that I would make had there been an inn.

Besides a refuge for writing furiously, this room has became a chamber of contemplation, for I can hardly rest, thinking constantly as I do of the young woman. That she might be the last of her race is a thought to overwhelm any disciple of natural history. My daily plan is to convert the most precise of my observations to the pages of my journal, and then continue, in letters to Professor Jameson in Edinburgh and the dear Hodgkin, now at Guy's Hospital in London. And to you, my good friend, in Liverpool.

I do hope you are finding Liverpool to your liking. It must, *at least, be more suited to you than Prince Edward Island.*

Please do not take my haste in bringing this letter to a close as any more than the need to portion my time wisely in allowing for the full measure of my experience is be set to paper.

Yours very sincerely,
William

☙

28th October, 1827
Exploits Island, Newfoundland

Doctor Thomas Hodgkin
Guy's Hospital, London

My dear Thomas,

Were you not as impassioned as myself on the subject of the aborigines I would not be writing again so soon.

I have the sad news to relate, now that I have had further opportunity to converse with Shanawdithit, that not only are the Boeothuck of the 'feeble races' (as you would suggest), they are indeed on the very edge of extirpation! At such a prospect your heart must sink as soundly as does mine, and I must quickly convey, in as much detail I am able, my plan to go again in search of the tribe. This time it will be directly to Red Indian Lake where I now know them to have their wigwams.

In preparing for this trip I will, of course, rely on Shanawdithit for assistance in setting forth the route I shall take. Today I laid before her a map of the interior, drawn, as best I could, from what had been told to me by the fishermen of Exploits Island. I wish you could have been seated beside me to share the intricacies of her reaction.

Shanawdithit raised the map to her eyes and for some time examined it, turning it first one way and then another. Finally, she put it to rest on the table and, taking more paper and a pencil in her hand, proceeded to redraw the map, punctuating her deed with what was clearly derision for the original. The young woman bears the primitive (and, I will admit, unsettling) trait of not attempting to disguise the fullness of her feelings.

Her sketching went on for some time, during which she hardly took her eyes from the task, such was her concentration. She would stop and stare at the paper, seemingly to recall the years she inhabited the land she was now depicting. On one such occasion her eyes moistened and, before she was able to wipe it away, a tear fell to the paper. Once it fell, she did not attempt to blot it, but left it to dry as if it were an inherent part of her drawing.

I was able to again study the woman, so deep was she in thought and inattentive to my stare. She would mumble quietly to herself, as if she were not in the room at all, or beside me, but rather in a world of her own choosing far away from the Peyton house. She would sometimes mumble as if in conversation, perhaps with her mother and sister as Mrs Peyton had said, even to the point of chuckling at some remark of her own that she had made. Her mood might then suddenly turn and her mutterings turn likewise, into something morose and brooding. One might think her not of steadfast mind had one not seen her demeanour before and after this display. Following much observation I have concluded hers to be anomalous intelligence, one that does not easily separate thought from action.

When she finished her drawing she appeared well satisfied with her delineation of the land and the river leading through

*it to Red Indian Lake. She laid the map before me and
awaited my judgment. I offered a smile, though she failed to
rejoin with one of her own. I turned to the map and studied it,
and was lavish in my praise, for indeed the drawing was
remarkable in its detail.*

*Shanawdithit had no trouble accepting my praise, and
appeared not in the least timorous about it. We have been
inclined — and I boldly include you in my company in this
regard — to think of female aborigines as a more demure
breed, and not given to forwardness in their conduct. Yet the
Boeothuck has about her a surety, one that indeed defies her
experience of white men whom she has encountered in the
wilds. The dear unfortunate woman bears the scars of two
gunshot wounds — one in the leg, the other the hand —
inflicted by the English, yet she has no fear of moving among
the settlers whom she now encounters day-by-day as one of
the Peyton household. It is a tribute to Mrs Peyton and indeed
her husband that they allow Shanawdithit such freedom as to
make her so at ease. They are no doubt attempting to undo
the mistreatment inflicted on her people, in the most severe
case by the senior Mr Peyton, thankfully now back in
England, the father of the very man in whose home
Shanawdithit is now dwelling!*

*Despite this, the overwhelming feeling I have for the
woman is one of regret that I do not know her more deeply.
Her mind is perhaps the last remaining receptacle of knowledge
about the Boeothuck, and as such deserves to be drawn upon
for as much as it will reveal.*

*'Where are the homes, the wigwams of your people?' I asked
at one point, with as much compassion as I could render
without forsaking the science at hand. It is imperative that,
once in the interior, I not waste time exploring terrain in*

which there is no promise of finding trace of the Boeothuck. Shanawdithit did not respond, and instead stared to one side with what I could only take for rebuke of my question.

'You not know words.'

At first I mistook the rebuke for anger, and recoiled slightly.

'You not know my people.'

I could only think the young woman had no wish to converse with me, except if I spoke the Boeothuck tongue.

I could not oblige her, as she realized. I could only hope that in her heart was a willingness to teach me the words of her tribe.

'Mamateek,' she said.

I took on the word as best I could. 'Ma-ma-teek.'

'No wigwam.'

I will not repeat the offending 'wigwam' in her presence again, and have chosen to use the word only before someone of my own race who would not otherwise know my meaning.

She proceeded then to draw a replica of such a dwelling place. The Boeothuck woman's facility with a pencil leaves me astounded, even though Mrs Peyton has on several occasions remarked to me of her eagerness to draw. Surely the Boeothuck in the wilds have not access to pencil and paper, and surely drawing on sand with a stick, or scratching with splintered bone on rock, cannot account for such skill. Is there then something inbred, taking no account of race? It is a matter I pondered at length in the letter penned earlier this evening to Professor Jameson.

The mamateek in Shanawdithit's drawing appears substantial and many-sided, not entirely round as I would have thought. Upright poles form the walls, converging in a high cone of poles, through the peak of which I assume escapes the smoke from the fire pit inside.

'What prevents the rain from entering?' I asked politely. 'Or snow?'

Then, in a most spontaneous fashion, she took me by the hand and, standing up, led me through the house to the back door. There she handed me my coat, which I donned as she waited, having thrown a woollen shawl about herself so that it covered her head as well as her shoulders and arms. She opened the door and advanced to the outside.

I followed, hurrying to keep up, into the yard, past the vegetable plots and animal sheds, and into the edge of woods beyond the back fence.

There I discovered her standing, arms wrapped around herself, atop a blanket of moss, a clump of birch trees to her side. I stopped before I reached her and stood motionless myself.

At the risk of sounding as if I have moved beyond the demarcations of science, I must confess that she appeared to me as an extraordinary vision, the truest of primitives. Had she been wearing her Native dress she would have been wholly a part of all that surrounded her, a sovereign and rightful creature of this land.

If I could have turned back time I would have done so at that moment, and placed her people beside her, standing as they would have stood before any white man ever set eyes to them. Hers was a deeply innocent and blameless pose, forever immaculate.

What a cruel and senseless creature is man that he would bring these Natives of the forest to within a breath of their end!

Yours faithfully,
William

SHANNON

HE HAD WARNED HER not to bring her twenty-first-century sensibilities to bear on Cormack. 'A very different world. Keep that in mind or you won't do him justice.' It had been her first meeting with Lucus, newly assigned as her thesis advisor.

As the months went by, especially after she returned to her job and struggled for time to work on the thesis, Shannon found Cormack increasingly tiresome. There was no keeping academic distance from his colonial, class-conscious attitudes.

She had no doubt he was sexually repressed. 'Definitely in need of a place to poke his john thomas,' she had emailed Marta, the latest in a string of such comments, this one coming after a long week at work. With the added assertion, 'I don't know how much more of him I can take.'

By then she had been three years toying with the thesis. It was long past the time to move it out of her life. Given that she was in somewhat of a sexual wasteland at the time, she wasn't surprised to find herself venting so loudly. It would be another three months before Kim would parade into her life.

Now, back in Newfoundland and Labrador, Shannon works at putting her past experience with the Cormack material to one side. She attempts a fresh view of it, in the context of wider Aboriginal history. Ingeborg Marshall's six-hundred-page compendium, *A History and Ethnography of the Beothuk*, never leaves her work area. She does a search of the online periodical indexes at Memorial University and uncovers several new and relevant articles. She arranges through the university's Centre for Newfoundland Studies to have them photocopied and sent to her.

Yet, no matter what she reads, in the back of her mind is Cormack. The journals and letters came to light well after the publication of Marshall's seminal work, but, as much as she wants it otherwise, she finds it impossible to read the book without Cormack forcing his way in. Shannon was one of the first to examine the newly discovered material. In an odd, illogical, supercilious way she feels an ownership.

WITH SOME DEGREE OF gratefulness, her attention is abruptly deflected from her job. Her sister Patti phones, to float the idea of visiting for a week with her thirteen-year-old daughter. She wants to show her daughter where she grew up. Shannon, though skeptical, readily agrees. Except for their mother's funeral, it will be the first time the two sisters have been together in Newfoundland since Shannon was in her early twenties.

Shannon is certain of the get-together turning awkward. She and Patti have even less in common than the last time they were together. Which was in the airport in Toronto while Shannon was waiting for a flight to Vancouver. She had deliberately chosen a later connecting flight to give her two hours with her sister, who had driven from Oakville to the airport to see her.

It did not go well. There was resentment from the beginning that Shannon had only made allowance for a fleeting rendezvous, in spite of the fact she had not seen her sister for four years.

'You could have stayed over. We have room. You'd like Oakville.'

She'd hate Oakville. Although she had never been there, and likely never would. She could have endured it for a couple of days had there not been stronger reasons to keep her distance — Patti's husband, Jeremy, and her two kids, Quincy and Rianna. To be fair, her first-hand experience with the kids had been minimal. Phone conversations and email exchanges with Patti had proven sufficient to conclude she'd be happier staying away from them.

Jeremy, on the other hand, is only too well known to her.

Their first encounter had been at the wedding. Shannon's instantaneous response was that Patti could have done considerably better. Obviously, by that time there was no point in making her feelings known to her sister. And now that the reality of Jeremy has long settled in, there is even less.

Shannon was a bridesmaid. Not out of choice, she concluded after she arrived for the wedding, but obligation. There was a gaggle of Patti's girlfriends there, any one of whom would have been a better fit under the easy warmth of the Cuban sun.

The wedding had taken place at a beach resort called Paradisus Rio de Ore. Neutral territory, since Patti had no family home to return to. Shannon had been rather taken with the idea of a Caribbean getaway wedding. It was October and snow had already arrived in Baffin.

The charm dissipated within two hours of the flight touching down. Jerm, as Patti called him, was proving an ass, preferring snorkelling and the rum punch to any serious attempt at helping with preparations for the wedding. His mother, Sophia, to whom Shannon took an even quicker and stronger dislike, excused him at every turn, making it entirely permissible for him to be an ass.

Shannon hardly knew her sister. She was not the person Shannon had seen at their mother's funeral. The year following their mother's death Patti had changed jobs, and in the process moved from Halifax to Oakville. She so completely embraced her new Ontario surroundings that she could just as easily have been second-generation Italian-Canadian, just like Jerm.

Jeremy's father was into real estate, but the son had neither his father's business smarts, nor his ambition. He was indulged by his mother, and, from what Shannon surmised, had turned into a disappointment for his father. The one and only son had not outgrown his teenage jockdom. He had been a very good hockey player, but not quite good enough to make a career of it. He was still smarting from what might have been. To make it worse, one of the gaggle of women who had flown down for the wedding was engaged to a former teammate of his from junior hockey days, who hadn't made it to the wedding because he was playing yet another year with the Detroit Red Wings.

Jerm drank too much. He was unfailingly cheerful and full of sophomoric quips that were in need of a locker room to gain their full effect. He enjoyed being seen at the end of a cigar. He made tasteless remarks about the resort staff behind their backs, and acted as if he and the bartender had been buddies their entire lives. The fact that the bartender was more handsome and intelligent, and could see through Jeremy's facade, only added to the pathos of the situation. Shannon learned that the bartender was in fact a doctor, earning extra money to help his family, with the hope of one day getting them all out of Cuba. Shannon said nothing to anyone about it, but stood back and watched the pathos deepen.

The wedding coordinator, Maria — who, to quote Patti, was 'a dream' — had assured the couple of a stress-free wedding. The wedding did indeed go off without overt complication, despite Sophia's attempt at rearranging what Maria called 'the wedding package.'

During the ceremony, as the public notary read in Spanish from the Cuban Code of Family Law, Maria translated the perfunctory words to English. Sophia, whose deepest distress had arisen over the fact there would not be a priest performing the ceremony, somehow held her tongue, taking consolation perhaps in the fact that the extra flower arrangements she had insisted on for the oceanside gazebo were in place. For a brief moment Shannon thought it all rather beautiful, with sea and blue sky filling the background, and found particular pleasure in the fact that as the couple, duly wedded, kissed, a round of applause rose from an assembly of snorkellers just off shore. Sophia smiled begrudgingly. Jeremy gave them a thumbs-up.

From all that Shannon has gathered, the beach wedding has been the highlight of their life together. Rianna followed in less than a year, Quincy two years after that. Jeremy is in furniture retail, and Patti is hanging in at her semi-managerial position with an insurance company. They have a more substantial home in Oakville than they could have afforded on their own, but Jeremy's parents continue to be generous. Patti has never hinted she is anything other than happy. Shannon suspects otherwise. The kids sound like nightmares, but then again, given Shannon's lack of familiarity with modern married life, she realizes they could just be normal. As the time for the visit approaches, she promises herself that she will be open-minded and not quick to judge. It is the least she can do.

THEY ARRIVE AT ST. ANTHONY on Provincial Airlines, having connected through St. John's following their Air Canada flight from Toronto. Patti wears tight capri pants and strapped sandals that glitter, and daughter shows a copious stretch of midriff. They have obviously come from someplace warmer than St. Anthony. Both appear tired, and Rianna still somewhat unnerved by the Provincial flight, it being her first time aboard a propeller aircraft, and one without an inflight entertainment system.

The sisters' reconnecting after such a long separation lends itself to a prolonged hug and to genuine satisfaction that they're together. There is no mention of Jeremy, or even thought of him it would seem, which further loosens the sisters' affection for each other.

The apartment in St. Anthony is small but adequate for three people for a week. Rianna is given the single spare room, which she accepts without deference to the adults. Shannon has cleaned her own bedroom, and insists on Patti taking it. She herself will sleep on the living room sofa, a way of insuring she gets late night and early morning time alone.

Shannon has prepared a safe, uncomplicated, baked chicken dish and Rianna, not having eaten much all day, takes to it with reasonable civility. Following dinner, they watch an episode of *Canadian Idol*, which, to Rianna's relief, has found its way to Newfoundland. Unlike her mother and her Aunt Shannon, she chooses not to support the Newfoundlander in the group, even though he is by far the cutest of those still in the competition. Shannon is not sure what, if anything, that says about her niece.

THE FOLLOWING DAY THEY are on their way to Conche. Shannon had mentioned Patti's planned visit to Bertha some weeks before, but decides not to phone ahead before they leave, thinking it would cause Bertha unnecessary stress. Better they drop by unannounced, providing good reason, if need be, for staying only a short while.

Shannon doesn't know what to expect of Patti once they actually arrive in Conche. They have not discussed going there, yet it is the unspoken understanding that Conche is their primary destination. They conveniently shift the focus to Rianna, allowing the sisters to approach the trip as a tolerable, detached lesson in family history.

Shannon takes them first up a hill to a recently built viewing platform that overlooks the community. She tells Rianna, 'This is all of it, this is the place where we grew up. It was home.'

Like Shannon a month before, Patti has never seen Conche at this height, as one complete panorama. She is numbed for the moment, and then her eyes begin to fill with tears.

Shannon is surprised by her sister's emotional turn. Rianna is mystified, then embarrassed.

'Mom,' she says under her breath. 'It's a tourist lookout. Give it up, will ya?'

Patti gives it up by turning away for a few moments. To divert Rianna, Shannon begins to name the various points of land, the coves and inlets. The girl is not interested, but by the time Shannon is through Patti has rejoined them, dry-eyed, as if nothing has happened.

They make their way back down the path to the vehicle and drive into the community. Patti says little. Shannon points out the church, the school, the hills where she and Patti, growing up, went berry-picking. They are of no interest to Rianna, who chooses to direct her attention to the teenage boys hanging out in front of the convenience store.

As they approach what was the family home, Shannon slows down so Patti can see along the path. Shannon is not planning to stop, but Patti cautions her against it just the same.

'I couldn't bear to go inside,' Patti says after they have driven by.

'It's only a house,' Rianna pronounces. 'Is it contaminated or what?'

SHANNON WISHES SHE HAD phoned ahead to Bertha.

'Bertha is amazing,' she says. 'She's the heart and soul of this place.'

'Soul?' is Rianna's reaction. 'I don't believe in souls.' A reaction the two adults ignore.

'You'll love her.'

'She sounds old.'

'She's your only great aunt on my side of the family,' Patti tells her.

'That's nice,' Rianna says.

Shannon would like to believe the physical presence of Great Aunt Bertha will bring out something better in the girl. She is near the point of dismissing Rianna as a spoiled and inconsiderate brat when they enter the house, Shannon leading the way, not bothering to knock.

They find Bertha on the living room sofa, knitting while watching television.

'Precious Saviour, it's not Patti?'

Shannon helps Bertha to her feet. Patti wraps her arms around her. Patti's eyes moisten, unexpected emotions loosening inside her once again.

'I wouldn't know you from a distance. But you're the same Patti.'

Shannon is reminded just how close Patti and Bertha had been at one time, especially during the years Shannon was away at university, before Patti herself left Conche. Patti, it appears, has a stronger tie to their aunt than her sister ever did.

The emotion quickly disperses, for Rianna is now at centre stage and not being co-operative. She has never met her Great Aunt Bertha, and that seems sufficient reason to be put off by Bertha's sudden show of affection. She has had no basis on which to react, her father's family not being particularly affectionate. Bertha's bosom against her own pubescent one, Bertha's frail lips on her cheek evoke an audible groan.

Get used to it, twit, Shannon thinks to herself. And don't be such a bloody pain in the butt.

Fortunately, Bertha's senses have been dulled by age, and she doesn't gather in enough to be offended, making Patti's quick lie about her daughter being a very private person unnecessary.

Activity shifts to the kitchen. Shannon convinces Bertha to sit down, while she proceeds to fill the kettle and set it on the stove, demonstrating the comfort level that the last few weeks of visits have given her. Bertha is just a little befuddled. Had she known they were about to show up she would certainly have baked something. As it is, the tea buns are days old and, she insists, hardly fit to be put on the table.

Rianna has no interest in tea buns no matter what their age. In tea either. And Bertha has not had soft drinks in her refrigerator for several years. Shannon knows a bottle of instant coffee lies somewhere in the far reaches of the cupboards, long stale-dated, but, as tempted as she is to mention it, she holds back.

'Try the tea, Rianna,' she says, 'you might find you like it.'

It is plenty to provoke Rianna into a shameless comeback.

'Tea is for old people.'

A simple-minded remark in a Newfoundland outport, where tea soon follows breast milk in the diet of most children. Shannon dares not admonish Rianna, leaving that to her mother. It is more laughter than a rebuke, though no less a slight to the girl.

Rianna retaliates. 'Tea would make me puke!'

She is on the brink of being an embarrassment, yet Patti is leery of further censure, not being in control of where it might lead. She will avoid at all costs a scene in front of Bertha.

Shannon blames Patti as much as her daughter for what's happening. Fortunately, Bertha at that moment is some distance from the table where the other three are sitting. The clash of wills is lost on her, leaving Shannon alone to ruminate on what it reveals about Patti's life in Oakville.

Rianna eventually has sense enough to remain quiet, and is rewarded by her mother's suggestion that she watch television in the living room while the adults drink their tea. Off she goes and through the table conversation is heard the constant stuttering change of television channels.

There is a repeat of much of what Shannon already knows of Bertha, Shannon filling in details Bertha finds hard to communicate. Nevertheless, there is obviously a reconnection taking place. She can see it in Patti's face. Not unlike her own, but more intense. She would have thought Patti had hardened over the years, had left Conche behind with a vengeance. When Patti starts asking about classmates from high school and finds that indeed a few of them are still living in Conche, married and with kids, there is a whole level of conversation that Shannon would never be able to duplicate.

When a suitable length of time passes, it is Shannon's suggestion that they leave and give Bertha back her peace and quiet.

'And that's what you're not. You're staying and having some lunch.' What she has in the fridge are a few fresh capelin that a neighbour brought to her the previous evening.

'The capelin are not in, are they?' Patti says excitedly, and in an accent that could make it seem she had never left Newfoundland.

'Yes, maid, they are so.'

Capelin are small, smelt-like fish that roll on the beaches of New-foundland to spawn in early summer. Running barefoot into the ice-cold surf to catch capelin was their yearly ritual as children.

The smell of them frying eventually fills the kitchen and drifts into the living room. Shannon catches a glimpse of Rianna, a hand shielding her nose. She seems to have found a program she is interested in, enough to prevent her from surfacing in protest right away.

Lunch is a different story. She finds the general sight of fish repulsive. 'Gross!' in her cliché-driven vocabulary. To face a pair of the fish, lined up on a plate with their fins and heads intact, is so far outside Rianna's realm of food choices as to be incomprehensible. Her mother refocuses her attention with a ten-dollar bill, directions to the convenience store and the suggestion of buying a prepackaged sandwich.

'What a shame she doesn't like fish,' Bertha says when she is out the door.

'She'll grow out of it,' Patti responds, though she is not fooling anyone.

Having lived long enough in the North to have seen all manner of fish and game consumption, Shannon is amused by what has transpired, though she hides the fact. Once Rianna is out of the house, Patti slides the fish from Rianna's plate to her own. As if she can't get enough of such restorative, comfort food. To Shannon's mind, her sister is overplaying the role of outport girl returned.

'You're not all mainlander then, Patti,' Bertha says. 'Conche is still in your blood.'

Just how much that is the case is apparent later in the afternoon. They convince Bertha that she is up to coming with them to the beach, and all four make their way to where the capelin have been landing. It is only by chance that there are still any capelin to be had, but as it turns out a few dozen people are lined up at the water's edge, eyeing schools of the fish just offshore.

Rianna finds it all rather peculiar, and is further disoriented when Patti discovers a classmate from high school. The woman, overweight and with a twin of boys a year older than Rianna, had once been Patti's best friend. Although their lives are now worlds apart, the bond between them is for the moment restored. Rianna is drawn into the reunion, against her will, and is duly embarrassed. When there is the opportunity to retreat, she does so by standing next to Shannon, as if Shannon's mainland sensibilities would bring an understanding of her situation.

Rianna growls under her breath, not to Shannon in particular, but as a general vent for her frustrations. 'Get me outta here.'

That is not to be. Her mother retrieves her at the point that her friend's two sons emerge from the water, dip nets alive with capelin. The fish are dumped into empty buckets set along the shoreline. The overflow ends up on the sand near Rianna's feet, flicking about, madly in need of water.

Rianna jumps back. The boys laugh, one flicking a couple of capelin caught in the mesh of the net toward her. She screams.

'Fucker.' Rianna's reaction is instantaneous and beyond her control. Bertha is taken aback. Her mother is embarrassed. Shannon thinks she is seeing Rianna in her truest light so far.

The boys don't quite know what to make of her, though they are obviously stirred by the sinuous young creature and the glimmer of loose morals.

At this point Rianna regains some sense. She feigns a stumble on some beach rocks, and a slight twist of her ankle. The grimace on her face is enough to override the effect of the expletive.

Her mother obliges, and stays on the beach only long enough to collect a few capelin for Aunt Bertha in the small plastic bag Bertha has brought along. They make their way back to the car, Rianna favouring her foot, but managing to lead, Shannon and Patti arm in arm with their aunt, together navigating her over the sand and rocks.

Bertha's outings are rare these days and she has enjoyed this surprise venture immensely. She seems to have forgotten Rianna's little outburst, and is happy enough to sit by her in the car on the way home.

Rianna is just relieved to be away from what she refers to as 'Mom's heritage moment.' It demonstrates to Shannon a wit and intelligence she had not given her credit for. When they say goodbye to Bertha after returning her home, it is Rianna who initiates the inevitable parting hug. It is a calculated move to further suppress memory of the outburst on the beach, but a clever one nonetheless.

All the way back to St. Anthony she feigns a level of interest in her surroundings to placate her mother. On subsequent outings she separates herself from her iPod often enough that Patti can generally relax and enjoy herself.

BY THE MIDDLE OF the visit, one morning when Rianna has not yet emerged from the cocoon of her bedroom, Patti enters emotional terrain which Shannon sees as open to pitfalls she would rather avoid. As teenagers the two had talked their way through the family upheavals, but communication in their adult lives has been reduced to infrequent emails, and more infrequent phone calls.

Patti has the greater need to talk. Yet Shannon is not about to open up to her sister in the way that Patti seems to expect.

'What do you think of Rianna?'

Not a good starting point first thing in the morning, the coffee not yet perked. Shannon is certain Patti knows the answer.

'She's a teenager. Teenagers have a lot of growing up to do.'

'Her father spoils her. I wish you could meet Quincy. He's a whole different set of genes. He would have loved this.'

'Boys are different.'

'This trip is meant to be a mother-daughter thing.'

'That's good.'

'She's over the edge. She'll soon have a steady boyfriend and that'll be a problem. She's already started to lose interest in school, and that's sure to be another blow-up. She's more into makeup at thirteen than I was at eighteen.'

Shannon won't say what she really thinks. Neither does she feel she has any basis on which to offer advice, having only sporadic, structured contact with today's teenagers. She knows Patti doesn't even expect her advice, just her ear. She would be supportive of her sister, but she detects dangerous ground. She goes back to what they both know.

'We had a very different relationship with Mom, and that was twenty years ago. And Conche is not Oakville.'

All true, but of no use to Patti, who is looking for confirmation of a gulf between mother and daughter that is not to be spanned.

There's more.

'I don't think Jeremy and I can last much longer.'

Shannon is not surprised, although she shows a certain shock.

'I'm serious,' Patti says. 'I've been sticking it out for the kids. And they're hardly kids anymore.'

'What would you do?'

'Split. Go through a messy divorce. Get half of something, including the kids most likely. I'd take Quincy and move back to Newfoundland. Possibly. Not here. Maybe St. John's. The company I work for has an office in St. John's.'

'All your friends must be in Oakville.'

'Half of them are Newfies. They'd probably do the same thing if they were in my position.'

Shannon so despises the word 'Newfie' that it colours her reaction. 'And they all have this unrealistic dream of coming back home.'

'Look yourself in the mirror, Shannon. It's exactly what you did.'

'I didn't come home to get over any problems.'

'Why then?'

'I was offered a job.'

'You told me you went looking for the job.'

'Only because it could lead somewhere else.'

'Bullshit, Shannon. I'm betting it was some guy. Either you were getting away from someone, or you are on the lookout for someone here. I know you, Shannon. You can't go for very long without a man. You never could. You like your sex too much.'

The final bit was a last-second add-on. It slipped in unannounced. It could have been funny, or taken as funny even if it wasn't.

Shannon takes control. 'You don't have a clue what I like. You haven't been in my life for twenty years.'

'How much have you changed?'

'This is not a conversation I want to get into. What do you take in your coffee? I'm making toast. Do you want some?'

Patti always did know how to get under her skin. Or try to get under her skin. Shannon is shutting her down before she takes it any further.

As for Patti, she is a guest and knows she needs to act like one. She can't piss off Shannon and expect to get through the week.

Not long afterwards Rianna emerges from the bedroom in a seventies retro nightshirt that ends halfway up her thighs, clutching a stuffed animal of indeterminate species, her mass of hair in need of civilizing. Her aunt and her mother glance at each other.

'Your hair is like a birch broom in the fits,' her mother says.

Rianna glares through sleep-skewed eyes.

'It's an old Newfie saying.'

'Whatever.'

'The word is *Newfoundland*, Patti. *Newfoundland*.'

CORMACK

15th September, 1827
St John's

I am not naturally a chronicler, yet I know myself to be at the
centre of an important juncture in the history of this Island, and
therefore it falls to me to put my thoughts and perspectives to
paper. In future, should I have the urge, I may well take what I
will have written and make a more permanent record of it.
Certainly, it is of more interest to me than to be tallying figures
in a ledger.

By birth I would be ranked a Newfoundlander, though there
are few who think of me as anything but a Scot. Those with the
intelligence to see beyond the rumble of my speech realize I know
no temporal borders. It was commerce that brought me to this
Island, though it be merely the means by which I grant myself the
luxury of other, more engrossing, more profitable endeavours.

My father had the mind for business and what mild facility I
have for it I no doubt inherited from him. His adventures in the

Newfoundland lumber trade were the reason for my birth in its capital city. The event, I admit, is hardly cause to keep revisiting the place. But Newfoundland, of the places onto which I have set foot, is the one that seems to hold a lasting allure. Lasting, indeed. Infuriating, no less so.

When my father died in Newfoundland in 1805 I was a lad of but nine. Suddenly, I was sailed back across the Atlantic and into the matriarchal shelter of Scotland. The Lowlands are what have come to mark me as a man, for it is there I grew into one, as restless as my mother was immovable. The place is imprinted in my person no less than my speech, yet I cannot say I ever considered settling there permanently, beyond the fickle ruminations of youth. It is a place to revisit, a place to seek what may not be there to find.

Odd that I would think it so, for in academia I assumed I had found my vocation, that there could be nothing more satisfying than to work in the prodigious shadow of the renowned naturalist and mineralogist Robert Jameson.

'Mr Cormack,' he said to me on one occasion, standing before a particularly prized stuffing of a short-beaked echidna in the Museum, the famed institution that will undoubtedly be his legacy, 'have you given thought to the East India Company?'

'I am not one for the heat, sir,' I replied.

He looked beyond me. The good professor, his face tight, his hair stiff and unruly as always, said gruffly, 'Nor I. True enough — one makes one's mark alone, not in the company of equals.'

I took time to absorb his words — overly long if I am to recall my demeanour in those days — for I have always held the greatest respect for the man. The words indeed would not fade from my mind.

My fondest recollections of academic life are of his Society's meetings. We met fortnightly in the professor's room in the

Museum. The room itself had nothing to credit it — no furniture of any note beyond an adjoined pair of oak tables and their monastic benches, bare walls and a bare fireplace. If the discussion required it, then an exhibit might occupy the centre of the tables, bereft upon a stained panel of linen. What it did have was a spate of minds, Professor Jameson's at the fore, loosened on a succession of topics, from the larvae of molluscs to the sequence of rock strata on the Isle of Islay. Most interesting of all would be the unveiling of a new specimen which that week had arrived unannounced in the Professor's office, likely from a former student who had made his way to some distant part of the globe. It was there I laid eyes on my first marsupial, the femur of a Maori tribesman, the beak of a Great Auk, a bird which I saw this very year in the flesh in Newfoundland.

There are those who think of Jameson as being as dry as a dead stick. Darwin for one, though we know full well that The Flycatcher is not fond of being lectured to by anyone but himself. Even he is not without his copy of Jameson's *Instructions for Naturalists*.

Jameson is a man who recognizes scholarship when he sees it, no matter what the specimen, or the vocation of the person holding it. That is what has kept us fast friends long after my departure from Edinburgh. At times when I most doubt the route my life is taking, it is Robert Jameson I turn to for advice. His words to a student of twenty-one years of age follow me, and it is to his door that I invariably return each time I again set foot in Scotland.

'Mr Cormack,' I recall him saying, in the midst of our last field outing, to the Salisbury Crags, 'the New World awaits you.' He persisted in calling it the New World, though from what my family knew of Newfoundland, it had long since ceased to be anything but set in its ways. Nevertheless, it was back across the Atlantic I was about to go, though I would have a brief sojourn on another, more timid, island before setting foot again on the island of my birth.

～⌘～

The less recorded of my stay in Prince Edward Island the better. Certainly, I left no mark on the district. I shouldered my job as land agent well enough, but never could I rouse enthusiasm for the place. It failed my faculties and left me brooding insanely for something beyond tedious pasture. The island lacks wildness. It is not a place that Jameson would ever have set foot of his own accord, for one can practically traverse its widest point in a day, and not be winded at that.

I am a man — a specimen of one taller than most, agile, hardy — who needs the challenge of intemperance. Crag and bog and land notched by the mightiest forces of nature are my longing. It surprised no one (least of all John MacGregor, my one true acquaintance there) that once I had dispensed with my debt and accumulated sufficient funds not to be tied to work straight away, I crossed to Nova Scotia, and set sail for St John's, my soul its most forgiving since leaving Scotland.

It was the dead of winter, 1822. That the year would be forever imbedded in my mind was hardly to be anticipated. But if there is one attribute which I bear which stands above all others, it is the swiftness to act once I set myself to a plan. I have no tolerance for indecision. It bespeaks a lameness of intellect that is the downfall of many people and, at the risk of sounding more authoritative than I am, whole nations.

My mind has come to rest on the question of vacillation much too often. My dealings with governments have more than solidified an answer to it. Unfortunately, and against all hope and ambition on my part, the authorities governing Newfoundland are the most grievously dithering of my experience, surpassing, if it can be believed, even those of Prince Edward Island. Dithering, yes, for they are like old ladies, old incompetent ladies, when they act under the most critical of circumstances.

Let me set to paper the political scene. Newfoundland, discovered by the Venetian Cabot — Caboto, if birthplace be a matter of any consequence — in 1497, claimed for Elizabeth in 1583 by Humphrey Gilbert, by all accounts a misfit. The Parliament in London ignored the land for two hundred-fifty years except to appease its West Country fishermen, then in 1822 ruled the lives of its citizens as if God had handed the English a sealed charter.

At its helm was Charles Hamilton. Its helm most certainly, for Sir Charles — in all but seal a peer of the realm which would have to await his return to England — was a Navy man. Suckled by the Royal Navy since he was barely ten, in time a vice-admiral, commander-in-chief of Newfoundland and of Labrador. Then its Governor. With all the sense and propensity for fair play that seamanship engenders. The man was a short-sighted narcissist of the kind only the English could breed and think they do themselves credit.

It was Hamilton who disregarded the proposal of mine laid before him, a proposal in all measures for the utmost good of the country. It was he who failed to offer me any assistance when in the fall of that very year I undertook what I suspect I will be most remembered for — my trek on foot across the whole of the Island, to access the potential of its minerals, and to seek the remaining home of its Red Indians. A proposal ignored by the very one who should have been the most eager to support it.

Yet undertaken nonetheless, Micmac guide at my side. That venture duly recorded in *The Edinburgh Philosophical Journal* of Doctor Jameson.

I failed to find Red Indians, yet that does not stop my thirst to continue the quest. For what greater mark can a man make on a country than to learn more of it than anyone before him?

By all accounts I am a man still fit for the quest. I submit not only to my own appraisal, but to that of others whom I have encountered since departing Scotland. Their commentary on my willingness to venture to the outdoors, and my fitness for such excursions, is steady, and entirely unsolicited. 'A devil for the wilds' is the one I most remember. I have even been accused of having Indian blood coursing my veins.

'You were born in St John's, Mr Cormack, but was your dear mother by chance frequenting the coast? Your father had dealings in salmon after all.' That said by a fellow so filled with drink and with so much raillery that I felt no reason to defend the honour of my mother. Instead, on that occasion I let it lie, let it add to the tide that was turning in favour of my new proposal.

My closest friends were deep in the details, the earnestness of their voices a testament to their approval. 'You best have an Indian with you, William. Indeed you must, if you are not to put yourself unduly at risk. These people have an uncanny sense of the wilderness.'

And so, five years on, here I am, once again about to set off in pursuit of the Red Indians. And, if my plans come indeed to fruition, as they must, this time it will be with the foreknowledge offered by dialogue with a young woman from the very tribe itself!

30th October, 1827
Exploits Island, N.F.L.D.

In short order, following confirmation from the Boeothuck
Institution, I secured an Indian. Indeed this time I have secured
not one, but three — a young Micmac, a Mountaineer from
Labrador, and an Abenakie from Canada. My reasoning is that
they will bring their multifarious instincts to bear on the
whereabouts of the Boeothuck. The journey will commence
tomorrow, daybreak on the 31st. It is later in the season than
I had hoped, and we are bound to encounter snow, but we
proceed with every confidence of success in our endeavours.

   With me I will bring a copy of the list of Boeothuck words
obtained from Demasduit following her capture. I have noted a
few of my own collection, taken from Shanawdithit. When I
have the opportunity I will also add words from the languages
of the three Indians, and in that way ascertain if there are likely
any affinities between the races.

⤳

3rd November, 1827
Badger Bay Great Lake

I write this at the end of a long day, in twilight, alone in my
corner of our encampment. My Native comrades remain around
the fire, smoking their pipes, conversing in a mixture of
languages, none of which I comprehend.

Our route in search of the Boeothuck has taken us inland,
northward to within reach of various inlets of the Bay of Notre
Dame. After four days of arduous travel we have come upon a
cluster of decaying mamateeks. They still hold moss between the
poles, though in many places it has loosened and sunlight shines
through. The birch bark which covered the roofs has weathered
and will not withstand many seasons more. It draws me to
the woeful conclusion that it has been many months since the
shelters have been occupied, perhaps not since the time
Shanawdithit remembers. What lies before us was once a
thriving Boeothuck camp, one perhaps abandoned under the
worst of circumstance. The remnants of Boeothuck life today
that we lifted from the untrodden ground — the shaft of a spear
still red with ochre, pieces of skin garments, the frame of an old
canoe — only lead us to despair of what became of those who
last rested here.

In the days that follow we will likely venture further north
and west, to where the Boeothuck might have come in their

hunt for caribou. We hope to find a peak from which we will be able to survey many miles in every direction, and with good fortune the sight of Boeothuck fires.

❧

20th November, 1827

We have ventured both north and west, both without reward.
There has been only an eerie stillness, and a second covering of
winter's snow.

We have at last reached Red Indian Lake. The snow has
deepened, yet the land has not frozen hard enough to ease our
passage. Here our hopes have slumped even further.

For the Indians it has proven a severely discomforting time.
To my mind they feel themselves usurpers in the domain of the
Boeothuck. The old Mountaineer of Labrador in particular
has been overcome with emotion. I know he feels a singular
attachment to the Boeothuck, for he strongly believes the two
races were once one, that the Boeothuck are his kindred. I agree
with his assertion, though there are many who would refute it.
I long ago reasoned, from the viewpoint of natural migration,
that the Boeothuck likely arrived on the Island after crossing the
Strait of Belle Isle from the southern shores of Labrador.

When first we took sight of the lake, the Indians surveyed
its broad expanse, no doubt pondering the history of the only
people ever to know its magnificence. That of the Boeothuck
had been a secure and rightful hearth, one they were compelled
to forsake. It is left for us to follow in their wake, to decry a
forlorn and haunted vestige of a home.

The mamateeks, found clinging to the margins of the lake,

are in ruin. While all about them are signs of a once flourishing refuge for the aborigines — birch trees expertly stripped of their bark, a smokehouse for venison unscathed, a little-used canoe set in the bushes near the beach. The occupants of the latter have drowned perhaps, and the canoe cast onshore, for inside it we found scattered iron nails. Stolen nails, I surmise. Goad to a crucifixion.

22nd November, 1827

It is the perplexity of our age — the scientific mind seeking
pathways through the sacred. All the while we survey the shores
of Red Indian Lake I feel it a hallowed domain. And no more
so than at the discovery of the burial hut of the Boeothuck.

Upon forcing away the posts which secured its entrance, I
could only stand silently for the moment and breathe the full
significance of the tableau set before us. When we stepped forth
and investigated the raised platform at the centre of the hut it
was as if all the injustices of the past were there displayed.

Before us lay the bones of Demasduit. The bones have been
wrapped with muslin inside a white deal coffin, the one in
which she had been returned to her people. And nearby, the
bones of an infant, her own we surmised, the child who, as
Shanawdithit has related, died shortly after her capture.

Stretched the length of the platform were the remains of the
man we can only think is her husband, Nonosabasut, Chief of
the Boeothucks. He had been struck down in his attempt to
prevent the capture of his wife. At the side of Nonosabasut —
a bow and quiver of arrows, and an iron axe. Other relics of
the Boeothuck past were spread everywhere about the platform.

While my three Indian companions stood mute, and after a
short time withdrew, murmuring what I could only think were
prayers in their own languages, I remained, transfixed by this

rarest of sights. In my mind seethed the desire to share this experience with those men of science who most wish to know the world of the aborigines. My thoughts took me to the reception the masters of natural history would give to an account of this scene. In truth the world beyond the wilds of this remote Island must hold a record of these people, for all trace of them can not be lost to the passage of time and the expurgation of decay.

With the Indians gone I carefully removed to my knapsack objects that I judge to be in utmost want of preservation: a model of a Boeothuck canoe, a small wooden figure of a human and another of a bird, a drinking cup made of bark, a spear point, the outer garment of the infant, two firestones of iron pyrite.

In the dimmest of light my hands came to rest on the skull of Demasduit. I peeled away the fragments of decayed muslin. I dislodged it from the vertebrae, the sound a slight, arid crackle within the chamber.

I removed the skull to the knapsack. And so, too, that of her husband.

My utmost wish is to honour the Boeothucks. The world of natural history will forever hold a record of the ancient aborigines of Newfoundland. They will not be forgotten.

In darkness I set the pieces in moss at the bottom of the canvas bag atop some specimens of rock. My Indian companions are burdened in spirit and would never ascribe to these objects the importance they truly hold. Today, within sight of my companions, I filled the remainder of the bag with other vestiges of the Boeothucks found scattered through the camp.

24th November, 1827

We have quietly set to building a raft, parts held together by the nails found in the bottom of the discarded canoe. Our hope of encountering Boeothucks has sunk and no longer is there talk of such a prospect. If any of us expects the trip down the Exploits to yield fresh sign of them, we do not speak of it.

It would seem the Indians see my melancholy as equal to their own. Their words, in their native tongues, are brief and hang in the cold air like questions.

'The Boeothucks are not your people, Mr Cormack,' said the old Mountaineer after a long, silent stretch of work.

It was unlike an Indian to be so unreserved in his words. We have grown into the habit of keeping our most earnest thoughts to ourselves. The bond that holds us together is one of common purpose, not open friendship. Yet I was not about to dismiss the question — for indeed it was a question — but rather address it as I would any other.

'I am a man who seeks to know all the world around me,' was my answer. 'I think of no people as any less than others.'

At first he did not speak, and appeared willing to have an end to our exchange. But I suspect the Mountaineer reflected on how I was committed by necessity to them, and could see nothing to be forsaken by adding to the question.

'You a strange man, Mr Cormack. I not know English man

who not think himself better man than French man. And I not know French man who not think himself better man than English.' He was so content with his speech that he added, 'And two better than Indian.'

The others smiled at the old Indian's words, and in their own tongue spoke words I could only take for agreement.

'Strange then I am,' I agreed.

Their talk continued. Although they spoke different languages they seemed to have found something of them in common. I knew not what they said, nor do I wish to, for it is more important that we fix our minds on the raft and make our way down the river before the weather turns colder and ice begins to form in its waters. Still, I cannot say I do not reflect on his words, nor the other, unfathomable ones. These Indian words swirl about my head even now, these many hours later, in need of sorting and conversion and transcription.

29th November, 1827
Sandy Point, N.F.L.D.

Several days ago we crowded the raft to begin the journey
down the Exploits to its mouth and thus back to our starting
point. Miles of caribou fences remain along one bank of the
river, fences built of felled trees to channel migrating game into
the range of Boeothuck spears, fences now gaping with decay.
These fences are a final testament to a nation once noble. It is
unthinkable that the race will never rise to repair them, to take
their place again as the true inhabitants of this land.

Where waterfalls prevented passage, we portaged around
them, then constructed another raft to continue our journey.
At times the waters propelled us downstream with such speed
that I feared for a calamitous end to our expedition. But today,
with November almost at its end, after completing a circular
route we judge to exceed three hundred miles, we are once again
in civilization.

Our journey's end brought us by boat to Sandy Point, to
where the Peytons have moved for the winter months, as is their
custom. Here to meet us was John Peyton, Jr., though it took
considerable scrutiny on his part before he recognized me.

'Good heavens, Mr Cormack, but your journey has worn you
to a vestige of the man I knew before.'

The man overstated my appearance for, although it cannot be

called less than arduous, the journey was for certain less punishing than the trek I undertook across the whole of the interior of the Island in 1822. I kept pace with the Indians and they are quick to vouch for my being at home in the wilds. As to my physical appearance — wild game alone is hardly sufficient to sustain a man except when one is settled in the forest and not traversing the country with such speed as did we.

Nevertheless, Peyton insists that I rest with his family several days before making my way back to St John's. I have first to bid farewell to the Indians, my steadfast guides. They are anxious to return to their respective homes before the full brunt of winter sets in.

2nd December, 1827
Sandy Point

Following their payment and the securing of provisions for
their journeys, my trio of Indians dispersed. I bid them each
a safe return, and recorded their likely whereabouts, should
the Institution have need of their services again.

During my time with the Peytons I have of course
expounded fully on the journey. John Peyton has shown
little surprise that the traditional Boeothuck territory had
not yielded any sign of recent lodging. We have weighed at
length the possibilities of where the Boeothucks might have
gone, if indeed any are still alive. Peyton seems not to share
my faith in the possibility that some have removed themselves
from the territory just traversed and remain to be
discovered.

'The three women who came to us were starving, Cormack.
The few who lingered in the wild could not have been otherwise.'

'Did she say as much?'

'Nance has said little about what she left behind. She keeps
her memories to herself.'

I refrain from asserting my true feelings on the matter, being
as I am a guest in his house. But since my first knowledge of
Shanawdithit I have held the belief that the woman has not been
encouraged to relate details of her people and that indeed if she

is holding these within herself it is because Peyton has shown little interest in them.

'The woman was saved from certain death,' he was quick to add, his benevolence not to lie obscured in our conversation.

I am not about to confront the man, but his words only confirm in my mind that his household is not the proper place for the young woman. It is a matter for the Boeothuck Institution and one that we shall soon address.

For the moment my attention is more properly directed to the Boeothuck herself. She seems increasingly troubled each time I near her.

My wish is to speak to her alone, but in this I wait out the opportunity. When work takes Peyton outdoors, and hopefully his wife at the same time to another part of the house, perhaps then I shall be able to beckon Shanawdithit away from the children long enough to converse with her.

⁓

KEVIN MAJOR • 123

4th December, 1827
Sandy Point

I wished I had good news to offer Shanawdithit. 'Your people
have gone elsewhere,' I said to reassure her, 'in their search for
food.' She seems to grasp the effort I have made to reach them.
    She harbours no less anxiety. Her past is not easily put aside.
    'Had we found them, and had they wished to come, we
would have brought them to join you.'
    'Guns?'
    I admitted we carried guns for procuring game. 'We were
careful not to discharge our guns except far from where your
people would have lodged.'
    'They no show themselves.'
    Shanawdithit fails to accept how valued her people are, or
that the Institution will protect them. Nor does she see how
important it is to the scholarship of natural history that they be
found. Her state of mind, dwelling as it does on her past, will
not allow it, and for that reason she can, of course, be readily
forgiven.
    From my reading of narratives by those who have lived
among the aboriginal races I have come to think of them as
secretive in the manner in which they view the world — a
manner, for that reason, difficult to fathom. They are not races
easily given to trust. Yet it is important that I win the trust of

Shanawdithit if I am to record the knowledge she holds about her people.

The time is near when I shall have to leave her to her life with the Peytons, although before many months pass she will board a boat and come to live in St John's. I cautioned her that it best remain a secret between the two of us, but that soon a formal letter will find its way to the Peytons informing them that the Boeothuck Institution has deemed it best for her to take leave of her surroundings, which hold such bitter memories, and then to begin a new and better life.

NONOSA

WINTER. THROUGH SHORTENED DAYS sunlight overwhelmed the sky and the land, erasing the boundary between the two, made of it an undulating mantle, frozen ceaseless white. It stilled unruly rivers, hardened bogland, smoothed the fractured, jagged rock.

Winter unleashed the landscape, made of it endless passage for the rawly vigorous of the clan. Winter unbound the lives of Nonosa and his people, freed them to the graces of ice and snow and the brilliant, saturating sun. Its charms outlasted the bitter cold.

Some wished it would never pass, so blissfully free it was of the bane of summer — blackflies, mosquitoes, airless sun, fire. And now, the same could be said of the sea. The seacoast in summer brought the breath of winter, and gave the Kanwashish the best of both the seasons.

With the food of one, the Kanwashish settled even more contentedly into the other. They celebrated with a feast.

It marked what they took for the shortest day and the longest night. The gathering brought a moon full and bright, hung splendidly low in the sky. Under it the Kanwashish built a robust fire. Melted the snow, produced a ring of bare ground for the celebration.

From frozen quarters of caribou they carved generous slabs — thawed, then pounded tender, skewered onto sharpened alder limbs and set into the fire. Not to remain there long, for the Kanwashish liked a good sign of blood in their meat.

The favoured custom of the old was to soak it first in the juice of squashed redberries. They had grown particular in how the fire was to strike it, so much so that one among them became their appointed cook. She would stake several pieces of meat, her eyes passing quickly from one to the other. Each piece had a rightful owner, and a rightful time to whisk it from the fire.

Coshee had grown especially particular. There was a seared edge of crispness he wanted in his meat that sometimes called for two and three returns to the flames. Only when it passed his strict inspection would he put it to his mouth, no matter how hungry he might be, or how impatient the others had grown. They said nothing, for they could all remember the many times there had not been enough meat to satisfy them no matter how long they waited.

Now the Kanwashish also had sea-fish and sea-bird as their choice, and walrus. Between the food came music-making and the dance. Drummers pounded new rhythm against their thin caribou skins. Chanters matched the rhythm, their song a creation of Tuanon, louder and more rigorous than the Kanwashish had ever known. The old ones were left to smile, caught in the memories of youth.

'Kanwashish, Kanwashish dance to dawn, dance to dawn. On and on, on and on. Kanwashish, Kanwashish, Spirits' wish, Spirits' wish. Kanwashish, Kanwashish!'

Nonosa had been one to help fashion the drums. But he had taken no part in shaping the chant, and at its boastful repetition he lost interest.

The dance he could not escape. His reputation at the dance would not permit it, though his pace was hardly a match for the vigour of the chant. And when Tuanon followed, Nonosa was left in his brother's wake. Tuanon spread his arms, a bold and soaring bird of prey, swooping past the children. He frightened and delighted them, the drummers drumming all the harder. It drove Tuanon to frenzied heights, until at its end he collapsed into a wind drift of snow.

Some old ones looked askance at his display. Without chastising words, for they were in an oddly agreeable mood. Except Teraset. Tuanon rose slowly from the snow and met her croak, words no one could understand.

NOT ONLY THE WORDS, the glimmer of pleasure in life which Teraset emitted fell away from her.

During the end days of winter, she died.

Teraset's body stiffened with the frost, the red ochre hardly holding to it. It was laid upon a slab of stone scraped free of ice and snow, covered with boughs weighed down with a few ice-encrusted rocks. It would be spring before the covering could be made proper and secure. At the gravesite came a sputter of words from Coshee, barely heard except by the cluster of the clan nearest him.

Death clutched Coshee by the hand, a wearisome companion. Coshee was not the same, for he knew he could not be far behind his wife. His silence filled quickly with rancour. For those who dared question him, he had an eager supply of scorn, expelled without regard for who else might hear his words. Bitter he was in his mind and equally in the face he showed the world.

His own health waned. He walked only with pain, his walking stick taking the posture of revenge, which he used freely to clear his way whenever he moved outside his lodge. One day, he inflicted the impatience of his stick on the legs of a child, sending her howling to her mother.

'Coshee needs a wife,' said one, the kindest defence to be found.

Others were less generous. 'When Teraset was alive, at least he kept a decent tongue.'

They turned to Nonosa, as if he were again the wise one of the clan, the person to pull them free of Coshee's querulous grasp.

There were three women whom he considered suitable for Coshee. Two had been widowed not long before, and one for longer than Nonosa could remember. The three shared a widow's lodge and there cared for each other. They bustled about, strong in mind and body, with chatter emerging from their lodge that made them seem younger than they were.

He was met with an eruption of words. 'None of us has the wish to be the wife of Coshee. Yes, he has his troubles. Not only in his legs! Do you think Teraset did not confide in us? Who would want to be part of that misery?'

'Not a wife he needs,' Nonosa interjected, 'but someone to relieve the aching in his legs.'

'And what is between those legs, Nonosa? Is there not an aching there as well?'

Nonosa could not help but smile, and when he did the mood of the three lightened. They fell against themselves in laughter, like young girls. The hope of finding someone to live with Coshee had come to a quick and certain end.

The three women then turned inward in a circle, whispering among themselves. When they had finished they turned to Nonosa and offered a proposal.

'Coshee's ways are a curse. Tell him we will come to his lodge each morning. We will work to rid him of his pain.'

'All three of you?'

'Yes.'

'Together?'

'Of course. We will rub his legs — only his legs — and work grease into them. We know the secret. Teraset told us everything.'

The vision of three women leaning over the bare legs of Coshee made Nonosa frown with misgivings. 'Will it not be embarrassing for an old man?'

'We have no reason to look into his face. Let him pretend he is asleep. Let him snore if he wishes!' They smiled at each other, then looked back at Nonosa, wonderfully satisfied with their solution.

And so it came to be that each morning, after the sun had risen and after they had taken their hot drink, the three women left and walked in a line to Coshee's lodge. The woman in the lead poked an arm past the doorway and shook a string of small bones to announce their arrival. They stood and waited until Coshee's grim 'now' reached their ears. Into the lodge they went and knelt around a pair of bare, old man's legs. No one spoke. The only sound was the drone of the women's working chant, and an occasional grunt of pain when their hands struck a tender spot. Halfway through they stopped and looked away, notice to Coshee that he was to turn onto his stomach and adjust the covering so that now it hid his rump.

No words ever passed between them and if Coshee met any of them during the course of the day, it was as if the visits to his lodge had never taken place. The progress in his walking, they agreed, must be due to the longer days of sunshine, to the fact that the bitter winter chills, so quick to stiffen old limbs, had finally passed away.

Coshee's walk grew stronger. Some days he could be seen outside without the help of a walking stick. The women told Nonosa they no longer saw the need to be going every day to Coshee's lodge. The next time Coshee emerged from his lodge the stick had returned, and with it a wearisome moan when the women came within his range.

What brought an end to the visits were the events of what two of the women came to call 'that morning.'

'That morning,' one of the pair bemoaned, 'Coshee crawled over the fence between right and wrong. He was no longer a patient.'

The women had not long started their task when the piece of caribou hide covering his loins began to stir unceremoniously. Eyebrows constricted. An exchange of scornful glances. It had happened once before, though the object of concern had fallen to rest as quickly as it had awakened, remembered as no more than a grudging flutter. That morning, as the hide rose higher and higher, if in fits and starts, the work of massaging the patient's legs lost its steadfast rhythm. In time the caribou hide resembled a slouching tent.

The work ceased. And what might have been mistaken for the time Coshee should turn onto his stomach gave way to a prolonged respite, to the disquieting feeling that it was Coshee's intention to remain in exactly the same position. To do so with a posture that was beginning to look like nothing less than pride. He certainly hadn't fallen asleep.

The three stood up and headed outside. The line of women started back toward their own lodge. Two of them were inside when it was discovered that the bowl of grease had not returned with them. And neither had the third member of the three, Marshuit, the youngest widow among them, in whose hands had rested the bowl when they left Coshee's dwelling.

Against their best predictions, Marshuit and Coshee became a pair, wife and husband.

'That morning,' Nonosa said in the women's lodge days later, 'Coshee changed.'

The remaining two women would hardly speak of what had happened. 'Some changes,' one said, the other nodding, 'come too late.'

NONOSA'S LABOUR IN GETTING Coshee a wife altered forever the relationship between the two men. There was now an alliance, if of a strange sort whose boundaries were hardly understood. Certainly Tuanon did not understand it, or think it anything but foolish that Nonosa had worked so hard to pacify the old man.

'Coshee long ago lost what sense he had,' said Tuanon.

'Put your temper behind you,' Nonosa told him, having finally lost patience with his brother. 'You grow feverish too quickly. Old age has torment you know nothing about.'

Tuanon would have none of it, and rebuked Nonosa for not stepping before the Kanwashish, not taking charge. Nonosa turned away, trusting time to mend his brother's ways, doubting if time alone could do it. Nonosa had much more than Tuanon's brashness to fill his days.

Shanaw was now crawling about the lodge, forcing her father to fashion a barrier that would keep her away from the fire. He strapped twigs together across a corner of the lodge, covered them with thick furs. He layered the floor with more furs to secure it against the cold, made of it a safe place for her to wander on her own. At first she found it strange and cried at being left alone, but she learned to pull herself to her feet and would teeter at the barrier, peering across the lodge. The curve of her cheekbones and her dark eyes caught the firelight, mesmerizing her father. He chattered constantly to her. It wasn't long before her babbling took the nature of words, the pleasure in her face a certain sign she understood what he said to her.

Her first true word came when her father touched her lips with a pulp of boiled fish. Her lips soured at the strangeness of it, though only for a moment. It seeped into her mouth, her quizzical look recast.

'Cod,' her father said. 'You are the youngest to know its taste.' He held her gaze as deeply as a child could allow. He said the word again.

It was a charmed smile that passed her lips, and then her first word. Only loud enough for Nonosa's ears. 'Cod.'

He smiled broadly, but kept his delight a secret. '*Our* secret, Shanaw,' he said and kissed her gently on the cheek.

WHEN NONOSA STOOD ON the seashore that spring the child bounced gleefully in his arms. When Nonosa let her bare feet skim the surface, she shrieked, not at the iciness of the water, but in delight. She kicked her tiny, fattened feet to have them skim the surface again and again.

On that sandy beach she took her first steps alone. She tottered to the water's edge, let it bury her feet in its swelling back ashore. Nonosa kept a watchful eye, for Biesta said it was not right for a child to wallow in such cold.

'No bother to her,' Nonosa said, not to admonish his wife, but to free his child. For her curiosity about the sea was boundless.

The delirium of the capelin's wild rush onto the beach secured its hold on her. She would sit in the midst of it, enthralled by its wriggling bounty, by its ebb and swirl.

At day's end the sand turned to a sponge of capelin eggs and milt. When she stood, a slippery fish in both her hands, she sank to her ankles. Had to be plucked from it, by a father playfully whirling her through the air to turn her mind to other things.

Biesta quickly covered her bare legs, red with cold. When the fish slipped from her hands Shanaw cried, and only when two more were set in place did she stop. She fell asleep at night exhausted, still clutching the fish. Only then could Biesta pry open her fingers, though her mother dared not throw the fish away for fear the child would wake in the middle of the night and remember them.

When Shanaw rose in the morning, she fussed until the hide door to the lodge was drawn back, until she caught the current of salt air. Nonosa could only laugh and call her sweet names, and treasure her impatience as he carried her in his arms to the shore.

Little one, wilful one. Beloved one, precious one. Washed in salted water.

And so she grew with salt water threading her senses. When her surge of language came she spilled back to her father all the sea words spoken to her. It was her game to concoct new ones for other faces of the sea. In the seasons to come it would be Shanaw who compared the many forms of spring sea ice and gave them names, who for long hours pondered the way the tide struck land, how on some days it crept ashore, on others it curled enough to made the pebbles sing, and how in the fiercest wind it came crashing down with a fury that drove everyone inland. It would be Shanaw who faithfully took the measure of the sea, gloried in its noble ways, warned of how fickle it might turn.

Shanaw's mind was her own, a truth that grew deeper each day. It pleased her father, but caused Biesta only grief. For Shanaw was growing independent of her mother, strange for a girl among the Kindred.

And strange for a girl to be clinging so to her father, thought Biesta, though she would not speak of it to him. 'You must not neglect your work,' were her words to Nonosa, 'to spend time with the girl.'

Nonosa was certain he did not, for his success at the fish was even greater than the summer before. And when a walrus showed up his spear was there to outsmart the beast and cause Nonosa to again surpass the other hunters in the glory of the kill.

Jealousy, he knew, was the reason for her bitterness, and jealousy would have to be confronted if it were not to split husband from wife. He took Biesta aside when Shanaw had fallen asleep and proclaimed his affection for her.

'Am I wrong, Nonosa,' she said, resisting him, 'to think you wanted me only as a mother for your child?'

Nonosa bared his chest and held her tight to him, for her to hear the beat of his heart against her own, to know the pleasures their coming together had wrought.

How much of it was thankfulness for saving Shanaw from certain death he could not say, though when he was alone it was still Biesta's sister who often filled his mind. When he looked into the face of his daughter it was the mother of her anguished birth he remembered.

He did not wish it otherwise. Nor did he think of Biesta as anyone but his wife, the one willing to share their lodge, to make her life a pair with his own.

'I am your only wife,' she said to him.

'That I know.'

'Do you wish another?'

Biesta opened her tunic and drew her husband hungrily to her. Pressed him tightly against her breasts.

Biesta forced her hands past the waist of his pants and closed them over his buttocks. They stiffened at her touch, though from the cold, not lust.

'Your wife needs you,' she said, at the same time sinking one hand between his thighs and feeling for his scrotum.

Nonosa had not known such boldness except in the seclusion of night. Reluctance washed over him. It seemed not the moment, with the child sobbing, daylight flashing past the door.

He drew back from her. Her hand clutched his testicles. Without strong grip, yet he moaned in torment and jerked his legs together to bind her hand in place.

Biesta laughed into the hollow of his neck, breathing pleasure at the way his whole body stiffened against her. Slowly she surrendered her grip and pulled out her hand.

That night when they made love his cock held back, though he thrust it as madly as he could. When he sank aside of her, exhausted, she seized his cock, stroked it to eruption. He fell to rest against her, her hand again searching out what she called his weakest part, this time with less surprise and greater care.

'You make of me a fearless woman,' she said before falling asleep.

CORMACK

St John's
2nd January, 1828

After a stop in Twillingate I returned to the city. It is pleasant
enough to be back to its familiar ways, although I am anxious
to complete the business at hand and be off to Britain. It is my
intention to pass the coldest of the winter months there and
return in the spring.

Only now has there been the opportunity to convene a
meeting of the Boeothuck Institution. In the meantime there
has been much to do in preparation for my voyage, including
outlasting the Yuletide. The inhabitants of the Island, whether
it be due to nostalgia or monotony, bedeck the celebration of
the Virgin Birth with so vulgar a display as to make it
unrecognizable to all but the pagan. Bands of the lower classes
rant drunkenly through the city day and night, as if it were
their right to circumvent civility at every turn. One can hardly
begin to envisage what they resort to in private, considering

what passes for humanity in public.

The most odious are the 'mummers.' The West Country mob has endowed its new home with the primitive custom of dressing up in disguise, in all manner of outlandish garb that, in the eyes of the costumed at least, turns delivery boy to Duchess, fishmaid to maniacal Justice of the Peace. Among the 'entertainments' to which they lend their wanton talents is a drunken piece of farce, a relic of the Middle Ages it would seem from the names of the characters, though, given the unintelligible performances, it matters not their names, nor their words, nor anything but that it finds a quick end without physical damage to the audience.

The audiences are the households which they swoop into for no good reason other than they suspect a bottle of brandy occupies a cabinet therein. Once King George and the Turkish Knight have duelled — the mantelpiece having been judiciously saved of its porcelains — the absurd Hobby-Horse has made its entrance, and Old Father Christmas has discharged his final petition, then begins the dancing and the rousing call for cake and drink. I suspect the merrymakers parted my front door only slightly less satiated than when they entered, for the house is without a woman, except for a cleaning maid every fortnight, and bore not the rum-soaked confections they had delighted in at other homes, as was their surly lipped compulsion to relate.

I sound the part of a miser given to dimming the winter solstice of the poor, yet I am not such a man, but merely one for whom manners have their rightful rank and decency in spoken word a precedence. My Yuletide was not without its revelry, and I not without my turn at the reels, though my choice of dance be a civilized Strathspey. Dr Carson, my fondest acquaintance in the city — himself the great champion of the destitute — would attest to both my empathy for the poor and the litheness of my step.

It seemed to delight the ladies who came within sight of the dance floor, and no less those who espied me in the pew of the Presbyterians on Christmas Day. My exploits into the Island's interior grew to be the talk of any of the Christmas gatherings I attended, and, but for the lack of interest I have in droning on, I could have regaled each and every buxom lady who gathered about the settees.

My mind was elsewhere, and try as I might to feign interest in speculating yet again on the demise of the aborigines, I chose to excuse myself and make my way home, dodging the rabble-rousers along Duckworth Street as best I could.

The day following, having by chance met Carson and some other of the guests from the night before, I had then to endure badgering about my early departure. Suddenly, it seems my marital state has become cause for inept speculation. For what reason I fail to see — the foul weather perhaps, the sight of a solitary man bundled and heading off to his rented lodgings consisting of an empty house and cold hearth.

'Not the man for the ladies,' Carson pronounced. 'For certain not one to court favour with his charm.'

'Not the interest in marriage,' I replied, my irritation beginning to show itself. 'For that is where favours would lead.'

'Not one given to amour then? Over which I have not known many to have much restraint.'

'Restraint is something I do have,' I told him.

Clearly, I had no wish to give myself over to the discourse. I had no wish to listen to anyone offering suggestions as to whom among the fair sex would be a congenial match for me. This did not stop him — or, at other times, any of my other married acquaintances, woman or man — from doing just that.

Then, in what I will admit was an unbecoming moment of exasperation, I said to Carson, 'You, good man, have a wife and eight children and a wage which must vanish in support of them. I prefer to direct my money elsewhere.'

A careless rejoinder, and with it I had taken on the garb of someone too selfish to wed. Carson, as was his way, pondered my assertion, allowing regret for the moment to gnaw at me. He then smiled and congratulated me on my resolve, though not without a parting barb.

'A man, except by necessity, should never think himself above the love of a woman.'

By necessity then. If I am to pursue the woman — for some are so bold as to point to the very one they deem most suitable, the daughter furthermore of the Presbyterian cleric — what would she make of my frequent absences? Would I not be constantly promising to return by a specific day or specific month, only to have that day or month pass and I not ready to return. The world, it seems to me, holds too many mysteries to conclude that the mystery of marriage is one to which at present I need expend my energy.

≈

3rd January, 1828

I should not be sounding so hardened to the ways of women. I am not unwilling to admit that I do not bear the experience of my peers in the matter of the female sex. And when in the company of such gentlemen I am at odds to say it otherwise. Thus am I willing to relate an episode, as a young man fresh to the city, one serving to illustrate the conundrum in which unsuspecting men find themselves, and from which they come away no more profited for the experience. It is an episode in which I take neither pride, nor moral. At the time I was led by what I now deem a tenuous conclusion — that it is better to have verged on the moment, and if need be, spurned it, than not to have verged at all.

It came to the matter of a certain lady, one whose station shall remain unnamed. The lady and the gentleman I had come to know within a week of my first arrival in the capital. And it was she who led me to the frozen waters of Quidi Vidi Lake. Pleasant indeed. Far beyond pleasant, in truth, for it began my infatuation with the art of ice skating. I recall the moment I was able to steady myself and for the first time glide over the sheet without fear of falling, my cloak and beaver sweeping the cold air. An unbinding it was, an extension beyond that of humankind. Birdlike in its dimension. I credit the lady with many things, admission to the most graceful of sporting pursuits among them.

Within a year, however, the lady was due to depart permanently for England, her husband's tenure at an end, and he gone ahead to secure the post. An afternoon meeting it was, the one she knew to be our last, it likely that she would never see me again, and I her. I was somewhat saddened at the prospect. I had quite enjoyed the company of the woman, she who had brought relief from a tedious arrival.

We passed several longish minutes of pleasantries, she citing the features of St John's she would miss, I countering with many she might not. Uncommon laughter spilled between.

'You wish me gone, then?'

'For certainty, not.'

'You'll not skate with such an interested partner.'

'Or patient one.'

'I shall think of you, William.' She was suddenly given to setting her eyes to mine. 'When you think of me, what will you remember?'

The next words, I knew, would be the most momentous of the afternoon, perhaps of all the time we had shared since our first meeting over tea.

'I shall most remember your charm, dear lady.'

She smiled, sweetly, but without the stir of new pleasures.

I took from it that she was wishing for more, for words that parted my tongue with less ease, with the struggle that accompanies a deeper search for them. I tried again to oblige the lady.

'And I shall most remember the curiosity of mind that dwells within that charm.'

She appeared ill-satisfied still with my endeavour. Then, with a bravery that thwarted my modest intentions, the lady extended a hand to mine, then her other, so that my own rested between them both.

'You are lost for words, William, and I see no reason to choose language to part from each other. Come with me, the servants are away to their errands, let us find other expression for our affections.'

Suddenly, I will admit, I was filled, not with an excitement at what that expression might be, but a dread of it. Not a dread of the act itself — whatever curiosity of mind the lady held — but dread of my own performance in the piece. And I thought of it as just that, a performance. Affection for the lady I held, in strong measure, but I was thinking it not the fervent drama that was needed for such an occasion.

Nevertheless, I rose with her and walked, hand joined in hand to a hallway, all the while her words filling the space between us. 'This house did not lend itself to amorous intent most seasons of the year. Fortunately, summer has not completely parted from us.'

What my intentions were I had but the murkiest of notions. The lady seemed a determined soul, and I was left to think myself soulless if I did not join in her concert. She led me to a room, vacant of any human scent, bare except for bed and dresser and a small landscape painted by the lady hanging above it, *Cottage in the Woodlands* its title. She had set the same painting in my hands during a previous gathering.

'It is said young Prince William rested here.'

Rest of a sort. The future William IV had visited Newfoundland indeed, some thirty years before, as a randy young man it was said.

'Do you not wish to lie where your namesake, Prince William, lay?' she asked, drawing the heavy curtains on the dull light of a late afternoon.

I was persuaded, guided by a steady hand and in the semi-darkness we filled the bed, both together coming to lie where the future King of England had lain.

The intricacies of that hour are difficult to relate. It is onerous to find the words, for there was no justice to be had in the entangling of the body and the emotion. I brought to it a passion, a willingness to meet the lady at her game. She proved sharper at the game than I, for I had not quickened in the manner to match her expectations. It would have been better had she not removed her petticoat in quite such a flourish, but eased her suitor to her monumental charms. Had there been a draft, I would have said I was numbed by it, but the reason my prowess tarried is not so simple to relate. The lady showed herself to be overwhelming in her carriage, where simpler, less warring ways would have been more fruitful. My mind was awhirl and failed to settle on the charge at hand, and she, dear lady, was no help, as if the flaccidity were my doing alone and she had played her part without fault. My hands did explore her flesh, as did my mouth her lips, but no such satisfaction would she embrace but that it were leading to something more.

The more was not to be and she fell aside of me unfulfilled, and most indiscreet for a lady, emitted a profanity. Mild though it was, yet a profanity, unbefitting her station.

In time, and awkward manner, she showed me to the door, and as predicted before I entered, I never saw the lady again.

SHANNON

S TANDARD PROCEDURE, GIVEN THAT the project relates to Aboriginals, is for Shannon to seek input from present-day Native groups in the region, to make them part of the process. The problem — if, in fact, it could be called a problem — is the uncertainty about the identity of the Aboriginals the Norse encountered. No definite link has been established between them and the present-day Innu or Inuit. Or Métis. There is also the possibility that the eleventh-century Aboriginals were ancestors of the Beothuk Indians, but of course the Beothuks are long extinct.

Which makes it difficult to pinpoint who has the strongest link to the site. In fact, even spiritually, some may have only a tentative connection to it. To put it delicately, some may well prefer to be spending their time dealing with present-day issues that have a direct impact on them. Nevertheless, to use the bureaucratic term, they are definitely 'stakeholders.' Shannon's plan is to arrange a meeting with representatives from the three groups as soon as the proposal she's formulating is ready for their response.

In the meantime, what she has to do is get a firm grasp of the site itself. Be certain she has all the facts. The only written documentation from the time are the Sagas, although there were a number of artifacts recovered at the time of excavation, all helping paint a substantial picture of life at the Vinland settlement.

She's read all the archaeological reports, the Parks' own internal reports put together prior to its National Historic Site and UNESCO designations. As well, there are transcriptions of interviews done with local people who were aware of the mounds prior to the Norse adventurer Helge Ingstad arriving on the scene in the 1960s. And a file containing a wealth of other items, many of them press clippings collected over the years. It was quite the news story at the time — the Norse proven to strike North America five hundred years before Columbus or Cabot.

The first irrefutable evidence came with the uncovering of a spindle whorl, a tool for spinning wool unknown in Aboriginal cultures. The scenario that Shannon included with her job application has Gudrid spinning wool, her baby asleep nearby, when she sights the young Aboriginal woman on the fringes of their enclosure, a woman perhaps wanting to trade, as the Aboriginals did when the Norse first arrived.

Much of the material in the files she's read before, so they serve only to refresh her perspective. She needs to be able to articulate the strengths of the site, from historical and cultural viewpoints, but also from that of the naive tourist. Shannon starts driving to the site at odd hours and in all kinds of weather. She wants to experience it from a variety of angles and light conditions. She wants to feel the impact it could have on a visitor who has come freshly upon it.

The reconstructed turf houses are remarkable structures, fairly large yet rising unobtrusively from the ground. They appear from a distance almost as undulations in the landscape. She finds it easy enough to set her mind back a thousand years, to when the Norse ships rounded the headlands, to when the Greenland passengers excitedly stepped ashore and settled in their Vinland. And not much more difficult to imagine the reaction of the Aboriginals to these strange, otherworldly humans.

AND NOW INTO THE landscape she has created steps Simon. Remaining there, unwilling to move off, imbedding himself in the frame, taking her from the excitement of that scene, to something of his own.

Simon is part of a group the regional Parks office has put together for when there is a need to consult what it terms 'the Aboriginal constituency.' He's one of the people Shannon approaches during the summer about the proposed reinterpretation of the L'Anse aux Meadows site, although it's September before they are finally able to get together for a meeting.

Simon is Métis — his grandmother was Innu, his grandfather white. This much she has gathered from the file. His grandfather had come from Scotland to work at the Hudson's Bay Company post in North West River. Simon grew up there. He's a teacher now in Red Bay, still in Labrador, but farther south.

He's not what she had been expecting. He's taller and straighter than the men she's met so far, and without the beer-bloated stomach. His face is angular, engaging, though his hair could use a cut and he tends to speak too quickly. More than anything, it's his warm, brown, clever, near brazen eyes that draw her in. From the very beginning, and against her better judgment, he has her searching for what's beyond those eyes.

His darkened skin tells her he loves his snowmobile in winter, his canoe in summer, loves hunting and fishing. But there's another, much less predictable part to him.

He's maybe mid-thirties. And that's trying to put his age out of her mind as quickly as it came in, deciding that he probably has a history she doesn't want to entangle herself in. Besides which, theirs is a prescribed relationship.

After all summer visiting the site, consulting with the staff and Park officials, and surveying visitors, she's anxious to get moving on the proposal she's drafted. Her recommendation is to reconstruct an Aboriginal encampment, at some distance from the reconstructed turf houses, but still in view of them, where visitors could go, just as they do now to the Norse reconstruction. Then to develop a small open-air amphitheatre where visitors would assemble to watch short dramatizations of the contact between the two groups, followed by a question and answer period with the performers, still in character.

Of the three people at the meeting, Simon is the only one to challenge the proposal. He doesn't oppose it, but neither is he willing to endorse it without discussion. Fair enough. That's the purpose of the committee. Shannon knows she would be doing the same herself if she were in his position.

'What stories would you tell?'

She had chosen not to go into the full details from the outset. So this leads nicely to them.

'In the framework of world history, of course, the linking of the two strands of human migration was quite momentous, the so-called "First Circle" — the descendants of the ancients who migrated east out of Africa meeting the descendants of those who migrated west. It's not well known, but it has immense potential for drawing more people to the site. One scenario obviously could be developed around that first encounter. I can see another around trading, using authentic goods and produce from the time.'

'Milk for furs, according to the Saga,' Simon interjects, turning to the other two committee members. 'The Norse quickly rejected the idea of trading weapons.'

Shannon presses on. 'The fact that one of the Norse women, Gudrid, gave birth to a child while she was at L'Anse aux Meadows is a story in need of telling. I would like to see it used as a way of drawing in the female Aboriginals, as a starting point to a maternal bond between them.'

'What about the killings?' Simon says, matter-of-factly. 'The two groups did end up slaughtering each other.'

The question, of course, was inevitable. She has thought this through.

'To me, it comes down to the choice of what aspect of the historical moment to portray. Given that in the beginning relations were friendly, that trading did occur, then perhaps a greater purpose would be served by focusing on that rather than what followed. Of course we wouldn't dismiss it. My sense is it is bound to be a point of discussion during the Q&A with the performers.'

She realizes she is sounding prepackaged. Simon listens, without expression.

'Do we want to revisit that conflict,' she says, 'or do we want to emphasize the abilities of the two cultures to co-operate? The overall human capability for good, or the regrettable action of a few impulsive individuals?'

'Truth or a sanitized version of the truth?'

It's obviously not the first time he's had this debate. The dialogue is civil enough, which is more than can be said for some of the meetings between Parks officials and Aboriginal groups that Shannon has attended over the years. No raised voices, no deep-seated resentment at the process. Is that for her benefit?

She continues to move things along. 'If we take the Sagas at their word, then we know that eventually there was bloodshed, that the Norse fled back to Greenland in the wake of it. But that initial sighting, that initial face-to-face trust, I believe, says more than the fact that, over time, the relationship deteriorated into the two groups attacking each other.'

'Parks Canada is a born optimist,' Simon interjects. Careful, it would seem, to keep the remark one step away from her. Then he retreats a bit more. And offers a disarming smile. 'Optimism is commendable. Unrealistic, but commendable.'

Shannon returns the smile. She's determined to keep the general tone as businesslike as possible. She's put a lot of effort into the proposal, and there is a specific process to be worked through.

'Hopeful we try to be. But not unrealistic. I can't see anything to be gained by having an out-and-out bloodbath on an open field in front of kids.'

'True enough, although I'm sure they see worse every day on their video screens.' He glances at the others before plunging deeper. 'We can't ignore the fact that this so-called First Circle lasted a very short time. Usurping another's domain is inevitably a nasty business. Will one race of people allow another race to take over its territory without a fight? I would say no, definitely not. That, in my view at least, is what it is to be human. In the end someone wins, someone loses, and they both pay a price.'

There is silence for the moment. Eventually Simon shrugs.

'That's the way I read history.' He's calm and soft-spoken still, which in some ways Shannon finds harder to deal with than if he were aggressive. He has adeptly yanked the others from her camp. But it's clear he doesn't want the meeting to turn into an open argument.

It doesn't. Eventually they all board Shannon's vehicle and drive to L'Anse aux Meadows. She wants everyone to see how well the physical elements of the proposal would fit into what's already there.

The stories to be told remain the sticking point. For the moment the committee and Shannon agree to disagree, and decide to meet again in a few weeks. In the meantime Shannon leaves them with a twenty-page printed version of the proposal, some photocopied background material, and encouragement to email each other as the process continues. Simon tells her he thinks emailing is a great idea. And then they all go out to dinner.

LATE THE FOLLOWING AFTERNOON into Shannon's inbox comes an email from Red Bay. Did she know, he asks, that the relationship of the Natives to the Basque whalers they encountered in Red Bay in the 1500s was generally a friendly one? That they traded in good faith and the Natives helped out with the rendering of the whale blubber to oil. 'They even looked after the whaling boats, which were left behind when the Basques sailed back home each fall.'

She did, of course, know that. But his attempt at being conciliatory is appreciated.

Then he drops a hint of his life beyond their business relationship. 'I'm off to check a few snares in the morning, before school,' he says to end the email. 'I love the woods this time of the year.'

Really, she thinks.

Shannon presses *reply*. 'Thanks for this. I love it, too, the woods, this time of the year.' Which she knows is sounding like conversation, rather than a formal response. Yet, he's trying to start on a fresh footing. She reconsiders the reply, then sends it anyway.

Later that evening there's another email from him. 'In that case, we should get together.'

So. This is it. Suddenly something more than business-as-usual. Does she keep it safe and unsullied by keeping her distance, or does she give in to personal temptation? Realistically, is there any question?

She knows the five-line bio, and nothing else of him, except for four hours together with two other people, followed by dinner with those same people. She doesn't know if he's single, divorced, or still married, has kids, doesn't have kids, is already in a relationship, what they have in common besides an attraction to the woods in September. Nothing.

The next night he calls.

'So, you want to go for a scun in the woods sometime?'

'Simon?' *Scun* — a word she hasn't heard since she was in high school. Since Jeffrey Walsh.

'Do you?'

'Do you mean a hike in the woods, Simon?' There is amusement in her voice. She fails to disguise it.

'Yes, Shannon, that's what I mean. I can meet you somewhere.'

Some neutral ground.

'How about Pinware?' he says. 'I know some trails near the river.'

He has obviously thought this through. Pinware is between L'Anse Amour and Red Bay. He has heard her talk about taking the ferry across the Strait. He knows her job encompasses these other two sites.

'That sounds like a reasonable idea.'

'I go salmon fishing there in the summer.' Further rationalization, of a kind.

'It should be lovely this time of the year. Some of the trees are starting to turn already.'

'We'll have a boil-up.'

Of course, a boil-up. Another reversion to her past. 'You bring the tea, I'll bring the food.' She doesn't miss a beat. They set the upcoming Saturday afternoon.

When she gets off the phone she suddenly remembers she's already made plans to spend the weekend with Bertha. She had talked her into taking a trip, down the Peninsula to Corner Brook, where she hasn't been in years. Shannon was planning to take her shopping and treat her to dinner in a pricey restaurant, something Bertha never gets to do. They were going to stay overnight in the Glynmill Inn. Shannon knows Bertha has been looking forward to it, but she also knows she won't mind having to postpone it for a week or so.

NONOSA

'I T IS TIME YOU found a wife,' Nonosa told Tuanon when they were next alone. It had been much on Nonosa's mind. Tuanon's glances had begun to fall on girls of his own clan, his envious stares on couples when they went off to their lodges for the night. He and his companions whispered incessantly, no doubts as to where their lust would one day lead.

'When?' said Tuanon. 'When will I find that wife?' As if to head off a false plan to pacify him.

'The gathering of the clans. It is the turn of the Nookwashish.'

Tuanon knew this. Before the clash between Remesh and his brother he had been eagerly anticipating it.

'Two winters have passed since the last,' said Nonosa. 'No clan has the right to put an end to it.'

THE CAMP OF THE Nookwashish came in sight at the first fall of snow. Thick flakes swooned from the sky, melted instantly at meeting the river. And did the same, with hardly more reluctance, after striking the land. When the Kanwashish reached the camp they were draped in winter, snow thinly mounded on their heads and shoulders.

Tuanon led the manoeuvring of canoes to shore. He rose to his feet as a paddler would only chance doing in shallow water. Simple and effortless, in all innocence.

The other young hunters feigned amazement at his balance. 'Wives behind the trees, Tuanon. You have won them over before setting foot on land.'

Tuanon jumped nimbly onto the beach, just before the canoe striking shore would have jolted him off-balance. He reeled on the sand and faced the clan, shook the snow from his long hair. He brushed it from his mantle with exaggerated vanity, then laughed aloud.

THE SHORE ABOVE AND below was crowded with other canoes, as if a place had been saved solely for the Kanwashish. With their canoes lifted ashore, Coshee declared that truly it was so. 'In the hearts of the Nookwashish,' he said, 'we are their people.'

The words had not left his lips before a jovial croak of a greeting fell from atop the riverbank.

'Coshee! You fox. You precious fox!'

Sabbah it was, now clambering down the riverbank as best she could, her arms spread wide when she finally made it to the water's edge. She wrapped them around Coshee.

There were instant, shameless tears when she discovered that Teraset was not at his side.

'My new wife, Sabbah,' he said after a time. Marshuit stepped forward, an unsettled smile on her face.

Sabbah embraced her, still wiping tears.

'You precious fox,' she murmured to Coshee. 'I remember when Marshuit was born. And you do, too, Coshee.'

'Long life brings many surprises.'

'It does, Coshee.' She turned to Marshuit. 'Agreeable ones.'

The riverbank swarmed with people. Ardent, boisterous voices filled the shoreline, the snowflakes swirling through the din, it never certain where they would land.

Remesh appeared on the bank above them. The noise languished until hardly more than Sabbah's voice was heard. Her son's words swelled over it.

'We have been anxious for the sight of your canoes.'

Coshee looked all about him, scanned the faces of the other clans. For a brief while his eyes rested on Sabbah.

'I have told them of your walrus,' called Remesh. 'They have no need of anything but caribou.'

'A man must hunt what he finds to hunt.'

Coshee said no more. He walked with Sabbah, leading his people into the camp of the Nookwashish and to the lodges set aside for them during the great gathering of the clans.

THE FIRST STORIES WERE clothed in unease. Though the time to sunset was unmarked by any sign of Remesh's discontent — in truth, he was brighter and more garrulous than anyone could remember — it was an anxious time, leading to the moment Nonosa and Remesh exchanged their first words around the mighty night fire. Their wives and children sat near. Shanaw squirmed in the arms of Biesta. Sojon sat quietly in those of Lerenn.

'Tell us, Nonosa, of the new life the Kanwashish have made for themselves,' Remesh called above the chatter when he finished his first round of caribou meat, wiping charred bits from his mouth. 'Were you not the first to come upon this place?' Smiling broadly, the generous host.

Nonosa looked up, assessed the charm in his cousin's voice.

'And what name do you give to it?' Remesh called, with Nonosa about to answer. 'Sea?'

'Yes. Sea. Salt water beyond measure.'

'Fish?'

'Boundless fish.'

'More?' said Remesh, with what Nonosa took for false eagerness.

'Yes.'

'Tell us, Nonosa. We are all anxious to know what excites the Kanwashish.'

Nonosa was determined to make of it an honourable story for his people, especially for Biesta, who sat, eyes cast to the ground, arms wrapped about her squirming child. His own eyes fell into those of Remesh, then turned to the wide and dense circle of solemn faces caught in the flicker of the fire.

He told them of his first sight of the sea, of the incredulity it stirred in him yet. He told of the store it held, of how there seemed no end to it.

He felt behind him the urging of his people. His voice rose. He told of his conquest of first the walrus, then the seal. Did so eagerly, with a pledge that the following spring he would lead any who wished in their own journey to the sea, to learn for themselves that all he spoke was true.

Young Kanwashish hunters spread before the gathering bundles of dried cod, walrus and seal. Passed it quickly through the crowd. Eagerly was it tasted, for there was nothing more enticing to the Kindred than food that had never passed their lips before.

The chatter grew louder, more clamorous. Some proclaimed the charms, some argued that only if it were eaten fresh could anyone know its taste.

'Think on it — more to eat than you have ever known before,' declared Nonosa. 'Think on it — the hungry days of spring no more!'

Remesh looked on without a word, letting the talk ripen in whatever way it would.

Nonosa again cast his voice above the others, announcing the new hunting ways of the Kanwashish. He filled the air with a nest of vigorous words. Failed to see that the tales of his fortunes had begun to breed envy. Now failed to see the other clans suddenly wanted an end to it.

'Why have the Spirits chosen you, Nonosa?' came the question from a Dohwashish.

The discontent in his voice startled Nonosa.

'Must the Kanwashish always think themselves the favoured ones?' called another before Nonosa had a chance to reply to the first.

Coshee struggled to his feet. The gathering fell to silence. He was an old man with his life behind him. Yet it would be the moment for which he would be most remembered. Coshee would be at the centre of a story all the clans would tell.

'The Spirits have chosen the Kanwashish to show the way. If other clans wish to keep to their old habits, so be the choice they make. Let it be their children's children who follow the Kanwashish to the sea.'

Coshee sat down again. What Coshee thought of as simple wisdom had fallen on the ears of the other clans as vanity. There was no forgiveness for his age, only a silent swell of ridicule.

When Nonosa saw their ire he said, 'There is more food to be had though the hunt for caribou will be good for many seasons to come.' His words fell away weakly.

The bundles of food the Kanwashish had brought lay scattered near the dying fire, some barely touched, some not at all.

Now rose the voice of Remesh, behind a heedless glare. 'Even the gamey milk of caribou has its reward. That you know, Nonosa. Well enough.'

NONOSA KNEW THE KANWASHISH would not be shunned, nor would they withdraw into themselves. The clans were held together by nature's inconstant ways — if not by food, then weather, shelter, marriage. They knew better than to think one clan would, some day, not have need of another.

For the young of marrying age, that day was upon them. Their elders might have their squabbles, but the young had come to find a mate. And if there was shyness at first in each other's company, it soon faded.

The eligible strode about in groups. They mumbled to each other shyly while others had sight of them, but their voices swelled the further they drifted from the centre of the camp. The pairings were more definite and as the days passed only the most particular were left unmatched. For them the urgency to decide was suddenly all the greater, for no one wanted to be left without a mate and have to share with another, or worse, wait until the next gathering of the clans.

Tuanon was not among the indecisive lot. He made his choice the first day. She had agreed the second. No one was surprised. What remained was for the girl's father to give his consent, and to agree when Tuanon might come to their camp to take the girl away.

Rokia was her name. When Tuanon first cast his eyes on her she failed to look away. The longer he stared the more determined was she to hold to his gaze. Not meek like the others, not modest in the ways she moved about the camp.

'Your name is Tuanon,' she said. 'We all remember you.'

'What do you remember?'

'How you bragged of your hunting skills and had yet to kill a caribou.'

'I did as I said I would do. Many times. And I have slain creatures you know nothing about. Walrus. Sea-birds. More sea-birds than anyone has ever killed. You would not grow hungry in my camp.'

'I do not doubt it,' she said, amused by his enthusiasm.

'What *do* you doubt?'

'Why do you think I doubt anything about you?'

'Is there anyone among us who does not wonder at the choices to be made?'

'You wonder about me, then,' she said. 'What doubts do *you* have?'

'None.'

'And what if I grumble and complain?'

'Do you do it now?'

'I have no reason to.'

'And neither would you when you are married.'

In truth there was no hesitation. She knew he was the one. No other could hope to excite her in the way that Tuanon did. No other could come close to doing it.

Rokia was a Nookwashish, her father a zealous hunter, remembered for the time he almost lost a hand to a wounded bear. Rokia was as striking a young woman as walked about the camp. As striking as Lerenn.

The two were cousins, though they came from different clans. They shared a resemblance, especially in the way light caught their eyes when they spoke.

In other ways they were different. It was unusual for a young woman to walk about with such surety as Rokia. That was expected later, after seasons of being a wife, of bringing forth children. Married men would counsel those looking for a wife to be wary of young women who were forthright in their bearing, though such warnings were rarely heeded. For those enamoured by such young women always thought of themselves as more than able to take charge of their married lives.

Tuanon was for certain a young man charmed by Rokia. When he went to his brother to tell him of his choice he found Nonosa in a lodge alone, fashioning a new paddle. Tuanon was so full of fire that

Nonosa would only stand back from him with his arms at rest and smile broadly.

'Tuanon has a heart surmounted by a young woman! He is stricken by her charms and hardly knows where to look but to the stars!'

'The stars are bright indeed!'

'And if you could you would gather them to your chest and present them to her one by one.'

'Brother!'

'Yes.'

'I am as eager as the stars to be with her.'

'That you are ... and to know her ways under them.'

'I have dreamt such a dream. Many times.'

'And are you now so stiff with anticipation you cannot think you must wait longer yet.'

'Yes!'

'Be patient, Tuanon,' he said, laughing once more. 'The longer the wait the greater the surge of starlight.'

Tuanon attacked him in fun, as if they were boys again and tumbling in the snows. As if his fondness for his brother could not be contained.

Biesta discovered them wrestling on the floor of the lodge, sweating profusely and grunting like beasts. She thought them bereft of their senses.

Nonosa stood to one side, recovering his breath, and assured her there was no cause for anything but thankfulness. 'For Tuanon has found the woman who filled his dreams. He has won her over with his skill at the hunt and the eagerness of his spear.' He doubled in laughter.

'Which one is she, Tuanon?' said Biesta. 'Tell me.' She was excited now, as if she herself were young again, one of those anxious for a husband.

Tuanon, reluctant at first, stood tall and full of conviction, pronouncing her name as if they were already a pair, already married and accepted by all members of both their clans.

'OUR FATE,' NONOSA SAID to Biesta when they were again alone, 'lies in harmony between us.'

'There is talk ...,' Biesta started.

He caught something in her voice.

'Some say we need a SpiritMan,' she said.

Nonosa drew back. He had not heard such talk. Though many seasons had passed since a SpiritMan walked among them.

'Some say it could be Remesh.'

Nonosa came near to laughing at the notion. A true SpiritMan led an earnest life, a wise and meditative one. What claim could Remesh ever make to that?

'If there is such talk,' he said. 'Remesh was the one to start it.'

'He says his strength has been a sign.'

'The chosen one?' said Nonosa, his retort of breath raw, dismissive.

Nonosa walked away. Not in annoyance at Biesta, but to find time alone.

He set his mind on a way of drawing the clans together, even though he knew his own words on the first night had been the start of strife between them.

He called for drumming and the dance. Celebration of the unions between young clansmen and the young women who had agreed to be their wives. The plan had not the blessing of everyone, least of all the shy couples who would be at its centre. Still, Nonosa pushed ahead with it.

That night, clustered near the fire, were all those who in the spring would be married. They shifted restlessly, gave an awkward gravity to the gathering. Nonosa forced them to their feet, to the full curiosity of the crowd — the old ones recalling the quandaries of their own first married days, the young ones gazing in alarm and suspicion at what awaited them.

Then the night gave way to dancing. Drums claimed the air, captured the youthfulness, the carnal ambitions yet untested. Tuanon had his night of it, flailing his arms about more wildly than ever he did before. One moment his swooping neared Remesh, so close Remesh drew back to escape a whirling limb.

None had seen the like of Tuanon. At once a strongman, an impetuous performer, one willing to turn his mind to dance with passions as strong as he brought to the hunt. Something in what they witnessed thrilled them, something made them think about how they made their own way in the world. Chatter encircled the fire, spiralled through the air. The eyes of the women fell on Rokia, many with envy at the heart she had captured and at the life that lay ahead of her, not the least of which the nights that awaited her between the furs.

Rokia's heart beat madly, though she would not look at Tuanon, even when he took to the ground next to her.

'Did I look the fool?'

'No,' she whispered shyly. 'Lost to the Spirits.'

When he danced he did feel loosened from all he knew of the world. What he felt now when he stared at Rokia was an intense, unrelenting love. He brushed his hand against hers resting on the ground.

Nonosa stood up.

Before he could speak a word Remesh was on his feet. The two stared across the fire at each other. It was in Remesh's camp they had gathered; it was his choice to address the gathering as he wished. Nonosa sat down again.

The clans could see Remesh had much stirring in his head. They shifted about in anticipation of what it could be. Remesh took a long and potent look about the fire.

Finally, he spoke. 'The Spirits walk among us. They consider the rightness in everything we do. Tonight they have not been pleased. We must act according to their wishes or pay with hunger.'

Silence fell across the crowd. For only a few, the silence of acceptance. For more, the silence of waiting, of urging someone forth with the courage to challenge the role Remesh had suddenly seized for himself.

Coshee could only struggle in frustration at the state old age had left him. Nonosa stood up again. Across a circle broken by the fire, he stood man-to-man with Remesh. Nonosa felt the weight of expectation.

'The Spirits have revealed themselves to you, Remesh?'

The whip of a reply — 'Yes!'

Nonosa scanned his rigid face. 'What do you say, Remesh, to those who do not believe?'

'Let them speak.'

They had not the courage to speak, and Nonosa would not have them stumble about for words. 'I speak for them,' he said.

'What do you know of the Spirits?' Remesh scoffed. 'Have you not denied them?'

'I deny you the guise of a SpiritMan.'

'You deny me nothing.' Expelled, not with the vehemence that gave rise to it, but with a crude and ugly calm.

The mumbling among the crowd steered a useless course.

At a moment of his choosing, Remesh wrapped himself in his cloak of furs and departed. Walked slowly back to his lodge, Lerenn behind him, with Sojon in her arms. The assembly came to an end, though many lingered in the sudden flurry of the talk, all of it of Remesh and his convictions.

BEFORE DAYLIGHT THE CLANS were awakened by a great commotion. Incessant drumming drew them to the fire, its flames rekindled to the height they had been that night.

The fire revealed the figure of Remesh, boldly naked, in defiance of the cold.

He strode among the drummers. His thick frame glistened with a greasing of red ochre. From time to time he fell limp and whipped into a dance, into a frenzied display he seemed to fight against. Eventually he drew out of it, resumed his measured strides.

The clans held at a distance, confounded by the sight before them. Their voices rose and fell with the ferocity of the dance, finally stuttered into silence. Remesh sank to his knees. He knelt stiffly upright, his hands folded between his thighs. He seemed hardly to draw a breath.

From his skin rose the frosted wisps of vapour like that arising from a late kill of caribou.

'*Know the passions of the Spirits. Know their wrath.*'

A perplexing stillness. Remesh remained rigid, unmoved by the chill of the night, the last threads of vapour drifting away. The crowd, too, fell silent, the huddle of bodies a ragged clump brushed by the shameless flicker of firelight.

The solemnity broke, the snap of a tree limb in winter. The oldest of the Nookwashish had fallen to his knees.

Someone near him tried to lift him back but failed. Another Nookwashish fell, then another. Then men and women of the Dohwashish, the Kanwashish.

In the end the number on their knees surpassed those left standing.

Nonosa stood with Shanaw in his arms, Biesta tight to him. Incredulous, powerless to alter the mood, all the while his eyes locked into Remesh, searching out the glint of treachery.

Nonosa turned and quit the gathering. Receded quickly, like a notion on cold, uncaring ears. Biesta followed, as did others, a bitter few.

Behind them, at the dawn, rose a burdensome, knife-sharp melody.

'*Spirit's sign. Spirit's sign. Ever now, ever after, waiting to be fed.*'

BEFORE DAWN THE NEXT day the Kanwashish converged on the riverbank. Between them passed words to quicken their exodus to open water. Only Sabbah was there when they took to their canoes, standing silently onshore until the last was out of sight.

The day before Tuanon had strode about the campsite with a walrus tusk hanging brashly from his neck. Now he held back nothing in his charge against those tangled in the spell of Remesh. 'He would have us believe he stands above us all. He the favoured one. The one clenching our secrets!'

Away from the camp Tuanon's words hounded the ears of the Kanwashish who had fallen to their knees before the man. Nonosa let Tuanon rage at will, for it was nothing more than what he himself held inside. In time Tuanon's words gave way to the bending of the river, to his labours at keeping his canoe on course downstream.

The further they receded from the Nookwashish less was the echo of its leader's voice. The air turned truly fresh. When they stepped ashore at the site of their winter camp Tuanon and his companions raced to its centre, called loudly into its vacantness. The others followed, and Nonosa drew them tight to one another, declared them the dauntless Kanwashish, the strong survivors who would forever feed themselves without worry.

The Kanwashish feasted that night on cod-fish and sea-birds. Though they had eaten more than enough to satisfy their hunger, walrus was brought forth to end the meal. They took to their sleeping pits fortified in the knowledge they could thrive alone. No longer was there need of other clans.

'Only for wives,' Tuanon said. 'For no other reason than wives and husbands.'

THEY LOST THEMSELVES IN the finest of winters. The cold was deep and hard, the sun unfailing. Their breaths billowed with particular grace, their rhythms like shadows undulating past snowdrifts. On such days the Kanwashish knew their lives to be equal to those of any clan that ever lived.

By day there was always winter work — keeping the lodges in repair, sculpting new canoes, cleaning and shaping hides, carving bone. Their nights brought stories, new and thoughtful, earnest stories, stories much repeated, shared in clusters around lodge fires, embers intensely red.

There was much talk of children, comparing one to another, granting each their distinctive ways. Shanaw took in their talk, gazed at the speakers in a stare that seemed far beyond her age. She treasured the nights among them, fought to stay awake long past the time other children had drifted into sleep.

That winter her mother led her to women's working ways, though her interest in them passed as quickly as it took hold. She would carefully set aside the strips of hide her mother laid before her, then fidget her way closer and closer to the door. She was happiest outside the lodge, even in the coldest weather. She wanted nothing more each day than to follow her father when he prodded free the ice-stiffened flap and slipped under it.

Many days he would give in to her, sink her in a deep hide pouch and strap her to his back. The thick fur inside would stave off the severest cold. From a cache of fox and beaver skins, Biesta had fashioned a bonnet, its edge of long-haired fur a perfect trap for the mucus that in the cold air seemed to flow perpetually from her nose.

At these times Shanaw was an appendage of her father. His habits, his labours filled much of her day. When exhaustion overcame her and she fell asleep in the pouch, he left her there, her form curled against his back, comfort to them both. Only when he thought his work a danger did he slip off the pouch and pass it under the flap door and into the lodge.

Each day Nonosa grew closer to the girl, though he took care she was not without the company of Biesta. That winter it seemed not to concern Biesta as it had done before, for there was a joy to consume her. Biesta's belly had begun to swell and was soon stirring with a second child, one all her own.

Nonosa was relieved, gladdened, too, at the thought of another child, if unsettled by his memory of childbirth. Biesta showed no fear and each day stroked her belly and sang songs of her own making, blissful, eager songs about the goodness of the Spirits and how dear her new baby would be to her.

THE CLAN WAS WITHOUT hard sickness that winter, without the grief of sudden loss. Coshee had his days of complaint, but nothing near that of his wifeless days. Marshuit knew how to still his grumbling, the noises from their lodge feeding sly jokes throughout the camp. Tuanon's mind had bred most of them, for his match with Rokia had swelled his thirst for all things carnal.

Tuanon himself was the target of another stream of lusty jokes, for he made no attempt to disguise his longing for the girl. He droned on to the other young hunters about the day in spring when he would return to her camp and sweep her away with him. The others had similar notions, though only professed among themselves, and then in half-whispered, reluctant tones between familiar bluster about their prowess at the hunt.

They spent part of the winter gathering poles to frame new lodges. They stripped them of their bark, stone-polished away the knots in readiness for the day when enough snow had disappeared to begin erecting them. They worked to make supple the hides to cover the frames, reckoning how they would overlap, separating any that bore spear holes. The women of the clan took to repairing the hides, for it was essential that new young wives joining the Kanwashish be assured how welcomed they were.

The thrill of young men bringing home wives was no mightier than that of the young women of the Kanwashish about to be gathered up and borne away by eager husbands from other clans. There was sadness at their going, but sadder still to some was the sight of the one husbandless young woman, left to wait out the time until the clans again came together. The older women tried to comfort her, but the girl had no interest in their sympathy.

For the girl, Oumou, was not as distraught as they suspected. She had decided she would be content to be a second wife. *Man tried, man true* were the wise old words, were they not?

'Bring the message to the other clans,' she told those who had been chosen. 'I will not be left bitter. Not left longing after someone I cannot have.'

'Too bold,' the old ones warned. 'Too brazen.'

Biesta stepped forward and took her part.

'No women among us would wish it, but who is to know what lies before us.'

'Spirits' will,' croaked another.

'Or is it the will of men?' said Biesta.

At first the women laughed as if Biesta were teasing them with boldness equal to that of the girl. But when they took in her humourless face, their laughter fell away.

Biesta's words were hardly to be believed. Odd, mysterious. Without heart, it was said by some, though Biesta was the wife of Nonosa, and for that the envy of most of them. Her question lingered through silence.

Truly, she could not expect to ask and not also expect their frowns. And now their mutterings as she receded from sight. To other women Biesta had turned herself into a curiosity. No longer the chosen wife of Nonosa, but the woman whose tongue could not be trusted to say what they wished to hear.

Biesta would not be shunned for her impetuous words, nor feared.

The Kanwashish were too few for that. Indeed for some — those stealing into womanhood — her voice was change from the drone of mothers and withered aunts. They dared not show any eagerness, but slipped into her lodge on winter days when Nonosa was away; there sought her daring words, and under the spell of them offered their own.

'But you have Nonosa and you are so full with your child.'

'Now I am content. Not always.'

'Then a second wife has her pain?'

'Perhaps if the husband were her choice to make ...'

'Then we would all pick a clansman exactly like Nonosa,' one said quickly. The others agreed.

'Why must the man choose and not the woman?' prodded Biesta. Most had never thought to question it. 'Because he is the man.'

'What fairness is that?' said Biesta. 'We are forced to find ways to make him think he is doing the choosing. Truly his mind is between his legs.'

The young women hid their faces. When one began to giggle it was a great relief. Soon the lodge was a noisy den of smothered laughter.

In the midst of it, through the door came Nonosa. The lodge fell more silent than a windless cave.

'What is this?' said Nonosa, looking around, amused, though no one but Biesta met his gaze. 'A gathering of the soon-to-be-married. A lodge full of husband talk?'

'Yes,' said his wife. 'I was telling them of a husband's never-ending charms.'

At that the young women stumbled to their feet and quickly filed past Nonosa to the outdoors, not one meeting his eyes. Only emitting a muffled mixture of embarrassment and laughter.

Biesta covered her amusement with the fuss of removing Shanaw from her pouch.

'Soon Shanaw will have her words strung together,' said Biesta, the child now the centre of their attention. 'Then who knows what you will hear.'

Even now Shanaw's words showed the turnings of her mind, if entangled with the words was senseless, mesmerizing chatter. She had discovered the pitch and roll of her own voice, and headstrong she was in filling every corner of the lodge with it.

Nonosa prodded her into a louder frenzy, echoing her sounds, pitching back her words, until Biesta pleaded for silence.

In the calmness of the night Biesta made love to him, whispered sweetly deep, within the furs. Nonosa slept a contented man and once more dreamed wild hunting dreams.

WITH WINTER WANING, BIESTA gave birth to a girl.

She was pleased it was a girl, and, though Nonosa had been expecting it to be a boy, there was not the briefest sign of discontent.

'A companion for Shanaw,' he said. 'A deafening pair of girls.'

Nonosa smiled at his good fortune. For Biesta's birthing pain was short and the delivery of the child without distress. She sat propped up in her sleeping pit the same day, nursing the newborn, hardly an ache remaining.

Shanaw was the bewildered one, gazing at the infant with intense curiosity, searching to understand the swarm of faces passing through their lodge. When her father held the child, his delight even stronger than the others, her face turned sour.

He took Shanaw also in his arms. It did little to appease her and soon the lodge resounded with wailing, the older child's cries rousing the infant's lungs. Nonosa bounced both children in his arms to no effect, and had finally to pass the newborn back to her mother. Shanaw's tears came to a sudden end.

It was a portent of the seasons ahead. Shanaw grew to tolerate her sister, and to love her in a way that bound them together, if the measure of that love was never certain. To Nonosa it seemed his first born held to him in ways no other child ever could, that such a circumstance was natural, though he never spoke of it, either to his wife or to the child.

Biesta named the new child Patria, after the mother she did not know, and vowed that Patria would be as loved by a mother as any child ever was. Within the lodge there was harmony, for each child had her favoured parent, and each parent a favoured child, and both pairings their secrets.

SHANNON

THE AREA IS MORE thickly treed than anywhere else along the southern coastal strip of Labrador. The Pinware River makes a deep, unexpected cut through the landscape. As she nears the bridge that crosses it she finds a place to park, behind what she knows to be Simon's truck. She catches sight of him not far away.

It is a crisp fall Labrador day. Frost-tinged, but not too cold. The air has a clarity that sharpens the senses. The forest is breathable, the water surging over the rocks of the river gorge starkly scenic. They have caught it at a classic moment. Before many weeks pass the gush and spill will be encased in ice.

The rendezvous itself doesn't disappoint, but Shannon is wary of exuding delight. She knows better than to give herself over to the experience without reservations.

The boil-up. On the rocks near the river's edge. The ones they eventually reach, having taken a trail from the highway. An expert fire and over-hanging stick to hold Simon's well-used tin kettle. Tea steeped on a low boil. Into a pair of previously stained mugs, unequivocally authentic. What other women might have shared the same mugs she does not ponder, although his ease with her leaves her feeling he is hardly new at the game.

The food. After much deliberation she had settled on the commonplace and substantial — cheddar cheese, oranges, yogourt. She is somewhat uncertain about the yogourt. Hardly rugged enough. And homemade muffins — a touch too domestic on her part? Given that Simon's contribution to the lunch consists of bottled caribou. But there it stands. She knows food and drink are secondary concerns at this point.

Primary are: she's fallen for the guy. It's a resoundingly heavy fall, and she has yet to steel herself for what she expects to be inevitable disappointment. That salt of fatalism, wounded as she has been in the past, is not surprising. As for what she does with the moment at hand — she lets it wash over her. Does anything make sense but to give in to the charmer? To keep a head between her shoulders and tread cautiously. Watching like a hawk where it leads.

Where it leads is deeper into the woods and, as darkness descends, supper at the Northern Light Inn. And following the meal of pan-fried cod for him and scallops for her, they retire with a bottle of white wine to one of the advertised 'five suites with Jacuzzi.'

Not so entirely predictable as it might sound, she would argue if there was need. She did give serious thought to his casual 'why don't we get a room?' Well before it came out of his mouth, realizing it was inevitable. And the Jacuzzi was overplaying his hand.

Still, at this point in her life, no longer does she take the chance of living with regrets. Besides, she has fallen for the guy with an audible thud. The sex is delicious. With the whiff of woodsmoke still in his hair and his muscles tautly sinuous. *Dark* is the word that comes to her, in all its simplicity. The chardonnay having loosened the graduated levels of inhibition that remain, the Jacuzzi delivers a full serving of aqueous dessert. Smirk, she thinks, whoever the hell wants to.

Sunday morning brings conversation of the type that is to be feared but entirely necessary. Not to forget inevitable.

Simon is divorced. A twelve-year-old daughter living with the mother in Goose Bay. A post-high school relationship that lasted, off and on, for six years. He worked airport maintenance and snow-clearing until, after the divorce, got it in his head that he could go to university. Did a year of courses in Labrador City, then made the plunge into St. John's. Graduated in Biology and Education, moved back to Labrador to teach school. A year in Cartwright, now two years in Red Bay, this year as principal.

'I've restarted my life,' he adds at one point. 'Though it's impossible to leave the old one behind. I want to spend time with my daughter.'

There's regret there. Shannon decides it is not for her to pursue. They talk instead about his teaching, his life in Red Bay. His need to consider other options.

He assures her she is more than another option. He smiles when he says it, demonstrating a sense of humour about the upheavals in his life. Shannon relishes an easy sense of humour.

'And you, Shannon. What's your story?'

Casual, non-judgmental, as if everyone has a narrative stored away. Which, of course, everyone does. Shannon relates the whole of it, not in any detail, but enough that she considers it honest and upfront, as he seems to have been with her. Has he really been? Who can tell at this point.

They have known each other a little more than a week, and a night in a hotel has come and gone and, she thinks, what does she know anymore? She knows that she likes him more than anyone she's met in a long time. She knows she has been honest enough with him that if he wants to get entangled he understands what he'll find at the other end. She's been around the corner too many times in relationships to go through another contrived buildup leading to the clamorous letdown.

SHANNON STUDIES THE PLANET Earth calendar she has hanging on the wall to the side of her computer desk. She counts backward and forward, confirming she is roughly halfway through the term of her contract. She feels good about what she's accomplished so far. The proposal for L'Anse aux Meadows, the largest and most significant of the three components, has been written, the Aboriginal committee set in place. She has some ideas formulated for L'Anse Amour. The site in Red Bay she hasn't given much thought to as yet, but that has been deliberate on her part. It will all follow in due course.

She's not a fool; she knows significant obstacles have emerged. They have not caught her off-guard, which she feels is as important in dealing with them as the obstacles themselves. She has, in fact, never dealt with an Aboriginal matter in which there have not been obstacles. It comes with the territory. In every way she can think of, what's before her now pales in comparison to what has surrounded some of the situations in the past. She thinks of the hunting rights issues on Baffin and takes comfort in the memory of what faced her at the time, including the constant presence of a CBC microphone, and the snarky young reporter behind it, dying to turn it into a national story. She thinks of the land issues in BC. Prolonged and protracted beyond belief, with an access road blockaded for two weeks.

She is relieved that it is only Simon that she has to deal with. Obviously now on more than one fundamental level, but she has always been good at compartmentalizing.

WHEN SIMON CALLS THE next evening she allows herself to breathe again. Her fear was he would slip out of the relationship as easily as they had slipped into it, that the appetite to continue was hers alone. He is sounding completely at ease, as if it's been a month, not a week, that they have known each other. He's had a stressful day at school and Shannon is overly sympathetic. He shifts the conversation to her and what she's got planned for her evening.

'I'm working my way through this book.'

'Sounds like it's painful.'

'The end is in sight.'

'What book is it?'

She tells him.

'I've read it. I liked it.'

'Didn't you think it's unrealistic?'

'What do you mean?'

'Too modern in the way the author deals with issues.'

'Not primitive enough? Like what ... the sex?'

'Well ... yes, the sex. Among other things.'

'You mean the surprise blow job?'

She tries not to miss a beat. 'I haven't got to that part yet.'

'There is no blow job. That's another book.'

'Simon. You're embarrassing me.'

'I mean, there could be. It doesn't go against Native sensibilities. As far as I know.'

She doesn't know what to say. There is silence. Neither of them is sure they want to be the first to laugh.

'I'm sorry,' he says, chuckling. 'It's been a rough day.'

ALL THAT EVENING SHE is preoccupied with just that — freeing Simon's penis from the confines of his jockeys and pleasuring him. Building him up to the point he's crazed with lust. The image has worked itself into her mind and it's not going to leave.

She gets nowhere with reading the book. She switches on the TV and tries to lose herself in something, anything. Not the news. Definitely not the news, and the beautiful brown-skinned announcer with the unpronounceable name.

She picks up the phone and dials. 'Simon?'

'I'm just getting into bed.'

'Don't tell me that.'

'I'm not getting into bed. I'm sitting at the side of the bed, buck naked.'

'Jesus, Mary and Joseph.' She laughs and hangs up.

IT'S FRIDAY NIGHT AND this time it's the Plum Point Motel. The motel is not far from the terminus point of the ferry from Labrador, and Shannon proposed she'd meet him there. It saved Simon from driving the hour and a half it would take to reach St. Anthony, after dark, through prime moose country in the midst of hunting season. Simon didn't argue. He knows too many stories of vehicles slamming into twelve-hundred-pound moose.

Shannon drove out in daylight late that afternoon. The Plum Point Motel turns out to be surprisingly big, and anonymous. From what Shannon could tell, it caters to a constant mix of tourists, hunters, and transport drivers. To the rear of the motel itself are a dozen or more self-contained cabins. When Shannon checks in she chooses one of those, and later texts Simon with the unit number so he won't need to go to the desk when he arrives.

The cabin is basic, but adequate. By the time Simon knocks and opens the door the cabin has warmed up, coffee is perking, and Shannon has stretched out on the sofa, a blanket covering her legs, the talked-about novel open in front of her.

Simon drops his overnight bag and greets her with a smile that turns to a contrived smirk and back again. Without taking off his coat he seats himself in the space remaining at the end of the sofa and rests one hand on the blanket covering her legs.

'So, you've discovered paradise.'

'Of a sort.'

'Did you know, dear lady, that into this very harbour sailed Captain Cook in 1764?'

'Yes, I believe I did know that.'

'But what you didn't know is that not far from here the surveyor Cook came upon a pair of rather well-endowed islands and after duly charting them, turned to his journal and ascribed them the name *Our Ladies' Bubies*.'

'Truly?'

'Later, renamed to the ubiquitous *Twin Islands*. But yes, at first impulse, indeed he did. Which goes to show that even the great monoliths of history need their gratification.'

At which point Simon falls across her, burying her in himself and his coat.

They find gratification. It is straight forward and familiar. Shannon has little cause to analyze what she feels about Simon. She is determined to enjoy the successive rounds that play out over the course of the evening, between the pizza and television. Novel reading does not make it into the mix.

THEY ARE BOTH UP relatively early on the Saturday morning. Simon first. He showers and shaves and pulls himself into fresh clothes. Pads about the cabin in bare feet, his head a mass of still-wet hair, cleaning up the dishes from the previous night and setting the coffee machine in motion.

During which time Shannon takes full charge of herself, including washing and drying her hair, donning casually coordinated sweater and scarf and jeans, emerging in the end as if she were from a page of L.L. Bean.

'Nice,' says Simon.

'It is not a transformation. This is the me you get if you wait long enough.'

'I'm game either way.'

'Thanks.' She pecks him on the cheek.

'The coffee is not great.'

In any case they had decided on the motel restaurant for breakfast. The food is fine, the coffee several notches above the cabin variety, but it all slips by, largely unnoticed. Simon has discovered a friend sitting in the restaurant and she has invited them to share her table.

Shannon is surprised that Selma Barkham, the person most responsible for the discovery of the sixteenth-century Basque connection to Red Bay, should be sitting in the restaurant of the Plum Point Motel. In Shannon's eyes, her fame far and away transcends the environment. Shannon has seen any number of pictures of Selma Barkham, generally taken thirty years before, when her research first came to light. Then as now, a tall, good-looking woman, with a shock of stylish hair, easily the determined and intelligent person behind the research.

'I spend my summers here. And quite often September,' she tells Shannon, with no pretension that she is anyone but a regular customer at the restaurant.

Simon seems to know this already. 'Selma and I have been friends for a long time. Since I showed up at one of her conferences.'

'Simon likes to ask questions,' the woman says. 'Competent questions, I would add, for an unschooled historian.'

'Thank you, Selma.' He smiles, then reaches across the table and momentarily rests his hand on hers, in acknowledgement of her humour. It's the gesture of friendship as well, and not in the least patronizing, which, in any case the woman would not have tolerated.

She would have to be in her eighties, Shannon believes, and no longer as steady in her manner as the pictures showed her to be. But she retains an air of confidence and security in her view of the world. Cordial and generous, and still holding opinions hardly to be toyed with.

Shannon knows her story well. An historical geographer, mother of four young children and suddenly a widow, who transplanted her family first to Mexico to learn Spanish, then to northern Spain, to work for years in the ancient archives at Oñate, uncovering indisputable evidence of an annual expedition of Basque whalers to Labrador, in what amounted to the first industrial complex in the New World. All with very little money and general indifference on the part of academia.

It is a story that is near legend, one for which Shannon has always held deep admiration. That she is now sharing the breakfast table with the woman at the centre of it continues to surprise her. She guards against appearing intimidated, but, unlike Simon, she is, somewhat. She has yet to ask what Shannon works at, and Shannon hopes that she doesn't. The woman is holding court, not intentionally, only because she is the repository of so much experience and knowledge, and Simon is probing for her opinions. There is mention of what each of them has been reading over the summer. Simon alludes to a couple of pieces of historical fiction. He has deliberately struck a nerve.

'If properly done, it has a place. Otherwise it clouds the truth.'

'There has to be room for speculation, don't you agree?' Simon asks.

'Any theory is speculation.'

'Informed speculation. Not a writer letting his mind go to the four winds, without any evidence to back it up.'

Shannon agrees and says so. She is sure Simon only opened the topic for her benefit, given their recent exchange about the novel she's been reading.

'I've just finished that Basque short story,' he says to Selma. He explains to Shannon that the story, set in sixteenth-century Red Bay at the time of the Basque whaling, was recently published in a collection of contemporary Basque fiction in translation. He turns back to his friend. 'I think you know it.'

'He knows I know it,' she says to Shannon. 'He likes playing the devil's advocate.'

Selma is on the one hand amused, for she is clearly fond of Simon, but on the other chafed by her recollection of the story. 'It could never have happened. It is not the Red Bay I know. There was a real whaler named Joanes de Echaniz in Labrador. He had a daughter and a wife, Domicuça, back in Spain. I uncovered the documents in Oñate. I uncovered his last will and testament! He died in Labrador on Christmas Eve, 1584.'

She is holding back her opinions, likely because she sees herself being prodded into reacting. She looks at Shannon, repeating her point. 'He knows what I think. He doesn't have to ask.'

The two women share a moment of agreement at Simon's expense.

'What I find interesting in fiction is not what I know,' Simon adds, 'it's what I wonder about.'

'Interesting is hardly the point.' Selma can't resist the temptation any longer. 'Interesting but distorted. And the average reader can't tell the difference.'

'Joanes de Echaniz — how did he die?'

'Scurvy most likely.'

'Speculation?'

'Informed speculation.'

'He should have been eating Labrador berries. The Natives would have known that. Perhaps they kept that knowledge from him. Perhaps they wanted him to die.'

Neither of the women react, or, as they see it, take the bait.

'In your eyes what I'm saying at this very moment is fiction,' says Simon, which sounds like a pronouncement, despite his roguish tone. 'Perhaps there's truth in that.'

'Your truth,' Shannon says.

'Exactly.'

'You're playing games, Simon. Shannon and I refuse to join in.'

Through it all the two women have become allies of a sort. They silently agree that they see through his scheming and prefer to leave him high and dry.

Simon has reached his limit and knows it. He smiles pleasantly, as if to say he's happy enough to have made his point. He comments on the quality of the homemade jam that has appeared with his toast. The conversation fades into another direction, turning rather duller in the process. Once it makes its way to the weather Simon hints to Shannon that it's time they were moving on. Shannon can see that Selma likely tires more easily than she lets on, and in any case there will be other opportunities for them to chat before the weekend is over. Simon kisses her on the cheek as they leave.

THAT AFTERNOON THEY TAKE the highway to Port au Choix, eighty kilometres south, the location of the most extensively excavated archaeological sites along the coast. Shannon insists they use her vehicle. She can claim the mileage as a work expense, she tells Simon, who goes along with it, though it's obvious that he's not used to being in the passenger seat. To Shannon it is a test of sorts. One she's initiated a number of times before with other men.

The test is always to see just how much effort it takes on the man's part to remain quiet and let her make the decisions. Kim, she remembers, could not have cared less, especially given the price of gas at the time they were together. Kim was very good at giving in to her wishes, and she never did decide if it was something she appreciated. She came to think of him as being fiscally submissive. The fellow knew the limits of his wallet and made adjustments accordingly.

Simon, on the other hand, would have no such concerns. Shannon assumes he is paying child support, but, given that he is a school principal, and even though the student numbers are likely low, she knows he'd be making a reasonable salary. The driver/passenger income dynamic is about equal.

He doesn't fidget or talk excessively. That would be the most predictable, commonplace reaction, one she noticed constantly in the North when she would jump into the driver's seat before others of the Parks staff. Some took it as if she were being aggressive, asserting herself unnecessarily. In fact, she's always liked driving, and she is good at it. She's never been in an accident, not one that was her fault.

'Selma is amazing,' Shannon says. 'It's remarkable what she did.'

'Put Red Bay on the map, that's for sure.'

'And never lost her exuberance. I want to be like that at eighty.'

'I suspect she actually enjoys having to defend her opinions. Of course, she's always been very good at having the last word.'

Shannon is not sure how far to take that, given that it's striking close to home.

The scenery gathers their attention. The conversation is left in the air, and in some ways, Shannon concludes, that is the best place for it. It is leading to discussion of their relationship and she sees no point in that while driving a highway, with no escape from what might be said.

The afternoon is enjoyable, no more than that on a personal level. On a professional level it proves profitable. The interpretation centre is modern, the displays well designed, with substantial artifacts, and a centrepiece of a life-sized, diorama-like animal skin and whalebone dwelling, staging a domestic scene dating back to the time of the Dorset Palaeoeskimos. Port au Choix has been home to four different prehistoric peoples, including the Maritime Archaic, the same group who inhabited L'Anse Amour.

As they walk about, the Maritime Archaic artifacts are the ones that draw them in most powerfully. She talks about what they see and, although she doesn't force it, she feels it good that Simon experiences a bit more of her professional side. He's absorbed, whether by her or the fragments of information. One artifact in particular, a hand-sized piece of black stone, shaped and polished into an effigy of a killer whale, captures him. Or is he truly captured, Shannon wonders. It's likely he's seen it before. It is not the first time he's been in the Interpretation Centre. Shannon doesn't ask.

Simon bends forward to look at it more closely. 'The Basques killed right whales and bowheads. As far as I know, never killer whales.'

'They wouldn't have been in commercial numbers. The Maritime Archaic revered them because they were such fierce killers of seals. Likely the stone piece was an amulet, or made by a seal hunter as a good luck omen.'

At several other stops in their walkabout Shannon's narrative enlarges the experience, drawing them closer, to the point that Simon slips an arm around her waist, Shannon's words momentarily losing their balance.

She leans against him, taking it for what she wants it to be — a fleeting but deliberate note of affection, as firm an indication of his interest in her as she is likely to accept. She knows she is analyzing it too much, but that is her mindspace at the moment.

The drive back remains low key, only occasionally animated. She took the driver's seat, habitually, and there is no perceivable indication that

Simon would want it otherwise. Shannon's radar has relaxed, and as she drives her thoughts mostly fall to the upcoming night.

The night unfolds as she expects, as she wants it to, and she lets herself fully succumb to the moment. At one point during the night she wakes to find herself cocooned within the curve of his naked body, an arm of his secured across her breasts. She holds her own hand to his, shuts her eyes and in time drifts back to sleep.

NONOSA

WITH THE END OF winter near, Tuanon's passions only heightened. In him was a desperation to get himself to the camp of the Nookwashish and draw Rokia away.

He waited only for the word from Coshee and Nonosa. Finally it came — the pronouncement that enough river ice had melted, that what remained was no menace to his canoe. Before daybreak the next morning he was at the water's edge, his canoe packed and set into the water.

Nonosa was there to bless him with a summons for good weather. His heave at the stern of the canoe helped set it free from shore. 'Soon to be a man struck dumb, his spear finally put to use!' Nonosa called, laughing, thankful his brother was about to gather what he craved.

Tuanon did not look back, but shouted over his shoulder, 'Not struck dumb, brother!'

'Remember the stars,' Nonosa called. 'They hear every moan.' A trace of the smile held to Nonosa's face until the canoe was out of sight.

SEVERAL NOOKWASHISH CAUGHT SIGHT of him from the riverbank, offered their habitual words of welcome when Tuanon's canoe struck their shore. They had been expecting him, if hardly so soon. While among the Nookwashish, Tuanon would slip into their ways, for they would want to be assured that Rokia was leaving with someone not unlike themselves. They returned to their work. Tuanon took to a task of lodge repair.

It was only later, around the cooking fire, that his glances fell on Rokia. The pair stole a sweet, heart-quickening moment. The clan took no notice, feigning disregard of Tuanon coming among them.

This was the way of wife-claiming, the day unfolding as it should.

Remesh had not appeared and Tuanon had no wish to see him. It would be the girl's father who would bestow the final, parting words to Rokia, at a gathering at day's end.

At dusk, his work done, Tuanon rested alone inside the spacious lodge set aside for the gathering. The first of the Nookwashish to enter built a fire and each one to follow carried a single stick of wood, shaved at the end to a dense mat of curls.

'For Rokia. For her new husband,' each said. And with the stick held to the flame there sprang more words, 'Flame of life together.'

'Light,' Rokia's father added. 'Light, Rokia ... light, Tuanon. Flame of life together.'

There formed a line of men, each gripping a pair of sticks. They struck them to the fire, then slowly, with measured, tramping feet, encircled the wayfarer. Struck the torches sharply together. Struck a rhythm in his head.

Marked, he was, a separate man, forced to rise out of what surrounded him — now a circle of loud, chanting clansmen — and prove himself worthy of taking Rokia away.

The chant grew even louder, the burden more intense. Through it all Tuanon caught sight of Rokia, if only for the moment it took for her to be guided out of sight. The glimpse roused his courage. He stood straight, free of timidity. From a pouch he retrieved his walrus tusk and hung it around his neck.

Tuanon defied the Nookwashish to think of him as anything but deserving of their treasured daughter. Still they chanted and encircled him. Added to the throb and pitch of night.

'Tu-a-non, Tu-a-non.' On and on. 'Tu-a-non!'

They stopped their tramping and widened the circle, all the while beating together the flaming sticks. Tempting him to conjure up his display at the gathering of the clans.

Ignore their abandon he could not, nor the sudden wildness of their words.

Animals flailing free of hunters, birds set to wing. Escape, escape. Like a bird he danced. Like the everlasting bird that lurked within his arrows. Sweeping bird, swirling bird, defiant bird on taunting wings, everlasting creature twisting through the night. Enduring bird of light.

And when he did not end his dance, but kept circling, the men grew tired, failed to keep up the beat of their sticks and sagged to the ground.

Tuanon, too. No longer able to dance the dauntless dance, he let his feet slip from under him, though as a bird might, bringing its spiralling body to rest.

The lodge fell silent. The light of the fire had turned to embers. The Nookwashish stared, in wait.

From outside the lodge came the rumble of a new chant. Distant, measured, building until it came to stand just beyond the door. Fervent now, anticipating its entrance.

Tuanon brought himself to his feet. His narrowed eyes scanned the lodge for Rokia, without reward. They came to rest at the door.

The door hide was drawn aside. Into the lodge drifted a solemn line of women chanters, their voices muted now, their shuffling feet the new rhythm of the night. Near its end, Lerenn, and asleep in her arms, Sojon.

Then Remesh. Singular, imposing Remesh. Whose face held scant emotion, whose presence suddenly bred full measure of it in the witnesses to his entrance. Only Tuanon stood unmoved. The others swayed, one against the other, like a herd whose lead had turned one way, then quickly turned another. The stature they regained was a weakened, servile one.

Remesh stood in full view of the clan. Unchanging until he held the eyes of every one of them. His face broadened into a thick, immodest smile.

'What have you to say, young Tuanon, bearer of that *walrus* piece about your neck? Fearless hunter about to bear away our Rokia?'

Tuanon held his eyes to Remesh. Words failed to pass his lips.

'You are a strong one, Tuanon. Strong young hunter. Proud man. Proud dancer. Rokia's head must swirl when her eyes set on you.'

'Our liking for each other is equal.'

'Astounded by you, she is? And you by her?'

'Tomorrow she will come away.'

'Do you not know what the Spirits are saying to the Nookwashish?'

From those crowding the lodge there was only silence.

'The Spirits look with anger on Tuanon,' said Remesh, 'for he has no modesty in his ways. Does he not fear for his people?'

Tuanon, staggered by this, called out, 'The Kanwashish are strong. Our storehouses brim with meat and fish. Rokia will live among a people without fear of hunger.'

Remesh cast off his reply. And cast off, too, Tuanon's boldness, as if he were an insolent, thoughtless youth. It a quick, decisive spit of anger, such bitter foil to his entrance.

'The Spirits renounce your claim to her! The Nookwashish refuse to have the wrath of the Spirits hurled on us!'

The Nookwashish recoiled. Tuanon stood untouched. Remesh's words could never mark his fate. Consent had been given at the gathering of the clans.

Rokia's father stepped forward. Remesh turned to him. 'What do you say to this young Kanwashish?' The urging of his SpiritMan. What filled the father's head was uncertainty. What numbed his tongue was dread. He offered timidly, 'I fear for my daughter.'

'You need have no fear!' exclaimed Tuanon. 'And what of Rokia? Has she not declared her will?'

Remesh looked on Tuanon with pity, with a face turned to disdain at his outburst. As if Tuanon had disturbed a venerable calm.

Remesh turned back to Rokia's father. The man stepped slowly forward into the remaining firelight. He was hardly steadfast enough for the moment, though Remesh betrayed no impatience, but waited out the words that formed in the air with desperate slowness. Fragile, tenuous words, words that waited for other words to follow, though none ever did.

'Rokia has no hunger to become a Kanwashish.'

TUANON PADDLED TO HIS people, skeleton of the man who had first fallen in love.

The next fall he married the young woman of his own clan who had thought of herself only as a second wife. They made their lives in the lodge Tuanon had built near that of his brother. Before their second fall Oumou gave birth to a boy.

For many seasons to follow the Kanwashish saw nothing of other clans, which was as they wished. The women who had come from outside the clan sometimes spoke of their lives past, but now they were Kanwashish and knew themselves to be fortunate ones.

The Kanwashish became more and more the clan of the sea. The days by the sea were their happiest for they were skilled in ways the other clans knew nothing about. On rare summer nights when the wind had died completely and the tide had reached its height, the Kanwashish would gather on rocks around a fire close to the water's edge and there sing new songs of thankfulness. Though the words had yet to fall from their lips with ease, there was excitement in knowing they were the first ever to sing them.

Their singing took away but little of Tuanon's melancholy. He was often sullen and quick to anger. He had not the interest in singing beyond a scattering of the words, and forever dismissed the notion he might charm them with a dance.

Only in the hunt was he as keen as he had been. When he returned from a kill with his brother he was not satisfied unless he had been the one to stalk the most birds, or fell the biggest caribou. Tuanon became the undisputed master of the walrus hunt. In his lodge was hung a gleaming collection of polished tusks.

ON A DAY NEAR the beginning of one summer — a day the Kanwashish would mark forever — a stray member of another clan appeared among them. Stumbled in, shrivelled from hunger, a young Nookwashish, remembered by Biesta and other of the wives. He fell to the sand, numbed by the sea that lay beyond it, more so by his craving for food. He ate relentlessly, most of it of a taste that had not passed his lips before.

When he did speak it was to plead for help for the Nookwashish. 'Load my canoe. Already some old ones have died. Sabbah is now the weakest.'

The Kanwashish had not gone hungry only because they had the bounty of the sea. There had been those who wished to take food to the Nookwashish in fear their caribou hunt, too, had been poor. But they were few, their voices drowned by Tuanon's.

Now his claim — that the caribou hunt was poor because the Nook-washish had taken more than their need — had been proven false. Tuanon showed no remorse. Rather, his bitterness was even stronger. 'Now what does the SpiritMan think he is hearing!'

'What of our beloved Sabbah?' said Nonosa.

'Deny Remesh a share. Let him starve.'

It could not happen. That Tuanon knew.

'I will go with the food,' Tuanon said suddenly. 'The boy has not yet the strength to paddle back.'

Nonosa filled with the gravest doubt. But the headstrong Tuanon would not see it any other way.

'Together,' Nonosa announced, in a voice the equal of his brother's, 'we will paddle a canoe filled with fish and meat, with a single reason in our hearts.'

They loaded a canoe with the best of their food. They balanced the bundles and strapped them in place. The next morning they set off upstream at daybreak, in wonder at what would face them when they came in sight of the camp of the Nookwashish.

NONOSA HAD NEVER FELT more weary in the presence of Tuanon. Their mother had called Nonosa the charmer, the peacemaker; Tuanon the stubborn one, the wilful bird building a nest in a blustering squall. Nonosa lingered on their strongest days of kinship, but doubted their return. There remained a potent bond between them, one near the point of breaking.

The heat of summer fell upon the brothers. Nonosa and Tuanon paddled bare-chested though the morning's river vapour, the scant wind barely disturbing it, the sun slowly burning it away.

With the sun brewing the bogs came the blackflies — the plague paramount in the lore of the Kindred. Men had been known to die of blackfly bites, though it was the swelling from the bites, the misshapen heads and limbs, that proved its unrelenting curse. Nonosa and Tuanon kept themselves lathered with red ochre mixed with cod oil. And, to their infinite relief, it kept the cruel hordes at bay, even better than the old way of mixing ochre with animal fat.

'What do you say, Nonosa? Are we not a match for Remesh?' Suddenly, Tuanon was one to abide a brother when he did not agree with him. 'A fine day, Nonosa. We will make the most of it.'

The sun beat down so relentlessly it drove the blackflies into the shade. At its most intense the brothers discarded their waist-hides, plunged into the water. They cringed at the shock of it, half in and half out of the still frigid water, reliving their heedless youth, their summers long past.

THE BROTHERS SLIPPED ONTO shore at the camp of the Nookwashish. The sun left a cloudless sky, the end of a second punishing day. The long light of summer would linger, and when it did finally go, it would be gone for but a short while before showing itself again. What night there was filled with a skydance of other, coloured light. The dome danced its irreverent dance, above a famished clan dragging itself toward a covenant of food.

The two brothers, messengers from a far-off bounty, cut apart the bundles and walked among the hungry, feeding them, reassuring them there was more.

'Under a Kindred sky,' Tuanon said to them, 'the Spirits have their words for us.' Strange stirrings in Tuanon's embittered mind.

Nonosa led him to Nookwashish too weak to leave their lodges, then made his own way to the lodge of Sabbah.

Sabbah lay alone in her sleeping pit, withered, in the dimmest of light, the air surrounding her thick with the smell of piss.

She barely stirred. Nonosa called her name, and then a second time, a little louder. She opened her eyes. For her nephew she offered only a most uncertain smile.

He brought forth food, hoping it might do what his voice failed to do. He made for her a paste of cod-fish and water, brought it quickly to her lips.

Sabbah ate some of it, closed her eyes and fell asleep. Nonosa stroked her dry, wrinkled forehead, smoothed her vermin-ridden hair. Such ache he had not known since the passing of Démas.

In the early light of morning Sabbah opened her eyes, began to moan about her sorry state. Nonosa carried her weightless body to a lodge where the strongest of the other women took her in, fed and washed her back to tenuous health. Nonosa dragged away the filth and that of the dead ancient ones who had shared her lodge, and condemned it to a fire.

Only then did the brothers lay eyes on Remesh. He stepped through the doorway of his lodge, a shadow of himself, yet without the gauntness of the others. He walked with a limp toward them.

'Left your own mother to die?' Tuanon taunted.

Remesh peered at him through crusted eyes. 'The Spirits forced the Kanwashish past their greed. Had you come before, you could have proclaimed yourselves the saviour of us all.'

Tuanon lashed at him, without a sliver of fear, for not one of the Nookwashish had the strength to turn against him. 'Your vanity, Remesh, has brought nothing but starvation!'

'Starved because you forbade the Nookwashish to come to the sea,' said Nonosa.

'Starved your own mother with your pride!'

Remesh slouched to the ground. His hand fell to a rock. Nonosa kicked his hand away, sent Remesh sprawling.

From the lodge of Remesh emerged Rokia, tattered and fatigued. Tuanon turned to her in a mad rush of emotion.

Rokia's body tightened at his gaze.

'I have not hungered as much as some, Tuanon.'

'You have made a home in his lodge?'

Her eyes narrowed. 'I am his second wife. Did no one tell you?'

Tuanon cringed, a great weight thrust against his chest. For the moment, a body stilled by pain.

Tuanon threw himself on Remesh, tore loose his necklace of polished teeth.

Tuanon heaved his weakened hulk of a cousin onto his back, held him there, rigid hands across his throat. Nonosa tried in vain to wrench his brother loose.

Suddenly, the SpiritMan drew a knife. Sunk its stone edge deep into Tuanon's chest. Tuanon's hands fell away. His body slumped with the weight of rock. It quavered, folded in upon itself.

Remesh wormed from under it, sodden with blood, clutching his throat. Croaking a few words.

'Spirits damned him! He would have murdered me.'

TUANON, BROTHER OF NONOSA, was dead. Remesh, their cousin, had murdered him to save himself. A hateful death, the most vile story yet to be told of the Nookwashish. For the death was needless, of a clansman who fed his people well. Of a lover lost to the uncertainties of love, to passions ravished by pride.

Nonosa paddled downriver with the body of his brother, bound tightly in hide to keep off the blackflies. He wept for Tuanon and for Oumou and their son. Nonosa knew now the boundaries of families, how love overlapped them, how hate wedged between them. He wept the most for Démas, whom he could no longer press against his heart.

He paddled through the night, slowly, as best the night would allow. When the moon was covered by cloud and he had to stop, he did not rest ashore, but waited solemnly in the stern of the canoe, the bow touching the riverbank, until the moon glinted on the water once more.

Nonosa's journey, like that of Tuanon before him, was the journey of a broken heart.

For families, and for the clans once bonded together, now slung apart.

His song unsung gave way to mournful words, of a journey's uncertain end.

NONOSA

Nonosa's song found its end in the river giving way to the sea. There, under the broad light of day, Nonosa brought his brother home. When the mourning had reached its crest the body of Tuanon, covered thickly by ochre, was carried out to sea and buried on the island. In the place where he had killed many sea-birds it was given back to the Spirits. When, on future nights, the coloured lights danced in the night sky, those of Tuanon did strange and curious things.

For days the young widow Oumou remained numb with grief, until Biesta gathered her into her lodge, and told her what she believed to be the hollowness of men. Together, in secret, they lamented the unfolding of their lives.

'But you have Nonosa,' Oumou said. 'I have no one.'

'I have one who wishes still for his first wife.'

'Is it so, Biesta?'

'In the eyes of others, men have their notions of what they must do. Secretly, they have their wishes.'

'And women, we have our secret wishes.'

Biesta showed her great compassion.

'To have strong children and be the only wife,' Oumou said. She began to cry again.

FOR NONOSA THESE WERE solitary times. Even his fishing days he spent alone, offshore or along a secluded finger of rock. When he returned with his catch there was no more of the banter, the mock boasts cast among the young hunters.

These were his days to take the measure of the Kanwashish, to anticipate what lay beyond the summer on the coast. To take the measure of himself, for it was to him the Kanwashish had turned, stupefied, in turmoil.

Even the oldest of the Kanwashish could not recall one man's death at the hands of another. From deep in the past there had come such stories, but had not their lessons been committed to memory? 'Yet there is no learning the ways of jealousy,' Coshee said to him, 'when they entangle a man and a wife.'

'Should not hunger, above all troubles, bring peace, Coshee?'

The old man pondered Nonosa's words as if there was wisdom to be wrought from what had become of Tuanon. He could find none. For the first time he thought himself an old and tired man, and, like the others, turned to Nonosa. 'He was your brother, Nonosa.'

A headstrong brother, Nonosa would not deny; a raging one. Would Remesh have died by his hands? It was the claim croaked from his cousin's lips. Staggered to his feet he did after he made the kill, struggled for breath. When others of the Nookwashish ambled near the body, it was Remesh's piteous words they clung to.

The talk of the young Kanwashish hunters was revenge, and Nonosa had no mind but to hear them out, for Tuanon was forever his cherished kin. The moment of the killing, when he turned over Tuanon's body and beheld the knife driven into his brother's chest, his own wish was merciless revenge. To draw his own knife and sink it into the wretch. He stood and watched Remesh slink away, his hands to his throat, beast struggling to his lair. What clasped his own hand to his sheath and held it there? While his brother lay a woeful, lifeless mound. Had he not been the peaceable one, the one to settle discord? Did he not wish to quell the poisons in men's minds? What fearsome echoes would fill Kindred lives if he were to slay a SpiritMan? As if revenge were the answer to it all.

Still, he could barely live with the vision of Remesh abounding as daylight, while sea-birds screeched over the mound of rock covering his brother's body. Nonosa's fish spear raged against the dark and endless swarms of cod, and filled the storehouses beyond all craving.

SHANAW DRAGGED NONOSA FROM his despair.

After the fishing she sat in his arms on the shoreline rocks, their talk marked by the lapping of the waves.

He wanted to talk only of their fishing and the sea, but Shanaw's mind was quick to fill with questions. 'Do fish hunger? Do Spirits hunger?'

'We know not enough of Spirits.'

She looked intently at him. 'Where is Démas, my mother?'

Nonosa let the question linger, as if it were another for which he did not have a ready answer. When he turned back to her he saw tears had collected in her eyes.

In the seasons to come, stronger, harder questions formed on her lips and Nonosa found himself struggling always for answers to satisfy her.

'Why are some Kindred without food? Are they hateful to the Spirits? Why do the Spirits not feed us all?'

THESE QUESTIONS HAD COME with the arrival of the Nookwashish and the Dohwashish. The clans came in early summer, without warning.

They arrived haggard and worn, with a few mangy belongings, in numbers hardly more than one clan had been before. Their canoes huddled at the mouth of the river, filled with disbelieving faces, their dignities restless with bewilderment at the sighting of the sea.

Remesh alone retained the visage of their former strength. When the Kanwashish saw him, they filled with enmity.

'I took the life of Tuanon to save my own,' he pronounced. 'Is there a man among you who would not have done the same?'

Their eyes swept over the canoes. Their dear Sabbah was not to be seen. Sabbah was dead to the grip of hunger, she who had forever embraced them with the best of food.

In the end it was only within the Kanwashish to welcome the clans, with hearts set on restoring them to health. They led them out of the canoes and spread before them all they could ever wish to eat.

It took many days for the clans to rise from their stupor and make for themselves a life along the shore. The Kanwashish taught them all they knew of reaping food from the sea. But not before the middle days of summer were they forging a place for themselves, independence showing through.

Remesh took in the talk of the Kanwashish from a distance, holding back from them, setting off on his own to explore the coastline in canoe, fish spear at hand. Each day he returned with a catch greater than the day before. One day he returned with a decision that the two clans were ready to move to camping grounds of their own. Though some thought it too early to be separated from the Kanwashish, there was no questioning the one clearly still their SpiritMan. They packed their canoes and set their lodge poles afloat, making their way along the shore to a place a half day's journey from the Kanwashish. There they settled, both clans together. They made of the coast a summer home, and like the Kanwashish, would turn back and head inland in the fall.

THOUGH NONOSA SET GREAT distance between himself and his cousin, their bitterness was forever present. Their few encounters — unforeseen, abrupt — only deepened it. It was easier when the clans moved apart, when again it was only his own people to fill his days. In his body Nonosa felt himself renewed, and on some of those days, for his own peace of mind, he would test his endurance as he did when he was younger, straining with the weight of lodge poles until sweat drenched his torso, until his muscle was near as taut and wiry as when he was first a man.

In the minds of other clansmen, he was their silent, unquestioned leader. Coshee had not the energy or resilience to assert his ways, and was resigned to living his life among the meagre pleasures his wife provided. Nonosa conferred with him, more out of respect than for any counsel he could offer. One day Coshee said to Nonosa, 'I would strike Remesh from our land.' Then turned his mind to other things, until, as Nonosa was departing his lodge, he added, 'Destroying a SpiritMan would bring no end of misery.'

It was Nonosa's great predicament. There were many times when the Nookwashish first settled among them that Nonosa would have overpowered his cousin, had him slink away, weak, defenceless. Would he have broken Remesh's hold over them? Would not another SpiritMan rise up, one unleashing greater vengeance?

One evening, after the other clans had gone, Nonosa arrived back in camp to find several Kanwashish men — once the companions of Tuanon — gathered around a fire set among rocks at the end of the shoreline. Nonosa neared them. Their voices faded.

'What have you to say,' he asked, 'that you must talk in secret?'

'You are fearful, Nonosa.'

It was true. These days he walked about wondering if his will was the will of a leader.

'What do you wish for us, Nonosa?'

A troublesome question, so curious in its abruptness.

'Will the Spirits turn from us if their SpiritMan has his way?' another asked.

Were his people still clinging to Remesh's notion of himself? Or were they looking for more reason to put an end to him?

When Nonosa did speak it was with doubts, not the voice he wished for himself. 'Remesh killed one of us.'

'Why then did you let him live! Did you fear what the Spirits would do?'

'I have no fear of Spirits!'

Now it was them who were struck dumb.

'The Spirits have no fear of you, Nonosa.'

Had he turned a madman? Risking his fate, that of his people.

With their turn of mind came a hardening of their will.

'Each of us,' said one, 'knows his own way.'

'We have been without a SpiritMan to guide us,' said another.

'We have prospered!' Nonosa declared.

'For how long will it last? You are vexed, Nonosa. You are no longer sure of your place.'

If some challenged his right to be leader, surely there would be many who would not. But Nonosa foresaw the great peril of the Kanwashish, of them falling into chaos.

There surged a torturous answer to his plight.

'I have no fear of Spirits,' said Nonosa, 'for I perceive their will. I know what they desire of the Kanwashish.'

The clansmen stared at him. 'The Spirits call upon you? What are you saying, Nonosa?'

Nonosa fell silent before them, as if overcome by what he had revealed.

'You have been chosen by the Spirits?'

'They have made of you a SpiritMan?'

Indeed it was so.

THE AVOWAL OF NONOSA AS SpiritMan drew the Kanwashish together with the strength of rock. As if their lives had been building to this day. Despite the abundance surrounding them, they had not thought themselves complete. A SpiritMan fortified their time, cleared a path beyond shelter and the hunt, beyond breathing. For a SpiritMan was solace in death even more than in life.

Nonosa cloaked himself in the aura of the Spirits. He gave full measure to the calling, brought to himself everything his people wished of him. And where before he ambled sullenly about the camp, now his stride bore wisdom, drawing his people together in near reverence to his words.

He became the tongue of Spirits. Nonosa's way with words added the strength of the heavens. Like the most polished of stones, like the wistful shimmer of the moon, they fell from his lips and charmed away the last of the unbelievers. It was his wish to grow into the most hallowed of SpiritMen, far truer than Remesh could ever hope to be.

Nonosa knew himself to be the SpiritMan for he bore the finery of place. He held steadfast with words and motions becoming of a Messenger. He would serve his people well. What they wished of him he would give, what he held forth they would eagerly grasp. At the centre was the wellness of the Kanwashish, and of them he would make a staunch and eager clan. If his deepest convictions he held tight to his heart, it was because his people had no need of them.

The ceremony to affirm his place filled a late summer night. The chill of fall tinged the air, kept far-off by an intense and robust fire. For the first time since the death of Tuanon singing could be heard, and in honour of Nonosa's brother his companions danced an untamed, gangling circle dance and shouted his name into the sky. As if Nonosa had ordered it, coloured lights embraced the night, bonded the living with the dead, ages past to ages hence. Made of the Kanwashish a whole.

To the neck of Nonosa they affixed a chain of walrus tusks. And when he stood before them, his stiffened shoulders bearing the finest seal fur, he was undoubtedly their SpiritMan. When he spoke it was mighty witness to their choice.

'The Spirits watch over the Kanwashish with boundless favour. They give us the finest of their store. Their blessings reach no end. The cherished children of the Kanwashish will be forever strong.'

Nonosa stood tall before them, regaled in the finest trappings of the sea, counsel falling from his lips. By every measure he was the one to reveal the vastness of their Fate.

TO BIESTA HE WAS her husband, never the SpiritMan.

She was filled with doubt, for in their lovemaking he showed no change. He lusted after her and when he thrust his penis between her thighs it was with the same feral moan.

When Biesta worked her will and failed to bend his ways, there was no thought to absolving him because of his new station in the clan. For Biesta was the mortal she had always been. Nonosa expected new virtues of her in keeping with the honour now accorded him, but she played poorly the part of wife to the SpiritMan.

Biesta, as she had always done, gathered at work each day with the other women of the Kanwashish. She was no more constrained or modest of manner, no more the guarded keeper of secrets, even if the other women now expected it of her.

'The SpiritMan has his yearnings, the same as all men,' she said, and turned her expression bluntly to an exaggerated scowl. It brought guarded laughter. 'And what he wants he finds a way to get.' Lest they would think she was revealing an unkind truth about the man, she let loose laughter of her own.

She took to referring to him as 'husband,' no more as 'Nonosa,' to brace the bond between them. For she refused to lose her husband to his Spirit world.

'Husband, you are my protector,' she said, expecting from him a sign of his devotion to her. The sign was a hand raised, a clear blessing, a sudden, frightful entangling of his private obligations with those of the SpiritMan. At that she scoffed, so forcefully it brought him quickly to his senses.

'Do you think no more of me than one of your clansmen setting forth to the hunt?'

'Biesta ...'

'Husband.'

He embraced her, more rigidly than she had known before. She held strong, her eyes fixed to his.

'Yes,' he said. 'I am your husband. We share this lodge. We raise fine children. Our lives we live together. Is it not enough?'

She did not answer him, but turned to a wife's work and to lament in silence.

That night when he slipped between the furs, she was rigid, unyielding. He persisted, and in the end she gave way to him. For she would not have it said that their SpiritMan was ill-content because of her.

HIS AFFECTION FOR SHANAW was never in doubt. She knew him only as a father, and would have nothing of any distant ways.

Shanaw was now the determined one, the talkative one, the girl stretching herself free of childhood. Nonosa no longer spoke with her but that he heard the cleverness in her voice, her sharp and insistent mind at work. Her questions were not to be set aside, nor his attention turned to anyone but her. Biesta watched them grudgingly.

'What do you think, father? Are you a wiser SpiritMan than Remesh?'

His stomach twisted at the question but he answered quickly, hoping that would bring an end to it. 'There is no doubt.'

'Then the Kanwashish shall have no fears. No one else will die.'

Shanaw's faith in her father had only swelled with his new station. If in her mind before there were limits to his prowess, now these had passed away. This Shanaw held inside herself.

But to Biesta it was no secret. It drew her closer to Patria.

For the women of the clan Biesta gave her wifely face. Her sly talk of her husband the SpiritMan carried on, with an added, measured sting. With an undertow of laughter she now hinted at some dogged, foolish pride. As if he were losing the compassion that had always been his finest trait.

'But is that not the way of SpiritMen?' the women said. 'For they know much that we can never know.'

'Or have us think they do?' With a shocked face Biesta berated herself for allowing such words to escape her lips. 'Let not the Spirits hear me.'

The others forgave her careless tongue and said no more about it. Only then did Biesta become more guarded in her words.

AS HAD THE NOOKWASHISH and the Dohwashish before them, the Kanwashish returned to winter lodging. First came the hunt for caribou, and then the clan turned to the prospect of quiet, uneventful winter days.

What restlessness arose did so among the young men and women who had recently come of age, those now eager to find a mate. During the summer past, some had encountered likely partners, but many of them were weak, too preoccupied with mere subsistence for promises to be made. Now the young Kanwashish were anxious to deepen the romance, yet saw no way of bringing it about.

One of them, Kalif, led several young hunters secretly to the Spirit-Man. The man who had once been so quick to play their joking games, was now the cheerless harbinger of sober news.

'The Spirits ask for patience.'

'Surely the Spirits do not expect us to live without the comforts of women,' said Kalif. 'We will go in search of women, as clans have always done.'

'Remesh would not welcome you.'

'What then are we to do?' asked Kalif urgently. 'We must find partners for our marriage beds.'

'The Nookwashish and the Dohwashish, they have each other,' said a second hunter.

'While the Kanwashish linger in despair!'

Their SpiritMan looked at them sternly. They left the lodge, and at a distance their voices cut the air with anger. Damn and curse what had befallen them. Their voices trailed away.

Biesta entered. 'Your young clansmen lament their fate. Muttering in desperation.' More words spilled out, in a stiffened, caustic tone. 'You have found the Spirits have no favour for them?'

Nonosa did not answer her, but left the lodge to survey the night sky alone, his wife's words in his wake.

It was a momentous decision now before the SpiritMan. Would he send off young hunters to risk the wrath of such an infernal will as Remesh's? For Nonosa was certain it was within his cousin's heart to stir both clans against the Kanwashish. If only to prove it was not success at the hunt alone that determined the prowess of any Kindred clan. In his swirling, troubled mind Nonosa foresaw only the swell of new hatred and its consequence.

NONOSA, SPIRITMAN OF THE Kanwashish, set forth from their camp when the deep frost of winter had passed. Over the ice and crusted snow of the river, solid still, but with the sun holding higher and higher in the sky.

He was not alone. Sometimes beside him, sometimes in a sled behind, was Shanaw. Her dear mother was a young woman raised by the Nookwashish, she herself an infant nourished by them. Surely the clans would see virtue in holding strong to the Kindred past.

The Kanwashish women had balked at the notion of her going, but Nonosa's mind was set. 'Children have always bred goodwill,' he told them, in the unyielding voice of their SpiritMan.

Biesta's few words had given way to rigid silence, her indifference to doing only what was asked of her to prepare them for the journey. When the time came to bid them goodbye, she stood at the edge of the frozen river with near pleasure at their going.

For Shanaw, it was an infinite adventure, especially with only her father by her side. Before long the excitement of snowshoeing was calmed by the struggle over crusts of melting snow. But even at that the cold air seemed constantly filled with vapour from their chatter.

'Domain of the caribou,' her father said, catering to her wonder with an outstretched arm, his eyes sweeping into the distance. 'The caribou led the Kindred here.'

'Where there are no caribou, are there Kindred?'

'I do not think it.'

'What do the Spirits say?'

'They do not tell of such things.'

'But you are the SpiritMan. You must ask.'

He lifted her in his arms and placed her in the sled, atop their provisions.

'The footing has turned to ice, furrowed and uncertain. It is not safe for a heedless, babbling girl.'

Nonosa bundled her in furs and wiped her running nose. She fell fast asleep.

Where the water of the river had met its many boulders, it had frozen haphazardly. It was a raw and gruelling task to drag the sled over the sharp ridges of ice, to keep his precious load from toppling.

In places the ridges gave way to expanses of wind-levelled snow, the surface swirling in broad, erratic patterns. It was joy to bound over it. His exuberant yells Shanaw mistook for calls to the Spirits, until he turned and broke into a deep and lasting smile. It was the Nonosa she remembered, from times before her uncle died.

The first night Nonosa made a shelter in a thicket of spruce not far from the river. He dug at the snow until he uncovered the frozen ground, layered it with caribou furs. Surrounded it with boughs meshed tightly together and packed with snow, forming walls that rose to a canopy. Just outside the shelter he built a fire, lit a stick from it later to ignite seal oil set into the hollow of a stone lamp. They peeled off their outside furs, hung them against the walls to dry.

Nonosa roasted frozen strips of caribou. Followed it with dried sea-bird egg. As darkness fell and stars filled the sky, they lay back, contented by the comforts encasing them.

'Weary travellers,' Shanaw sighed, in the voice of men back from the hunt. 'We will sleep well this night.'

But the day that followed did not repeat the pleasures of the first. They awoke to but a slit of daylight. A heavy layer of snow sagged their canopy of boughs. They crawled into their furs, the snow falling outside now turning to rain.

When the rain stopped they escaped the shelter. Only with great strength did Nonosa free the sled from its tomb of melting snow. They set off again, progress slow and tedious, for now water and slush together coated the river ice.

Before they had gone far the sled upended. Shanaw struggled to her feet, only to slip and fall into a pool of icy water. Nonosa rescued her, lifted her up and wiped her face. She bravely held back her tears.

Nonosa carried her to a sheltered spot on the riverbank. There he made a fire, strong enough to keep her warm while he again built a refuge of boughs. He warmed sleeping furs with heated rocks, then tucked her naked between them. On sticks before the fire he hung her clothes to dry.

He told her stories of when he was a young boy hunting with his father. At their end she said, 'I will be a hunter like you.'

'Boys are hunters.'

'Then I will hunt like a boy.'

He smiled at her innocence.

'What do Spirits tell you?' she asked.

'They say nothing of such things.'

'Then you will show me how to hunt. SpiritMen can make hunters of girls. I will become a better hunter than Sojon.'

The next day Nonosa entranced her with the secrets of the hunt. She clung to every word. They stopped, started cunningly again, pretended to stalk a partridge, then a bear, then a young fox.

With a hand in the air Nonosa traced the pattern of the caribou fence, now hidden beneath a line of mounded snow. Near it they stopped to build a fire. He warmed water and set dried leaves from his pouch to steep, regaled her with more stories of the hunt.

'As young as you my first time,' he said. 'I stood at my father's side, watched the way his hand gripped his spear, the way his arm swayed to narrow his aim. How then the spear sprang from his arm as if lightning cut the sky!'

'Did the caribou fall dead?' Shanaw asked quickly, her voice pitched with excitement.

'Dead.'

'Some need their throats cut to die.'

'Yes,' Nonosa said.

'Yearlings, too?'

'We hunt the biggest animals,' said her father.

'But yearlings are food. Meat that is so tender.'

'We would not waste a spear on a young one when its mother trails behind.'

'I would not wait. I would drive my spear into his heart.'

At that she stood, steadied the grip on her imaginary spear. Her arm swayed at the sight of the yearling, then snapped in the air. Shanaw crept over the snow toward the prey. With her knife slit its throat. She

jumped in celebration at the kill, triumphant hunter like her father.
Bearer of meat for the clan, teller of stories.

'Show me how to stalk a walrus.'

NONOSA SAT UPON THE shore. Rest, he would, for as long as it took to
regain his strength, for never would he enter the camp but that he
was the equal of their SpiritMan. So sapped of energy he was that he
did not look up, or he would have seen his cousin.

The sight of Nonosa, and young Shanaw in the sled behind, brought
a sudden halt to Remesh's survey of the melting river ice. He stared
with deep distrust. Why would any clansmen travel such a distance with
a child? Why would Nonosa struggle over ridges of ice, drained of
potency, some wounded, winter beast.

Remesh continued to stare, relishing the secret glimpse it gave him
of his rival. What now was in Nonosa's mind? Since the time they were
boys, Remesh had not trusted what worked itself through that mind.
Nonosa was the one with the headful of words that Sabbah was forever
savouring, as if her own son could never find a match for them. Even
when she praised Remesh for his keenness at the hunt — when he
brought her more food than she could ever eat, while other mothers
lolled about in envy — there lurked the notion that she wished for
other talents in a son.

A lump of shit, thought Remesh, now slouched upon the shore.
The little one, with a mouth equal to her father's, squirming to be free
from the sled. Remesh watched Nonosa loosen her from her nest and
set her on the snow. A queer pair. A doe and her gamey calf.

WHEN NONOSA AND THE girl entered the camp there was surprise, but
little commotion. Even the presence of Shanaw failed to stir them from
the consequences of their wounded pride. For Nonosa, the death of

Sabbah was never more keenly felt.

There was but one exception to their half-hearted ways — the throb of voices from the few young ones of marrying age. What did he know of Kalif and the others? Would they see them on the coast again? Theirs were shy and hesitant words, spoken in haste so others in the clan would not hear.

For Nonosa it affirmed the virtue of his journey. If clans were held apart, it was not the will of the young. If they were to hold together, it would be the young who would bring it about.

Shanaw bore not the burdens of her father. Other children drew to her and she to them. There was memory of the summer past, no hesitation in their play.

'Sojon,' she said, when she found the boy, 'Come. I will show you how to stalk a walrus.'

'You are a girl.'

'But I know how to stalk a walrus and you do not.'

Sojon studied the look in her eye, and grinned. 'You do not own the spear that will kill it.'

'He will think *your* spear is no more than the bite of a mosquito.'

'Hah!'

'He will swim off with your spear. You will never see him again. Come. I will show you how to make a spear that will keep him from escaping.'

Sojon could not resist. The pair played together, the rest of the children trailed them, joined in their fun as much as Shanaw and Sojon would allow. At once they were the unquestioned leaders of the group. When they could not agree on how to play, their group broke into two.

'Sojon! Cousin! What are you about?'

Sojon halted what he was doing and scowled at her.

Shanaw knew the tie between them. And she had overheard woman's talk about Biesta being the one to give birth to the boy. She told him so.

'Lies,' Sojon said, thinking it a way of Shanaw making herself more powerful.

Shanaw would not back away, though she recalled her own alarm when she had first learned it. Sojon stalked off to find his father.

Remesh bore himself close to his son. The boy had never feared his father. Remesh was always the one he sought if he felt he had been mistreated.

Remesh took him aside, out of the sight of the others. Sojon felt a strangeness in his father's grip. Tears welled in his eyes.

'The girl tells the truth.'

A deeper unease circled the boy. Not fear, for Sojon knew the power of his father to protect him. 'We are cousins?' he said.

'Yes.'

Sojon stood bewildered. 'Like you and Nonosa are cousins? Like you and Nonosa are enemies? For the girl says now he is a SpiritMan. A better one than you.'

At first Remesh thought it child's talk.

But when he laid his eyes again on Nonosa he saw him to be a clansman he had not known before.

THE FIRE WAS LOW, built only for its heat, for daylight stretched long into the evening. Nonosa searched the faces that surrounded it. He uncovered a soreness of heart at the death of his brother. Their words spilled out — short, uneasy notices of regret, only for the ears of Nonosa.

Set before the clans were two SpiritMen. If it were to be a match of words Remesh had no hope of rivalling his cousin. Yet Nonosa was wary of appearing the wiser one, again the outsider with the answer to what assailed the Kindred.

'Why is it you've come, Nonosa?' said Remesh, the question for the others, not himself.

Nonosa looked at Remesh, still the slayer of his brother. 'To secure the bond between the clans. The Kanwashish have no wish but to live as we once did.'

'The Kanwashish grew fat by the sea, while we were left to suffer.'

Remesh — the determined one, the quietly warring one. The circle held to the imperious rhythms of the man.

'Your clans made their way to the sea as they chose,' said Nonosa. 'We gave them all they wanted when they came.'

'Too late to save those who died in hunger.'

Why did his people not hold Remesh to account for what had befallen them? Nonosa thought it fear. And despaired that it be so, for suddenly there was no sign of the compassion he saw when he first walked among them. Remesh had stirred them once more to his own end.

How to reclaim their fickle trust? It was a fragile risk Nonosa was about to bear, one there was no turning from.

Nonosa brought Shanaw to her feet. The young girl stood straight, but not without a child's timidity when all eyes turned to her. The clans knew her well, for hers was the face of Démas and Biesta.

'This child owes her life to you,' Nonosa said. 'You snatched her from certain death in the most cherished moment of our lives. You aided the Kanwashish in their need, so the Kanwashish have done the same for you.'

Remesh was about to expel his reply, but Nonosa's voice swelled again above the crowd.

'We must not divide one from another. Or there will be no Kindred! Only two peoples torn apart in anger! Do we not wish to call upon each other in times of torment? Do we not wish to share our young in marriage? One day when she is grown Shanaw will seek a husband among you. One day Sojon will search among the Kanwashish for a wife.'

Remesh's thunder sliced the air. 'You! Kanwashish! You have no judgment of what my son will do! Never will he bring a Kanwashish into this camp.'

'One day!' Nonosa shouted. 'One day Sojon and Shanaw might join together in the marriage bed! Just as her Nookwashish mother and her Kanwashish father have done.'

Remesh sprang from where he stood, launched himself past the fire, to within an arm's length of Nonosa.

'Is this the wisdom of a SpiritMan?' bellowed Nonosa. 'Is this the wisdom of one guided by all the Spirits in the heavens!'

Anguish enveloped Shanaw. Panic struck at the heart of Sojon. Words ceased, except for startled cries encompassing the fire.

Nonosa had unleashed his cousin's ire. By any measure a torturous sacrifice. The seasons past had weakened Remesh, yet his strength regained more than matched the challenge. The brute of a SpiritMan had revived in almighty rage.

Remesh flung himself at Nonosa. He latched his hands to Nonosa's throat, to finish what he once began.

The battle was brief, for Nonosa was not able for his fury. The two fell into a crust of coarse, half-melted ice, Remesh on top, Nonosa sunk below. His head of hair swirled through the ice water, his eyes and mouth one moment submerged, the next barely breaking the surface.

Shanaw screamed, delirious with fright at the sight of her father desperate for breath. She pounded at the back of Remesh. In a piteous gesture tugged at his covering of fur.

Then in a frenzied, vicious moment of despair Shanaw clutched her father's spear. Raised it barely off the ground, thrust it in the direction of the beast! Thrust its sharpened slice of rock into his side. Pushed it past the fur and into his flesh with all her strength.

Remesh sagged atop her father. The moan of the wounded no match for the great communal cry.

Hot blood streamed from the gash. Reddened the snow, swirled into the ice water, like the pith of any creature. Shanaw fell back in terror.

The weight of the wounded Remesh pinned her father in the water, barely allowed him to bend his head out for air. Clansmen loosened their SpiritMan, dragged him free and righted him, his face vacant to the sky. There was no hope the bleeding would stop, none that Remesh would ever rise again.

Lerenn stood over him, seized by grief, Sojon sobbing in the stiff folds of her mantle.

There descended over the gathering a great solemness. Grief and incredulity at the slaying of their own. Fear of what would now befall them from the Spirits. They would not draw near Shanaw, but let her curl away in fright.

When Nonosa dragged himself to his feet, and heard the scorn lashed at his daughter, he cradled her in his arms and walked among them all to show that she was but a child.

Nonosa held Shanaw tight against him and stood before the crowd. Remesh dead at his feet.

Nonosa led them in mourning at the death of their SpiritMan. He proclaimed the innocence of a child desperate to save her father. He led the Kindred in their chants to the Spirits, in their cry for mercy.

The body of Remesh was dragged to a vacant lodge, there prepared for burial.

In the darkness, by only the fickle light of the dying fire, Nonosa shed his clothes and, boldly naked, declared himself SpiritMan for all the Kindred.

His voice rose and fell with the waves of mourning. His body swayed in the firelight as if burdened by an impenetrable grief. The despair gave way to petition, the petition to an affirming that the Spirits were contented still with the Kindred despite the killing of a Messenger. Nonosa's words encircled them, drew away their terror, wrapped it in a conviction that all was well, that the next day would unfurl in hope.

'Before you I am. Bearing goodwill. For the Spirits lie content. For two great hunters — Remesh and Tuanon — have taken their places among them.'

Nonosa raised an arm toward the sky.

'Soon the nights will flare with the fire of our hunters.'

He stopped and crouched before the gathering. His voice bore a sudden edge of fear. 'What of hunger?' He veered toward them. 'What of hunger?'

Nonosa emitted intoxicating words, now a web of brilliant words that caught their ears and eyes and calmed their fearful minds. They longed to be led out of their misery, willing followers, as Nonosa knew most men to be. All Kindred longed for what Nonosa promised them — bodies free from hunger, in calm, untroubled times.

He fell to his knees, his hands folded between his thighs. And under the night sky, with Remesh barely gone from them, they declared now their faith in Nonosa — their Messenger, their SpiritMan.

Nonosa covered himself and, with Shanaw asleep in his arms, walked among his people to the silence of a lodge.

Only the heartache of Lerenn and Sojon lingered, filling what remained of the night.

THE CLANS WAITED OUT the days until spring. They carried the body of Remesh to high ground and there set it in a rock hollow, covered it with a noble mound of boulders. Their new SpiritMan cast forth words to help the dead man on his journey, then drifted away. Lerenn and the boy held back once again, in solitude.

When Nonosa looked at her from a distance she seemed no longer to hold to her heart anyone but Sojon. The boy himself moved about with a hardened look set in his face. Ignored the world, as if he were no longer part of it, but part of a world he made for himself and fiercely guarded.

Shanaw was as worrisome for Nonosa as the boy was for Lerenn. The severity of what she had done set into her mind, dislodged the sweet trust that normally settled there. She followed her father about constantly, never straying, even to sleep. Nonosa would wrap an arm over her to help her through her troubled dreams. And sing to her the songs he sang when she was a fretful infant.

For a child to have killed such a giant was beyond the comprehension of the clans.

When the eyes of the Nookwashish and the Dohwashish met Shanaw's it was to judge if a poison lurked there, if she were a child possessed by some wickedness that might spring at them again. They warned their own children to keep their distance from her.

Shanaw begged her father to begin their journey home. Nonosa would not rush away, for if the Kindred were to hold to him, he had to be with them in their days of greatest sorrow.

The river ice had begun to break apart. When there was a channel wide and free of it, then Nonosa and the girl would go with the Nookwashish and the Dohwashish, on their second spring journey to the sea.

As he had wished, it fell to Nonosa to lead them there.

SHANNON

IT'S LATE. SHE'S INTERESTED to see what the author does with the boy. That is how she has come to think of it — the author's manipulation of characters on the Labrador landscape. She flips through to the end to see how much more she has left to read, then sets the book atop a pile of others on her bedside table and turns out the lamp. In the few minutes before sleep she thinks of Simon, of telling him he has good reason to be smug, given the book kept her awake for so long.

She would have finished it, but for the fact she has so much to do the next day. The apartment has to be tidied and cleaned, the beds changed, groceries purchased. In two days Marta will arrive with her husband, Lars, and their three-year-old, Markus. Shannon was surprised Marta had followed through on her promise to visit, although she should not have been. She has always known Marta to be impulsive.

'Lars has a window of two weeks before he must start to get ready for the Christmas season. The SAS fares to North America are really good at the moment. We decided yes we can do it, so why not.' That was three weeks ago.

They spent a few days in Montreal, flew to Deer Lake, where they rented a car, spending time in Gros Morne, where they were the day before, then began the drive up the peninsula to St. Anthony. As they get closer, the anticipation builds, as does the unease. All these years Shannon has thought of Marta as her best friend. She wonders, when they finally reconnect, if there will be the same bond between them, or a significant measure of it. At least she is more relaxed than when Patti proposed her visit.

All the while cleaning up the house, she is thinking of the boy, Markus. A couple of her friends in BC had young children, but never has she had a child so young staying with her. She is conscious of keeping breakables out of reach, of covering sharp edges, of blocking access to electrical outlets. She wonders what he will eat. She buys lots of milk and juice. And yogourt, though it is likely not the type he is used to eating in Norway. She is tempted to buy cookies but she is uncertain if Marta would approve.

From pictures she has seen of Markus, she knows him to be a handsome boy, resembling his father more so than his mother, although Shannon was never very good at deciphering facial features. Lars she knows relatively little about, other than the fact he's a chef. Again, it is the pictures that come to mind. Much taller than Marta, lean, trim, blond. Nordic, if only because there are several pictures of him cross-country skiing, with Markus in a carrier on his back. An outdoors person, it went without saying, given Marta's interests, and the fact that Shannon remembers her as not being a particularly good cook.

It all happened so quickly after she went back to Norway. Shannon concluded Marta had known him before she came to Canada, even though he was not someone she had ever mentioned. Shannon now suspects they never completely lost touch, that going back home was in part a last effort to see what might become of their relationship. For the longest time Shannon felt hurt by that, since she herself had opened up so freely to Marta.

Obviously, it worked out for her and Lars. Shannon had been invited to the wedding, of course. She could have been the maid of honour, or the Norwegian equivalent. She could have gone had she really wanted to.

Marta had said, 'Come. Please. I'll introduce you to some of Lars's friends. You could end up meeting some great guys.'

It wasn't worth the risk, or the money. She had decided it was just too far away and the wrong time of the year. It would likely have cost her three or four thousand dollars, and it came just when she was about to take time off for her term at UBC. She ended up with the full details, of course, the pictures, and eventually the long emails. There were groups of thirtysomething men, all looking too handsome and too sure of themselves, all likely with girlfriends they would have been fools to give up. She felt hopelessly overshadowed, not that it mattered, although there were times later, when she was in one of her funks, that she thought it might have been worth it for a few Norwegian nights in bed with one of them.

THE DAY IS HERE and she is as prepared as she'll ever be. Marta has called ahead to give an approximate time they should get to St. Anthony, and Shannon gave directions to her apartment. In any event it is hard to get lost in St. Anthony. As the time nears, Shannon is back and forth to the window to snatch a look outside, to be sure there is still a vacant parking space.

An hour past their expected time, they arrive. They are out of their car and heading toward her entrance before she sees them. She rushes downstairs and opens the door shortly after the first ring of the doorbell.

Shannon's arms fly instantly around Marta. She reciprocates and the two are again friends for life. Except that now there is a tall husband with their child in his arms standing next to her.

Shannon draws back, quickly wiping her eyes. 'Sorry, guys. It's just so wonderful to see everyone.'

Lars extends his hand, smiling broadly, 'And you, too, Shannon,' in free-flowing English, enriched by its Scandinavian inflection. 'And this is Markus.'

Markus turns shyly away, sinking his head into his father's shoulder. 'Say hello to mama's friend.'

'He has been practising all the way in the car.'

Shannon leads them inside and up the stairs to her apartment. It is a comfortable fit, and, unlike when Patti visited, there is no need for manoeuvring around past relationships.

In the centre of the living room floor Shannon has left a box, with the lid open, of large Lego-type building blocks. Markus is torn between it and the security of his father. With Lars's encouragement the blocks win, freeing the three adults to sit and talk as the coffee perks. Some of Shannon's best memories of Marta are set against a background of dark, black brew.

'I told you,' Marta says to Lars when it's poured. 'Shannon makes the best coffee.'

It sets off a chain of reminiscence — anecdotes of the Parks staff on Baffin and their personal quirks, what Shannon knows of any of them now. Their winter outings into the open country with the local Inuit. Their gaffes with the food that faced them at some of the community gatherings. The recollections jump back and forth, and are always of the most humorous incidents. Lars sits comfortably on the outside, but remains the foreigner for the moment. After she and Marta end a particularly effusive exchange, Shannon attempts to draw him in with her description of the incredible landscape that surrounded them daily, although she knows he would have heard about it from Marta many times before.

Shannon is all the time reading him, trying to make a clear judgment on what's at the core of the attraction he was for Marta. She knows it wouldn't have been a matter of claiming a man, any man within reason. Marta would have come back to Canada before doing that. Lars isn't fiercely attractive physically, although there is plenty about him to appreciate. He appears to be a very good father, but that, of course, came after the fact.

Shannon sees an attentiveness to Marta that she first thinks endearing, but then realizes that if it were her, and it went on for too long, it would likely start to drive her crazy. He is soft-spoken and compliant in a way that seems to overcompensate for the unfamiliarity of the situation in which he finds himself. Shannon knows she should not be so quick to judge, and sets herself up to be wrong — in fact, she wants to be wrong — but it has always been her nature to do just what she's doing. Marta, she can tell, knows precisely what is going through her mind.

Shannon is nervous about cooking the meals. She has considered going to restaurants, but the best of them are closed until the tourist season rebounds in the spring. She has researched the Norwegian diet on the Internet, and concluded that fish would be her safest bet for their first meal. She debated trying Bertha's recipe, but decided it would be a gamble and that morning went in search of something fresh, managing to find cod. She knows that, since the moratorium on fishing cod, what's available is by-catch from fishing other species, but she's assured it was caught the day before, that she couldn't get it any fresher.

Their first meal is not cooked by Shannon, as it turns out. Lars seizes a chance to take over the kitchen. That is how Shannon sees it — commandeering the kitchen, although it's a deed for which she is grateful. Her relief at not having to cook more than offsets the revelation of the shortcomings of her kitchen in the eyes of a professional chef. She has no fresh herbs for one, no *fleur de sel* for another. But Lars makes do, and, in fact, seems to have come unceremoniously alive.

What faces them at the supper table is something far beyond what Shannon might have prepared. She does score well with the wine, appropriately white and dry.

'*God appetitt*, everyone,' says Lars upon the unveiling.

The cod, baked in foil with thinly sliced vegetables and mushrooms and served with lemon butter, is unquestionably delicious, though Marta assures Shannon he is capable of much more. Dessert is Shannon's mix of vanilla ice cream, drizzled with golden-yellow, locally made bakeapple syrup.

'You'd call it cloudberry. We call it bakeapple.'

Lars is fascinated by this example of localisms. The berry, which also grows in Norway, is neither apple-flavoured, nor has it been baked. Shannon is unable to explain the origin of the word and a momentary retreat to *The Dictionary of Newfoundland English* is of no help, since it doesn't offer an explanation, only early incidences of its usage. Lars is admiring of its quality, which is a natural lead-in to the suggestion that the following day they visit the premises where the syrup is made. The meal has worked well for everyone, including Markus, who took to the fish as eagerly as the adults, something which Shannon finds curious in a three-year-old. Curious, but another instance of good parenting, of expecting the child to eat what's put in front of him. She momentarily imagines her niece, Rianna, as a three-year-old.

THEY ARE A HARMONIOUS lot and when that evening they are away to bed, Shannon makes a quick call to Simon. She knows he's been wondering how her day has gone. She speaks as quietly as she can, and for only a few minutes, but long enough for him to taste her buoyant mood. She wants him to meet them. They decide on Saturday, for supper.

Before she has tucked herself away on the couch, Marta emerges from the bedroom. Shannon had almost expected it. Some of their best times when they lived together had been that last half-hour before each of them went off to bed.

'Look for a solid sleeper in a husband,' Marta says, curling up in an armchair. Shannon tosses her a woollen blanket.

'Someone who doesn't snore.'

'Once he's asleep, he doesn't move.'

'Marta,' Shannon says, 'he's lovely. And Markus is adorable. I'm very happy for you.'

Marta doesn't reflect on her own happiness, which Shannon takes as acknowledgement that it is as strong as it appears.

Shannon brings up Simon, without any prompting, a way perhaps of levelling the field. Marta is not surprised there is someone new in the picture.

'I want to meet him,' she says firmly, as she would have said ten years ago.

Shannon informs her about Saturday.

'Is he ... you know?'

She can't think that Marta's English has slipped so much that she can't remember the word. What does she want to say? Handsome? Sexy? The one?

'Is he good to you?' Marta says.

'He is as good as it gets.' Which is not what she would ever have said, had it not fallen off her tongue as a clever comeback.

'You deserve the best, Shannon.'

The exchange has taken an entirely clichéd, meaningless turn. Which leaves Shannon feeling that a gap has opened between them that neither would have tolerated in the old days. It was all brutal honesty then. Time passes. Shannon figuratively shrugs. 'He's the very best, for a very long time.'

Marta walks across the room and hugs her then, on her way back to the bedroom. And Shannon sheds a tear, if not of happiness, then certainly for a steadiness of heart as she turns out the light and listens for the low interplay of sounds that will take her into sleep. The blend of the computer and the refrigerator. It works for her, much better than no sound at all.

THEIR EXCURSIONS FROM ST. ANTHONY must start with a visit to the Norse settlement at L'Anse aux Meadows. Shannon has no expectations except that there be a vague visceral reaction of some sort on their part, given that the ancestors of Leif Eiriksson came from Norway, as did Helge Ingstad, the adventurer who discovered the site in 1960.

Lars stands before bronze busts of Ingstad and his archaeologist wife, Anne Stine. 'They are quite famous in Norway.'

'He lived to age 101,' adds Marta. 'He lived in Oslo?' She hesitates because she realizes Shannon likely knows a great deal more than they do.

'Yes, Oslo,' says Lars. 'Just outside. I saw him once, at a bookstore when I was a boy. And many times on television, of course.'

They take in the site largely through Markus. They move about the interpretation centre as a foursome, their own interest subsumed by a need to interpret for the boy. Shannon falls back, for the time being, as if she were a bystander. She sees their slow walkabout, their narrative partly English, partly Norwegian, as a prolonged skim through history. The Marta she sees is a mother above all, one very good in her role.

Lars is her match, taking on the responsibilities of parenthood with parallel confidence. Shannon comes to think of them as a well-integrated team, near-model parents in the Scandinavian mode. Markus will grow up to be a happy, well-adjusted boy.

It is later, when they go outside again and take the path to the reconstructed sod huts, that their qualities as parents truly take hold. Markus, initially wary of the costumed, bearded Norseman who greets them, is brought around to embracing the moment as if it were a storybook come alive. Björn the Beautiful becomes his friend and there spreads across the boy's face an enchantment that Shannon thought was only ever fabricated in movies.

On their way back to the parking lot Markus falls asleep on Lars's shoulder, freeing the parents to fall back to being adults. They pull Shannon back again into the circle.

'Explain to us exactly what you've been doing over the past few months,' Marta says.

It's for the benefit of Lars that she's made the request. Marta, if she had read Shannon's emails, would know exactly what she's been doing. Shannon keeps it simple, but the use of the word *Aboriginal* generates more interest than she anticipated.

'Who are these people, how would you say — aborigines?'

Shannon draws back again, putting it in a framework. She wonders how typical his response is. Typical of Europeans perhaps. She recalls they have a strange fascination with North American Indians. She remembers stories of re-enactment camps in Germany where people come together to dress up in Indian garb and dance around fire pits.

She had not intended to mention Simon's heritage, but it drops naturally into the narrative, a way of modulating Lars's take on the present-day Native situation. He has heard the reports about the desperate state of some Native communities, the glue-sniffing, the neglected children. All the world has seen the pictures. He is looking for an explanation, but it doesn't lend itself to anything simple.

Shannon is relieved when they finally see the sign for Dark Tickle and Lars turns into the parking lot. She's hoping his interest in Newfoundland berry products will take over. Dark Tickle calls itself an 'economuseum,' part artisanal production, part museum. A chance to watch how the jams and syrups are made, but, of more interest to Lars, a trail out back leading into a Newfoundland marsh, where berries are to be seen in their natural habitat. The only berries remaining this late in the fall are partridge-berries, but Lars is head and eyes near the ground with the newly awake Markus.

This is the sight Shannon wants to remember of their visit, and takes several pictures of all three of them, set against oranges and reds, the changing fall colours of the marshland.

Berries in situ do not comprise a complex subject, however, and once Lars has spoken for twenty minutes to the couple who runs the enterprise, he has exhausted the subject to his satisfaction. Lars departs Dark Tickle with a collection of produce that will find its way back to his homeland and which he says he'll use as a comparison to Norway's own berries, and incorporate into some complicated dessert for some special Christmas reception.

Shannon enjoys Lars very much on this level, and even though it is all about Lars and his cooking, forcing Marta's interests to the sidelines, Shannon appreciates its lack of complication. The more the visit moves along, the more it becomes clear that Lars has a considerable reputation in Oslo as a chef. Marta explains from the backseat of the car that he does private catering, often for high-level government functions, including receptions for international heads of state. He is in the process of searching out financial backers so he can open an upscale restaurant.

This is where Shannon would prefer the conversation stay, and she does what she can to keep it there, but before they are long on the road back toward St. Anthony it has reverted to Native issues. Marta knows about Shannon's thesis topic, having been a sounding board for the failure to bring the thesis to its conclusion. The mention of the Beothuks is enough to take Lars on a whole new path, for indeed he knows something of their demise.

What Shannon has to say stirs a new intensity, Marta unwittingly stoking the fire. Lars first wants to make sure he is pronouncing Shanawdithit's name correctly, and once he has it mastered, it is as if he's been given a secret combination to whatever tidbits might lie impounded within Shannon's research.

She has discovered his penchant for the arcane, the secret for which few others are privy. He likes the feeling of being ahead of the game. He locks onto the notion that Cormack appeared to her to be sexually repressed, and how that affected his relationship with Shanawdithit. As much as Shannon thinks it herself, she knows it to be as yet a theory, and comes to regret bringing it up.

Lars doesn't need any more than a theory. He runs with the notion, seemingly with a passion to see history rewritten.

'Like the medieval Norse. They were really brutes. They wouldn't think twice about killing.' He checks in the review mirror to be sure Markus is indeed asleep in the car seat. 'I mean, their helmets with the horns are fun for kids, but they were animals. Cultural terrorists.'

'I wouldn't go that far.'

'How far would you go? If you are reworking the site, how far would you go?'

'I'm not sure I call it reworking.'

'Whatever the word is.'

She has no intention of debating him on the issue. She skirts the question, which doesn't mean it goes away, merely that it lies in the background, only to re-emerge that evening.

SIMON IS THE PERFECT conduit for Lars bringing it back to the surface. Shannon absorbs the whole irritating exchange as she sets the dinner table and uncorks the wine.

On meeting, Lars and Simon fell into a cordial relationship. All the more conspicuous since the two are very similar in physical stature. Except for skin tone and hair colour, they could have come out of matching gene pools. Simon shook his hand and commented that their meeting might be called 'Full Circle Revisited,' which requires an explanation, one that Simon seemed to have practised, and which Lars finds unreservedly appealing.

Shannon keeps her distance, but it doesn't stop them opening the lid on several topics, all thorny in Shannon's experience, but which the men seem to relish, indifferent to her not joining in.

'Frankly,' says Lars, 'I'm sick to death of this business of Vikings as a tourist attraction.'

Shannon feels herself standing alone, Simon's eye catching a momentary sting of alienation. At which point he attempts to move the conversation along. Damage done, thinks Shannon. She would like to feel gratitude for the effort, even if her attention to setting the table fails to show it.

The lull prompts Lars to check on what he has cooking in the oven. 'A traditional recipe,' he announces to Simon, 'from northern Norway. We call it *lofotlao*.'

Once Lars discovered salt cod in one of the grocery stores, he knew immediately that he wanted to prepare this dish. Simon's dinner with them turned out to be the ideal opportunity. Shannon saw no reason to argue, other than, being a good host, to suggest that Lars should not be spending his holiday in the kitchen.

'Not to worry,' he had said. 'It's very simple. I could make it with my eyes closed.'

The salt cod was put in water to soak for several hours. Besides slicing potatoes, onions and red peppers, and preparing a garlic and tomato sauce that took all of ten minutes, there was very little to do. The dish was assembled and in the oven an hour before Simon had arrived, and now it smells wonderful.

'Simple,' Lars says, bringing it to the table, 'but delicious. We shall see. It is a peasant dish. My grandmother's speciality, to which I add some black olives, jalapenos and oregano — fresh, I would have preferred — just to make it a bit more interesting.'

Of course it is delicious and generates an outpouring of compliments. Wine flows freely, as does change in the conversation. Shannon feels a return to something more sociable.

Simon wants to know about Norway, and what differences they've found between it and Canada. 'Would you live here?'

'People are people,' says Lars. 'It is where you feel most comfortable, where you choose to make your life. Marta loves Canada, but we love our home, too.' He looks at his wife. 'I think we would say that. We are not people who want to escape our families. Or our politics. We make a good living. What more is there?'

'The best restaurant in Oslo?' Marta offers.

'Maybe so.'

'Then what?' Shannon questions. 'Maybe the best Norwegian restaurant in New York? Nuevo-Norwegian cuisine.' She is laughing, too, a bit more loudly than the others, but she finds it hard to tone it down.

'What opportunities arise in the future, who's to know?' Lars says. 'More questions. Right?'

'Who knows where we will be in ten years? That's the exciting part.'

'Excitement,' Shannon says, 'will likely have a lot to do with it.' She raises her wine glass and waits for the others to join her in a toast. 'To excitement.'

CORMACK

17th January, 1828
aboard the brig George Canning

Dear John,

This letter finds me en route to England and Scotland. When we dock I shall entrust it to the Mails, and in due course I shall be arriving at your doorstep, as my previous letter forecast. Let us hope this one has found its way to you before I myself do.

You will be pleased to hear that the Boeothuck Institution met finally on 12th January in St John's. We came together in the courthouse chambers, under the Honourable Chairmanship of Judge Des Barres. There passed generous good wishes for the New Year, whereupon the meeting turned to the principal reason for our gathering, the presentation of my report on the recently concluded expedition to the interior. A summary of the same constituted much of my previous letter to you, so you

may well have been privy to it prior to the members
themselves.

To a man there was vigorous admiration for what has
been achieved. Since my arrival back in the city it was known
that the expedition had not led to an encounter with the
Boeothuck as had been hoped, yet they were all well satisfied,
not least with the amount of territory covered in the course of
thirty days.

I described each site of the Boeothuck and, with the interest
in my narrative at its peak, I displayed before them the articles
of Boeothuck manufacture which I had collected, and, in
addition, the numerous outstanding specimens of rock and
minerals that it had been my good fortune to secure. The
others were astonished at the exhibition, even more so when
I brought forth foolscap bearing the Boeothuck words
previously collected from Demasduit and augmented with
those I myself had gathered from Shanawdithit.

There was great interest in Shanawdithit, of course, and it
was readily agreed that for her well-being the young woman
should be brought into St John's as soon as it proves judicious
to do so.

In the meantime, there is much remaining to be done to
answer the question of whether there are Boeothucks in the
interior. As I pointed out to those gathered, it is my conclusion
that those of the Boeothuck tribe who remain alive are either
west of Red Indian Lake, or, more likely, farther to the north,
in the vicinity of White Bay. A motion was passed that again
three Indians be hired to undertake an expedition, at my
suggestion to be led by the same Abenakie, to travel inland in
the spring and inspect this territory, and not depart from it
until they have succeeded in befriending any Boeothuck they
encounter, and then return with that Indian to the Peyton's,

being duly aware of the need for prudence in travel should the Boeothuck prove to be in a poor state of health. For doing so it was agreed that, in addition to their customary payment, they should receive a bounty of one hundred dollars.

The meeting strengthened our mission. We again firmly resolved that the injustices served the Boeothuck be righted, that what remained of the once noble nation be protected from further harm. In this, John, had you been seated among us, I am sure you would have vigorously concurred.

As President of the Institution it is my duty, and privilege, to work diligently to that end, the next step of which will be to lay before the Colonial Office in London the proceedings of the Institution; hence, one of the paramount reasons for my forthcoming visit to London. By the time I reach Liverpool I will be able to report on that meeting. I look forward to doing so and to recounting in detail considerable and positive results.

Yours very sincerely,
William

Tuesday, 29th January, 1828
London

If I write in haste, it is because my exasperation will not allow
me to do otherwise.

Today, again, I arrived on the steps of the Colonial Office. In
the position of Secretary for the Colonies is one William
Huskisson. Word is that Huskisson has embroiled himself in the
Corn Laws. I have come to the conclusion that the man is more
concerned with the trade in grain than with the extirpation of a
whole race of aborigines.

Again I waited in the antechamber of the Colonial Office off
Downing Street, again my notes neatly and concisely assembled,
as was the case the whole of yesterday.

To put it as mildly as I am able, the gentleman behind the
desk displayed all too brisk a manner, and derived untold
satisfaction in doing so, without the least regard for how great
a distance any of the people seated in abeyance had come. It
was as if the steady stream of black and eastern faces were
common business. It made no difference that mine was white
and that he did not have to ask for my words to be repeated
and fail miserably at masking his irritation.

'Please inform his Honour, the Secretary, that I have
ventured deep into the interior of Newfoundland and bring
knowledge of the Red Indians.' These were my words on my

first approach to the desk.

'New-found-land?'

'Yes.'

'The place bears more of interest than cod?'

I was not amused by his oafish questioning, and unfortunately my impatience at his manner showed.

I waited two full days in the antechamber. I did not see Mr Huskisson.

It but confirmed the opinion I held on the governance of Newfoundland. One had greater hope of bending the ear of its masters if one resided in Dorset in fish-merchant luxury than if one actually ever set foot on the Island.

Woe be it that the matter of a vanished race should add to the burdens of the Colonial Office! I leave London no more satisfied than when I arrived. More scornful, yes! More dispirited, yes!

4th February, 1829

I arrived two days ago in Edinburgh.

My coach ride was an awkward one, for my valuables I was unwilling to let part from my sight, and as the collection of rock and mineral made the case intolerably heavy, I began to be looked upon with suspicion. What could be in a case that a man would go to such lengths to keep it so near him? By the time we neared Edinburgh the bag had attained such outlandish attributions that I was obliged to open it and remove one of the specimens of rock for viewing, such was my fear that I would be pursued through the streets of the city and robbed of its contents.

At the office of Professor Jameson there was not fear, but euphoria. I unwrapped the rock and minerals first, though our discussion of them, together with a firm identification, would come later. For I was quickened in anticipation of the reaction my Boeothuck pieces would bring. My passion was not without justification, for with each successive unveiling the man was even more deeply affected. I had never seen him so — his eyes, veterans to such unveilings, suddenly narrowed, fraught with intensity, his head inclined sharply toward the specimens. He quickly sat down at the table, in one of those sudden motions which characterizes him when something seizes his attention. His head he propped against an upright arm, studying the objects in silence, not yet willing to touch either of them.

Only at the end of the retrieval from the case did Jameson's eyes turn to me, and then only for a moment before resuming their gaze at the pair of Boeothuck skulls which I had carefully set down, uncovered from their fresh wrappings.

I presented the chronicle of the skulls and under what circumstance I had retrieved them. My excitement was near equal to his own, although I would not have it show. It would have diminished the alliance which at that moment was set between us. In future years I am sure to mark it as the moment I became a significant benefactor to the study of natural history.

Jameson stretched out his hands and held first the skull of Demasduit. No ordinary hands, but ones which knew well the shape and textures of bones, hands that had held the bones of innumerable tribes. He ran a row of four fingers from above the eye sockets, over the crown of the skull and down the other side. He did it a second time, and then from ear socket to ear socket, pausing after each motion was complete. Jameson was not one given to effusiveness, yet in the way he held the skulls, the way he rotated them in his hands, inspecting each to the last detail, I could tell with certainty that these would become distinctive additions to his College Museum.

He seemed particularly fascinated by the skull of the Red Indian chief. He joined the lower jawbone to its upper companion. Although only a few of the teeth remained, the pairing gave the observer a clear indication of the magnitude of the man.

'A coarse wound to the lower jaw,' commented Jameson.

I nodded. Having examined the bones in great detail myself, I was well aware of their points of irregularity. I did not provoke comment on the perforation of the maxillary bone, but waited his conjecture.

'What would you say, Cormack?' He had turned its interpretation to me. 'You know the circumstance of his life better than I. What do you make of this fissure?'

'Gunshot, I would suspect. The man had been accosted by settlers. His slayers claim they were acting to save themselves.'

'Woeful fellow then.'

It was the first time I had heard Jameson ascribe sentiment to the human whose bones were before him. It was uncommon for such bones to be personally delivered, and more uncommon still that an individual's story be ascribed to them.

'The year this happened, what was it?'

'1819.'

Jameson seemed surprised. 'Not ten years. These specimens — hardly relics then.'

These, his words to me. As near to being his confidant as ever I would be.

20th February, 1828

At variance with my will, given my last sojourn in the city, I have returned to London. It took a visit with Hodgkin to be good reason for my return. It has been that, if in equal measure unsettling.

I have just come away from his museum rooms in Guy's Hospital. This Museum of Morbid Anatomy holds few bones. His is a collection of diseased tissue and muscle. Indeed we had hardly exchanged greetings before he gathered me in front of a specimen, freshly displayed in a large tray, a human heart with which he had been occupied prior to my arrival. With a surgical probe, and his habitual zeal, he fell into an explanation of what he called the 'retroversion' of its aortic valves.

'The leaflets of the valve drop back against the ventricle, making them unable to function as intended. Do you see?'

Rare, of course, is the layman who has stood before a specimen of human heart. At its sight one could not be anything but enveloped in emotions, if also at a loss to delineate them.

Obviously, the heart was not to be taken into the hands as are specimens of other sorts. Hodgkin handed me the probe and motioned me to incline my head nearer it. 'Blood flows backwards,' he said, his voice precise, yet edged with the flutter of new discovery, as had mine many times I should think. 'Thus causing the heart to strain and the pulse to vibrate extraordinarily.'

'The cause of such a condition, Hodgkin?'

'In this case syphilis. A young man, no older than ourselves.'

I exchanged a look with Hodgkin, the Quaker. Unlike other bachelors of my circle, Hodgkin has never been one to speculate on the sporting pursuit of women, or, as in this case, its consequence. Before us was the bleak price of an errant path.

His Museum shelves and their mass of glass containers — the contents each a grim reminder of the misery to which the human body can succumb — made remarkable surroundings. Each specimen had been sunk in preserving fluid, the container covered by a glass plate, and the two sealed with wax. Besides my admiration for the labour its assembly must have required, it did bring disquiet for which I had not been prepared when I entered the rooms.

'A constant lesson in one's mortality,' I said to Hodgkin.

'Undoubtedly.' He answered quickly, and thought no more of it.

In such environs how could a man not be left to wonder at what disease awaits him? Yet Hodgkin is invigorated by the scrutiny of dead men's viscera. A diseased heart incites him, sets him forward onto a quest.

A quest not unlike my own, I thought, and to my relief we left the dissection trays for the perfunctory arena outside the rooms of the Museum, where on a table Hodgkin cleared space for a display of the treasures I had brought.

At seeing them Hodgkin demonstrated no less enthusiasm than if they were his own, an amazement to me, coming as it did from someone who in a short time had attained such a high standing in his profession, with, one would think, little time to devote to pursuits other than his medical ones. He examined each object with fascination worthy of a scholar of natural history.

Just as I expected, the man was especially engrossed by the skulls. I related the story of my journey to Red Indian Lake.

'Come then, Cormack. What were you thinking when you gathered these vestiges?'

'The same as you with your hearts.'

'Some look upon the Museum as a repository for the desecrated. Accusations of grave robbing fly through the air like vultures,' he said, with a cursory smile at his own humour. 'What does one do but go about the business of science.'

My fondness for Hodgkin grew from his unwavering beliefs, his defiance of regulation. He cares not what others think of him, only what he considers right in the face of God. Unlike Hodgkin, I am not cloaked in religion. I have my creed but it is unwritten and bears no imprint, Quaker or otherwise.

'That we do,' I said. 'We seek the virtuous, and spurn corruption.'

'And these Red Indians, we must be their Protector. Nothing less.'

I gathered up the objects, wrapped them in their cloths and put them away.

'The world thinks us odd,' said Hodgkin.

For the moment his words left me silent.

Hodgkin is right, of course. 'I should think the world odd,' I answered, tightening the straps of my case.

'More than odd.'

I stood up and clasped its handle.

Then he said, 'Would you agree, Cormack, that first cousins should be allowed to marry?' The question he thrust at me, seemingly plucked from nowhere.

I quietly released the handle. It was clear the question bore down on him with considerable weight. Hodgkin was suddenly and uncharacteristically chagrined, but determined to see the subject through.

He sat me down again. His was a startling revelation. The man, against my prediction, is preoccupied with a woman. And indeed she is a first cousin, a young woman whom he has known since childhood and with whom, as much as he has tried to quell his emotion, he is dearly smitten. His parents are against the liaison, and more importantly, the Society of Friends forbade it.

'It is against church law, but it has no basis in Scripture,' he declared, his view as earnest as that displayed toward the aborigines. He has tried in vain to persuade the church elders of the soundness of his views, but it has done no good.

Exceedingly dispirited he is, yet he will not part from his church. The bonds are too strong, the consequences for his family too great. In the meantime the young woman and he have parted, and she is now engaged to be married to another.

I have little experience in such matters. And no advice could I offer, except that perhaps immersion in work will put it out of his mind, that with time the frustration will pass.

'But I am consumed by this, Cormack. Have you never been consumed by the adoration of a woman?'

'As yet I have not.'

'Then it is you who is odd.'

I was taken aback by his words.

Hodgkin assured me he meant no insult. 'The time will come when romance will overwhelm you.'

'Perhaps.'

'And my wish for you is that you will be free to do as you please, that you will not be compromised by the stubbornness of the dogma surrounding you.'

I am seeing Hodgkin in a new light, a less compatible light, for a time at least. The man's passions concerning the welfare of the aborigines will, without doubt, cause us to cross paths many times hence. But, at that moment, my foremost compulsions, for which I had sacrificed my own welfare, he chose to obscure with his private life.

7th March, 1828
Liverpool

In contemplating my previous entry this I have concluded —
about the most dedicated of men swirl their public passions, yet,
overwhelming these passions, seemingly beyond their control,
are their private ones. Must these men then forfeit the will to
govern themselves outright?

My voyage to Britain has yielded but one person with whom
I can share my thoughts completely, and who reciprocates with
the time to dedicate to them. John MacGregor, since our
acquaintance in Prince Edward Island, has set himself up as a
merchant and a commission agent, although, now have I
learned, his truer endeavour is that of writer. It was with some
trepidation that I found myself at his doorstep, trepidation that
swiftly dissipated as he welcomed me into his home.

I should think I have not found myself more at ease than
what I had been during the first days of our several together, for
ours has proven to be a deeper friendship than we had at first
thought, and our sharing of experiences has only served to
draw us closer. For we are indeed of a similar disposition — at
times anxious to move ahead in our ambitions, impatient with
incompetence, especially given to irritation about governance.
Moreover, we readily forsake the day-to-day business of
commerce for greater aspirations — his, to publish his wealth of

information about the North American Colonies; mine, to be the discoverer and purveyor of such knowledge.

While in Liverpool I have taken to visiting the offices of the *Liverpool Mercury* to inform them of the decline of the Boeothuck of Newfoundland and the aspirations of the Boeothuck Institution, and I have made the rounds of Liverpool's mills and foundries on behalf of my mercantile interests. With our business dealings completed for the day, MacGregor and I spent our evenings in deep discussion of the Colonies we each have left.

It is, of course, the subject of the Red Indians that most occupies us. I have instructed my friend on the native language and we are able, where possible, to dispense with the common English words and use instead the true language of the Boeothuck. At the sight of the Boeothuck objects I claimed for preservation from my inland journey, MacGregor was at once in awe and admiration. He saw immediately the value of the pieces, being particularly taken with the model of the canoe and the skin dress of the young child. I afforded him as much time as he wished to hold them and inspect their detail.

I told him, 'I have acquired also the most momentous Boeothuck bone relics to ever have been discovered.' It was not boasting on my part, and we both understood it as such.

His interest reached its pinnacle and I found myself feeling again the emotion I felt on first laying eyes inside the burial hut. I withdrew the skulls from the case and gently unwrapped them. I lay them then in the centre of the small table that separated us, MacGregor having set aside his glass of port.

The man's voice was stilled and for the moment all that could be heard was the dull rumble of wind at the rear of the house. I sat back in my chair and sipped port while MacGregor held the skulls one at a time. Such was my pleasure at seeing his reaction that I could barely refrain from commenting. Yet I held back, knowing there is that private moment between a profound object and its viewer that should not be interrupted.

'Cormack, these are rarities. Who could wish for more sacred remnants of a people?'

The man shares my conviction that these are treasures that need to be in the hands of civilization, and that when I return with them to Edinburgh they will find the place of esteem to which they are entitled. MacGregor, for a moment, drew back, realizing the privilege of viewing the pair, openly, intimately, not behind the restraints of a museum.

I think it a mark of our friendship. As day faded we raised our glasses in the firelight and on our honour declared that the Boeothuck would not pass from the earth but that every effort be made to save them from such an absolute fate.

I spoke to MacGregor then of Shanawdithit. I created a portrait of her which would have it seem she was in that very room with us. Her facial features, her manner of speaking to her dead relatives, her ease at drawing — all this and as much more as I could recall from memory. I retrieved this journal and read directly from its copious entries, all the while keeping a sharp but unobtrusive eye on my friend, exultant at the glimpse of him immersed in my words, making of him someone as truly concerned for the welfare of the aborigines as I.

'Cormack, she may well be the only one of her race. When you return to your island she shall consume you, completely.'

Others of close acquaintance have suggested such to me before, but coming as it did from the lips of the man whose perspective of the Natives seems most in keeping with my own, who has voyaged not far from them and known their aboriginal neighbours, the Micmac, I suddenly felt a tangible weight, a cross of a sort, though one that I will shoulder most willingly.

I said little, modesty of speech being the most truthful of rejoinders.

In these several days together we have talked of other things, of course, though none with the same interest or intensity. I have not known anyone quite like MacGregor. His is a generous and unabashed intelligence and he has little patience for those who would concern themselves overly with the minutiae of daily life. The band of his interests is as purposeful as my own, and his need to attend to it as earnest.

We have spent the most pleasurable of days traversing the countryside, for the mere satisfaction of escaping the staleness of the city and taking fresh air, and of course, indulging our appetite for discourse. The joy is in seeing where our conversation leads, on which of many tracts, all equally captivating, we will eventually settle.

It is refreshing that the conversation has not come to dwell solely on the fairer sex. Certainly neither of us is averse to the subject, although MacGregor, I gather, is, at this particular moment, no more interested in marriage than myself. He has already struck one hasty retreat from the altar, and in me he has found for once someone for whom its humour outdistances its pathos.

'I could have settled in Charlottetown and lived the life of a gentleman and husband, and charmed all who encircled me,' he said.

'Wholly predictable,' was my counter.

'Wholly regrettable.'

I laughed, and MacGregor correspondingly. 'The time may come,' he said, 'when I shall embrace the holy sacrament with zeal.'

'I, the same.'

'Until then, let it be said that freedom is relief, and I the sovereign of my soul.'

What can one do but admire the self-assurance of the man. And seize the companionship it offers, for rare are the makings of true friends and rarer still a willingness among men to concede it.

This evening, after our jaunt through the hills, we took supper at the Wayfarer's — prime mutton doused in the blackest and tastiest of gravies — drank a full bottle of claret, and sauntered home like fools. Scarce have been the times when I relished an evening more, for it was without pretense or the travesty of false honour.

At the house, before retiring, we warmed ourselves with a goodly dram. MacGregor thought he should end the evening with a poem, one of his own composition, one he considered most appropriate to the day. I think it a wise and knowing piece. Its final lines, I feel certain, will never escape my memory.

> *He who takes a man at his learned word*
> *is oft the foe, more oft the wretched Master*
> *But he who shares with man his learned word*
> *is at once the peer, the Compatriot long after.*

The words, I confess, have kept me from sleep. To my mind MacGregor's future as a writer is assured. One can hardly credit what the well-chosen line will do.

⨊

17th March, 1828
Edinburgh

Only now, in the wake of days of reflection on my life thus far,
a life strewn with its frustration as well as its triumphs — in
that no different than anyone who passes time on this earth —
will I confess I have dwelt on that single night more than any to
have passed before or since. My fondness for MacGregor was at
that hour as deep as any I have known, for man or woman. I
have not the wish to conceal it from this journal — for what
reason, I would ask, for seemingly I have no kin but history —
but think of it as a great wave that swept under me and receded.
A wave that crested again at each successive day in his company,
and one that I shall ever deny.

For what is the fondness of one man for another but to that
end a curse. Fondness, I will confess, that runs through the core
of my being. Would it be that he felt at that moment the same?
Could I tell by the brush of his arm against mine, his hand
tightening on my shoulder as we bid each other goodnight and
took to our rooms?

Me to lie awake much of the night in confusion at what had
overpowered me. I dared not think it outright, but had the
yearning saturate my mind until I knew not what was dream
and what was truth. My body thrusting against the bed in release
of the delirium. And sagging in guilt at the failure of restraint.

The endearment kept me at Liverpool three days longer than were my plans when I arrived. These were as wrought with pleasure and with ultimate inhibition as the others. My judgment — though, in truth, judgment is too precise a word — is that MacGregor was as confounded as myself. After that night he began to add to the simple pair of friends, and made of it a circle of other acquaintances, perhaps to ease the attention my presence alone was giving him. I do not know. Perhaps the enjoyment of our first days in one another's company had faded. I do not know, nor had I the courage to seek the answer.

One makes of life a portrait, a framed likeness, with the wish that those who view it will see what the person desires them to see. A smile there, a charming manner, a gesture, a wise word. Most others are accepting of the likeness, for they themselves have made their own. Some, like Jameson, see only the intellect, and hardly have interest beyond it. Or, like Hodgkin, like Carson, live in such a swirl of purposes that they glean from each whatever time allows.

To MacGregor I have drawn more of the portrait than I have ever. Tentatively, it is true, for one is forever wary of rendering oneself in so much detail that one appears the fool if the deed is not reciprocated.

MacGregor seemed to me to dwell on that portrait, to give it attention that left me to think it had stirred in him an admiration, a caring beyond mere sympathy. Whether he knew it to the depth that I knew in beholding him, I have failed to conclude. And ultimately, failed to pursue the answer.

It came the time when my leaving was not to be further delayed. Perhaps neither of us would admit it could be otherwise. When I made my departure known with certainty, it was in the light of a profuse invitation to return, and that alone made the departure tolerable. One could think it all the effect of the dearth of friends, of the lack of bearing, in a country I cannot think to call home. I fail to trust such thoughts. My obsession — that it is, for to deny it would be to embrace falsehood ultimately for my mind alone, and for what purpose ... my obsession may well have left me the fool.

~

2nd April, 1828

Newfoundland has become more home than any place I know.
Indeed as I write this, in the restrained comforts of the ship, I
have to confess a lure back to the Island, one I felt before I left
England once more for Scotland and took a last audience with
Jameson.

In summary this is what transpired.

At a summoning of his Natural History Society I unveiled
the cache of Boeothuck discoveries for the final time before their
presentation to the Museum. I was accorded the admiration of
members with the grace due a seasoned naturalist and to them
I am very thankful. Newfoundland might not be as far-flung as
the Indies or Tasmania, but it holds new and singular fascinations,
for never before had they held council with someone conversant
with a race on the threshold of extinction.

No longer do I feel the remotest urge to settle in Scotland.
To it I rightly accord my gratitude for fashioning me in the
way that it has, and it is indeed the fitting repository for what
marvels of natural history I have secured. Yet, beyond the
affinities of food and drink and speech there is little but loyalty
to Jameson holding me to that place. The man was wise indeed
to lead me as he did — I was destined for expanses beyond its
shores and in them I have found what contentment there is to
be had.

To say that I felt at odds while lingering in Edinburgh and Glasgow would not be excusing the truth. I grew anxious and at times must have proved an aggravation to the relatives in whose homes I had taken my lodging. My mind veered from the business dealings that were partly my mission there. I was too far removed from Newfoundland.

When it came the time to set passage back across the Atlantic, I did so on a ship leaving England. Before I boarded I wrote to MacGregor to inform him of my expected whereabouts in order that he know where to direct his further inquiries about the colony's fishery, and, should he begin to write about them as he intended, his questions regarding the Boeothuck.

I look forward to a spring crossing though I know the Atlantic at this time of year can have its turmoils. Physical turmoils I am well able to withstand, and think nothing of them, when their end is in sight.

20th April, 1828
St John's, Newfoundland

I spoke too soon of spring. Once across the greater expanse of ocean, we again encountered winter. We were forced to navigate past the icebergs that descend from Greenland, and find their way down the coast of Labrador. At night we took our bearings without the benefit of the moon and by day through the fogs of the Grand Banks. Strange then my thoughts — that it be home.

As we sailed over the Banks, arrayed as it was with Portuguese, Spaniards, and French, besides our own, one could hold no doubts but that we had arrived at the most prosperous fishing grounds in the world, every vessel and its dories intent on cod. Even our own dispatched a small boat, and in a short time returned with dinner enough for all aboard. Secured by lead jiggers sunk through the frigid waters, the fish was as fresh and lusty as any ever to be had, its flesh, as fishermen say, as white as the driven snow. We had our splendid taste of fish, and with it our first sight of the Island.

An odd, foreboding one she is, her headlands showing themselves like ramparts through the fogs. Sheered grey-black cliff much of it, although in some parts its clumps of wind-warped trees thicken to spruce forest inland. Salt sea ice filled crevices in the faces of the cliffs and snow in patches over what we could see of level land. The shoreline waged its own fight to rid itself of winter. In some places pans of ice had been heaped against the rock, waves flogging them, desperate to scour them to nothing.

'That will take days,' I told the onlookers, 'more likely weeks.'

In other places, ice had broken to bits so small it meshed into a broad blanket, quelling the waves beneath it. Dense surging sludge, lapping onshore.

'Slob ice, the Newfoundlanders call it,' I said with some authority to the Irish huddled around me. 'A vivid term, if an odd one,' thinking it no odder than many of their own.

By this time it was well known throughout the ship that I held far more knowledge of the Island than most. The passengers frequently sought me out with their questions, more so when we had our first sight of the place. Many of them had never set foot there before and were, with some apprehension, about to make it their new and lasting place of residence.

I did my best to set their minds at ease, painting a picture of the land in summer and fall, rather than the tumult that passes for spring. There were plenty of the Irish aboard, the vessel having stopped at Waterford after leaving the coast of England, assuredly the more eager of the lot, if also the more coarse of manner.

It is the years of a great Irish surge across the ocean, the peasantry clutching after another life for themselves. St John's is the destination of a good many from Waterford and the country surrounding it. The port has made its wealth on supplying the Newfoundland fishery, and few are those who don't have family lodged here already, turned fishermen from farmers.

'It'll soon be in your blood,' I told them. 'Once you set foot in a skiff and get your sea-legs, the fish as thick as maggots.'

It was what they wished to hear, the promise that made bearable the last days until we sailed past The Narrows and into

St John's Harbour. Then their Catholic souls settled, for what lay before their eyes could have passed for Ireland on a sour day, it being but a duller green. The blighted cadence of the voices to greet them as they ambled down the gangplank, all their worldly goods in two hands, assured them they would not be without their tot and tin whistle. They took heart and disappeared to the home fires of cousins prepared to cram them into their dwellings, there to await the building of their own.

I, too, now can't help but see it for the home that it is.

St John's, in truth, has all the promise of becoming one of the great Colonial cities of the world. What she lacks in cleanliness and architecture, she more than makes up for in physical beauty. No harbour I have entered is more perfect. The narrowness of its channel, quickly broadening into a basin of substantial, yet highly practical proportions, leaves one imagining the Creator could not have done a finer job.

Of course, upon actually stepping foot on its thoroughfares one is immediately overwhelmed by the fishiness of the place. It is, after all, a cod port far out of proportion to anything else. Its waterline, at least that on its northern side, is so dense with finger piers one would think it possible to leap from pier to pier the full length of the harbour without danger of falling in. Set back from them are the storehouses and cod-drying stages making up a merchant's 'Room.' All this and the heart of the world's greatest sealing enterprise besides.

It is the March seal hunt that proves the most amazing sight to one mellowed in the herbage of England. Around the time of St Patrick's Day — that in itself a dizzying circumstance to witness — the pathway closest to the harbour and running parallel to it teems with men, young and old, every one of them anxious for their voyage to the ice floes. Many have made their way from the villages outside the town, from places with which I am now familiar — Bay Bulls, Renews, Portugal Cove. One would think the waterfront is the centre of enterprise in the Americas, and I would venture to say, for that moment it is. Surely there could not be more bustle in Boston or Brazil.

The harbour sees the arrival of countless schooners in addition to its own, all gathering what provisions they can at the best prices to be found. Each schooner captain eventually settles on his complement of seafarers, the luckiest bearing their own muskets, the others clubs especially fashioned for the killing of their game. I have never laid eyes on a prouder lot of vagabonds.

'It's a ten-pound note I'll come away with, sir. In me hands, sir. You'll not do better than that in six weeks.' I wouldn't deny the man his ardour for the adventure. For by the look of him — in threadbare coat and poor excuse for footwear about to set all day on ice — he is in desperate need of cash. Though it was not himself he is thinking of. It is a wife and children. I never dare to inquire as to how many.

'They'll have their molasses and their flour, that they will,' he said. 'And you, sir, what might you be? Besides a Scot, which I can tell well enough. A trader then, an agent?'

In truth I am, though hardly one of the better known it would seem. I have not devoted the time to set myself up as well as I might, though at that moment with some regret, for it was obvious there was money changing hands, and once the schooners returned, the commerce could only increase.

That moment comes, as is the sealer's promise, but a few weeks later. The first of the returning schooners makes its way through The Narrows in weather hardly less frigid than when it left. There is jubilation — nothing short of it — at being the first, and before the schooner is near enough to the wharf to clearly make out a face, comes the count of pelts and a sketch of success for all the vessels.

'Not one lost!' hopefully is the shout. 'Not a man.' For that more than anything is what the crowd wants to hear. For no doubt about it, sealing is a treacherous affair. Scampering over the vast fields of sea ice, the wind and sleet no better than ice candles prodding at a man to get the job done, get the seal flattened to the floe and a knife run the length of him, the pelt with its blubber hooked and roped for hauling back to the ship. From what I surmise, the bloodier the laneway over the ice to the ship, the broader the smiles on their faces. Certainly the broader the smile on the Captain's face, and the merchant's whose ship it is, waiting on the wharf at its return. For though the sealer will have his ten pounds, the merchant will have hundreds times that and more.

The world it seems is mad for seal oil, mad to have it fill their lamps. And it is the oil that I now have my fill of, on days I make my way from the wharves to Water Street, and on towards my residence on Duckworth. Indeed, I have my fill in more ways than any man with a pair of nostrils could care for. Since my return the wharves and premises have become the domain of the seal skinners whose job it is to separate the fat from the pelt. They have their seal-skinning knives and their seal-skinning pidgin talk, the use of one as fast as the use of the other. Despite myself, I can do nothing but stop and stare at the line of them set in front of their broad makeshift tables — wool-capped, bearded men, apprentices at their side, lords of the wharfs and grease-dandies at their trade.

It is not this business that is the cause of my constraint. It is that of the blubber once it makes its way into its vats, left to render in the sun. Newfoundland has no spring to speak of, as I have said, but once the sun does take hold and give the blubber the heat it is wanting, then the odour that issues from it is hardly to be described. I have to say that I have encountered nothing to rival it in the bilge of any ship. And can one but imagine a port whose waterfront is home to a succession of these large squarish wooden vats, from one end of it to the other! One's imagination is best left stored for other purposes.

I would have thought the mud — of which the thaws of spring now slick my boots with their undue share — would be an equal deterrent. But I, the returning St John's man, have learned to navigate the streets, winding though they do, and retracting in width numerous times, and for no apparent reason than the whim of a store builder on any given day.

It is a bracing town then in which to reside. Yet what it lacks in breeding it more than makes up for in an exuberance of spirit. And I have much more than profits to hold me to Newfoundland.

I had not long crossed the threshold on Duckworth upon my return, my boots removed and scraped of their globs of mud outside, before I was alerted to the fact that in my absence my partner in mercantile trade had helped to refill my dwindling coffers, and that the goods which I had arranged for in Liverpool would soon arrive and refill them more. What else will arrive from Liverpool in the months to come I also wonder — what word of MacGregor, of his state of mind, what in his words to hearten me?

NONOSA

NONOSA PADDLED THE HEAD canoe, Shanaw curled against his legs, caribou fur wrapped tightly around her.

Despite the heartache of his daughter, Nonosa felt the promise of the days ahead. He held fiercely to the notion that the Kindred clans would prosper by the sea. That by the sea he would hold them together.

The death of Remesh had lifted a burden from the Kindred, though Nonosa dared not utter the thought, not even to his daughter. Least of all his wife. He no longer trusted Biesta to keep private the words between them.

With one person only he shared his relief. Coshee looked at him with hard and knowing silence, turned to the Nookwashish and the Dohwashish waiting at the water's edge, welcomed them with more eagerness than it seemed his frail body was capable.

His wife Marshuit went to Lerenn, held her hands, poured out her words of sympathy. The other women of the Kanwashish followed, all except Biesta who lingered at a distance from them, atop the riverbank.

Shanaw ran to Biesta, clung to her and to Patria in her arms. Biesta led her to their lodge. She gathered her close, retrieved from her the story of the death of Remesh.

'You are a brave woman,' Biesta said.

She was the first to call her a woman. Shanaw took comfort in it, and in the uncommon gentleness of Biesta's voice.

'Some are frightened of you — I have seen it already — but do not be frightened of them. Think only what a courageous thing you have done. For Remesh was a wicked man.'

She drew Shanaw even closer to her. The two cried in each other's arms.

In some ways for all clans it was a wearisome, awkward time, in others a revelation. For pride and ambition, such crosscurrents filling the air when last the clans had been together, were finally put aside.

Biesta and Lerenn avoided each other, though neither turned away when finally they met. There grew an understanding between two women who had shared the same marriage bed, who together had known many faces of Remesh. Both had been numbed by his temper, and both felt relief they would not have to endure it again.

Lerenn shed tears at the death of her husband, only because of the pain it caused the boy. For Sojon was the one to grieve most deeply. His triumphant world had suddenly been crushed. He was unable to be the boy he had been, as much as he yearned for it. He became the constant centre of attention, for wretched reasons he could not control.

The other children sought out their leaders in the games they played, but walked away sorely disappointed, for Sojon and Shanaw could not bear the presence of each other. There reeled a fearfulness between the two that Biesta and Lerenn knew must be brought to an end. The mothers decided that when the clans began their journey downriver to the sea, it would be the four of them together in canoe. But even there Shanaw and Sojon held to their silent, unspoken strife. More callous it was than ever.

THE DEATH OF REMESH drew Nonosa to Biesta. There were times when Démas faded from his memory and only Biesta remained.

Within the darkness of the sleeping furs he probed for relief from the burdens that had recently befallen him. He wished an eager passage for his hardened cock, the sounds of waves a rhythm for his craving. Biesta had no wish to deny him.

But what Nonosa discerned when the deed was done was relief, not pleasure. When during the night she curled away from him, he found it strange, as if she had grown used to sleeping alone and it was to her liking. He questioned her.

'A woman has her ways,' she said. 'Ways that change as she grows older.'

What did he know of woman's ways? In some things — in her new closeness to Shanaw — he found reason to be pleased. He curled away himself and fell asleep.

The truth was Biesta had taken someone into their bed after Nonosa had gone away. No one knew of it except the young clansman himself and no one would ever know unless he chose to tell.

Kalif had been bursting to find a place for his cock. Each time Biesta's eyes fell on him it was as if every muscle in his body ached for it. A glance between them confirmed he would turn crazy with lust if it did not happen soon. Yet it was her choice, her lasting stare that drew him to her lodge late one night, the rest of the camp asleep.

It was she who stripped him bare, ran her hands slowly down his smooth, lithe frame, seizing his buttocks, relishing their firmness. It was she who felled him to the furs and opened her legs to him, covering his mouth with one hand so his ecstasy would not wake the child. When he erupted so quickly, she laughed in his ear and told him he should be proud to bear such a lively spear, one a wife would crave.

She swore him to silence. Pored over his nakedness as he dressed and slipped away.

Was it wrong to lead the young clansman to relief from his craving? She had seen his torment in being without the prospect of a wife, through no fault of his own. Where might he have gone to satisfy his lust? Already there were young girls of his own clan fearful of him.

Kalif's life changed when the three clans came together. Suddenly every choice in a wife was before him. The night with Biesta he confided to the past, as did Biesta, though she would remember it more often. When Biesta saw him drifting among young women of the other clans, his pleasure obvious, her heart she forced to turn, against her will, for the night had been one to thrill her. She took pleasure in curling away from Nonosa knowing that the strongest, most virile young clansmen had taken to her with lust worthy of women much younger than herself.

IT WAS SAID AMONG the Kindred women that wise men made senseless lovers. In lovemaking Nonosa chased the head of his cock, and was satisfied when it was satisfied. He liked Biesta well enough, and truly thought her the best wife for him. But he now grew suspicious of her tongue and gave little thought to their life together except as father and mother to their children. He was beside her when he was needed, and she beside him when he needed her. That was as he wished it, and never in his head did he hold the thought of another clansman stiffened against her.

His thoughts were of the fortunes of his people. He stood tall as their SpiritMan, irrefutable leader of the three clans together. As was their wish, he led them to the sea and there set to directing their lives. By the sea they would unite, he proclaimed, and hold together as one Kindred.

He declared a communal marriage of the new young couples. 'To celebrate the rebirth of the clans!'

It was the most exuberant, the most harmonious ceremony any of them could remember. The clans feasted endlessly on fish and seal and walrus. Marvellous stories were told of the Kindred past. Long into the night they sang and the eager new husbands danced around the fire with fervent charm. At the end Nonosa arose and spread his arms, his words filling the night sky.

'Now our young couples shall know what it is to revel in desire, their bodies certain match for their yearnings. Tomorrow those same young men will paddle to the islands and slaughter sea-birds until the canoes can hold no more. Return home they will to wives who will clean the kill and feed every one of us until we are glutted with food. We are Kindred basking in the favour of the Spirits.'

That they were favoured by the Spirits was beyond doubt. The supply of food was the most they had ever known.

Even Lerenn walked about the camp with a contentment, sheathed though it was by her solitary ways. Lerenn had changed. She did her share of work, equal to that of any woman. She did not complain. It was much more than many had expected of a leader's woman so violently made a widow.

Lerenn took to confiding in Biesta, yet there was the awkward circumstance still of Sojon. The boy kept his distance from Biesta as he did Shanaw. Try as the two women did to get him past his suspicions, they only sank deeper within him.

There was solace to be found in Shanaw, for the girl it seemed had gained new courage. And she was not without her quiet moments of abandon, especially after her father had taken the long hollow leg bone of a bird, bored holes in it and made of it a curio of sounds. Shanaw played with it endlessly, by herself, then with prompting while her parents and sister watched. More and more often she withdrew it from inside her mantle and rendered its few notes before other children. The flute was above all a mystery, a fascination sparking their envy. Shanaw became once again the centre of their attention. She poked at it, chose her times to give attention back, gradually attached herself to the world outside her family.

Over the summer Sojon grew more peevish, a constant aggravation. Finally, with the consent of Lerenn, Nonosa took Sojon aside, to put an end to his quarrelsome ways. Against the boy's wishes, he set off with him in canoe, paddled away from shore, until his mother Lerenn was a speck in the distance.

There floated the two of them alone, nothing to hold to but the open sea. He made Sojon turn and face him from the bow. 'You are of an age, Sojon, to know the ways of a man. This sulking will not bring your father back.'

Sojon stiffened in anger. 'Remesh would strike you dead. He would drive his spear into you and watch every drop of blood drain away!'

Nonosa peered deeply into his eyes until Sojon's head fell forward. 'Look at me, Sojon! Look at me!'

The boy lifted his head, tears streaming down his face.

'The Spirits brought peace between our people ...'

'Trickster!' Sojon sputtered. 'You are no SpiritMan!'

'A boy full of lies and hate.'

'You were not chosen by the Spirits!' the boy yelled at him. 'Wife-stealer!'

Nonosa could not stop himself, though it was a mere boy he was condemning, though he knew it was Remesh's words the boy had spoken.

'The Spirits will strike you, Sojon, like they did your father.'

'Trickster! Fool!'

'Strike you they will!'

Suddenly — as if in answer to his warning — the waters near the canoe turned black. The rounded back of a whale sprang from the depths, broke the surface, grazed their canoe.

Nonosa had seen whales many times before, though always from a distance. Never had the massive hulk come so close to a canoe. Never this shiny, black, endless expanse of hide.

Silenced they were, struck frantically dumb.

The whale's tail, a colossal spread of briny wings, rose clear of the water, then followed the beast into the abyss below.

Just when the pair thought the whale gone, it rose again from the depths, a thick, colossal heft of rock, its head pockmarked by white, encrusted mounds. The whale rose straight up, then fell forward, its massive mouth agape.

A fibrous horde of baleen leered at them. The head smashed against the water, narrowly missed the canoe, sent it reeling in its trough. Sojon cowered, clutched the gunnels where they narrowed at the bow. Nonosa seized his paddle and with frenzied strokes thrust the canoe into calmer waters.

As they escaped the worst of it, the hulking whale resurfaced. Its broad back rose behind the canoe, bore down on it. Nonosa stood up, turned, lunged at the expanse of hide with his paddle, a desperate bid to force the canoe out of its path.

Sojon seized his own paddle, sprung upright in wild, maniacal rage. Flung the paddle spear-like at Nonosa. It struck blunt into his back. The SpiritMan arched in pain. His body pitched. Toppled from the canoe.

Nonosa struggled to the surface in the wake of the whale. The beast had curved under the canoe, rose up, set the boat to rest along its back. Swam with it in the direction of the shore. Then set it down to float again. The whale swam free. Sojon clutched the remaining paddle and made his way to shore.

The sea had left him dazed, unscathed.

From that day forward the whale was thought a demon. Savage whale, Sojon called it, attacking the canoe, hurling Nonosa overboard. Sojon had made it to shore on his own, without sign of Nonosa. He bore little expectation their SpiritMan would again be seen alive.

Sojon secretly wallowed in the pain that engulfed Shanaw when a voice rumbled from a lookout. 'Nonosa!' It drew the frenzied camp to the water's edge.

Kalif and the strongest paddlers had dragged their canoes into the water and now sprinted away in search of him. Alive indeed he was, though barely able to hold to the side of a canoe when they finally found him.

They dragged Nonosa through the water to lie prone onshore. Biesta and the two children crying over him, the rest of the Kindred hovering nearby. There came his words, brief and scattered. He said nothing of how he came to fall from the canoe, told instead of not losing his mind to the water, to the whale, of the fight to keep his nostrils free in the air. When finally the boy Sojon stood over him, there passed between them a bitter wordless stare.

Nonosa recovered, was left to ponder in silence what had happened. And so, too, the boy. Sojon drew even further into himself, though gone was his querulousness. Replaced with a deep, impossible gravity.

AN UNEASY TRUCE SETTLED between Sojon and Nonosa, between Sojon and Shanaw.

One day, several seasons after the near-drowning of Nonosa, when the Kindred had again come together on the coast, Biesta went with Lerenn in canoe to an island offshore to collect yellowberries. At the insistence of the mothers, Sojon and Shanaw went with them.

The warm weather had turned the treeless island orange-gold with the prized berry of the Kindred. A stiff wind kept away the flies, made of it a cherished summer's day.

Sojon, forever the rival, turned sour over how quickly Shanaw picked the berries, how her container brimmed with them well before his own. When Shanaw stood up to take it to Biesta, Sojon pushed her aside. The berries spilt onto the ground.

'Spirits curse you,' he hissed.

It frightened the girl. For now Sojon was stoutly muscled, had grown into a bullish boy.

Yet she did not let him go unchallenged. She ran at him and struck him to the moss-covered ground. He was quickly atop her, had her pinned to the ground, one of his knees lodged between her thighs. He seized a heavy stone, drew his hand above her head.

Just at that moment Biesta reached them, struck the weapon from his hand.

'I would not have done it,' he shouted. 'I am not a coward! One day she will not have her father to answer for her.'

Shanaw was left in tears, though she kept courage enough not to turn away from him. Sojon strode off. When Shanaw reached the camp at the end of the day, she ran to Nonosa and told him what had happened.

'What will become of him?' she asked in tears.

Nonosa had no answer, except that she stay away from Sojon. For it seemed he would be forever sheathed in cruelty.

'What would the Spirits have us do? Are you not their Messenger?'

Nonosa stopped. It was not just more of her questions. What did the Spirits wish him do, for the sake of all the clans?

'The Spirits have no desire for the Kindred to suffer at the hands of Sojon.'

A statement of their SpiritMan. One reasonable and wise. One with consequences he had no wish to ponder.

ALONE AND AWAY FROM his people, only then would Nonosa dwell on his days as the SpiritMan. Sometimes it was to the site of Démas's grave that he escaped.

How his life had twisted since she died. If the Spirits had not taken her away, would there not be another history of the Kindred, one not of wife quarrels, of vengeance and slaying?

What answer was there but that he had prevailed above all others, that the Kindred had grown stronger for it.

What mattered but that? The clans' survival. That of the child he held to his heart, in the likeness of her mother. He would not have her grow to womanhood tormented by Sojon. Nor the Kindred the victims of his wrath.

Sojon's hateful ways had lodged ever more deeply among the Kindred. Nonosa went first to Coshee and his wife.

Coshee, feeble now, spent his days outdoors. Marshuit hovered nearby, covered and uncovered him with furs, brushed away the flies. Coshee sat eager for attention, though he knew full well Nonosa was now the only one the Kindred followed.

Nonosa came with the grave secret of Sojon the cause of his near drowning.

'Why, Nonosa, have you kept this to yourself?' Coshee said, his hands quivering even as he held them together in his lap.

'For the Kindred's sake. But now I see an evil lurk that will never leave him.'

'He is still a boy,' said Marshuit.

'Too soon a man.'

Coshee pondered Nonosa's words. 'Take him with you, Nonosa, in the canoe once again. Give him the chance to purge the past.'

The notion spread among the Kindred. Nonosa considered it. He would do as they wished.

Sojon could not escape the gravity of what was set before him — the dire warnings, the frightful price of ignoring them. Lerenn pleaded for him to change, for she worried desperately about what would become of the boy.

The Kindred set their minds on the journey of Nonosa and Sojon. As if it were a final treaty with the past, a final clearing of a path ahead. The clans gathered in a half-circle on the shoreline, grimly chanting their praises.

The sun had begun to show itself from behind the morning's bank of fog. Coshee declared it would turn a fair, near-windless day, a favoured day from the Spirits.

Nonosa stood beside the canoe as it lapped onshore, half in, half out of the water, its bottom scraped by restless pebbles. He placed his spear inside the canoe. 'What of their store will the Spirits bestow on us today?'

Nonosa stood a solemn man. Sojon, his ward, a tamed and limpid boy, at least in the face he showed the world. He withdrew reluctantly from the clutches of Lerenn and took to the bow of the canoe.

Nonosa broke the chant with another one, the old and familiar one.

'*Motherfather, feed me. Strong of heart, strong of head, ever now, ever after. Fathermother, feed me.*'

Coshee raised his hand as best he could, proclaimed his fiercest hope. 'Spirits within our SpiritMan, steer them on their journey.'

Sojon faced the open sea. Nonosa pushed the canoe into the water and thrust himself aboard in one unbroken motion. The first push of their paddles freed the canoe from the shoreline.

The Kindred held together, squinted into the sun with muttered expectations. When the canoe turned a distant mark, they began to drift away. Left Lerenn and Biesta alone, unmoving. The two remained apart, planted to the sand, each holding to her thoughts about the boy.

A pair of mothers for the child, fearful of the place he had made for himself in the world, fearful of the power of a SpiritMan on such a headstrong son. The morning's breeze no longer brushed their furs. They drifted away, though all the while they clutched to their hearts the hope that this was the day the boy would find a proper home among his people.

ON THE OPEN WATER Nonosa couldn't help but think he was once again following his heart in making a journey in the direction of the rising sun. Nor could a child feel anything but wonder at how the sun filled the sea and sky, perpetual in the way one poured into the other, the way the Kindred shrank into its vastness.

What was such a day as this, thought Nonosa, but one the Spirits had fashioned to change the Kindred fortune. Sun streamed past the remaining strands of fog, burned it away until the glint of sun on the salt water surrounded the canoe, made of it a charmed, prophetic shelter. Could Sojon do anything but embrace the brilliance of the sea, succumb to the world that overwhelmed his own?

The boy said nothing. He kept a steady pace, mute as if mesmerized at the thought of what might follow. Straight on they paddled, the sun rising before them, the morning's chill retreating. Nonosa filled the air with talk about the weather, about the islands in the distance, about the fish that swarmed the waters beneath them. Sojon paddled on in silence.

Soon they were far out of sight of any Kindred, even those with the curiosity to take to the lookouts. From time to time Nonosa would stop his paddling, tell the boy to do the same. Would raise a bare arm in the air to study the nature of the wind.

They reached the bird island where Tuanon lay buried.

Nonosa drew the canoe to the far side of it. The canoe drifted toward shore. Sea-birds — gulls and guillemots and dovekies — filled the air in screeching confusion, arced and spiralled and let it be known they had no need for creatures who only ever came for slaughter.

The young had learned to fly, joined in the screeching hordes, bold and brash. Followed the lead of their elders in the way they swooped and swirled, displaying prowess they had not earned.

Nonosa knew it a fitting place for the boy.

Nonosa's brother, Tuanon, first victim of the turmoil between the clans, lay within the island's rock. Spirit voices charged the air, life's canopy of birds cried ceaselessly. Nature's covering, Spirits' words of consent.

On the mind of the SpiritMan were thoughts of raucous Spirits drawing back their own, binding the ends of a course begun with the snatching away of Démas. *The Spirits deliver. Now they take away.*

They alone shaped the pathways of the Kindred, resumed their charge when the clans fell from them. He, Nonosa, but their voice, the Spirit voice acting through him, through him.

It frightened the child, what Nonosa told him was the cleansing of his ways. Sojon could hardly bear the words, for they were vacant, passionless. They loomed over him, drove themselves beyond him to another time.

At the island's only landing spot, Nonosa ordered the boy from the canoe onto the sea-bird home. He the stranger, the intruder among creatures whose wish was to be rid of him. The birds scattered, encircled Sojon, marked his boundaries.

'Sojon,' said the SpiritMan. 'No longer are you the fighter. The moaner. The one who would strike another man into the water and leave him there for dead.' Then even louder — 'The measure of a man you'll know. Ready to plunge into that water and atone for your treachery.'

Sojon was now a diminished clump of a boy, hardly the wilful menace. For the SpiritMan had cast himself the commander of the child, the rightful master of his mind. With a piercing cacophony to embed it in his very bones.

Sojon held tight his fear, showed Nonosa a mute, neglected soul.

But when the final, truthful moment came, when Nonosa the Spirit-Man made him walk the beach to where it turned to cliff, to where it gave way to sheer, unforgiving precipice, then did Sojon rise up and hold his own. For his terror now was absolute, his only hope to confront the man blunting his every move.

Sojon suddenly dodged him. Raced for the canoe.

He seized the spear Nonosa had left behind. He turned with it in his hands.

Just as Nonosa lurched after him. Lurched straight into it. Just as Sojon thrust it forward.

Sojon saw the spear tip sink into hide, saw the spear fall away, the end of it snag the hide. Sojon grabbed the length of cord and jerked it tight!

The SpiritMan fell to the rocks, hands clasped to the wound. Rose again. Staggered onward in pursuit of the boy, the boy at the other end of the cord imbedded in Nonosa's gut.

The boy stumbled. The bloodied hand of Nonosa latched onto him. Hauled him to his feet. In his savage grip Nonosa drove him along the cliff edge. 'Your father's son!' yelled the SpiritMan. 'His kind the Kindred must never know again.'

Sojon's hatred unbound — 'You would have me dead!'

It incited the SpiritMan, inflamed his stride. Sojon stumbled ahead of him, at the end of his outstretched arm.

The terror-stricken boy flared again, words his only hope. 'The Spirits damn you, Nonosa!' He turned and twisted to wrench himself free. Nonosa gripped him harder, jerked the squirming boy further up the cliffside.

Once he reached the fateful height, he clasped his hands to Sojon's shoulders and held him tight to his own chest, the boy face forward, straight at the open sea.

'The Spirits are calling, Sojon! Their cries fill your heart!'

Sea-bird squawks bore into the boy, his exhausted body sagged, then jolted erect one final time, in senseless defiance of the sea. Clung in desperation for reprieve.

'The sea!' Nonosa called. '*Ever now, ever after!*'

And with those words Nonosa, SpiritMan, raised Sojon stiffly upwards with both hands. For a moment saw the boy's feet dangle free of the rock. Saw the wind blow through him.

With a sudden thrust of his arms, Nonosa flung the boy away from him, flung the boy beyond the precipice!

Heard his screech above the screeching sea-birds, heard him wail toward the deep, fomenting sea.

Nonosa had himself been flung, had himself been torn out and over the godless precipice!

Felled by the end of cord wound taut around young Sojon's hand.

SHANAW HAD STOPPED PLAYING her bone flute when the canoes struck the shore. But her bid to charm the Spirits had passed to nothing.

She lay the flute on the sand at the bottom of the pit. Fires burned on either side, thin tongues of flame flickering against its walls, lighting them, lighting the faces of the Kindred who ringed the edge of the pit, looking down.

In silence the naked body of the child was brought forth, then draped into the arms of Coshee, though he could only hold him up with help. Chanting charged the night, brought vague, restless streaks of coloured light across the sky.

'As the Spirits wished,' Coshee said, his voice an aged croak.

The body of the boy passed into the arms of Kalif, who descended one end of the pit, sand foundering before him with each step. Kalif laid the body face down atop the flute.

The Kindred buried Sojon in sand deeper than the height of a man. They buried him, head to the west, feet to the east. Shanaw placed the tusk from her father's first walrus kill next to the head of the boy, in thankfulness to the Spirits for taking away the scourge of her life.

Next to his shoulder Lerenn, her grief the deepest of them all, placed the pair of knives that were his favourites. The boy's skill as a hunter had barely been tested, but every person of the Kindred clans knew there would come days when they would long for a hunter with such skills as those Sojon would have acquired as a man.

Biesta, at his head, set down a handful of darts and a bow, for killing birds he would meet on his way to face the Spirits. Where his drowned body had been found afloat, on the far side of the island, hovered a mass of screeching birds.

Perhaps, said Biesta, the birds screeched at the body of Nonosa, sunk to the bottom, a cord length away from the boy.

The clansmen who found him had wrapped Nonosa's body in their own body furs, befitting a SpiritMan, and laid it in the bottom of one canoe. In the other was laid the equally sodden body of the boy, now the cursed boy who brought the long-loved Nonosa to his death.

Into the burial pit was carried a broad flat stone. Coshee called for Kalif to lay it atop the back of Sojon, to keep forever buried what was lodged within the boy.

The pit was refilled with sand, boulders carried from a stream nearby and piled to cover it. Then did Coshee speak once again to the Kindred, who had encircled the mound with their chanting. 'Now among ourselves — peace.' Declared with what strength his withered body would allow.

Nonosa's body they laid in a crevice, one as close to Démas's grave as could be found. They mounded it with rock. The Kindred stood together, chanted and grieved. Grieved for many days more.

Among them were those who said Nonosa was happiest now, being with the one he had always loved the most.

BIESTA GRIEVED FOR NONOSA, but more for the boy who had been born her son, whose short life had amounted to nothing. What would become of her, she wondered. She wished for a clansman. Perhaps Kalif would take her as a second wife. Before long she began to dwell on such a plan, though it would never come to be. Kalif was happy with the woman he married, who was now close to giving birth. They wished it to be a boy.

Shanaw, without her father, became a lost and melancholic soul. She drew herself to Biesta, although there would be forever a distance between the two. She held to her father's independent ways.

Shanaw turned into a woman. She struck a hardened, resolute figure each time she stood on the rocks of the shoreline and looked with hunger out to sea.

SHANNON

O N SUNDAY SHANNON, HER visitors, and Simon cross the Strait of Belle Isle to Labrador. They explore a bit of the coastline, driving a short distance into Quebec, then backtrack and make their way to the historic lighthouse at L'Anse Amour, and finally to the Maritime Archaic burial mound along the same road.

The essence of the burial mound is, of course, what took place below the boulders several millennia ago. Simon relates to Marta and Lars the story of the twelve-year-old child who was buried there.

The image is implanted in Shannon's mind in a way it has not been previously. The night before, with Simon asleep on an air mattress nearby, she had read the last chapter of the book.

There's a profundity to Simon's telling of the story, the more so because of Markus playing in the sand at the edge of the mound. Simon would have it appear the Maritime Archaic child is related to them all. To Simon himself at least, Shannon thinks. In time there may well be proven a genealogical link between the Maritime Archaic and the Innu.

Simon makes no attempt to disguise the fact he's bothered by the mound. The grave itself is empty. The remains were removed when the site was excavated, and have never been reburied. Shannon has always assumed the study of the skeleton to be ongoing.

'It's been thirty years. A bit of a long process in that case.'

'There are new research techniques being developed all the time,' Shannon replies in mild defence.

'They could easily make 3-D computer records of the bones,' says Lars.

'Of course they could,' says Simon. 'Let them keep one or two for future analysis and rebury the rest.'

It is left to Shannon to point out that it's a delicate issue. Lars wants to know more.

'Because,' says Simon, 'it involves Aboriginals. Real, live Aboriginals.'

It's getting late. Markus is getting fussy. He needs a nap and they need to catch the return ferry. Except for Simon, who will drive on to Red Bay for school the next day.

He makes his farewell to the others, wishing them a safe return. They are all genuinely pleased to have spent time together. He has a moment alone with Shannon before he boards his truck. 'Next time you'll have to come to Red Bay.' Which she takes as a convenient way of saying there will be a next time.

'For sure.' She kisses him lightly on the cheek.

There's a touch of his hand though her hair, lingering at the back of her neck.

THERE ARE TIMES IN the days that follow when she feels consumed with the anticipation of spending more time with him. After her visitors no longer take her attention.

Marta and her family stay another day before packing up their car for the drive back to Deer Lake, where they will catch a flight to Montreal, then another back to Norway. Overall, the visit has gone very well. They've connected to the place, and all three have been at ease with each other. They insist Shannon plan a holiday to Norway.

'We'll show you all the sights of Oslo,' says Lars. 'You'll eat very well.'

'Sign me up.'

Such a reality is a long way away. She's never admitted to Marta her regret at not going to their wedding, and she's long ago given up the idea of making amends.

'Bring Simon if you like,' Marta says. There's the subtext of a moment's eye contact, a knowing half-smile.

Shannon bends down and kisses Markus goodbye. It is the first time she has kissed him, or any child, for a long time. It is the softness of his cheek, the young child smell. Unexpectedly, he wraps his arms around her neck and hugs her tightly.

'Now you absolutely have to come,' Marta says. 'You've won his heart. He never does that, only with family.'

Shannon buries the embarrassment of her emotion in Marta's embrace, in the genuine affection she has for her friend. She embraces Lars as well, stiffly, lightly, only glancing the physical reality of it.

And then the three of them are gone, out of her life as quickly as they came in. The apartment seems strangely silent, but full of them still.

It is morning — not the time to be calling Simon.

She lounges about for an hour, unable to think about work. Early that evening she and Simon talk on the phone. Evening follows evening. The familiarity with each other accelerating with each call. And where is it all leading? That will make itself known. Give it time, she thinks, although she has never been one to allow time for relationships to unfold.

For now she'll admit she is the one thoroughly smitten. He no doubt has more control of his affection, having been previously smitten to the point of divorce, a youngster in the wake.

THEN, JUST AS SHE sees something in the future, the past collapses around her.

'It's Jerome. Is this Shannon?' She inwardly flares at the fact that he would have her phone number.

'Yes it is.'

'I got some bad news. Your Aunt Bertha. I'm sorry to have to tell you. A heart attack. She was found dead this morning at her kitchen table.'

There are other details. They fade past her. She mumbles something.

'I'm sorry, but I knew you would want to know.'

'Thank you.'

'Will I call you when they decide the time of the funeral? Her daughter has to get here from Alberta.'

'Yes. Please.'

She hangs up the phone and gathers herself into a corner of the sofa. The weight of the news holds her there. Bertha was old and not well, which should have been warning enough. After a long while the phone rings again. It's Simon.

She had mentioned Bertha briefly to him. She hadn't gone into any details, anything about how fond she had grown of her. Or how she hadn't seen her that weekend as she had planned. How Marta's visit had then come upon her so quickly.

'I'm really sorry.'

'I know you are. I'll call you tomorrow. I'm not up to talking about it much at the moment.'

'Sure you're okay?'

'I'm okay.'

Shannon is surprised at how hard it has hit her. All the years she was away she felt there was something. That Conche, in whatever small way, was still the place she could come back to. It wasn't home anymore. But it was the place where as a child she had been happy, where there was someone who remembered that, who had some of those same memories of her.

It's a severing of a connection to her mother. Now there's no one. She always knew that eventually it would have to come to this. But somehow she thought there would be time. For what? Time to hold to that connection a while longer, to strengthen it. There would never be the trip to Corner

Brook, a long talk over dinner, the night in the Glynmill Inn, breakfast looking out on the fall colours.

Later that evening she walks to a grocery store and buys salt cod, potatoes, and salt pork. She cuts up the fish and puts it in water to soak overnight.

The memories cause her no end of heartache. An intense aloneness imbeds itself in her. Nothing seems to help much. Not her call to Patti. Not another of Simon's calls to her.

She takes another day off work. That evening, with the notebook open on the counter, she makes a meal to remember Bertha.

THE FUNERAL IS AWKWARD. She knows few people, although they all seem to know who she is. Gail from Alberta, Beverly from St. John's, neither is surprised to see her. Word had circulated before she arrived. She is an outsider, a step removed from the inner family circle. Jerome and Marie make a feeble attempt to gather her in, and, when she resists, are satisfied to have tried.

There has been a wake in the good Catholic tradition. Which she prudently stayed away from. Bertha was a formidable pillar of the church and the funeral service reflects it. It includes a prayer in Latin, at her own request from what Shannon overhears from the pew ahead. All the while there are only the memories of Bertha shuffling around her kitchen to make any of it real to Shannon. The priest offers a eulogy of a kind, about Bertha's faith, her work for the church. Nothing of the Bertha she knew. She is distracted, and seems to focus only on the coffin set at the base of the altar steps, in a church she recalls vividly from childhood.

At the gravesite she stands close enough to still see the coffin, but removed from the family members. She knows she can't possibly bear the grief of her daughters, for she knows that depth of grief well enough. What she bears is a sorrow-filled heart, for Bertha was the only new family friend she'd had in years. A singular friendship for them both, gone now, still fresh. Just as the service is ending she slips from the scene, unwilling to endure it to the end.

A gathering at the house follows, and it would be wrong of her not to be there. It seems the great weight of family mourning is past. The kitchen is full of stories of the woman who spent most of her life in that very room. If the noise ceased surely there would be the strains of her voice. Shannon has her stories to contribute and then she prepares to leave. There are promises made to see each other when she is next in St. John's, or if she's ever in Grand Prairie, promises that, most likely, won't be kept.

THE DRIVE AWAY SCATTERS her. There's little that seems to matter.

Eventually she stops the car and calls Simon on her cell. He's just arrived home from school.

'I need to see you.'

'Where are you now?'

He has school tomorrow. She doesn't expect him to drive to St. Anthony. Besides, the last ferry from Labrador has already left.

'There's a late ferry crossing from your end — six o'clock,' he says. 'You should be able to make it. I could meet you.'

She tells him where.

'You're sure?'

'Yes.'

'It'll be after dark.'

'It doesn't matter.'

HIS TRUCK IS PARKED by the side of the road when she gets there. The sun has been down for an hour. There is some light, a partial moon.

Outside the vehicles Simon draws her to him, holds her head into his shoulder. She has control, but not enough. Her eyes fill with tears.

He's brought a blanket. He leads her over the side of the road, onto the sand dune. There is light enough to find their way to the mound.

Night visitors to the ancients.

'Why did you want to come here, Shannon?'

'These people wandered all that way,' she says to him, thinking as she says it she's making sense only to herself.

He spreads the blanket atop the sand at the edge of the mound. They sit with the stunted trees at their backs, the only shelter except each other. They huddle together, what's left of the blanket draped around them.

'My great-grandmother spent her life wandering Labrador,' he says. 'My father hardly travelled ten miles from where he was born.'

She gives back only silence. He, too, is staring past the boulders, to the glimmer of the shore.

'The child,' he says. 'You would think the grave would have been his end.'

She draws the blanket tighter, leans deeper into Simon's embrace.

The silence settles around them. From the distance comes the lingering murmur of the sea.

CORMACK

St John's, Newfoundland
27nd October, 1828

Dear John,

I trust this letter finds you well. This week there has arrived another of yours, the second since my return to St John's. It was received with great interest, I assure you. Its arrival was delayed, by the fall winds no doubt. As you will appreciate, the Mails to the Island are far from dependable.

I feel the greatest urge to share my latest dealings with the Boeothuck, Shanawdithit. I know these words have an eager ear.

You will recall my anticipation at the foray into the Boeothuck regions, in my absence, led by the Abenakie, and my disappointment at the news when it came to nought. The shores of Grand Lake and the territory to the west of Red Indian Lake were all without recent sign of the tribe.

Sad again to relate, a second excursion to the French Shore in White Bay has also yielded nothing, even though the reward for discovering someone of the tribe was raised to one hundred and fifty dollars. At a meeting of the Boeothuck Institution I attempted to convince my fellow members that the last of the tribe could well have retreated to the vicinity of Baie Verte, perhaps inland on the peninsula between White Bay and Bay of Notre Dame.

They were not won over by my optimism. But I assure you, John, neither will the notion rest easily in my mind that, but for Shanawdithit, the Boeothuck have vanished completely from the Earth.

I have taken some consolation from the Lord Bishop of Nova Scotia. Our Patron has praised the Institution for doing all that was possible in finding the Boeothuck. I have had no misgivings in regard to our own efforts. Those of the Governor and the Colonial Office are the ones derelict, and without the least regard for the urgency of the situation. I reiterate what I expressed to you during my visit, that my utmost regret has been in trusting to the humanity of the powers in London.

That aside, my attention now rests on a much more immediate circumstance. Shanawdithit has been brought to my house in St John's. Indeed she has been here these past few weeks. She has come for her personal welfare, of course, but now, such is her ease in my presence, that I feel myself on the brink of a great unbinding, the release of the vast reservoir of knowledge she holds about her race.

There have been some who contend that it is unbefitting a bachelor to have a young lady reside in his home. I reminded the gentleman that the young lady in question is an aborigine and the reason for her being here is the advancement of natural history. Would the gentleman deny the ease of collaboration and the accumulation of knowledge that such an arrangement would doubtless provide?

I have heard no such puerile remarks again. That is not to say they have not been uttered out of my hearing. Strange as it appears to some, I am past debating what is said of me. It is a trait I always possessed in some measure, only reinforced by having spent time in the company of men such as yourself. As we agreed, one fares no easier in life by giving way to public expectation.

My only concession to the civic prate has been to have had within my home not one, but four aborigines. For a time resting there, in addition to the Boeothuck, Shanawdithit, were the searchers, the two Abenakie and the one Mountaineer, just returned from White Bay. It called for a piece in the Royal Gazette so that the whole of the citizenry might wallow in the thought of it.

Such is public ignorance of the human race. These Natives were a stupefying curiosity still — the Gazette, to feed its readers' appetite, saw fit to print the heights of the men, sparing the dignity only of the woman. Passersby made of my home a curiosity shop, lingering near the gate, anxious for the gawk to which they deemed themselves entitled. The bolder entered and let their eyes seize on the aborigines. Then took it upon themselves to speak to them, and in the simplest manner, as if they would have no comprehension of anything but the wilderness and wild beasts.

My patience for such demeanour wore increasingly thin. It would seem that to encounter the aborigines directly was suddenly a mark of social standing, and their presence in my home was undoubtedly the sole talk of a good many of the gossipers. The only profit in many of the visits was the parcels *of food that arrived with them. Invariably they consisted of game or berries, accompanied by a self-congratulatory smile. But they did serve to lessen the expenses of the Institution, and for that I forcibly emitted my gratitude.*

On my part there is particular interest in Shanawdithit, of course. She was withdrawn for much of the first week after her arrival on the boat from Twillingate, overwhelmed by the attention cast on her. She spent much of her early days in the room I had made ready for her with the help of the woman hired by the Institution to come, as is the need, to cook as well as clean.

When she emerged Shanawdithit declared her intention to assist with the preparation of our meals. I assured her gently, but unreservedly, that she was not to be a servant. When it is her wish she ignores me and goes about the kitchen, engaging herself in whatever tasks she had been used to doing at the Peytons.

She clearly misses the Peyton children. I suspect it from the dimness of spirit that surrounds her much of the time. On one occasion when Dr Carson arrived with two of his offspring, it seemed to vanish. The children were shy and clung to their father, but Shanawdithit pursued them and finally, to her satisfaction, succeeded in summoning their attention.

Although on that occasion her melancholy did retreat, at no time is it entirely gone. I have not yet known her to smile.

Dr Carson has given her a vaccination to prevent her contracting smallpox, though he has been unable to do anything to assist in her struggle against consumption. She has lived with it all these years, since it took her mother and sister, and though at times one would not suspect her illness, she is often given over to tiredness and will retreat in the middle of the day to her bed. Only after two weeks had passed did I

detect a cough, and that only in the early morning. She eats
well, as she did with the Peytons, and I detect no loss of
weight as is common among consumptives.

My dear John, I say without reservation that Shanawdithit
has proven a mesmerizing house guest. I wish you could be
here to share in her company, for how worthwhile would it be
to discuss her behaviour with someone whose interest is the
equal of my own.

For the time she shared the house with the other aborigines
she exhibited the most unexpected aspects of her person.
Contrary to what I might have predicted, she seemed not to
look upon herself as part of the same race, but rather part of a
race unto its own. She drew away from the others to her own
room much of the time. On more than one occasion, through
the closed door, I heard her reciting words which I could only
take for the Boeothuck tongue. Then, standing in the hallway
and listening more intently, I heard, much to my incredulity,
sounds that resembled nothing so much as laughter. I recalled
Mrs Peyton saying how Shanawdithit often talked with her
dead mother and sister, and I was forced to conclude that what
I was overhearing was that very act of illusory communication.

Only at mealtimes did there seem to be a bond between the
aborigines. They savoured the caribou equally, though it was
cooked in a fashion very different from what any of them
would have known in the wilds. Shanawdithit, having been
several years among white settlers, was no doubt most familiar
with it being stewed with root vegetables. I doubt if the Peytons
were given to it being flavoured with red wine as is my
preference. Yet all four of them took to it with vigour. It
disappeared, as did the partridgeberry tart that followed,
without a trace left on a plate. Their manner of eating —
the crude use of the knife in particular — was hardly to be

overlooked, yet I did, and did so with aplomb, for at my table were primitives of extraordinary variety and extraordinary fashion. The Gazette was right in that much at least — the four together offered a fascination such as is not likely to be met with again.

It is my contention, and I am anxious to hear if you would agree, that the most primitive of beings, given the opportunity, and with the incentive of reward, will rise to the occasion to act in a manner in keeping with that of the leader. I find there a cusp of truth — no matter the race, no one wishes himself to appear less, in what I would call the grace of conduct, than the host to which the person is indebted.

Unbeknownst to the aborigines, my mind filled with details of that very conduct. It is one circumstance to be at home in the wilds, yet quite another to dispense with its trappings as the occasion calls for. All four had eaten at the table of settlers, of course, and copy their manner, as best as they are able. Our use of the knife at the table, as I have said, proved a particular intricacy. But it was other details that I thought most revealing of the differences in races — the slightly angular posture in the chair, the way the hand encircled the water glass, the verbal offering to denote satisfaction. I am not certain that it would ever be possible to eliminate the differences, and perhaps unwise to wish it.

There were those of my acquaintance in what is called The Reading Room, on Water Street — though limited has been my time to frequent it — who contend that with strong training an aborigine could learn to conduct himself in a manner that would never reveal his origins. That it would only be his facial features and the shade of his skin that would give him away for who he really is. I argue against the notion. It is my contention that there are features inborn, not to be *changed, that make a race what it is. Jameson would be of the opinion that the differences are due to the physiological, that the nature of bone structure perhaps, or the nature of the blood that flows through the veins, alters a person, makes the representative of one race different from that of another. What is to account for the colour of a Native's skin, he would argue, but that one body contains matter of a sort that another does not?*

Such is the debate that lingered in my mind after the three Indian men left St John's for their respective parts of the Island and Labrador. Two of them travelled first to Green Bay, for from that coast had come rumour of a sighting of the Boeothuck. Word arrived today that the rumour has been put to rest, making it now more certain than ever that Shanawdithit is indeed the very last of her tribe.

My commitment to the cause of the Boeothuck is impassioned, as you have been witness, but it is not without challenge. Please accept my apologies for this letter of undue length, but the need to put my experiences to paper, to share in the excitement they offer, has overwhelmed me. Might I be so bold from time to time, as I feel the need arise, to write of what transpires with the Boeothuck woman? I find to do so a much-needed mental calming.

In closing, let me extend my best wishes for good health, with the hope that the fall season in England has proven to be a pleasant and invigorating one.

Yours very sincerely,
William

29th October, 1828
St John's

From what had been a flurry of Natives in my house, I am left
only with Shanawdithit. The work of gathering from her all
manner of information has begun in earnest.

At my request, friends and members of the Institution have
ceased their near daily visitations. I have asked that they restrict
themselves to one day a week, and by prior arrangement. A
stillness has settled in, an atmosphere of contemplation. The
house is suddenly and profoundly quiet.

Her health remains a concern, and always I take stock of it.
Yet, I am trusting of Shanawdithit to realize the urgency of our
endeavour; in this she has not disappointed me.

I began with the most rudimentary of undertakings — adding
to my list of words in the Boeothuck tongue, together with their
equivalent in English. There were some simple to garner — the
features of the face, the movement of limbs, and so forth. I
pointed to fire in the hearth, the water in our cups that turns to
tea, and, outside the window, the sky and its weather. Always
I had Shanawdithit repeat the word until I was certain of its
transcription. When I exhausted all that surrounded us — for
most of which the language does not hold the words — I
directed her attention to drawing with paper and pencil.

It is with these in hand that Shanawdithit has turned her

brightest. The young woman has a natural faculty for drawing and, as I witnessed while she was with the Peytons, silently relishes the opportunity to display her talents. In due course she has provided drawings of the Boeothuck dwellings, both summer and winter, and of the structures that surrounded them, for curing and storing their food. She drew drying platforms and filled them with the profusion of animal and fish which her people have consumed. As she completed each one she sat upright until I had verified the specimen and labelled the drawing accordingly. Several times Shanawdithit emitted great sighs befitting the memories which had no doubt collected in her mind. There lay such reason for anguish. For what once was a thriving tribe, with food surrounding them in abundance, has, with deplorable swiftness, been forced to surrender to starvation.

The cooking vessels of her tribe fills another of the pages, as does their weaponry. She sketched their spears and their methods of using them to kill wild game. She put the spears in the hands of members of her band, and then at my request, took each of these people in turn and drew their likeness. She held to a quiet moment to bring them to mind, then with a quickness and surety, rendered their profiles to paper. Such was the clarity in her mind that she would often draw a face a second and third time to get it exactly as she knew it to be.

With each drawing I have been taken inside a private world and there brought to an understanding of the Boeothuck that no white man before me has known. She embraces my good intentions, if slowly and cautiously at first, and from this rises promise of even greater reward. As I had so earnestly hoped, my thirst to discern the extirpation of the Boeothuck is now being satisfied. At some moments I can barely contain the tumult that races through my soul, though I give Shanawdithit no indication of this for fear she will mistake my enthusiasm for pleasure at her misfortune.

When the prospect was right I guided our attention to the tribe's encounters with white men. She started first with maps of portions of Red Indian Lake and the river Exploits. Onto these she has drawn trails of men — the Boeothuck in red pencil, the settlers in black — depicting the expeditions which were sent upriver in pursuit of the Boeothuck. Because of our daily lessons Shanawdithit's use of the English language has advanced markedly and she is now able to explain much for which she had previously been without the proper words. Now there issues a sputtering stream of words, English and Boeothuck together, that can barely keep pace with her drawing.

And with it emotion that she is no longer able to hold within herself. Over the drawing of the capture of Demasduit and the killing of her husband, Nonosabasut, Shanawdithit wept. And, while I could not share the depth of her feelings, I felt myself moved beyond all expectation. For a long while I withheld my pen from the paper, feeling it unfitting to perform such a dispassionate task in the midst of her grief.

Into the privacy of her grief she settled, until she deemed herself willing to return to the world that presently surrounded her. I sat with patience, storing in my mind my observations, but anxious to assist the aboriginal woman in her journey.

'Shanawdithit, I see a heart struggling to emerge from its misery.'

She looked at me, her eyes reddened, her mind wounded by what the universe has set on her.

I offered what counsel I knew. 'You have endured more than is just. Your people have been lost to greed and cruelty, struck from their world. I, too, fervently wish them to return.'

I sensed a hardening in her countenance.

'My most solemn desire is for you to be circumscribed by your own race,' I said to her. 'To live as you most earnestly would wish it. I long that you live again unencumbered by the rancour of our world.'

~

2nd November, 1828

I suspect Shanawdithit is rarely one to exhibit gratitude. Seeing
to it, as I did, that she was removed from the servitude that was
her fate among the Peytons, to the Institution which provided all
the comforts necessary to her well-being, I anticipated some
offering of thankfulness. Indeed it was only with great effort
and sacrifice, and against the considerable resistance of the
Peytons, that we drew her under our protection, at a time when
those governing the land, the ones who should have been charged
with that responsibility, ignored her and the desperate plight of
her race, without contrition.

Perhaps it is a Native trait, common to all such races.
Certainly, when I bring to mind the Natives who were my
guides in the wilderness, I do not recall any acknowledgement
from them of the devotion to the Boeothuck demonstrated by
myself and the other men of the Institution.

Shanawdithit is not ungrateful. Rather, I think her uncertain
of her place among us. That I take as reason enough for the
aberrant direction of our discourse. One provides the means
for discourse, she being conversant in English far beyond
what she was when she arrived, but one knows not to where
it will lead.

She chose to speak to me of her people as I requested, and
did so with goodwill and an understanding of the importance of

her task. It has not been entirely harrowing for her, because I do believe it serves to give release to her feelings. That she should step aside from her narrative and bring her attention to bear on other matters with equal fervour, matters private and less crucial, leaves me to wonder at the nature of the aboriginal mind.

I have come to the conclusion that it is less given to reason than our own, that it is easily overwhelmed by emotion. Constantly I have had to remember that Shanawdithit's understanding of civilization is narrow, confined as it was to the outlying regions of the Island. Her days spent among us have not been sufficient to grasp the way opinion is properly exchanged. It is beyond the development of her brain perhaps, if I am to follow Jameson's logic, to realize that language is governed as much by appropriateness as it is by diction.

After two afternoons of inquiry on my part and of drawing and explanation on hers, Shanawdithit put aside her pencils and turned to me with the most formidable expression, as if I had been the reason for a sudden, and indeed physical, torment.

I said to her, 'What is it? Are you not well? Perhaps it would be best to rest in your room.'

'What is it? You say *adore*?' Her straight black hair, in need of cutting, framed a sombre, at moments severe, face.

'I do not understand.'

'*Adore*. White people say *adore*. What it mean?'

'I have not said the word.'

'You do not know it?' she said, more quickly than I anticipated.

'Adore means to like very much.'

'Like *person* very much?'

'Yes, a person. Or something, food perhaps. I adore herrings.'

'I adore caribou.'

'Yes,' I said.

'Do you adore Shanawdithit?'

It was a cumbersome moment. An unmanageable one, knowing the artfulness of language is beyond her grasp. Shanawdithit has not the knowledge of nuance.

'The word has a strength that alters its meaning.'

'Mr Cormack not adore me.' She drew her hand from the table and raised it to her chest. I could not fail to notice the wildness of that hand, rough in a way uncommon to young ladies. It excused her forthrightness.

I raised my hand to my chest. 'Nor Shanawdithit me.'

She stared even more intently, when someone of our race would have known it wise to look away for a time.

'You not like me?' she said.

'Like? Yes, truly, I like you. I like you very much.'

Now her sternness turned to puzzlement. 'I not understand. *Adore?*'

'*Adore* is a strong word, a word perhaps for two people in love.'

'We not in love.'

As always, I accepted her innocence. And did so meekly and with a smile, though not one broad enough that it chanced offending her.

'No, we not in love.'

'Who you *in love?*'

'No one.'

Her head drew to one side, though she continued to stare. 'No one?'

· 'No.' I knew it best to turn her attention away from these questions for which she could bring no understanding. 'Would you like to finish your drawing?'

'I in love. I have man by the lake, when my people together.'

'Yes.'

I did not say more, with the hope of her not revealing her private thoughts unnecessarily.

'Good man. Strong man. Strong heart.'

'Yes.'

She waited for more. I chose to ignore these new expectations.

'The older children call it "prick." You have no woman for your prick.'

For a moment I could not think I had heard the word. I felt myself claret-faced, naturally.

I knew I would have to speak for fear she would continue on, unbridled.

'I have no woman ...'

'No?' she interrupted, dismayed by my state it seemed. Only for the moment was I left mute by the strain in her stare.

'I think it best if we end our work for today.' I moved back my chair in anticipation of rising from the table.

'Then you sad sometimes. You cross. No woman and no children.'

I stood up. 'No.'

Her questions had been thoroughly innocent and simple-minded. I smiled at her ignorance still of the intricacies of life beyond her tribe.

'Not happy man,' she said as I began to part the room to attend to some business matters that I had neglected in order to confer with Shanawdithit. Though I chose not to turn back at her voice, what I heard I took for a mild scolding as I had seen her use with children when she resided with the Peytons.

To offer an explanation to Shanawdithit would have been fruitless. To contradict her thinking, mere folly. Shanawdithit is deserving of compassion above all else. One can never hold her accountable for the plainness of her thoughts.

I remain perplexed by her manner. There have been other

times when the innocence of the aboriginal mind has led me to do just as I did at that moment — withdraw from the discourse until the matter passes. It has continually proven the wisest choice.

The episode has caused an outpouring in my mind — a vast reflection on intelligence and the weight of experience in its advancement. I know myself to be unquestionably fortunate in having at hand an illustration of a people who have traversed an infinitely narrow path in the world. Until she came to live among the Peytons, Shanawdithit's orb had been no more than the shores of a lake, a strip of seacoast, and the river spanning the two. That and a canopy of stars. Before the incursions of settlers, her concerns were but protection from the vagaries of nature. The bonds between the Boeothuck were simple of design, in all proportions practical. The choice of partner for marriage, or what in their race constituted marriage, could have been but sparse. Attraction was purposeful, and romance, as in the European custom, unknown.

Yet the woman possesses a strength of mind disproportionate to her knowledge and experience. It had been my prediction that she would have receded from all but the most rudimentary of questions. Holding to mind her near-starvation at the time of giving herself up to our care, one would have thought her preoccupied with her health and well-being to the exclusion of all other matters. Oddly enough, though she continues to cough, unmanageably at times, it seems not to concern her.

For another incidence, she is indeed taken by clothes, and likes nothing better than running her hands over bolts of new dress material in the shops on Water Street. I requested a seamstress from one of them to come to the house and attend to her, taking her measurements for a dress and letting her select a reasonable fabric — a modestly yellow floral calico it was —

for its construction. I had not seen her any happier than on the day the dress was fitted. When the garment was delivered, Shanawdithit retreated to her room with it, and with the scraps of material left from the fitting. From beyond the door I could hear her singing. Chanting, perhaps, better described it. When she emerged I saw that she had sewn strips of the material to the lower sleeves, in a most unattractive fashion, though one immensely pleasing to herself. And, with a second piece of fabric the seamstress had given her, had fashioned a charming pair of infant boots, a piece of ribbon serving as a closure for each.

She was not smiling to be certain, but I have grown never to expect that expression. Her mood I deemed equal to it. There are times during her stay at my residence, I will admit, when I call in the seamstress as a respite from a period of her unremitting gloom, or a restlessness following my refusal to follow the course of her questioning. She continues to prove an intriguing soul, one whose inclinations are not to be predicted from one day to the next, and certainly not to be counted on to satiate the inquisitive members of the Institution when they arrive on their appointed day to spend time with her.

It is only me that she holds in her confidence. I look upon it as an honour, as straining as it is on occasion. As the weeks have advanced, the accumulation of hitherto unrecorded knowledge of the Boeothuck has been remarkable, unquestionably warranting the effort required to gather it. Shanawdithit is proving a marvel, one whose contribution to the appreciation of her people will last long into the future.

SHANNON

IN THE DAYS THAT follow their visit she discovers herself dwelling again and again on Marta returning home. When Marta had set off back to Norway after their time together on Baffin Island, Shannon had been stupefied at how keen she was to go. She had been forever talking about how much she loved Canada. She said she would go back home for a year perhaps, but even at the time Shannon could tell it would be permanent.

Shannon had talked to Marta endlessly about her escape from Conche. How she had deliberately cut herself loose. For good reason.

Leaving her no choice but to find another place to set roots. Without the husband and children to do it for her. Shannon became the rover. The rover with no home to fly to at Christmas.

There is Conche now, as distant as ever. She hasn't been able to set herself right, despite the realization she risks edging toward despondency.

That's the other 'd' word, the milder one. The one for which time is supposedly the healer.

SIMON IS NOW THE constant. And for that she knows she should be thankful. A plausible course would be to give herself over to him. But reading men has never been her strong suit. For whatever reason, trusting him shrinks in reverse proportion to how compatible he tries to make himself.

As easy as it would be to collapse into his arms, she holds herself back. She won't risk anxieties compounding, working themselves into a hard, crystalline knot.

'Your aunt was in her eighties and she had cancer, Shannon. It wasn't unexpected. She had a good life.'

She doesn't react. She wonders how Bertha would have characterized her eighty years. How good were they? Bertha would not have questioned. She had her God to tell her.

Her fierce faith took her through whatever heartache came her way. Took her through three miscarriages. Once, in the prime of her teenage religious indifference, Shannon had wondered aloud to her mother why her sister hadn't the swarm of children that would have been her Catholic duty. Only then did she learn of the miscarriages, one right after the other, barely three years apart, and one late in the second trimester of a pregnancy. Right in her own house. She almost bled to death. Bertha put a firm and deliberate end to having children.

Shannon had come to the conclusion that her aunt's religion had its limits, after all. She can only speculate that Bertha laid down the law to Uncle Bill, that they would have turned to birth control, papal encyclical or no papal encyclical. Condoms, she imagines, acquired covertly at great risk of embarrassment to himself, from heavens knows where. Not Conche, that's for certain. The religious contortions may have been the prime reason behind his temper flares. In any event God or the Trojans saw to it that Bertha was never pregnant again.

Shannon's mother had only two children, years later, but little less of an anomaly in a Catholic community. She'd had a particularly difficult time when Patti was born. The doctor had warned her about the risks of a third pregnancy, so, as they said in those days, she had her 'tubes tied.'

She was one step ahead of her sister, only to have her sister outlive her by thirty years.

It's her mother who Shannon thinks about more than anyone. By the time her mother was the age that Shannon is now, her two children were teenagers. Again and again she finds herself doing that — thinking of the life her mother was living at a particular age, in comparison to her own.

She knows she is not much fun to be with at the moment.

ONE WEEKEND WHEN HE comes to visit, Simon manages to bounce her from her lethargy. They are watching a movie, about someone on the track of her birth mother, when he pauses it to open a bottle of wine.

'Have you ever thought there might be Native blood in your family?' he calls from the kitchen.

All that time alone in the great outdoors has hardly done much for his tactfulness, she thinks. He re-enters the room and hands her a glass of white wine. She stares at him without answering.

'Your complexion. Some of your facial features ...'

'You should be so lucky.'

'I'm serious.'

'Coincidence.'

'Could be.'

'Irish, Simon. County Waterford. Well documented.'

'You don't look Irish.'

'You don't look Scottish.'

He catches the whiff of her irritation and does not press the point. Nevertheless, it lingers, and though he doesn't raise the suggestion again, it has planted itself in her mind.

When she catches herself in the mirror in the full light of the next day she has to concede there is still something there that would give rise to the question. Age hasn't diminished it.

Marta had mentioned it jokingly several times. Shannon told her it was a pigment of her imagination. Droll, but not entirely so. The sea-kayaking sisters joked that she blended in well with the Haida.

Of course it came with other implications — that her appearance had something to do with the success she'd had negotiating with Aboriginal groups. It was likely some advantage. But in the long run, not much of one. She knew better than to think she'd been given a job for some reason other than the fact that she had proved she knew what she was doing.

THE DAY BEFORE SHANNON'S follow-up meeting with the Aboriginal group, Simon emails a copy of a letter he's received from the Provincial Department of Archaeology in St. John's.

> *The decision to retain the human remains from the burial mound at L'Anse Amour was made for the purposes of scientific research. Since so little is known about the Maritime Archaic it is felt that the opportunity for ongoing study of the remains is of prime importance in increasing our understanding of these, the first human inhabitants of our province. You can be assured that the skeleton is being stored with utmost respect for it as human remains.*

He calls her a short while later.

He is ripe with skepticism. 'Do you buy this?'

She doesn't, but then again, she is not surprised. 'You didn't tell me you wrote to them.'

'You had enough on your mind.'

She still does. She really doesn't want him drawing her into it.

'It's the bureaucratic runaround,' he says. 'Make it sound like you know what you're doing and hope they swallow it.'

'Do you really want to take this on?'

'It bothers me.'

'If it's just you that it bothers, then I think you have your answer. One complaint is not what stirs them to action.'

He's silent for the moment.

'Are you expecting me to join in?'

'The site means a lot to you. You said you thought the skeleton should be reburied.'

'It's not my fight.'

He hesitates.

'I can't afford to jeopardize my job,' she says.

Silence, then, 'Can't afford in what way?'

He must sense her irritation rising. Before she answers, he says, 'Okay.' That's it.

She hangs up. And when he calls back right away she doesn't answer. Or open his emails.

THE MEETING HAS TO go ahead. Arrangements for the other people have been put in place.

She knows she could have done better. She has always made a point of keeping her personal life separate from her job. Two distinct territories. Not always easy especially when you live in a small place. On Baffin she did it. In BC.

Here it's turned into a different story. She's let it become a different story. She knows she needs to back off. She needs to get her head in order.

She emails Simon and tells him that. 'I need space, Simon.'

Space. She's knows she's the one who can't settle, who still feels like the goddamn outsider.

The meeting is a disaster. She and Simon keep their distance. When she doesn't respond to the looks edging her way, he gives up and retreats into himself, the air thickening with his resentment.

He finds wording for a position on the proposal, then entrenches himself in it — the choices made for any reinterpretation of the L'Anse aux Meadows site will have to include substantial reference to the confrontations between the Norse and the Aboriginal people.

He has the other two on side from the beginning, which means he's likely emailed them and they've found a position in common days before. It pisses her off further. She ends consideration of the proposal. She knows she is in no frame of mind to be arguing with them.

'We'll leave that for now. Let me take time to consider the options, talk to people in Ottawa. In the meantime, we'll move on.'

There is only one place to move to, for she knows exactly what he'd say about L'Anse Amour.

'Let's open preliminary discussion on the site at Red Bay. Since Simon lives in Red Bay, perhaps he would be good enough to give us his impression of the site, rather than me begin with the Parks Canada version.'

Simon is caught off guard, but has no trouble rising to the moment.

'Sure. Okay. As far as I know the evidence uncovered by Selma Barkham in the research that led to the development of the site indicates a positive relationship between the Basques and the Native People.'

Overly cautious, Shannon can see. He stops, but, without a response, continues.

'It was the sixteenth century, of course, and these were whalers and the written record was in the form of business transactions and legal documents, not specific accounts of life in Red Bay at the time. From what I understand, references to the relationship between the two groups are sparse.'

There's an urge to question him just to vindicate herself, but she holds back.

'There was trading of goods, though not of weapons it would seem. The Natives apparently helped with the processing of the whales once they were brought to shore, and took care of the Basque whaling boats, the *chalupas*, over winter during the time the Basques were back in Spain. One would assume if there was violence then it would have found its way into the documents. That's not to say there wouldn't have been a clash of cultures on some level. We just don't know for certain what form it took. It can be imagined, but there is no written record of it.'

'Are you suggesting interpretation be developed from what could have happened, without concrete evidence?'

There's a clipped, efficient tone to her voice that she can't seem to control. There's no escaping the urge for retribution.

But Simon shrugs. 'I'm not suggesting anything. It's a possibility.'

For the first time Shannon detects sustained discomfort. He doesn't want to give her more grief. By now the shell around her has turned hard and impervious.

'The story I was talking about ...,' he says, another olive branch it would seem from the tone of his voice. He shrugs again.

From his satchel he retrieves a book, a bookmark protruding between its pages. He hands it across the table to Shannon. 'Contemporary Basque Short Fiction.' She looks at it front and back.

'Borrow it if you like.'

She won't say no. That would be unbefitting her position, against the spirit of the committee. She sets the book on the table, to one side of the binder of material she has open in front of her. She will take it home, and eventually she will read the story. She expects to hate every minute of it, but she won't have it said that she didn't do what the job expected of her.

JOANES

'SWEET VIRGIN OF SAN Sebastián!' The harpooner bellowing like God's chosen.

A chalupa load of six, the harpooner filling the bow, the others working their long oars like madmen. Men mad for the kill, dead set on the whale. A right whale — right for the taking, right because he is a slow-roaming beast, because he will float still with the last spoutful drove from him. Right because the blessed Saviour has brought him within our reach, good Catholics He knows us to be.

The harpooner Ramos, his carbuncle face blood red with anticipation, his grip on the shaft iron-hard, he eyes the barb, it sharpened that morning, not an hour before the bell-clatter burst from the lookout, before the keener had sighted the monstrous trail of black just below the water. Hard sighting too, this day, the sky brooding rain, the ice not yet gone from the shore.

'Row, bloodsuckers! You'll not lose this one!'

What a place is this for a Basque man. Colder than a fishwife's tit on Epiphany, and this what should be summer. Man was not born to face what winter brings to this scruff of barren rock. Think, you would, after five weeks of galing over the sea, there'd be something worth the gawk. There'd be — whales, more than ever a man could know in Biscay Bay!

IT BE A HEATHEN crew of aborigines that comes to see what we're about. Heathen as the knolls of lichen rock upon this *Tierranoba*.

Peaceable enough. We have no fear of them, and they none of us. They tend the chalupas we leave stored on shore, after we're gone then in the fall, as much as anyone can tend what is pounded with the wind and mauled with ice and godless freezing rain.

They're a strapping crew, taller than us. Muscled so much there's hardly a whaler among us lot who would think of taking one on man for man. Even Ramos has his doubts, and good for it, too, though the Bilbaon would have us believe he could flatten one to the rocks if there be call for it. More mouth than brains be that Ramòs.

All for all, like us, a swarthy, steadfast crew. We've yet to take one in the whaling boat. Ramos knows he would have the poor devil afeared of his life. But onshore they work like horses. Not that they have ever seen such a beast, or ever will.

Work — slicing the walls of blubber now with the best of them. Dancing atop the beast, in time, too. And a hearty laugh they have, when inclined. You would think, if you hadn't set your eyes square on them, that they're no different than yourself. And perhaps they're not, except they have not been blessed with the Catholic faith. Still for all I can't think the good Lord Jesus would look with scorn on them, their lack of faith being no fault of their own. At least they not be one of Luther's misbegotten hordes.

This voyage brings a man for the job of instilling the love of Jesus in their pagan souls. A Grey Friar has come along, not, as he would have us think, to bring the light of the Saviour to good Catholic whalers wherever they roam, but for a bigger challenge. He has his lusty apostolic eyes on a greater reward for himself in paradise — to bring the heathens into the heavenly fold. The man strolls about the shoreline looking all the world like he is walking hand in hand with the blessed Virgin herself.

Alfonse de la Bastida is his name. French by birth. Franciscan, follower of the virtuous St. Francis, by virtue of his robe only. Why the man should think himself able to bring into his fold heathens of whose language he does not speak a single word is beyond my head to understand. It be better that he devote himself to his own soul, or to ours, for there are plenty among us with souls in need of a good stiffening until they again fall into the womb of the Mother Church in Spain.

Such be the wonder of *La Provincia de Tierranoba*. Ah, what weeks at sea and months on wild and brutish rock do to a man! As for me, I keep my wits about me and stand aside, remembering every hour my dearest Domicuça and our angel of a daughter.

LET IT BE SAID that I know my place and keep it. Unlike some what think anything could be better than in the boat most of any day, escaping danger with every wave, knowing any day could be your last if you do not heed your own good sense. Ramos is a braggart, but the man knows the sea. The graveyard lasting proof that he be one to smell a moody sea.

For no Christian man can bear that thought — to die in such a place as this. Whether it be natural, or by the fury of the trade. Buried then they be, or half buried, for earth is scarce. To be laid in the rock of Tierranoba, and not the rich dark loam of the homeland, that is the fear of every one of us.

I sometimes think I am a fool, but my dearest ones will have their stomachs full another year, and a strong roof over their heads, and fine new dresses for the Feast of the Annunciation. There's plenty in Orio who cannot make such a claim. Or anywhere in the Basque country for that matter.

Alfonse de la Bastida for one. Lord, forgive me my wicked mind, but a snigger at the expense of a man claiming himself so close to Jesus, knowing what I know of him, might not be a sin. He has no wife to feed, or dress, or provide a roost for his lively rod. And it is lively from what has been told, by certain women in Orio, as he passes through, doing his good deeds for the Lord.

The man does say a fine Ave Maria, and a finer Credo and Salve Regina. I'll say that of him ten times over. He leads the prayers with such potent reverence it would make one think he had just that moment quietly closed the door behind him after his audience with God.

Little wonder that he has turned his mind to those who have no means to question his godly regard. Namely, the new legion of Native heathens who descend down the river in their canoes and make their way along the shore. They stand at a distance, as if to give us time to brace ourselves for their arrival. Then a few men step forth. They are taller and leaner, and what they wear is a curious clump of animal skins, though they wear them well and without any dishonour, as if they had been prepared by the cleverest tailor in San Sebastián.

They leave their hunting spears behind with the others, then venture close, greeting us with shining eyes and with a deep, but civil gaze. With the last few steps their mouths widen into a show of their good nature. Not a smile as we know a smile, but one guarded in its range, as if they need to judge the merits of each of us, one man at a time.

Our Grey Friar is there, quick as a witless dog. He bounds to the fore-front, vying for a broader greeting than that offered even the Captain, someone they saw but half a year before.

'An honour to greet you, good Native man,' the Franciscan says to the head one of the band. To himself he adds, 'In the name of Jesus, bless this unbeliever.'

The Natives are dumbfounded by this brazen foray into their lives.

The Captain steps forward to regain his station and set their minds at ease. 'Come,' he says to them. 'First we must trade.'

They know the word 'trade' well enough, and the Captain's eagerness for them to walk on to what has become the customary trading spot sets their minds at ease. They see us gathering there with goods brought from our Basquelands for that very purpose. Alfonse de la Bastida is suddenly ignored, for the man has brought no earthly goods for trade.

Soon the other aborigines descend in a chattering mass, each with a bundle. At first gaze they seem bundles of furs alone, but this is hardly the case, for once they are untied, revealed are shells, walrus tusks, animal teeth of all kinds, bird beaks. What would we want with bird beaks?

I myself come away with as fine a pelt of beaver as the one I acquired last year. From the very same aborigine at that. He remembered me and knew my fondness for the fur. What he doesn't know is how it will delight Domicuça de Arbe to give her winter coat the full trim it deserves, how at Christmas Mass that garment will be the talk of all the women.

Before the thought is gone from my head, a pious cock has joined the bargaining, having scurried back from his place of lodging.

'And who among you has something for this?' he announces. And what he hangs in the air before him is nothing less than a string of rosary beads. With no shame at that! 'For,' he says, 'Jesus would wish these put in the hands of his children who have yet to know him.'

Indeed Jesus would, I am sure, though what I doubt is whether He would wish a pelt of muskrat in return. What the dear and holy Friar, forsaker of earthly goods, wishes with fur I do not know. Perhaps to warm his neck while he sleeps. Perhaps it, too, will find its way to the coat of some lady of Orio, on a night when he has some generous soul to lie against, helping him to keep his neck warm.

The rosary beads will not remain rosary beads for long. They will no doubt find themselves a new life, scattered about the hides of the aborigines, for their men and women alike have a fondness for decorating what they wear. Holy glass beads will add much to the intrigue of their clothes, more than what it will ever do to boost the parade of their souls. Souls scarce in need of parading.

WHO THESE ABORIGINES PRAY to, I am not certain. But pray they do. I have seen them gathered together in the most solemn manner, and chanting in a most woeful tone, not unlike what is to be heard from the altar of San Nicolas in the depths of February, but a tone that changes, grows louder and more lively, one that then gives way to dancing. They like the drum, as do we, though our drumming would not dare show itself inside church doors. I have seen, too, a simple flute among them. They seem to have a fondness for the flute, the same that we have for our glorious *txistu*.

And their dancing! Many are the nights we work at cutting up blubber to the sounds of drumming. For their people will not work far into the night as is our habit. Some nights I have slipped away to watch their dancing. At one moment they move stealthily to a single strike on the drum, and then, within a flash, shout together and pound the drums madly, and jump about like the Holy Spirit has grabbed onto them. Holy Spirits more likely, to judge by how they toss and turn and call names into the sky.

NOW, UPON THE ROCKS of this place, looking out to sea, has stepped a curious young woman who has struck me dumb. This I can do nothing but confess, even if it should lead straight to the confession box once I step ashore in Orio.

None among us has seen her like before. She arrived with the rest of the aborigines, but only now has chosen to come forth. She has been with the aborigines these many seasons, but she is suddenly a young woman. It is as if this is the summer a veiled angel has chosen to reveal herself.

Rough I can be in my talk, but when my eyes alight on the angel, I have no mind for it. God might strike me down for thinking so, but when I see her alone walking over the rocks and looking out to sea, yes, it is the Blessed Virgin who comes into my head. There it is and have I not gazed upon the face of the Blessed Virgin in the Church of San Nicolas so many times that I know the grace of the Lady when I see it.

This aborigine has that face, as if there has been more for her than life among these rocks. She has a far-off, unearthly stare. As much as I can tell, she is not discontent with her place, but bears a mind that dreams of things others of her race do not. Strange she is, for want of a better word. But more than strange.

I am not the only one whose curiosity is stirred! The Franciscan foremost among them. Yet the man is married to the Church, is he not, and has renounced all earthly pleasures. If the pleasures of looking on a woman be the measure of his sin, then he has drowned in it ten times over.

There has never been a time I was more dispirited at not being able to speak the Native's tongue. And while, when I pass her, I smile and dip my head slightly in respect and honourable intention, I can hardly do more than that. On occasion I will say her name, for this I have learned from careful listening when she is around other of her people.

Sha-naw-dí it is. And it is Sha-naw-dí that I say. Shanawdí. Careful to pronounce each part clearly, while trying to say it all together, as you would an ordinary name. When I speak her name it is then she looks up and occasionally returns my smile, though she is not one to do more. On one meeting I present to her an extra earthen bowl I brought from Orio. Though I wish nothing for it, wish it merely be a gift. The next time we meet she hands me a portion of a hide, a handsome fur I had not known before. She smiles, says nothing, and continues on her way.

I have now the sense she knows the route I like to walk when I have an evening ashore not consumed with work. She deliberately walks the same route, knowing we will pass. On evenings when I am feeling bolder than I truly am, I nod my head even deeper and in the course of speaking her name I comment on the weather and gesture perhaps to the sky, or rub my hands over my arms as if to demonstrate how deep is the chill in the air. She now anticipates the encounter and looks up before

I reach her, expecting I am sure that I will have something other than her name to say, though she has no hope of understanding a word.

At my boldest yet I say my own name — Joanes de Echaniz, tapping my fingers against my chest as I speak the word. First, 'Shanawdí,' veering my right hand in her direction, then, 'Joanes,' as I turn the same hand toward my chest.

On the first such occasion, she hurries past, as if I should not have been so bold. But, the second time, less so. The third, she speaks my name. I should not be thinking it or feeling it, I know, with a wife and child, but meeting her and conversing with her, if it could be called that, lifts my spirits to a height greater than they have been since I left the shores of Spain.

In the rogue Alfonse de la Bastida I have my rival. If he could be called rival, for the lady in truth would seem to spend time with men of her own race. At least she converses with them with no hint of unease. I am certain she is not wedded to any one, for none share the shelter where she bides, only other women and a pair of children.

The Franciscan plots for her attention. You would think he would have the care of proper Basque souls to fill his days. Why is it that he chooses her to lavish his attention on? If conversion to the Church of Christ were his true intent, then would he not seek first the leader of the aborigines? Let it not be said that I have lost my Catholic faith because of one way- ward man. I have stood and watched the heretics be driven from the Basquelands, and cheered their going, like the best churchmen did. I do not associate with Moors, Jews, or Protestants. A day does not pass that I do not recite the Paternoster and the Ave Maria. The Lord God's Ten Commandments come to my lips as easily as they do to those of Alfonse de la Bastida, of that I am certain.

What I lack in humility I make up for in holy innocence. For I never fault a man, but that he has faulted me first. I never bring words against a man, but that he has stirred words against me first. Such is the depth of my holy innocence.

Some nights when I am laying abed, in the brief moment before my dead tiredness overtakes me, I pray to God to give me the strength to forgive the Franciscan his indiscretions. I pray earnestly and justly, without undue hatred seeping into my head. In my hand is clutched my most treasured possession, a copy of the *Tercer Abecedario Espiritual* of Francisco de Osuna. The page is carefully marked, and it passes over my eyes again and again, until the light faded beyond use — his twentieth treatise, on temptation. Although I find it hard to tell one word from another, I know it by heart, its Chapter IX, on carnal thoughts. *Renounce, renounce your bestiality. Remember that you are to be the companion of angels, the child of God, the friend of virgins, sufferer with the martyrs, and citizen of heaven where only the chosen gather. Be a man in your heart. Do not allow yourself to fall, but rise up.*

And each night rise up I do, as the book falls from my hand. For, though I am want not to, I seem only to dwell on the passage regarding friendship with virgins. Dark and tortuous friendship with virgins that give way to mighty thrusting forays of bestiality. Conquered I am each time, by a hand that goes from book to bold arisen manhood, thrusting until my seed is cast again into the boughs that line my bed, and dripping somewhere onto the ground. In a final thrust I lodge the hairy poker deep into the prickly boughs. Let the spruce needles savage the head of it. Torture, deserved torture in the name of Christ.

Be ashamed to be conquered when there are so many conquerors. Accomplish virtue through God, for he will bring your enemies to nothingness.

Ashamed I am of my weakness, but a man is a man and confounded I am that God has attached such temptation to a man's very being. I miss my Domicuça so, and three months ahead of me before we strike again the shores of Orio.

Every day now I long for the call from the lookout and the dash aboard the chalupa. Then my mind is set where it should and wanders nowhere but to the scheme to outsmart the whale. We harness that beast and sap it of its colossal urges. We conquer the mightiest beast known to mankind and turn it to what God intended.

On what God has intended for me I do not dwell. Instead, I hold steadfast my Christian heart and pray that temptation passes from me. And for a time it does, for when I am on the salt water in pursuit of the whale, my mind is nowhere but upon the task before me. I play my part as soundly as any man aboard the boat, and when that whale is lashed lifeless at the shore station, I stand as proud as any one of them for the job that I have done. Excellent crewman I am, and no man will say different.

It is when the job is done, and I have time to think on matters other than the call of whaling, that temptation lifts its bloodied head. Unseemly of a Christian man, unseemly of a Basque, who takes the fiercest pride in the firmness of his faith. A man sprung from soil where there are no more pure Christian men anywhere in Spain. Some days, when my faith is at its strongest, I sit on the rocks, my eyes out to sea, my tongue in the confessional at the Church of San Nicolas. Every word I utter I do so from my heart and make my confession to the father beyond the wooden slats shiny with spit, and to the dear Father in heaven.

Forgive me Father, for I have sinned.

'What is it, Joanes de Echaniz?' comes a voice behind me. 'Are you in need of confession?'

I turn to find the prick of a rival perched upon a rock, looking as much like a slovenly alley dweller as any I have ever seen. Except that here he is on the rocks of Tierranoba, the wind thrashing his hair, his hands swollen from the bites of mosquitoes.

'No, Alfonse de la Bastida, I need confess nothing to you. I have no business with Lucifer.'

Though he suspects I have slighted him, he looks on me as someone to be pitied. 'What is it, Brother?' He has taken to giving that name to whalemen, as if it were a sign of him drawing them close to God. I will have none of his false benevolence.

'My thoughts are mine alone.' I will not have it said that I was publicly insolent to a Franciscan, though it pains me to keep a civil tongue.

'But I am grieved to see you hold the Lord at a distance.'

'Grieved? You have no cause to grieve for me ... Brother.' I know only that to call him. If my tongue were free, it would be 'moron.' 'Fool' could do, or 'idiot.'

'I have made this voyage to provide for the souls of men left without the comforts of their Mother Church.'

Such is the persistence of the man, and his falseness. For there is much more to his roaming ways than the eternal salvation of our Basque souls. To begin, it is said he spent his youth in Moorish Granada! He will have to do more than walk among us to be a Basque. I myself think he boarded the ship to rid himself of his past, perhaps before some poor trollop flopped with a bawling youngster at his door. God absolve me from my aspersions, but I can hardly bear the sight of him, the way he clutches his Franciscan robe.

'Why have you taken to the rocks?' he asks. 'Alone and troubled.'

'Troubled. I am no more troubled than you ... Brother.'

'I have seen you gazing at the aborigine. Is there lust in your heart?'

What is now in my heart is loathing! This ... this ... Franciscan — curse his blundering soul. He knows how much he has angered me, yet still he gazes down from his windswept perch as if he were the Lord salvaging the lifeblood of a mere mortal.

I rise from what I had claimed as a private refuge and walk away without a word. For to speak would be to acknowledge that he deserves to be spoken to. To look his way would concede him to be more than pestilence.

Just as I rise and am about to make my way to where true Basque men might be found, my eyes fall on the Mary, the aborigine Shanawdí, herself walking about the rocks, now turned in the direction of us both. At once I am in a quandary, for to walk as I had intended would leave the scoundrel to encounter her.

Boldly, I change direction, without hesitation, once I have fixed in my head my course. For I am the one meant to gather her attention, not the

Franciscan. I am the one she wishes in her sight, perhaps the very reason for her excursion about the rock.

Alfonse de la Bastida is left a gangling shorebird fighting the wind. Not able now to control the fraudulent sheath of Franciscan habit encasing him. Suddenly the wind works a passage under it and the rogue billows up and is nearly lifted from the ground. As it is, he has been put at the mercy of the gusts, which toss him to and fro, then spill him onto the rocks. The heavens have dealt him an answer to his deceitful ways.

I cannot contain the pleasure, and as he flops about the rocks riotous laughter bursts from the very core of me. Such a fool he looks, and such a fool he proves himself to be. That it should happen with the aborigine woman looking on only makes it all the sweeter to the eye.

The woman is not as amused as I, though neither is she acquainted with the full measure of his trickery. She can be excused for running to him to help him contain his garb and regain his feet. So as not to appear callous and inhuman to his plight, I aid Shanawdí in her quest.

Soon the Franciscan is erect once more, now clutching the excess of cloth that forms his habit, embarrassed as he should be to be rescued by a woman. Though he smiles at her and babbles on as if his very life had been in danger and she had been one to save him from certain death. Stand upright, I have the mind to shout, stand upright and play the part of a man! Even if you have not the spine or the balls!

The heart of a woman is the same no matter what the country. She takes pity on the weak and feeble-minded. She has not the understanding to realize that Alfonse de la Bastida is a fraud of the highest order, a man in name only, a Christian man in dress only.

'Praised be Jesus Christ!' he shouts.

'For always,' I reply, out of habit. It is as good Catholics have been taught to answer since childhood. It is too late when I realize I have fallen into the Franciscan's trap, for he seizes my reply as an act of contrition for having laughed at him.

'And praised be the Blessed Virgin!' he shouts.

It startles the dear woman, the Mary of the Rocks as I am apt now to think of her. Though by the look on her face she is not alarmed at his behaviour. She must think him possessed by some strange spirit, by the Devil perhaps, if there is the Devil in her faith.

The Grey Friar is clearly relishing his sudden restoration, for now he has the attention of the whole of the multitude, both Native and Basque, within hearing of his voice. And those who have not heard are relayed the message by those who have.

'This woman has saved me from being cast by wind into the sea!'

It is a lie of course, but nobody save I and sweet Mary saw what happened and only I can render the truth in a language our men will understand. But now my truth no longer matters, for the Franciscan has woven his deceitful tongue about the incident and declared himself rescued from certain death.

'Saved I was! As I was about to fall into the merciless waters, a vision of the Blessed Lady appeared to me, then her outstretched hand turned into the hand of this dear aborigine.'

The others who had now gathered around peer with doubt into his eyes, for they know better than to trust his word. The spectacle is this: the Franciscan perched in the manner of the Christ upon a crest of rock, his audience of unbelievers below, behind them the flock of aborigines, and bewildered Mary suddenly at the centre of us all.

I am about to deny the charlatan, when it is as if every Basque man sees in Shanawdí what I have seen — the serenity of the Blessed Virgin to be found at the side altar of their own Church, whether it be San Esteban in Usurbil or the Church of our Lady of Yrun Urancu, or any of the myriad of Marys they gazed upon every time they found themselves at Mass.

They are pondering what I know not to be true — could the Blessed Virgin appear so far from the Christian world as this? So far from Rome, where dear Pope Gregory will never hear of it and cannot send his blessing? Yet I am mute, for to deny the Grey Friar is to deny what I myself have known for many days — that the aborigine has the face and benevolence of the Virgin, if not the flesh.

I am grieved to know that the Franciscan has used her likeness for his own devious ends. He wishes to make himself the worthy one, the one she has chosen above all others. And now, in horrid supplication, he falls to his knees before her, his hands clasped in appalling tightness, his face a mask of overwhelming rapture.

The dear lady, of course, does not know what to think of this, and is all the more confounded when one by one a scattered host of other Basque men drop to their knees, sheep following the cunning ram. Oh, but I am grieved for her. My heart is sore at the sight, for she is left bewildered, as are her people. There is not the language to explain the spectacle. They know nothing of our tongue beyond the whale and its parts and the simple tasks of turning blubber to oil. There is no way to make them understand the turning of their Shanawdí into a miracle of a Blessed Virgin. Dear God, what do they think has befallen them?

It is for me to intercede. I approach the lady and thankfully she has such regard for me that my forthrightness adds nothing to her misery. Indeed it calms her to see me lead her away from the scene and to her own people. I greet them all with strong and honest intent — they cannot fail to see it in my eyes — and assure them, with the kindness of my tone, that there is nothing that should trouble them. Only that I could make them see the Franciscan is a fool.

When I lead the band of aborigines away, back to their own patch of ground, at a distance from what has become the Spectacle, my countrymen who have fallen to their knees are left to look about themselves, ponder how absurd they appear to the others who have remained upright, who remain men with minds of their own.

Suddenly, the Captain of the *Maria Louise* appears and is met with a barrage of explanation that leaves him the most confounded of us all.

'Has there been a miracle here?' he asks, though hardly with the reverence one would think due such a deed.

There is awkward, tepid nodding from several of the men. The Franciscan, on his feet now, back to clutching his cloak, makes his way toward the Captain, to what he takes to be sanctuary.

There is a slovenly look about him now, his hair pasted to his skull with sweat, his body pained after its beating about the rocks. There is a cut above one eye and a plaster of dirt and blood from the eye to the corner of his slackened mouth.

The Captain is wary of him, having spent weeks jaw-to-jaw aboard the ship, their minds pitted across the supper table. The Captain is a clever fellow and knows enough of clerics to sift the honest from the rogues. His brother walks among the principals in Rome and spent many of his priestly years at the hearings in Trent. He no doubt told the Captain of the scheming minds of wayward clerics, the ways of routing them from their lairs.

Yet, woeful though it be, the Captain fails to rebuke this scornful, mocking act of the Franciscan. It does not come easy to him to denounce a miracle and that I can only take as pardonable. What mortal, without full knowledge of the Spectacle would risk an endless sojourn in Purgatory by denying it.

It is left to me, the sole witness to the scene, excepting the woman herself, to present the facts. I make no show of my account, but set it forth in as straightforward a manner as I am able, knowing the Captain to be a man of no patience for the garnishing of a story. He wishes a swift end to the upheaval among his whaling men. A miracle would disrupt the steady flow of commerce.

But the Franciscan will have none of it, and contradicts my words at every turn. Then to add fat to the flames, all manner of whalemen fall victim to his fervent tones, and their eyes having dwelt on the face of the aborigine for such a spell, are further convinced that they are the chosen ones, the ones God has culled for a glimpse of the Blessed Virgin walking about the earth.

I try as hard as I can to convey the gravity of my mission. And they know full well I am a man as eager in my faith as any of them, for I have made my pilgrimage to the Virgin in Itziar, and with the best of men kissed the rock. I have travelled all the way to Gasteiz and prayed before Virgen Blanca as earnestly as any man ever did. They dare not shroud me with the epithet of unbeliever.

Yet, unconvinced do some remain that the rocks of Tierranoba have not for a brief moment been touched by Mary, gentle mother of His Son. And woe is the man, Captain or otherwise, who stands between their blessed selves and God.

I have a notion of why this should be, besides the serenity encasing the face of dear Shanawdí. Who would not wish God among them in the midst of the danger of the hunt? Who would risk separating themselves from God with an ocean separating themselves from home?

As the day comes to its end, nothing has found a resolution. The Franciscan has his believers, I have mine, and between us the Captain and the mass of whaleman left undecided, unwilling to pledge themselves to either story. As for the aborigines, they are left skirting about their fires, mumbling to themselves, in tones that seem furtive, perplexed.

I cannot sleep this night and when I escape the hut and sit on the rock outside, huddled into a blanket for warmth, I can think only of Shanawdí and what must stir within her mind. It is not only her mind I think of, but her face and the full sleekness of her body. Imagine the delight of it I do. As any man would, I tell myself, though perhaps it be that I dwell on it more than most.

What takes my mind away from her is the echo of rock striking rock. And when I turn in the direction of the sound and bring my eyes to bear on it, the moonlight reveals the vague outline of someone moving about the very arena of the Spectacle, someone piling rock atop rock. When I stand in the shadows of the hut I can see the low square of rock that he has created, and at the seaward edge of it a wooden cross erected, rocks mounded at its base.

Who be the rock piler there is no doubt, though I cannot see his face.

It is lost in the folds of his cowl. The Grey Friar has made of the Spectacle a Shrine!

IT IS CALLED THE Shrine of Our Lady of the Rocks. He is the one to christen it, and I make nothing of the fact that the name has been stolen from under my nose.

The Captain refuses to grant the day of solemnization that the Grey Friar wishes, for he will not have the men distracted from the business of whaling. Already it vexes him to hear his shoremen arguing over it as they work the blubber.

'This Tierranoba is no place for miracles!' I have heard him declare, exasperated. I agree, though it seems one has been concocted in our midst, leaving the Captain powerless to stop it breeding.

The look I cast on the Franciscan each time I encounter him — more often than I wish, for continuously he cuts his route to cross with mine — is a look of indifference. To show him anything more would be to confess that what he has erected is something more than a lie, a shameless lie to bring attention to himself. And make of him a perpetual curiosity to the innocent Shanawdí. There are those among his followers who know not whether to cast their attention on the woman herself or on the shrine. The Franciscan is quick to make it known that he is the one to engage the aborigine, for fear, he says, that her confusion will lead to harm.

Bulls' balls, for always! As it is, the woman is confounded by the stares the men turn upon her. I do what I can to set her mind at rest, but our languages remain a torment, and I worry that I only confuse her more with my constant wordless smiles.

What she thinks of the Franciscan I fail to understand. The oaf follows her about and blathers on to her in the Castile tongue as if some notion of what has happened will seep into her brain. As if he thinks the earnestness of his drivel, and not the words themselves, is what will reveal the Spectacle to her. I have heard him repeat the Ave Maria again and again, continuing it when her patience and politeness have run their course and she wants to be free of him. Yet it is as if the Franciscan has some spell over her, for she comes back to him in time and endures his spouting once more. Out of the kindness of her heart it must be, for certain not any liking for the cork-brain.

Let it be said that the malice I bear toward the man I can put to silence. I would never strike the grey fool, though it long be in my mind to do. If he were an ordinary man, a man no different in pith from one of us, then I would have done it long ago and put an end to the idiocy now upon this shore. But something draws me from the act, something about the robe he wraps himself in, even though I know the pretense and the mockery it is.

The days pass and again it is the whaling that takes charge of our days and nights. Though the work saps all the strength I have and I want nothing more than food and drink and a dry bed, I am happy that it should be this way, for with each barrel topped and its hoops driven in place, that is one less space aboard the ship to fill, and one barrel closer to returning home. For one thing I do know for certain — the Captain will not have the Franciscan aboard his ship another year.

By midsummer there are days pleasant enough in their wind and weather. There is not the cruel heat of the sun burning down on us as there would be in our homeland. Nor does the Captain see the need for a midday halt in work — that is the luckless side of it. As long as there is a chance of collaring a whale then it is steady at it, with only wind to give us rest.

On one such day, a day not long after the erection of his shrine, I see the Franciscan sitting with Shanawdí, exchanging word for word with her, as if they are sacred and not words that any man would know. The Castile tongue is one we speak as well as our own, except the sheepmen, too far in the hills to know anything but sheep. The Friar boasts that it is the tongue Franciscans will spread throughout the world. What of the Jesuits, I have the mind to ask, for he hates the Jesuits. The Loyolas were bred from Basque soil, Ignatius among them. In Guipuscoa — I know it well. I will press the Captain for a Jesuit next season, for a Jesuit would surely teach me to read.

The aborigine makes the attempt to repeat the words. For some reason she is willing to sit with him and listen to his drone. No doubt all day while men are working themselves to the bone, he is spending his time wooing her with a deluge of words. Before long the single words have changed to two and three together, then three and four, with the Grey Friar prancing about the rocks in demonstration. 'I walk. I see rock. I carry a rock.'

'I see an idiot,' are my words when I can stand it no longer and stride up to him face to face.

'Ah, Joanes de Echaniz,' he says, as if I have uttered nothing. 'We spied you walking about the rocks, and wished for your company.'

Shanawdí, of course, understands not a word. Any wishing she might have done for my company was not for him to know. She does smile at my presence, however, and that is plain enough to the Franciscan.

She, in all truth, does much more than smile. She looks at me as if I have rescued her from torment. Why she would consent to the excessive word-passions of the Friar I do not know. His lust he surely cannot disguise with words, or his clutching of a book. I see a rock. I carry a rock. The Friar has no more heart than rock itself.

He looks at me, his eyes suddenly sharpened, as if now I am a heretic, an infidel out to thwart the wishes of Christ. Is it not a look culled from the Tribunal in Logroño?

'These people are as human as any one of us. Did not His Holiness declare it?'

The Franciscan does not take kindly to being lectured on the *Sublimus Dei*. He quotes stiffly, '*They are not only capable of understanding the Catholic Faith, but desire exceedingly to receive it.*'

And with that he turns from me, back to Shanawdí, who has been left bewildered by my intervention it is true. 'Praised be Jesus Christ!' he sings, and points to her with the words, 'For always,' giving himself over to repeating the two words again and again until she is willing to say them.

And when she does, and with the clarity that he deems righteous and true, then he sings again, 'Praised be Jesus Christ!'

'For always,' she chimes.

A face of joy and contentment relieves his earnest brow, for her words are all that he wished to hear. They confirm the righteousness of his ways.

'For always,' she says again. And again, when she sees the reaction it evokes, as if he were a marionette and she the holder of the strings.

Her own face is now pleasure-filled, for she has found the answer to his perplexing questions. Two words it required. Of course, she knows not what they mean, but that is of no consequence. In the Franciscan's head the first step has been taken. The only one left confused must be the Lord himself.

Ah, but who am I to cast judgment on the foolish Friar. Perhaps chained to the gates of Purgatory I will be. Yet it is not for my own self that I question him, but for the pure and innocent aborigine, heathen though she be. When I look upon her face — as true to that of the Holy Virgin as is upon this earth — I am moved close to tears, and close to driving an unholy fist into the mouth of the Friar. He seeks to save his soul, and gain the affection of Shanawdí in the process, the logic of which is beyond any decent man. I doubt even he is stupid enough to believe the aborigines are any closer to the dear Christ by the blathering of a pair of words.

That the runt of a man has more than conversion on his mind is as plain as the smile that never leaves his lips once her two words are spoken. As for me, it is obvious he wishes me gone. For the sake of Shanawdí I do not budge from the rock, but hold fast to protect her should there be the call. When he sees I have no intention of leaving, he unfurls an even bigger show of his righteousness, enough to sicken to the core any godly man.

He spreads his arms wide and to the heavens, then sweeps them to the hills and the sea, then touches his hands to the earth, all the while pronouncing 'God, God.' Then falls to his knees and bends his body to the earth in a display of holy supplication. Display it truly is, for all the time one eye of his is on the woman, and when she draws back he suddenly returns to his feet, and extends both hands to her hand covering her face in bewilderment. He holds it and, bending his head, presses his lips onto the hand. In the most unholy manner one could conceive.

Bared his soul for the fraud he is! What manner of Franciscan would so fix himself upon a lady! He has the soul of a syphilitic Frenchman, and the debauchery of a Moor! I would have nothing more to do with him except that I am the only hope of protection for the lady.

I should not say the only, for it is not long after the wanton kiss upon the hand that a male aborigine appears, and several more of their band in the distance behind him. They, too, must be more than wary of the Franciscan, and the time he spends with one of their own.

The Friar's manner changes quickly at the sight of him, not the least because he is a head taller than the Friar, with a frame that bears only hardened muscle cased with sun-browned skin, all of which, except his loins, in plain view of Franciscan eyes. The heft of flesh beneath the Friar's robe must quiver, for the aborigine's rigid smile is deeply pursed with consternation. I cannot say it an angry smile, but one that could turn easily so, should the Friar not withdraw himself from Shanawdí, as he is more than quick to do.

Then, as is his way, the Franciscan overwhelms the moment with a flurry of words, all of course, the Natives hear in utter ignorance. 'God looks down upon you all with love and mercy. You are all His precious children, awash in blessed innocence, worthy of the place Your Lord has set aside for you.'

The aborigine hardly changes his expression, until the Franciscan runs out of words. Then the Native spews forth a torrent of his own. Just as vigorous and with no more regard for our understanding than the Friar had for his. It is lunacy, a comedy of wills. Shanawdí and I, we catch each other's eye and share secretly the madness.

Oh, but it is a sweet, sweet moment. The two of us loose, then touching in a way that needs no words. I chance a second glance and this time I am certain it is amour I see. The faintest touch and for the briefest moment, but of nothing am I surer. Our hearts have met where there is silent, wordless understanding.

And that night, in the lull of darkness, we steal a moment together! I sit by the rocks of the shrine for so long she chances it is me. I sense her drawing near and I angle myself at the moon in a way that she will be certain who it is.

I catch first the glint of moonlight on a rosary bead that now adorns the fringes of her caribou hide. At that moment she is a Mary like no other. What is it about the night that frees our emotions? I know only that I have her in my arms, know not the detail of her face, as exquisite as it is. All I know, and wish to know, is the pleasure of my hand against her skin. The lifting of my heart at her breathing, the scent of wintergreen luring the good and godly man I know myself to be. I swoon at the touch of her hand against my skin.

It is strange. I am more shy than she. I am more wary of the raptures of night. She leads me away under the cover of darkness to a safer place where there is no chance of being discovered, a place she has had in her mind, it seems, for just such a chance. I think nothing, but embrace the holiness of the ground on which we lie. Moss-covered ground punctured by twigs. The twigs pierce my naked back, like thorns I think, like the pilgrims who pierce themselves at the ecstasy of Holy Week.

'For always,' she says. 'God,' she says. The only words of my tongue that she knows well enough to utter.

I know nothing of hers but her name.

That I do not repeat, for to me at this moment all I know is her body, mine for this mote of time. A chamber for my deep, abiding lust.

I wrap myself in her, side by side, loosened hide about my body, the scent of ochre colouring the blackened night. Oh, but I seek the place for my poker, and when her legs tighten around it, there I have found the refuge for the longing. Suddenly, she rises above me, such as a woman has never done before and it is she who is thrusting, up and down the shaft, her ravenousness equal to my own. I have no mind for anything but the delirious surge, the utterly sweet shutter of Paradise.

My face I bury in the delicious mounds of her breasts, my heaves lessen, drained as I am of the craving.

When she falls away from me, only then do I feel the full bloom of what the night has brought, more suddenly than I had ever thought possible. I lie with her, without speaking, for there is no use in it, until I grow weary of the night, not without fear of being discovered.

We part — she treading silently a path to her dwelling place, I dodging the moonlight to mine. When I take to my boughs, amid the snores of other crewmen, and ease to sleep with the memory of the night, I am a wildly contented man, for I have tasted the New World in a way few Basques, if any, ever have. And I have found a blessed refuge for my poker.

I AM WOKEN IN the morning by the sound of the *txistu*, its drum and flute, and of chanting, the voice of Alfonse de la Bastida in the lead. It is Sunday, that I know, and a day the Grey Friar conducts the Mass, if there are no calls from the lookouts. More than once the sight of whales have left him without a flock, or cut short the Mass, once with the wine and host at that moment on my lips. The whaling, the Captain has made it clear, is God's business, the first business of every day.

When I peer from my roost I see a morning thick o' fog, without strength in the sun to burn it very quick. The Friar shall have his way. But today, from the commotion I hear, he is in want of more than his way. My eyes squint at the sight that crowds them, for I hardly think it real.

A procession, of the kind that fills the feast days, be it in Orio or San Sebastián or any home of ours, has spread itself upon the rocks of this Tierranoba. In holy homage to the Blessed Virgin, the Franciscan leads a blustery throng of whalers over the barren land to the Shrine of our dear Lady of the Rocks. *Ave Maria, gratia plena. Dominus tecum. Benedicta tu in mulieribus, et benedictus fructus ventris tui, Jesus. Sancta Maria, Mater Dei ...*

I stand for a time incredulous at the sight, but then I see there are but a few scoffers busying themselves with work as a pretense who do not join the crowd. The eyes of the crowd descend on me, for they know I have had the attention of Tierranoba Mary these many days, and should I not be at the head, shoulder-to-shoulder with the Friar?

That I should, if only to protect the lady from his zealous foolery. This newest spectacle is fraught with trouble for the aborigines, that I can see straightaway, so I answer their stares by clambering over the rocks to the head of the pack.

Met with freakish gawks I am, and for what reason?

I do not know. And when some fail to hide their smirking faces I demand to know what about me they find to amuse themselves.

'Your face, Joanes de Echaniz, your face! It is smeared with red ochre, like the aborigines. Except they smear it over all parts of their bodies, we're told. Where has that face of yours been, Joanes, that it should be grimed with ochre?' Laughter spreads itself through the crowd, foul laughter, that of Ramos the foulest of all.

'Where has that face been buried, Joanes de Echaniz, that even your ears are coated. Deep between two hillocks?'

'His poker lathered in it.'

'More likely rubbed away!'

'And him with a wife back in Orio, and a sweet young maid.'

Their laughter stretches the length of the procession, growing only louder when I wipe the wool of my sleeve across my face.

The Franciscan is the only one failing to find humour in my state. He seethes with anger at what the others have proposed. Treacherous anger, of the most vile nature. For he attempts to conceal the depths of it, and pretends his vexation is defence of the aborigines, not fervid jealousy.

I make no pretense about what I have done. My silence inflames the Friar more. 'Is this the truth?' he demands of me.

I am not answerable to the cur, who is as well known in the brothels of San Sebastián as any man. Robed or naked.

'Is it? Have you preyed on the innocent aborigine?'

If to shame me into confessing is his game, he will be sorely disappointed. For what I make of any day, or night, when work is done, is my concern, no other's. Silence and my cold, indifferent stare are answer enough for him.

He turns away from the procession, in pious rage, and strides over the rock in full wing. His robe billows out behind him, making him the lofty sight indeed. To the camp of the aborigines he heads, there to find Shanawdí no doubt, as if he has a God-given right to make her confess what has taken place.

From the distance I can see what transpires. The Friar stands face to face with Shanawdí, and to his great dismay for certain, face to face with the Native headman. What few words he knows in their language he puts to zealous use, together with sweeping gestures of his arm toward me. All of a sudden the gestures end, his voice loses its severity. The Friar is left stunned, it seems, by the reaction of the aborigines, who now part from him and head our way, in a band similar to our own, Shanawdí at the fore.

What might be their intention I do not know, but they are now a lively breed, more lively than ourselves.

It is a meeting of our world and theirs, Basque men and aborigines, ancients both. Bizarre it is upon the landscape. Two trails — one garbed in woollen weave, shirts brick red and blue pantaloons, the other their furs trim about them, though for many what covers most of the skin is only ochre to keep away the flies. They are taller, yet our chests are as strong as their long, rangy ones. They, too, have a drum and their queer flute made of bone, which they play apart, not together as is our way. And a rattling sack that has the look of some animal's gut. Two bands roving the rocks, bound for each other, the Shrine of Our Lady of the Rocks the meeting spot.

Their eyes have fixed on me, and once the bands meet, I am the one to whom their words are directed, though, of course, I know nothing of what they say. Still, the words are jovial enough. Without the scorn which I feared when I saw them trekking toward us. Jovial, and in truth hearty in a fashion for which there is no accounting.

I have wiped my face as much as I am able, but at seeing me draw my sleeve once more across it, the head Native rubs his hand across his own face until there is ochre lodged upon it, then standing face to face with me, extends that hand and smears its ochre onto my cheeks.

What am I to make of this? For now the others of the band have circled me and drawn me in amongst themselves.

'Ramos, what is it they want?' Confused I am, though not fearful as I said, for they have still goodwill across their faces. All except Shanawdí, whose face is filled with something I can take only as affection. And pride.

'The Mary has a chosen one, it seems,' says Ramos above the din of the aborigines, his amusement hardly diminished.

Now indeed it is fear I have. What the aborigines wish is to embrace me, then the whole of our procession, for what reason I have no notion. Yes, but a lively troupe they are, drumming and chanting, now dancing about, as if they have set forth a celebration. They have swallowed our own procession and urged us to join their revelry. They gesture for more of our *txistu* playing, only livelier and louder, to which the whalers bearing them happily agree.

The Friar's homage to Our Lady of the Rocks has turned to a carnival of a most peculiar sort. Our Tierranoba Mary at the centre of it, to be sure, but it is not the godly deed the Friar wished, nor is he any longer at its helm. He is now outside, gawking angrily in, and that pleases me the most.

But fears I have. For now from their headman comes nudging, of me toward Shanawdí, that we might be closer to each other, as if at the centre of the circle should be the both of us, together. O, but this is troublesome, for Shanawdí has not the discomfort that I have, and now what I see in her eyes is anticipation that the two of us are paired, a match of man and woman. A match (I dread to think it true) of man and eager woman. But there it is in her eyes, through the shyness, an eagerness to be sure.

'O, Jesus Christ!' I cannot help but call upon my Saviour.

'For always,' is her steadfast reply.

Dear Saviour, am I not an innocent, a mere follower of my poker. A man is but a man, who wishes only that what God has put between his legs causes him no grief. Had I but known the consequence, would I not have cast my seed away again, and again, hoping I would not have to slice away the thing to stop my wandering. I wince, dear Lord. I draw my legs tight together at the thought of it.

The dear Tierranoba Mary is not the Blessed Virgin. She is a woman of this world, just as I am a man of it. She drew herself to me, as much as I to her, perhaps more so, if the truth were told. But I cannot speak the truth, for none will understand it. The only truth for them is what falls from the lips of their own. What I speak has no virtue to anyone but myself. Speak, lady, and the truth, and let me draw free, the innocent that I am.

She has no such intention, and neither have the other aborigines, of doing anything but celebrate the pair of us.

'They have taken you for one of their own, Joanes de Echaniz,' says Ramos, his amusement only slightly abated. 'It would seem to me that by doing what you did to young Tierranoba Mary, you have stated a claim to her, and they have happily agreed. There is no telling their pagan ways, Joanes de Echaniz.'

The man is right. Heathens have no hope of knowing what is right in the world. They have not taken the Saviour as their own. Instead they call upon the sky and make of it a god and make a dozen other gods of whatever surrounds them. No sense is there in that. This procession to the Shrine, this road to their conversion, of this they have made a mockery. I have my quarrels with the Friar, but neither do I wish anything but the saving of the aborigines' souls. It is my only hope, and theirs as well if this display is not to turn to disaster.

Alfonse de la Bastida stands outside the circle, a man in stature shrunk, annulled by the workings of the heathens. What thoughts are lurking in the Friar's brains that he is not clamouring for their attention? Does he ferret pleasure from the terror in my soul? I wish only freedom from this circle, to return to my lodging, to the whaling life that brought me to the rocks of Tierranoba. That is what I am here for, to hunt the whales, not to have myself displayed, a curiosity for the Natives of this place.

Now the headman would have me join hands with Shanawdí, and presses both our hands tightly together. I cannot know a word he speaks, but if I am to judge by the strength in his eyes, then they are fateful words, words about to change the man I am in their minds, and the woman Shanawdí is as well. Now I fear the worst.

My heart rises in my chest, as stiff as any rock to which I have set foot on this shore. There are words spoken by the leader of the aborigines — rough and mulish words, now that he sees the reluctance in my eyes. They bear great weight, for they have the attention of every soul in their band. They bring our own Basque whalers to silence, which strikes even greater fear in my chest. What notion do I have of his words? None. And yet I am expected to stand my full measure, and be looked down upon by the aborigine whose height is also far above my own. Stand and take his heathen words the same as if they were spewing from the good Father at the Church of San Nicolas in Orio.

I fear them, Lord, even more than what came from the dear priest when I last confessed to him. And that a matter of straying into a back street of San Sebastián. I did engage with the woman, and confessed soundly to it, and sat in the confessional, a man I was, unflinching with every utterance from beyond the panel wall.

But this is something worse, though I am unflinching still. Were it to do any earthly good, I would stand and confess my sins. But in their eyes it is not sin, dear Lord, and that I fail to understand! Were it sin I would gladly seek a churchman — even the Grey Friar, he being the sole choice to be had — and I would confess and seek the pardon of my Lord. To escape my allotted time in Purgatory I would slave at my indulgences harder than any man would know.

O, but this is a strange and fearful moment. When the headman has said his last, it is only then that the full weight descends on me. It is as if I have been struck from above, not by you, dear Lord, but by heavy weight indeed — of a thousand Purgatories! I sink nearly to the rocks. It is Shanawdí who holds me up, and with such strength that I am stricken in my heart even more.

For now she speaks. Their leader steps away, to the fringes of the circle. She is the focus of every eye there is upon these rocks. She speaks on and on to the assembled — strange for any woman. How strange these aborigines that one of their women would stand and take charge of all they see and hear, in charge with all the conviction of a man. Even the Blessed Virgin would not be so bold.

This woman can be no Mary. She is not deserving of the likeness. Holy innocence drains from her countenance with every opening of her mouth. Foolish I was, and sinful, Lord, to think her akin to the Holy Mother, sinful once more and that I openly confess, dear Lord.

Confession does no good. These aborigines are ignorant of confession. What in their breeding does it take to wash away their sins, that I wish to know.

That, I have no hope of knowing. I try not to show the dread that is within my soul, for to appear weak at such an hour as this would only seal my fate, whatever dreaded fate it be. Why must words loose such torture? If only these heathen men could see that I am but a man, the same as them. I challenge every one of them to lay bear their roamings from camp to camp in the middle of the night. I dare to think what I would learn. Guilty they are of seeking women, or they are not of this world, they are of some unknown race. Some unknown human race? Not human then. Wild, unknowable heathens, dear Lord. Savages then!

SHANNON

THREE WEEKS PASS SINCE she last spoke to Simon. It is well into November.

Three weeks of doing everything but what she knows she should be doing. She has yet to tackle the site at Red Bay.

She's been alone much of the time, even through the weekends. There is no interest in going to Conche, no reason to be going. Before long the full brunt of winter will set in.

On a particularly troublesome Saturday afternoon, without allowing herself to think any more about it, she emails Simon.

Would you like to get together for a drink? Maybe over Christmas. If you don't have other plans. She immediately regrets sending it.

He doesn't reply right away. Fair enough.

The next day he does. *I'll be spending Christmas in Goose Bay, with my daughter.* Double space.

How about New Year's?

She waits a day before getting back to him.

St. John's?

Single space. *You could try to set up a meeting with someone from the provincial archaeology department, for one of the days we're there. If you want to, if you're serious about L'Anse Amour.*

Silence for two days.

She emails: *Sorry. I'm being an idiot.*

That evening, another email back to her: *I've been talking to someone at the Labrador Métis Association. They're considering backing me on this, having me go as their representative.*

She replies. *I meant to tell you, the story was very interesting. Thanks for lending me the book.*

In fact she hardly knew what to think of the story. It was not what she had expected. ImagiNative? Affected? Was that his take on Red Bay? She is still thinking about it.

THAT DOESN'T STOP HER from moving it aside. A few more emails and there is agreement that, no matter what the Métis Association decides, Simon will fly to St. John's with her and they'll spend a few days there. Neutral territory. New Year's together.

There is nothing for Shannon to do but wait out the few weeks that follow. To make it through the crappiest Christmas she can imagine, with the expectation that New Year's will bring something, although she dares not think about exactly what.

SHE HAS SEVERE SECOND thoughts. No goddamn idea where it is taking her. By February she has to get a preliminary report in the hands of Parks Canada. With the understanding that the Aboriginal stakeholders have been consulted and their input incorporated into it. That they're 'on side.' With no danger of any changes to the sites blowing up in the collective faces at Parks Canada.

It's December. The site at L'Anse aux Meadows is buried in snow. There's no point in trying to revisit it. It's all there on her computer, a drawing of the proposed changes expertly overlaid on a wide-angle photograph of the site taken on a beautiful summer day. All very professional.

TWO DAYS BEFORE CHRISTMAS, Marie phones. She is not someone Shannon wants to talk to.

Marie works her way past the preliminaries. 'Your stepfather and I were wondering if you had anywhere to go on Christmas Day. Perhaps you'd like to come and have Christmas dinner with us in Conche. There's just the two of us.'

And the one of her. No, she thinks, she doesn't have anywhere to go for Christmas dinner, and yes, that would be the last place in the world she would want to spend it.

'It's very good of you to ask. Thank you all the same, but I have plans.' Plans to spend it alone, with a good bottle of wine.

'You're sure? We'd hate to think of you all by yourself on Christmas Day. Even if you just drove out for the meal. You wouldn't have to stay for long, not if you didn't want to.'

Acknowledgement of the idiocy of the whole situation.

'Thank you. But I'm fine.'

'Call then if you change your mind. Or just show up. We're sure to cook plenty. We'll be eating around one.'

It's goodbye then and hang up, the deed done.

For the moment she sits motionless, stunned that the conversation ever took place. Either it took unfathomable nerve on Marie's part to make the call, or she and Jerome are absurdly oblivious to the emotions that swirl around the real world.

Before she has time to recover, the phone rings a second time.

Marie, again. An apology for phoning back. 'I wanted to say something else, Shannon. I wanted to say we know you have a hard time understanding Jerome and me. He has his faults. But he's not whatever you got him made out to be.' Her voice breaks before she can get out the rest of what she wants to say. She manages, 'Have a nice Christmas.'

Marie hangs up. Shannon sits, stunned for a second and decisive time.

HER MOTHER USED TO call her 'a devil for punishment.' And shake her head when she said it, or close her eyes in frustration, whenever Shannon was being particularly stubborn, which, in retrospect, she admits happened regularly. She'd get it in her head to do things and she just did them. Nothing cruel or deceitful. Often for no other reason than to assert herself. Sometimes she'd live to regret it, but most times not.

Impulsive would be the kinder descriptor. She thought she was past that.

On Christmas morning, she lies in bed, fixated on why there is no need to get up. She has not gone through the exercise of putting up a Christmas tree, fake or otherwise. As expected, it has not turned into a pleasant holiday season.

In the midst of a particularly dismal chain of thought she gets it in her head to dress, board the CR-V, and drive to Conche. Absurdly, blindly. Rather than lie slovenly in bed on Christmas Day feeling sorry that thirty-eight years should have come to this.

By even her erratic standards, it makes no sense. Other than in the myopic context of leaving Newfoundland once her job is over, nothing changed.

To confront that, even she can see, is a tall order on a Christmas Day.

Nevertheless, within the hour she is in the vehicle, pointed in the direction of Conche. If nothing else, it is a beautiful, sun-filled morning, the woods sprayed with snow, the landscape glittering.

Her good intention, having duly steeled herself, is to provide the opportunity for something other than aggravation. Whether Jerome will turn opportunity to disaster remains to be seen.

Marie, predictably, is surprised by her change of plans. And now turns excessively enthusiastic, whisking Shannon's down-filled parka onto a hanger and force feeding it into the narrow closet. Shannon removes her winter boots and dons a pair of shoes and prepares to enter the kitchen, wherein she knows she will find Jerome.

She is right, yet only temporarily. At Marie's insistence, the three of them move to the living room. Jerome takes to one end of the overly florid sofa, Marie to the other end, and their guest to matching armchair opposite. An artificial Christmas tree, thick with crocheted ornaments, stands in one corner. Strings of multicoloured tree lights flicker — randomly, it would appear.

The conversation is strained, but not discordant. She gives Marie full credit for the effort she puts forth to make her feel at ease. The invitation was her idea, no doubt, and Jerome the innocent victim of her tenacity. And of Shannon's unforeseen consent. On this day life has its trials, twinkling tree the least of them.

Dinner brings additional challenges. The aromas evoke memories of her Newfoundland Christmases past. And now she must find a path to walk between being the grateful guest and a restrained eater with an ambivalent stomach. There is no denying the turkey, however, and several of its many accompaniments. Marie is a very good cook. Each time Shannon pauses, inadvertently observing the pair, it is clear that in Jerome Marie had found the perfect patron for her kitchen talents.

Christmas pudding drizzled with rum sauce follows. Then, back in the living room, weak coffee and the lingering touch of Marie's own partridge-berry liqueur. They talk for a while. Dinner settles somewhat. Shannon offers to help with clearing the table and doing the dishes, but Marie is adamant that she stay where she is. Orchestrated perhaps for her to be alone with Jerome while Marie busies herself in the kitchen, out of hearing range.

Shannon has come with a head tight with a single line of questions. The timing is as unexpected to her as it is to Jerome, leading as it does from a benign comment about the memory of an early childhood Christmas morning.

'Did you know him? My father, that is?'

It takes a while of shuffling about on the sofa, but eventually he does emit an answer.

'In a way.'

She's prepared to wait for more.

'We grew up together. He was a grade ahead of me in school.'

'What about the rest of his family?'

'It was his grandmother who reared him up. By herself, most of the time, her husband away on the boats. You would know that.'

Both had died before Shannon was born. Not even any pictures. Or none that she knew of. None even of their daughter, the grandmother she also never knew.

'Your grandmother went away. Married an American Air Force fellow from the base in Stephenville. Went to the States and never came back is what we always heard.'

For Shannon to have heard too, a family story rarely repeated, though never a secret, apparently.

'His father, then.... Was it ever talked about? Who he was?'

Jerome looks at her as if it's not right he should be the one she's asking. He makes no move to answer.

'You don't know?'

He shakes his head. There is no telling what that means.

'Was he from Newfoundland?'

'He would have to be, I suppose. People said your grandmother never wanted her husband to know she already had a child or he would never have married her. Said the father himself never even knew she was pregnant. That's what your mother told me, Shannon. That's all I knows.'

'Nothing else?' Not even her grandfather's name.

Jerome shakes his head. Then he says, 'Growin' up, whenever your father was in a fight the boys had a name for him. *Jackatar*, they used to call him. C'mon, ya little jackatar. I never knew where it come from. Until years later I used to be out to Stephenville and I heard it again.'

Jackatar. Jack-o'-tar. Jacky Tar.

She is as ignorant of the words as Jerome. 'Mixed breed,' he had said, 'half French.'

She is absorbed by that, thinking of Conche's long ties to France. Jerome had said nothing more. If there is more to it, it's for Shannon to find out on her own.

It doesn't take long. *The Dictionary of Newfoundland English* online. And again, *The Random House Unabridged.*

A Newfoundlander of mixed French and Micmac Indian descent. That, or the choice of *A Newfoundland Native of mixed French and Amerindian descent.*

A name given to the mix of the French from France and the Micmac from Nova Scotia, both of whom settled on the west coast of Newfoundland. No longer are they the Micmac. They are called now by what they call themselves — the Mi'kmaq.

No longer a pigment of her imagination.

She sits at the computer desk in the apartment in St. Anthony and thinks to herself that Simon will be pleased to have been right.

Perhaps not. Perhaps he would rather it wasn't all the more bloody complicated. She won't tell him yet. She knows the time will have to come.

As New Year's closes in she spends her days revisiting what she has written of the preliminary report, taking stock, deciding what's to be salvaged. She has three weeks after she gets back to put it into its final form. She still has the site at Red Bay to tackle.

She hasn't thought much about what she might be doing after that. There is the second component of the contract — to implement the proposals. If they are accepted. If not, there's the option of returning to her old job.

She left BC with the intention of never going back. She was counting on something permanent opening up with Parks somewhere in Eastern Canada. Now there's nothing in her head telling her what she wants to be doing.

CORMACK

7th November, 1828
St John's

As President of the Boeothuck Institution, I think it wisest
not to bring Shanawdithit into a meeting of all members, as
monumental as that might prove to be. Rather, from time to
time, I gather several of them at my residence to share supper
with Shanawdithit, trusting to the informal nature of the
assembly to set her at her ease, and with good fortune, uncover
yet more of interest concerning her tribe.

Try as I do to instill in her what is appropriate for discussion
and what might prove an embarrassment, it is never certain
what will emanate from her in answer to a question. One might
think the presence of five men, each of considerable stature in
the Colony, and suitably dressed to indicate this, would restrain
her thoughts. Such has not been the case.

The five gathered around the dining room table last evening,
on the day following the celebration of Guy Fawkes, and that a

near catastrophe because of the ludicrous number of fires in all parts of the city. Besides myself were Dr Carson, Attorney General Simms, Judge Des Barres, and John Stark of the Northern Circuit Court. We had much of interest between ourselves that would fill any supper table, of course, especially in light of the fact that Stark had just arrived from several weeks along the coast.

Stark was in the midst of relating his time at Trinity, one of the older and more prosperous of the northern outposts. Carson knew Trinity well enough, it being home to John Clinch, friend of Jenner, and the first on the continent to use vaccine against the pox.

'Shanawdithit, I should think,' said Carson, raising his voice slightly to be sure he had her attention, 'is likely the very first aborigine in the New World to have the good fortune to be inoculated. A circumstance duly noted to my colleagues in Britain.'

Shanawdithit did not appear to recognize the significance of the doctor's statement, but chose instead to devote her attention to the soup. The others exchanged glances and let the conversation change course and lumber ahead.

Stark brought it around to religion, as is inevitable during any gathering in Newfoundland, and to the new church in Trinity. He rendered the first lines of the hymn written by the Rector in celebration of its consecration, a most welcome diversion from the dialogue that had previously deflated the table.

'We love the place, O God / Wherein Thine honour dwells!' The words rang out in deep, reverberant tones.

'The man sings well for his supper.'

'The Reverend Bullock has composed as fine a hymn as the good Lord would wish.'

At the mention of the Rector, Shanawdithit raised her head. 'Bollock. His brains are in his bollocks.'

The gentlemen winced at the words. Coming as they did from a young lady, and not some urchin or slovenly fisherman. There was a sputtering of soup from the Judge, back into his bowl, as much as aim allowed.

'Mr Peyton always say the words,' added Shanawdithit. 'His brains are in his bollocks. What it means?'

'Mr Peyton has his crude side he fails to hide in company,' I said to her. 'In any case the man's name is Bullock.'

Her ear finally attuned to the difference, though the consequences of the utterance was still with us. I directed the cook to remove the soup bowls, which were near empty in any case, and to bring on the main course, in the hope the change of fare would change the direction of Shanawdithit's wanderings.

'Now, gentlemen. Let us continue our meal,' I announced, in a strong voice, gaily clad. 'And must a plot to burn the Parliament in London two hundred years ago be such an excuse for hooliganism?'

Shanawdithit took it, as was my worst fear, for a rebuke, a slight inflicted on her person.

'Bollocks,' she said again, most distinctly. Then announced, 'Gentlemen!' in such a mocking tone I could hold nothing but dread of what might follow. 'Bollocks! Show me bollocks! Then I understand.'

The gentlemen, of course, knew best to ignore the confusions of the aborigine. They took to their partridge and potato, with devotion to each forkful, oblivious to the young woman and her clatter.

Eventually Shanawdithit, a relief to all gathered, retreated into her meal, though not before a paganish long stretch of silence. Bruised by the episode she was, by the unfortunate consequences of her innocence. It seemed to be her nature to stumble into such episodes.

The evening advanced much more agreeably from that point. And in due course, after a respite from conversation to quell the waters, the table turned almost as warmly boisterous as when we first sat down.

With some effort on the part of myself and Carson, Shanawdithit was drawn again into the evening. Although she was given to monosyllabic response, we did, nevertheless, succeed in conveying the sincere concern of the Institution for her well-being. She could hardly realize, of course, the distinction it was to have so much time given over to her by a congregation of men who shouldered such an abundance of responsibilities in the Colony.

◈

9th November, 1828

The episode described in my previous entry proved an unfortunate one, causing the good Judge in particular to lose his way. These few days later I have put forth to Shanawdithit the subject of religion. In my judgment she needs to take on some measure of reverence, as appropriate to the subject, when again she finds herself in the midst of it. As well, I wish to continue my note-taking, seeking to understand the Boeothuck attachment to their gods.

One reason for bringing Shanawdithit to St John's has been to advance her instruction in the Christian religion. Bishop Inglis was especially insistent that this be attended to as soon as she arrived, and indeed she was not long in the city before I did just that. The Archdeacon at St John the Baptist came around in short order, returning on several occasions. And, I would note, with increasing frustration.

Try as he did, earnestly and with profound patience, to convert the woman, Shanawdithit has shown no interest in becoming, as the Archdeacon would have it, 'a lamb washed in the blood of the Lord Jesus Christ.' She has chosen rather to fasten herself stubbornly to her own beliefs.

Her spirit world has lent her contact with her dead sister and mother. Upon sober reflection, one would hardly think it surprising that she holds to her people in this way, for it could well be what keeps her from insanity in the midst of all the upheaval that has beset her. I cannot bring myself to join in the compulsion to make of her a Christian, knowing, as I do, what comfort Shanawdithit takes from her beliefs, even though there are some for which I remain a skeptic. Shanawdithit drew for me what she called *Aich-mud-yim*. The Devil he would seem to be, densely bearded, dressed in thick beaver skin. She knows of such a creature, she has said, on the shores of what she calls the Great Lake. He is the worst of the 'bad spirits' and so fearsome that the part of the shore where he appeared has never again been set upon by a Boeothuck.

Aich-mud-yim I think a wild embellishment of some trickster, a Micmac perhaps out to terrify his enemy. I keep this notion to myself, for to spurn the ethos of the Boeothuck is equal to spurning Shanawdithit herself, and for that the consequence could only be to estrange me from her. I sit and listen and I prompt her memory when I judge her to be of a mood that will favour it. The result has been a page of precise and extraordinary sketches depicting what I have labelled 'Emblems of Mythology.' Others have reported sightings of such hallowed staves, but never have they been certain of their significance.

By Shanawdithit standing and setting her hand above her head I estimated the staves to each measure six feet in length. Her sketches show precisely the carved emblems which top each one, some geometric in shape, others as explicit as the tail of a whale. It is not unlike the Cross, I supposed, though on no account would I make the allusion to the Bishop when in my next letter to him I reported on the progress made in the young woman's conversion. Neither did I allude to it to the Archdeacon when on the occasion of his next visit I displayed to him the drawing.

'What do you take them to mean, Mr Cormack?'

'They are part of an elaborate affair, a ceremony according

to Shanawdithit, to signify a great event. The hunt of caribou perhaps. Or to signify their reverence for the great works of God — the whale, perhaps.'

The Archdeacon is English-born, a Cambridge man, and these many years a missionary under the Society for the Propagation of the Gospel in Foreign Parts. He has traversed more of the outlying regions of Newfoundland than many born here. His religious path, however, is a narrow one and the tenets of the Church of England he holds to fiercely, to the exclusion of all others. If he has no tolerance for papists he can hardly be expected to give credence to idolaters of the spruce forests.

'She grasps onto her heathen ways as if her life depended on it,' he said.

'Perhaps it does, sir.'

He looked at me through eyes considerably narrowed by the frustration that had built up there over the past weeks. 'What are you saying, Mr Cormack? Are you sanctioning the paganism of the woman?'

'No. But not condemning it, either. She cannot be expected to embrace the ways of the white man in view of the treatment he has afforded her people.'

To the Archdeacon I sounded all the world like a libertine, and as such as abstruse as Shanawdithit herself. He suddenly lost patience with me, and turned to me as if I were the reason for the woman's lack of interest in the Christian faith.

'I have doubts about the woman, sir,' he said to me after he had donned his coat, in readiness to face the snow outside. 'And about you, Mr Cormack.'

'Doubts?'

'Doubts if her residence with you has been the wisest choice, or the most respectable, that could have been afforded her. She has been charmed by you it seems, beyond what benefits her in this life, and the one to come. She has rejected the Holy Scripture. Her soul is adrift, Mr Cormack, and you seem ill-inclined to steer it right.'

With that he wound his stream of a woollen scarf about his neck and chin, planted his hat on his head and with one hand holding it there, escaped the house, leaving me in the doorway. Not to regret his leaving, nor its petulant flourish. What concerned me was the effect on Shanawdithit, for although she was not present at his retreat, his words assailed the hallway and without doubt her ears. What sense she makes of them I do not know.

Upon looking at her as she stepped into view from the kitchen, I spoke. 'The Archdeacon is not well. He does not enjoy his time here.'

'Then he should not come. He is too full of his Jesus.' She turned then, back to the kitchen.

I am uncomfortable at her profanity, though I know she has no way of knowing it is such. Perhaps then, I am led to think, it is not profanity.

I wonder what Hodgkin would say on the matter. In his most recent letter he clings to his Quakerism as strongly as ever, despite how its tenets have thwarted his love for his Sarah. Today I read again his 'Essay on the Promotion of Civilization.' Setting aside its simplicities, having been written when he was barely a man, it puts the corporeal well-being of the Indian races before their conversion. Proselytizing, in Hodgkin's view, seems to be 'strewing seed on unploughed ground, to puzzle them with mysteries which even to the most erudite and piercing human intellect are unsearchable.'

I clench these words in the wake of the Archdeacon's impetuous flight.

❧

30th November, 1828
St John's

These weeks just past have seen my guardianship of
Shanawdithit soundly questioned. I, equally, have soundly
questioned myself and the direction I am leading her, or, more
truly, being led by her.

Does the woman need to be saved from her heathenism? I am
of the view that her beliefs derive from a life which even I knew
little about. It is her belief that when it comes time for her to
pass from this life she will be rejoining her family. She has no
desire to go to a white man's Saviour who, the Archdeacon had
said, will quell all her pain. Her pain is the work of white men.
It is a pain that can never be quelled.

Carson has come again to my house and earnestly bade me to
relinquish the aborigine to the Attorney General and his family
who, he assures me, are without the least doubt willing to take
her in. I hold no dispute about their suitability as guardians.
Shanawdithit would be well cared for, and no less content. That
is not the root of my hesitation.

Can my words to Carson be any more clear? 'I have work
to undertake if I am to further advance knowledge of the
Boeothuck. It requires a rapport with the young woman, a
rapport that has taken me some time to nurture.'

'You would still visit her, of course. The family would

provide a room for your meetings.' A preliminary offering to sustain his opinion.

'I would not be able to judge her mood, nor choose a time to raise a question. Much of what I have learned of her people has come at the most informal of occasions — when she is peeling a potato, or sitting with a cup of tea at a window, her thoughts cast to the outdoors.'

'There is talk in the town, Cormack.'

That, finally, the true tenet of his argument. 'Spread by the Archdeacon, without doubt,' I replied.

Carson would not deny it. 'Rumour feeds on itself. Consider the reputation of the Institution, if nothing else. If we are to expect the support of the Governor ...'

Carson, of all people, bowing to the wants of the Governor. I said to him, 'Cochrane, the dear man, has had no interest in the protection of the Boeothuck. In Shanawdithit residing in St John's he has had even less.'

The Doctor then accused me of failing to understand the seriousness of the situation.

'I have sacrificed my working life to this race, I more than anyone. Would you deny it?'

'It is your choice to make,' he said. As if that were sufficient.

'And you would deny me the opportunity of saving them from the pit of history. Who will remember them, but for what I have recorded? But for the drawings I have elicited from her and her words I have put to paper, what will be understood of them?'

He dared not question my assertion. 'Surely, you have had enough time with her to record all she knows.'

'You have not been versed in natural history, Dr Carson. Had you been you would know that as much time is spent in creating the tenor for study as in the study itself. What she has yet to reveal I do not know. I can only suspect it, too, is of lasting worth. We dare not chance it escaping our grasp.'

'For yourself you do this, not for the Boeothuck?'

'I do not leave it to others to recognize the value of my endeavours. I expect they would be forever blind.'

'Myself among them?'

'There is no more Boeothuck, Dr Carson. As much as I wish it otherwise, I suspect she is the last.'

It grieved me to openly admit it, and I swear I will not do so again while the woman is still in my house.

≈

St John's, Newfoundland
2nd January, 1829

Dear John,

I am afraid it is to you I turn when I am in most need of
someone with whom to share my disappointments.

I must first tell you that, beyond the venom of rumour, there
are those who have come to speak of my attachment to
Shanawdithit as strange. They have done so plainly, and on
more than one occasion.

I have assured the persons in question that there has been
no affection between us, not that of a husband for his wife,
nor a man for his beloved. I assured them that never have I
sought to caress her, even to ease her pain, for I know I can
never truly achieve such a purpose. Shanawdithit is not of our
world, and there is nothing I can do that will make her so.

I have kept my distance from Shanawdithit, and, I will add,
I have done so at the expense of her confusion. In front of a
mirror she will stand in her new dresses and comb her hair
until it shines, deeming herself an attractive woman.
Doubtless, to another Boeothuck she would be. To the
observer, the student of her race, who needs detach himself
from the emotion of what he observes, she is a woman of
great interest and conjecture. I am indeed overwhelmed by

her, but my amazement is not of a nature she understands.

As loathe as I am to do it, I have chosen to appear more often in public view with Shanawdithit, as·a means of demonstrating the nature of our companionship. At the milliner's on Water Street, the gossipers saw for themselves its propriety, swallowing their vulgar words before they had chance to spew from their mouths. I maintained an honourable distance and at the same time stood between her and the inquisitive to keep her from harm. Shanawdithit was fitted with a smart church hat of her own choosing, and I will say it was one in which she struck a self-respecting and independent figure.

We went one Saturday in December to the Amateur Theatre. There were those who found more of interest in the aborigine than in what transpired on the stage, though not one would have had reason to doubt the innocence of our association. The next day I escorted her by carriage to Church, and sat in the pew behind Doctor Carson and his wife and brood of children. The idleness of the children elicited more whispering than my companionship with Shanawdithit could ever have. Indeed, there were those sullen Presbyterians who took solace in my mild rebuke of her manners.

This week, we again ventured forth, navigating the snows in an attempt to reach the residence of the Attorney General for his New Year's fête. We started out well enough, with no undue attention falling on the young woman. But we had not gone far when an odious crowd of drunkards gathered. Shanawdithit quickly fell into a state of panic at their boldness. It forced a retreat back toward our house.

It took the discharge of someone to search out the night patrol from Fort Townshend to finally send the ruffians scattering into the streets, though not before their vile shouts of abuse had driven the poor woman behind the locked door of her room. It took some time to calm her. This morning I discovered she had slept under her bed, behind a barricade of all her earthly possessions.

The daylight and the normalcy of the street outside eased her upset somewhat, but she seemed to be needing more — reassurance of a sort I thought wisest to withhold. She was wanting to be embraced, I could tell, and calmed with physical touch. It is a childlike need of the most basic sort to be sure, but what it might lead to was my concern, how it might be interpreted in the aborigine's mind. More gravely, if word were to escape the house, by a slip of her tongue or a change in her manner toward me, then who is to say what might be the consequence.

Shanawdithit withdrew to the kitchen table and sat brooding, like a wounded bird. I made tea and approached with a cup, placing it in front of her. She glanced at it and looked away again, emitting a weak but mournful cry that I could only believe was her way of getting more of my attention.

'Please drink the tea. It will make you feel better.' These, some of my few words to her, and, as you will note, entirely innocent.

She has lived in my house long enough for me to know her nature, how she seeks even greater attention when a first response is not to her liking. She has an abundance of Native utterances and gesticulations, a near repertoire it could be said, if in doing so I risk sounding hard-hearted.

She yelped this time. Though not loud, I thought instantly of the wolf cries I had heard during my trek across the Island. It forced me to surmise that at that moment she reverted to a type of primitive who knows nothing but the woods and water that surrounded her tribe. Remarkable to behold if one is able to distance oneself, knowing as I do the mock passion in the sounds for what it is.

When that did not stir my empathy she again changed her manner. She sat upright and peered at me from behind her black eyes, made blacker by the tangle of hair surrounding her face.

I explained again that she had nothing to fear from the lewdness of the night before. She failed to take me at my word, at which I was not surprised, given her tribe's fear of bad spirits and the ceremonies they concocted to fend them off. In her mind the drunkards were not unlike the devil-men of her drawings, worse perhaps. Having spent much of the night awake, troubled by my need to understand it, I concluded it may well have unearthed memories of the Buchan expedition of 1811. On that occasion, you will recall, intimidation led to the Boeothuck capture of two of his men, whose heads they severed, displaying one on a stave and dancing for hours around it.

I dared not make my judgment known to Shanawdithit for fear of adding to her upset. Instead, I tried again to calm her with tea and the morning pleasantries to which we have become accustomed.

She, however, continued to stare, not the least forgiving of what had been her burden. 'Mr Cormack wishes me go from his house. He not want me here. I go back to Mr Peyton.'

I had, of course, done nothing to rouse such a conclusion. She was confused, pained still by what had taken place, her mind racing about in odd directions.

'You must rest,' I told her, my voice strong and unyielding, for her own sake. 'You are not yourself as yet. This afternoon perhaps the seamstress will come ...'

'I no want dress.'

'Perhaps when you are feeling better.'

'I no want damn dress.'

The coarseness of her previous life in Exploits was showing itself again. I quickly made it known that I would not accept her tone of voice, as much as I understood the reason for it.

'I not yours. I not like it here.'

She lifted her hand and began thumping her open palm against her chest. She did it for some time, then spoke again.

'You no like me. You no wish to take pain away. You no think I person like you. To you I Boeothuck, not person. I go back to Peytons.'

I had not foreseen this outburst. Shanawdithit is more troubled than one could ever have imagined. Her mutterings about going back to Exploits I knew to be a pretense, if a course she might stubbornly pursue out of vexation.

Against sound judgment and all that I knew of the bounds of relationships, I approached her and held her hand until I had stilled it. She did not stare at me as I feared she might, but rather gripped my hand and held it as tightly as I held hers. Her head fell against them, and then lodged against my chest.

She began to sob and did so for some time. Without embarrassment. Her womanly display was foreign to me, and it would be false of me to say it was a circumstance from which I myself took any comfort. I could recall in the recesses of memory a mother bearing the weight of her husband's death, a sister that of her father's, yet nothing prepared me for the awkwardness I felt at this need to be consoled.

I knew at that moment it was Fate that bore down on her, not solely the ordeal of the night before. Rather the ordeal of a history that made her the end of her race.

I must say, John — and forgive me if I lack complete coherence on this matter, though I am feeling calmer for *having written this letter — at that moment the shield of my own simplicity lifted. I had been blinded by my own convictions, in thinking that my work with Shanawdithit was best served by observation, that personal feelings for her be only those that would advance these observations.*

I realized she bears a need — a desperate, unrelenting need — to give birth. To herself bear a child who would continue her race, if but by half-measure.

I must close, for there are other matters of business, such as it is, that call urgently for my attention. I regret this haste, but be assured of my thankfulness for lending your mind to what I have set before you. It has turned much the more bearable.

Yours faithfully,
William

≈

13th January, 1829

In the days following her outburst Shanawdithit has displayed, as if it had been deliberately withheld, renewed pride in her appearance. She devotes even greater attention to her hair, which she has taken to tying back intricately with ribbon.

Shanawdithit is a curiosity now more than ever. If it had been a choice of resisting her informality, of re-establishing the comfort of a distance between us, I would have reset our course. But Shanawdithit is not now the woman who first entered my house. She makes her way from room to room with an assurance no longer in keeping with her circumstance as a guest. She has taken to directing me in the kitchen, of expressing a preference for some foods and not others. She speaks with an ease not common before. Her remarks come sometimes in a rush — simple, uncomplicated streams of words without her first thinking it a foreign tongue. This I deem a consequence of my teaching, one not altogether in keeping with what I have foreseen.

Our daylight hours generally unfold without impediment. Regardless, my business ventures consume much of any day and I am not averse to spending more time at the premises on Water Street as the need arises.

By late afternoon the daylight has gone. The light of tapers or lamp is inclined to add a secretive air to our evenings. Members of the Institution and other acquaintances make their visits, but most evenings are spent alone. They find me by the fireplace in the sitting room, reading a book or composing a letter. If I had the concentration I would sketch in words a broader likeness of Shanawdithit sitting at the opposite side of the fire, sewing perhaps, or completing small drawings using any pencils and paper that could be spared.

On several occasions since entering my house Shanawdithit has asked if I would teach her to read. I know there will come a time when she will be capable of doing so, and I assure her of this, that it is an undertaking for the future. Before she is able to recognize printed words, she will need a stronger facility with the spoken ones.

Perhaps even more so, she envies my writing, seeing the ease with which I am able to communicate with people I am not able to see.

'Where the letter go?' she has asked.

'England,' I told her.

It meant little to her of course, although she has often heard the word.

'Far away,' I told her.

'How far?'

'Two weeks by ship, perhaps, if no storm comes up.'

'Who the letter for?'

'A man I know in England.'

'He have house in England, like you.'

'Yes, in Liverpool.'

'He have wife and children?'

'No.'

'Like you.'

'Yes.'

'You like him?'

'He is a good friend. He is interested in much that interests me.'

'You adore him?'

I looked up from my letter, and answered her with a slight irritation at the length of her interruption. 'We are friends. Friends are fond of each other.'

She sensed that it was time to return to her own work and lowered her eyes to it. No more was said for the moment, although she was not without parting words when she rose later and made her way to her bed.

'I think the Liverpool man adore you for writing long letter.'

A miscalculation of words on her part, but a firm example of the nature of her mind these past days. I detect stronger and stronger opinions, ones she is not able, or no longer willing, to hold within herself. She still has not learned the boundaries of discourse, and until she does so she will not fit more comfortably among the people who are responsible for her.

In recent evenings there have been times when I refrained from showing patience with her many questions. If she sees that I am occupied with important matters, it is imperative for her to learn I am not to be interrupted. I have, in truth, such matters constantly filling my mind, for the trading enterprise in which I am a partner is seriously troubled. Since my return from Britain last spring my associate in business has grown increasingly critical of the time I spend on matters concerning the aborigines.

After one such outpouring I hastened to point out that in many quarters my name is praised because of it.

'Certainly the praise is in no way due to your reputation in business,' was his retort. 'The frequent absences that it has taken to secure that praise is the principal reason for the decline in the fortunes of this firm!'

I believe otherwise, and said so. The principal reason is our business rival, Patrick Morris, and his brigade of Catholic supporters.

Morris is a man whose reputation is hardly less in Ireland than it is in Newfoundland. The prices at which he is able to buy his goods in Waterford are considerably less than what we find is our lot in England. His business flourishes, seriously hampering our own. The prices he is able to charge for his goods in St John's drag away the slackers among the Protestants, in what would appear to be an unending stream. Bargaining, as is its habit, is quick to rise above the din of religion.

I am dispirited by my recent poor fortune and have begun to consider ways I might rekindle it, for the rent due the landlord Mr Roopes is becoming each week more difficult to secure. I am able to draw on the funds of the Institution to maintain Shanawdithit, yet her presence at times is more than a distraction.

My foremost concern remains an unabridged understanding of the Boeothuck. In that I have not wavered. It was the reason for the woman's removal from Exploits, and I will not rest without the knowledge that every detail possible has been gleaned from her.

In these days following her transfiguration, I find myself wishing her less familiar, and, for my blessed peace of mind, less forthright in her ways.

I returned home yesterday only to discover that Shanawdithit had taken to the streets on her own. When I questioned her after the misadventure had run its course, she related the story, with what could only be satisfaction at the deed. She had dressed in the winter boots and coat given to her by the Institution, wrapped around her neck and head the long, and sordidly bright woollen scarf that arrived with her from Exploits. And with that had donned snowshoes of mine, the very ones I had used for treks into the interior. Set forth then from the house despite the frost and snowdrifts, a sight the likes of which, I venture to say, could never have been seen before along Duckworth Street. All this despite the memory of our encounter with the drunkards not two weeks before.

'It was foolhardy,' I told her. For safety's sake, I would not hide my displeasure. 'You must not do it again.'

'I go in daylight. I want cold wind on my face. I want snow under my feet.'

'Then you must wait until I am able to go with you.'

'I no wait,' she said sharply, in what could only be called indignation, her simple manner failing to show any subtlety whatsoever. 'I live in woods many winters. You no live in woods in winter.'

I looked sternly at her childlike judgments, not to belittle them, but to show the unacceptability of her tone. For Shanawdithit had not gone far from the house when she did have fear for her welfare.

A woman whose house she passed on her tramp confirmed my suspicion. The woman had been standing at a window when she spied Shanawdithit trudging the street. She spoke to her out her front door, with the intention of convincing her to return home. Shanawdithit had stopped, peered at the woman through her getup, and pressed on.

What was Shanawdithit's intention, God alone might know. She had not gone far when a small crowd gathered. This time it was young ruffians, of no more than fourteen years of age, and certainly no wiser for being Catholic and Irish. They began calling out to her, in some ungodly misrepresentation of her name.

Then — though I was not there to see it, there is no reason to doubt the woman — a pair of the more brazen ones made snowballs and began flinging them at her. One struck Shanawdithit in the shoulder and caused her to stumble and fall.

The common sense of others in the crowd thankfully put a stop to it, and one helped Shanawdithit to her feet.

In an absurd display of foolhardiness, she turned and rushed at the boys who had thrown the snowballs. 'Like a goose in the fits,' the woman has related, 'hissin' and bawling.'

Not only did she chase them, she overtook one and tossed him face-first into the snow.

The crowd thought it great sport and, when she finished, cheered her as they would the winner of a drunken fight among their own. I would have expected no better. 'They shouted and whistled and called her their sweet Sheelanagig.'

Whether it was the best they could do with her rightful name or some foolish Gaelic parody, who would know. Whatever it was, Shanawdithit thought it wonderful and, to end any measure of sense that might have remained, she unwrapped the scarf from her head in a flourish and bowed to them. As if it were a stage and she a performer.

It was at this point that I happened upon the scene, ascending Custom House Hill from Water Street. She had been rash and untrustworthy, a danger to herself, for the excursion of hers could just as easily have ended in calamity. Indeed, whatever sense she might have had was lost completely.

SHANNON

O N THE AFTERNOON OF December 30th, Simon is on a flight from Goose Bay to St. Anthony, en route to St. John's. Shannon drives to the airport and boards the same flight. He has managed to save the seat next to him.

Once past the awkwardness of suddenly finding themselves elbow to elbow, past the regular banalities of weather and workload, there is little to add. Nothing that would even border the personal, for they are encased with two dozen other passengers and nobody flies Provincial Airlines without overhearing what the people within a ten-foot radius have on their minds.

Even when they are safely settled in the anonymity of the Courtyard Marriott on Duckworth Street, some reticence continues. There's the ungracefulness of attempting to reconnect after all that's happened since they last saw each other.

She wonders what Simon sees in her. What there is that still appeals to him, why he agreed to this.

'What are you missing?' she asks him.

Bluntness shouldn't disappoint. Not without the customary edge of

irritation. She seeks to avoid self-pity at all costs. What is he missing —
that nerve and spirit brewed in twenty years of naive wandering?

'Sit down,' he says. 'Let's talk.'

They sit next to each other at the side of the bed. Talk is not where it
should be leading.

'Tell me what's going on.'

Just play the charmer, the seducer, whatever works for you, Simon. It
won't take much.

Silence. He takes a chair some distance opposite her.

'Do you have several hours?' She is being the shithead she despises.

He looks at her and says nothing. Regret for ever agreeing to this
weekend. If he's sensible.

'Let's start with my newfound heritage. You were right. I've unearthed
some family past and I'm a fraction of something that is Aboriginal.
Mi'kmaq it would appear.'

'Really?'

'No, I lie, because I so desperately want us to have something in common.'

The man laughs. Looking squarely at her, his elbows on his knees, he
laughs.

'Now you're fucked,' he says. Shaking his head of hair and grinning
broadly.

'You're obviously pleased.'

'Of course!'

'To be proven right.'

'Your blood is laced with something, and it's not all from across the
ocean. Welcome to the family.'

'Be realistic, Simon. I'm about as Métis as Snow White.'

'The First Circle is coursing your veins!'

'Jesus, Simon.'

What is there to do but laugh with him, the ardent fool. He sits back
next to her. She grabs on to him then.

Clasps her head to his chest.

She drains herself against him, sunk in the exhaustion of the weeks past, the two of them curled together on top of the king-size bed. It is the holding she will remember.

The next day walking along Water Street she suddenly leads him, deflecting his protests, into a swank hair salon, an hour later emerging, his hair sheared into something from the 1920s. He is an embarrassed, slickly handsome northern hunting man.

The sex remains delicious.

WHAT HAS IT COME to? She doesn't know. What she figures she knows is that since leaving Conche at eighteen her life has had its moments. And here again, another moment.

If another, hopefully then another. These she deals with, can take a certain pride in. By forty she should be well able to drive herself past their complications, on her own, without help. Without a Marta.

Perhaps she will take a trip to Norway. Force herself into the charms of Marta's married life and emerge the stronger woman for it. For now — day after day. For years, when the moments were particularly remote, she would switch on the news, get past the golden-brown, unfailingly handsome guy reading it, to the story about some disastrous part of the world, and take heart in the fact that she was alive and healthy and didn't have an AK-47 in her face, or a hurricane bashing down her door. She had friends. She had good friends.

On Boxing Day she had phoned some of them in British Columbia. Maybe it was a matter of covering her bases, but it was Christmas after all, and a fitting time to be phoning. She spent an hour talking with Jillian and Ursula, a very pleasant hour overall. Uncomplicated, devoid of undertones, coloured with laughter.

'When are you coming back?' Ursula asked, knowing full well that was never Shannon's intention. Still, it seemed more than a necessary question, fulfilling a expectation.

'We'll see.'

'It was a leave of absence from your job, right?'

'Of course.'

Something Jillian said stuck with Shannon long after the phone call had ended. 'We miss having a Newfoundlander around.'

Shannon thought it odd for someone to think of her in that way, enough to make a point of it. For all the years she spent in BC she had never defined herself as being from Newfoundland. She didn't avoid it, but neither did she wear it on her sleeve. Practically everyone she knew had been born in someplace other than BC. She was one of them.

She hadn't said anything to Jillian in response, other than a benign 'Thanks.' But hours later she sat wondering if another twenty years living away from the place would eliminate all trace of it. Shannon would prefer to think of herself as being from somewhere. The complication is in the details.

She sees herself turning into the generic Newfoundlander, flexible by degrees, to suit the occasion. With the right group of friends she could even fall into dialect, given that her exposure to it over the past months has reinforced her proficiency.

Where the next few months will take her is not to be predicted. She knows it's wise to have options, not to back herself into a corner. She sometimes thinks of severing ties completely and looking for a job in some other country. If Marta could do it, she could. Someplace where she wouldn't have to learn a language. Someplace safe for a woman. A place where she could put her Parks experience to use. New Zealand. She thought she'd like New Zealand.

IT'S THEIR THIRD DAY in St. John's and they're inside the hulking new cultural complex overlooking the city, The Rooms. Among the museum's prized artifacts are a miniature portrait of the Beothuk woman Shanawdithit, a Basque harpoon head, a Norse pendant, the flute that lay beneath the child buried at L'Anse Amour.

Seeing the artifacts together in one space is surreal. It plays against the emotion she feels for their origins. She deals with it only moderately well, and that within the boundaries of her work life.

Even approaching them one at a time, pausing between encounters, leaves her unsettled. She ignores the storyboards and tries to absorb the artifacts in isolation. It is no less manageable. Especially when other people circle her, leaning forward for their own views.

She withdraws, holds close to Simon, tries to think what at this moment is inside him.

He says nothing. There is a silent level of understanding. They feel better moving to the restaurant, having lunch by the broad expanse of window that overlooks the city, intimate in conversation that purposely ignores what they have just seen.

THAT AFTERNOON SHE GOES with him to the Provincial Department of Archaeology, for the meeting he has set in place. Before they reach the offices, he stops.

'I'm fine. I can handle this.'

Whether he expects it, or she does, it doesn't matter. 'I want to be there.'

'You don't have to,' he says.

He smiles, running his fingers through his hair, expecting more of it.

'I'll keep my mouth shut if you want me to,' she says.

That is beside the point. They've both run out of places to go.

She walks beside him to the end of the corridor, to the double glass doors leading to the offices. She opens one, with the option of slipping inside ahead of him.

She lets him go first. She'd rather be the one to let the door glide shut after them.

CORMACK

14th January

My dear John, excuse this appendage to my letter, but these are Shanawdithit's very words, spoken to me this evening.

'You not bossing me, Mr Cormack,' she announced at the end of our supper together, the moment the cook had left the house. A meal of stewed cod, her favourite, which I went at length to arrange. She spoke loud enough to be heard clearly, if with none of the excessive emotion she displayed of late.

I turned to her, for I knew her sentiment could hardly be sound. She rose from the chair and went to her room. I resumed my tea and biscuit, no different than at the end of any supper.

Shanawdithit returned, in her hands a small pouch of hide. Over the months I thought I had seen all of her possessions. This pouch had escaped me. She held it before her with a pagan's reverence.

'What do you have?' I said, my friendliness not lost, for the sake of civility.

She did not speak. She extended her hand, expecting me, I assumed, to grasp it and rise to my feet. I accepted her childlike manner and followed her out of the kitchen and into the sitting room. There was not yet a lamp lit, though the fire cast considerable light. She wished me sit in the chair. I did so to oblige her.

It was all a circumstance I would have avoided had I not felt a trace of regret for the strictness of tone I had used with her in recent days. Boldly, she took my hands and placed them one atop the other on my lap.

'Close your eyes, Mr Cormack.'

Fitful as I was, I did as asked. It was entirely unbecoming to be led in this way, no matter it be an aborigine. I was about to protest, when I resolved it might well be a Boeothuck ceremony of some kind. Such was my errant thinking — a ceremony, to be recounted vividly to you, John, presenting a rare glimpse into the traditions of the race. My eyes remained tightly shut, my hesitation replaced by tepid eagerness. My expectation: that a secret was about to be revealed from within the soul of the tribe.

My mind surrendered into an orbit of grace. Would other scholars of natural history not have done the same? I knew well the significance such a ceremony would have held for these men. The forefinger of Shanawdithit traced a path across my face several times and in all directions. My thoughts fell again to you, John. You more than anyone have known my life as it has been lived with the aborigine.

My faith in the woman was such that to me her finger bore a warm paste of red ochre. I felt it drying to my face. Has not the Boeothuck liking for red ochre been the subject of infinite

*debate between us? It bears significance unmatched, used by
the tribe to coat both their living and their dead. Spellbound
I was at the notion of being received into a place where few
of my race have ever been privileged to go.*

I was lost to the moment, caring little what she asked.

'Do you adore me, Mr Cormack?'

*Or caring little if my answer were any more than the one
she sought.*

'Yes,' I said, such was my fever.

*The swirl of mind inside the darkness was like nothing I
had known before. Indeed, when she stopped her finger trailing
across my face, my elation persisted. And when the aborigine
did not speak I thought it the climax of the rite.*

*Such was the thwarting of my good sense. In time my mind
drew itself together.*

'Shanawdithit.'

There was no reply.

*I thought perhaps I had fallen into sleep. My eyelids were
weak-willed, but eventually I drew them open.*

*I expected the sight of her, for I felt her presence around me
still. I turned my head. She was not to be seen.*

'Shanawdithit.'

*When my senses returned, I rose to my feet and walked out
of the firelight and into the kitchen. She was not in the room.
I took the lamp in my hand and walked about the house, in a
stupor still, stopping finally at the door to her bedroom. I spoke
her name, to no reply.*

*My hand clasped the door knob. I felt the resistance of the
bolt inside.*

And still no answer to my entreaty.

*I proceeded to my own room and there held the lamp to the
mirror that hung above the dresser. I will not deny my*

incredulity, nor the disquiet that arose in my heart.

My face was indeed my own, coloured by nothing but tallow. If anything my features were brighter, reflecting the glow of the lamp, like damnable pale moonlight reflecting on a sea.

I remain

Yours faithfully,
William

17th January, 1829

Shanawdithit's pretense burdens me. My compassion for her is unresolved. By her own will she diminished my charity, for, although she would never reveal my humiliation, I cannot but be wounded by its intent. I am resolved to set the matter aright, yet know I cannot but fail to do so.

They are an aggrieved race, these aborigines. There are those who would insist they brought harm to themselves with their deceptions, those who avow that nothing was ever safe from them, that all possessions were the object of their sleight of hand. It can be no sanction for the extirpation of a race, yet does Shanawdithit's conduct not dull the discord over it?

I choose to look beyond the young woman, at the nation in its true primitive state before the white race was ever set among it. I seek the essence of their race, not its troubled remnant. For it is in man at his most primitive that the study of natural history has its foundation, and it is he who most willingly reaps our compassion.

18th January, 1829

When Shanawdithit emerged from her room this morning she
was more worn than ever. Try as she might to appear the
steadfast soul, she could not hide her anxiety. She coughed
through the whole of breakfast, a consumptive woman in need
of heeding her health more than her opinions.

She was the first to speak. 'It is a good day, Mr Cormack.
The sun will shine. Will we go to church today. Today we will
go skating on the lake, as you promise.'

'You are not well,' I told her. 'Your cough is worse. You must
rest.'

She chose to ignore my guidance and pretend that nothing
unnatural passed between us these last few days. Instead of
bundling herself in blankets and resting in the sitting room near
the fire as I advised, she made for the vestibule, taking it in her
head to don her winter coat and boots in readiness for the outdoors. I followed her.

'It good for my cough,' she said, striking her fist against her
chest.

I told her plainly, 'You have no suitable covering for your head.'

She took the ugly scarf, wound it twice around her head and
drew it tight.

I tore it from her. And for her own good tried to force away
her coat.

She screamed savagely. She broke away from me.

My hand rose, but stopped its motion. I did not strike her.

She huddled in the corner of the vestibule, her black eyes sunk into mine. I turned then and walked back to the kitchen, and took more tea.

I paid her no further attention, only to hear her go out the door. The sun streamed past the kitchen window, having risen above the hills on the south side of the harbour. A fresh layer of snow had shrouded the city overnight, and for the moment covered its grime. It being Sunday it would take longer for the grime to show itself again.

By the noise outside it appeared that Shanawdithit had not gone far. Her hacking cough was no better than the bark of a tobacco-rotted sailor. I heard less of it after a time, though perhaps only because she went into the street.

She finally opened the door to the house, stamping the snow from her feet. She discarded her boots and clothes. She looked in at me drinking tea and reading the Bible as I sometimes do on Sunday mornings.

'A fine day, Mr Cormack. The air outside is wholesome, good.'

I looked up, but by that time she had gone.

⌯

4th February, 1829

As I make my way to England, I think often of the aborigine. The distance between us brings a more lasting judgment.

Shanawdithit appears to be happier in the home of the Attorney General and his family. On the day of my boarding ship Carson told me he had seen her there the night before and thought her well settled. I expect the young children are a distraction for her.

As for our alliance, that will continue through my correspondence with the Institution. I had accomplished all I was able with her. The sheaf of her drawings, together with my many transcriptions, will consume me for several months to come.

If I appeared irresolute at our parting it was because of the many matters assailing me. One does not approach insolvency in business without regret for what might have been done to prevent it. My partner and I parted company on the most disagreeable of terms, and the legal proceedings bore heavily on me. Had Shanawdithit been my sole concern then her transfer to the home of Mr Simms might have been less disorderly.

All my household goods were auctioned. I sailed past The Narrows with less than what I had brought when I arrived from Prince Edward Island. A disheartening state of affairs, and one for which I am not about to disguise my bitterness, in view of

the contribution I have made to the knowledge of the Island —
its minerals, its fishery, its aborigines. There were many, if less
than I would have thought, who attempted to keep me out of
the financial mire into which I had been thrust. I was unwilling
to accept their charity. My pride would not allow it. Rather
I left the Island and will eventually make my own way to
dominions I have yet to explore. Australia holds a particular
allure. An immensely bigger island, and one, I hope, with a
more ample and generous heart.

After arranging Shanawdithit's transfer I did not return
again to the home of the Attorney General. Upon parting
Shanawdithit left me three keepsakes — two stones and a braid
of her hair. One of the stones is quartz, the other granite. The
latter was polished, most likely by the sea. Shanawdithit knew
of my interest in minerals, for she had often seen me display
specimens and examine them with a magnifier, and perhaps
thought this pair a significant addition to my collection.

The braided strand of her black hair I know to be the
most personal token she could have given me. I know she had
left such a token with the Peytons when she parted from them.
When I held it in my hand I offered an expression of my gratitude,
a smile. As was her way, she did not respond in like manner.

It is an artifact I thought first to bring to Edinburgh and
deposit there with the others, but chose instead to leave it,
together with the rocks, in St John's. I have left instructions
that they be placed in a suitable public collection, there to be a
reminder to Newfoundlanders of my diligence in preserving the
memory of the Boeothuck tribe.

I had no parting words for Shanawdithit, nor she any for me,
except for each of us 'goodbye.'

29th March, 1829

These past weeks I have taken a respite from writing herein, devoting myself instead to writing of a more substantial nature.

When my passage ended at the port of Liverpool, I was thinking less of the last months with Shanawdithit, and more of the months stretching ahead. I sent forth to MacGregor word of my arrival. He appeared shortly thereafter to welcome me and lead me to his house. Here I have rested, and will remain, if such proves reasonable for us both, until I have regained my direction.

MacGregor's own mercantile pursuits have not been without their troubles. Our commiseration has renewed the both of us. In its course we have discovered how deeply the maritime colonies have ingrained themselves on our lives.

Our compulsion is to propagate an understanding of them, for the British still fail to acknowledge their potential. To this end I have submitted to the Natural History Society in Montreal an essay which I titled "The British, American, and French Fisheries." It appears to have been well received and my hope is for it to be considered for one of the medals the Society accords the most exceptional essays presented to it.

My intention is to now use the information acquired from Shanawdithit in the writing of an essay for publication in the *Edinburgh New Philosophical Journal*. Jameson will shortly print therein my report to the Boeothuck Institution, written following my last venture in search of the Boeothuck. My furthermost intention, arrived at through the unrestrained encouragement of MacGregor, is an independent volume, *The Aborigines of Newfoundland*. Certainly, no man knows more of them than I.

MacGregor is busily preparing his *British North America* for publication in London, having had published two books already, both to enthusiastic reception. It is his confidence in my abilities that has propelled me as a possible writer of books, for I had previously felt I had neither the proficiency nor the assurance it required.

'Absurd,' MacGregor said, and with sudden levity dismissed my misgivings one by one. 'Above all, William, one must not plod through life with regret. One plods one's way to the grave soon enough!'

This impetuous change of tone he only displays over subjects for which ordinary speech is an insufficient instrument for his enthusiasm. He is sometimes embarrassed by the trait, but I think it a picturesque and charming one, and find myself joining in, my own reserve in abeyance. Whether it is mere release from the gravity of the past months, or a hitherto dormant attribute, I do not know. Nor care, for in Liverpool there is no one other than MacGregor of more than cursory acquaintance.

My days are spent then in writing, and, as a consequence, if somewhat against my wish, reflection. While I attempt to embrace MacGregor's advice, I cannot contemplate what the past years have brought me without some measure of regret. I will not deny the fact it has hindered the progress of the writing, rather than advance it.

As to our personal fondness for each other, that remains unspoken, and untried. As is to be expected, and allowed to be endured.

In truth, MacGregor has chosen to spend considerable time in the company of a young lady. I have grown fond of her, it could be said. She is altogether an agreeable sort. Pretty and forgiving of my moods.

29th June, 1829

A letter has reached me from Carson with news I much regret having to read.

On the 6th of June, the Native woman, Shanawdithit, died of consumption. She was the last of her people.

I am strangely less distraught than I would have anticipated. The distance from the event perhaps accounts for the restraint of emotion. I am not surprised at the course her illness took, though I would be less than truthful if I did not acknowledge that there may well have been other, equally significant, factors contributing to her death. The young woman's passing marks for me the end of an extraordinary portion of my life. It will reach a final conclusion with my submission of her obituary, and that of the whole of her race, to the *London Times*. As I have written, in a draft of the same, 'There has been a primitive nation, once claiming rank as a portion of the human race, who have lived, flourished, and become extinct in their own orbit.'

August, 1829

I have spent these past summer evenings alone or in MacGregor's
company, attempting to satisfy his renewed curiosity for the
detail of what transpired in Newfoundland following our prior
time together. My letters to him conveyed some of it, though
little compared to sitting together before Shanawdithit's
drawings. I decipher them, attempting as I do to suggest the
milieu under which they were composed.

'I have noticed your enthusiasm tempered,' John commented
to me this evening. 'Was there disappointment at what you were
able to glean from the woman?'

'Perhaps my familiarity with the drawings is to blame.'

'Was she not a fitting subject then? A true representative of
her race?'

'Indeed she was that.'

MacGregor was silent for the moment, bent over one of the
maps.

'She tested your generous nature. I concluded as much from
your letters.'

'Her time with the Peytons altered her irrevocably.'

'Were you drawn to her?'

I must have appeared puzzled. Indeed I was.

'She being a primitive, did she rouse your affections, in the
way that a woman of our own race might?'

I thought it unbecoming of MacGregor. Nevertheless, I answered him honestly.

'She was not in the least attractive to me.'

'Had she been, it would have made for a match to alter history.'

MacGregor, again to my surprise, has not fully appreciated the boundaries set within the study of natural history.

'Had you no thought to fathering a child, of allowing the blood to continue?'

'The thought arose in me, yes.'

Perhaps I sounded overly firm in my answer. He said nothing further for the moment. It was I who felt the urge not to pause at that.

'The aborigine gave me no cause to love her.'

'Did you not wish to halt the passage of the Boeothuck from the earth? Was that not sufficient cause?'

It would seem to me that only a long-lived life will offer such answers.

At that, God must know, they are likely not sufficient for all its questions.